Leading Lady

THE GRESHAM CHRONICLES

The Widow of Larkspur Inn
The Courtship of the Vicar's Daughter
The Dowry of Miss Lydia Clark

TALES OF LONDON

The Maiden of Mayfair
Catherine's Heart
Leading Lady

Visit *www.lawanablackwell.com*

Leading Lady

LAWANA BLACKWELL

BETHANYHOUSE

MINNEAPOLIS, MINNESOTA

Leading Lady
Copyright © 2004
Lawana Blackwell

Cover illustration by Paul Casale
Cover design by Danielle White

Scripture quotations are from the King James Version of the Bible.

Published by Bethany House Publishers
11400 Hampshire Avenue South
Bloomington, Minnesota 55438
www.bethanyhouse.com

Bethany House Publishers is a Division of
Baker Book House Company, Grand Rapids, Michigan.

Printed in the United States of America

Library of Congress Cataloging-in-Publication Data

Blackwell, Lawana, 1952-
   Leading lady / by Lawana Blackwell.
      p. cm. — (Tales of London ; bk. 3)
   ISBN 0-7642-2260-0
   1. Actresses—Fiction. 2. Women—England—London—Fiction. 3. London (England)—Fiction. 4. Theater—Fiction. 5. Revenge—Fiction. I. Title II. Series: Blackwell, Lawana, 1952-   . Tales of London ; bk. 3.
   PS3552.L3429L43   2004
   813'.54—dc22
                                     2003023499

LAWANA BLACKWELL is a full-time writer with nine published books, including the bestselling GRESHAM CHRONICLES series. She and her husband live in Baton Rouge, Louisiana, and have three sons.

This book is dedicated to
my editor and friend,

Ann Parrish

who encourages me every step of the way.

One

"See how she leans her cheek upon her hand!
O that I were a glove upon that hand,
That I might touch that cheek . . ."

The fine-toned male voice coming from the stage was reduced to murmurs when Jewel McGuire closed the wardrobe room door. "Now, that's what I call good acting," she said on her way to the drafting table. "We both know what he'd *really* like to do to that cheek."

Bethia Rayborn raised her eyes from the costume sketches spread out upon the table's surface, to give her a warning smile. "Funny thing about sounds, cousin. They travel out of a room as well as in."

Jewel winced. One never knew who could be passing by, and gossip raced through backstage passageways like sharp scissors through silk. Everyone even remotely connected with the Royal Court Theatre was aware of the enmity between its leading actor and actress. But as co-manager with her husband, Jewel was supposed to be more discreet.

Lighted by skylights, the wardrobe room was situated upon the top floor of the honeycomb of rooms to the right of the stage. Rolls of cloth formed a colorful pyramid in one corner; hats queued across shelves; strings of paste pearls and jewels cascaded from the branches of a coat tree; and stockings and belts, gloves and lace collars spilled from cupboard drawers.

The two sewing machines sat idle because seamstresses Mrs. Hamby and Miss Lidstone were at lunch. Noon was far too early for the actors and stage director to be thinking of their stomachs, for their breakfasts would still be digesting. During the run of a play they rarely left the theatre before midnight, which meant daytime schedules lagged accordingly.

As it was impossible to snatch back her words, Jewel wasted no time fretting over them. She picked up a sketch of a man wearing a Renaissance flatcap, an embroidered doublet over a long pleated undershirt, and silk tights. One-inch squares of fabric were glued along the bottom of the page. "Is this Romeo?"

"Count Paris," Bethia corrected, and picked up another sketch. "Here's Romeo. This green velvet will be his cloak for the street-brawl scene, and we'll line it with this black satin for the Capulet ball."

"Reversible? How clever." And only because it was her duty, not because she doubted her younger cousin's competency, Jewel asked, "Everything will be ready in time?"

She did not have to specify at which date, for the revival of Shakespeare's *Romeo and Juliet* was scheduled to open on the twenty-eighth of December. Afternoon rehearsals were taking place, now that evening productions of Sydney Grundy's *Over the Garden Wall* had been running smoothly since the end of August. But Bethia would be returning to Girton College tomorrow.

"In plenty of time," Bethia assured her. "The patterns are drafted, and the sewing will be completed well before the eleventh, when I'll be here for final fittings."

"That's a comfort. But I must say I'll be glad when you're finished with schooling."

"Not as glad as I'll be." Bethia hesitated. "I hope you don't feel obligated to keep me on because we're family, Jewel. I would understand perfectly if you'd rather have someone here every day."

"Nonsense. You've less than a year left. I'm not about to lose the best wardrobe mistress in London."

Her cousin rolled her eyes. "Now you're just being silly."

"Only a matter of time," Jewel said, patting her arm. "And you're the best *we've* ever had."

It was quite by accident, or then again, by providential design, that Bethia fell into her position. Her talent with a needle became evident when she was only ten and started asking the housekeeper for scraps from which to fashion clothes for her dolls. She learned sketching from a parlourmaid. And she had inherited her father's passion for history, the subject she was reading at Girton. The three interests merged when Bethia, home for Lent vacation in her second year, stopped by to watch dress rehearsals for R. Cowrie's playscript of Sir Walter Scott's *Ivanhoe*.

"I'm afraid Rowena wouldn't have worn padded undersleeves," she had whispered after drawing Jewel aside. "They appeared about three hundred years later."

But when Jewel, only seven months into her position and still quite intimidated by the staff, brought Bethia's observation to the wardrobe mistress's attention, Mrs. Wood's injured reply was, "I was costuming actors when you were still in nappies, Mrs. McGuire. I don't expect there'll be anybody in the audience from the twelfth century, so who's to know the difference?"

The drama critic for the *Times* happened to be one who knew the difference, writing with scathing pen, *The costuming was slipshod, apparently left over from an earlier production of Henry VIII.*

When Jewel steeled herself to inform Mrs. Wood that she would have to send all future costume sketches up to Girton so that Bethia could check them for authenticity, the wardrobe mistress resigned in a huff. No suitable replacement had been procured when the time came to plan costuming for Bulwer-Lytton's *The Lady of Lyons,* and as Bethia happened to be home for summer vacation, she agreed to step in.

The *Times* critic was much appeased, writing, *The settings and costumes were so authentic that at times I almost fancied I could hear the bells of Saint Jean's Cathedral in the background.*

"I just wonder how long you can burn the candle at both ends," Jewel continued.

"I *like* keeping busy."

Jewel smiled understanding. "It makes the time pass more quickly, yes?"

"I'm sure I don't know what you mean," Bethia said, but with a spark in her blue eyes. On both their minds was the absence of Bethia's longtime beau, Guy Russell, off in Italy studying violin at the University of Bologna.

"Well, at least you'll both be home for good, come summer."

"That will be lovely." Bethia's wistful smile made her seem younger than her twenty years. She was petite like her mother, with wide blue eyes and freckles scattered across the bridge of her nose. With neither the time nor the inclination to primp, she simply tied her honey-brown hair with a ribbon or a bit of lace at her collar. The plain style suited her oval face. Her even temper and good humor prompted the two seamstresses to work twice as hard as they had under Mrs. Wood with her authoritative ways.

When the seamstresses returned from lunch, Jewel and Bethia chatted with them of patterns and suitable trimmings until three o'clock, when Bethia packed what pages remained of her sketch pad into her satchel. She would be boarding the train tomorrow morning for college and planned to spend the rest of the afternoon with her family.

"I'll walk you downstairs," Jewel said, accompanying her out into the corridor. "Grady will want to say good-bye."

They wrinkled noses at each other at the odors wafting out of the open doorway to the scenic artists' studio. Paints were the culprits, from the filled jam pots on the long tables to the large framed canvases drying against the walls, waiting to be lowered by winches to the back of the stage. Bethia took the lead on the staircase, with one hand on the railing and the other holding up her sea-green skirt. On the ground floor they went to the office Jewel shared with her husband. Grady McGuire, in shirt-sleeves and waistcoat, and wiping ink from his fingers with a handkerchief, rose from his desk.

"Back to the books, is it now?" he said in his soft Irish brogue.

"She's never away from the books," Jewel said. "You should come up and have a look at the sketches."

She knew, of course, that he wouldn't, for he cared so little about costume that, if she did not choose his clothing, he would shrug his thick short body into whatever in his wardrobe first caught his color-blind eyes. But he made up in kindness for what he lacked in style, and Jewel was grateful for his confidence in her judgment in that department.

"I'll wait and be surprised at dress rehearsal," he said. He stuffed the spotted handkerchief into his waistcoat pocket and came around the desk to engulf Bethia's small hand with his two. "Do take care up at Cambridge. We'll miss your sunny face about here."

"Thank you, Grady," she said. "I'll see you in December."

He escorted them out into the corridor. Mr. Birch, head attendant, was limping their way. Tall, white-haired, and stoop-shouldered, he could have been anywhere from sixty to a hundred years old, and had actually acted in small parts in his younger days at the Adelphi Theatre. "Ah, there you are, Miss Rayborn. A Mr. Pearce is in the lobby, asking for you."

"Oh *no*."

Jewel turned to Bethia. Her cousin was staring in the direction of the lobby, her face drained of color save two crimson slashes across her cheeks.

"What is it, Bethia?" Grady asked.

She blinked and gave him an apologetic look. "I'm afraid it's Douglas."

"My cousin?" Jewel said. "Why would he ask for you?"

Bethia drew breath. "We happened upon each other in Covent Garden two weeks ago. I had just seen Guy off at Waterloo Station and was window-shopping, trying to distract myself from a blue mood before going home." She looked at Jewel. "You know how Mother and Father worry over me."

"Yes," Jewel said. She supposed it was because, now that Uncle Daniel and Aunt Naomi had reached their golden years, they were more aware of the frailty of life.

"Mr. Pearce invited me to join him for tea in one of the shops," Bethia continued. "I really would have preferred to be alone, but he was rather insistent. He said it wouldn't be improper, as we're somewhat related."

"But of course," Jewel assured her. After all, this was late 1897, less than three years away from a new century. Some of the more unreasonable chains of propriety that had bound their mothers were loosening. And Douglas and Bethia *were* distantly related, by the marriage of Jewel's parents, with Bethia being on her father's side, Douglas on her mother's.

"Just explain that you have a beau," Grady suggested. "And that, while he would understand meeting as you did by happenstance, he would object to a repeat of the occasion."

"I've explained," Bethia said in a flat voice.

"When?" Jewel asked.

"Many times."

"You mean he's courting you?"

"He sends me letters—sometimes more than one a day. He's even knocked on the door at Hampstead. The second time, Father warned him not to come about anymore."

Jewel traded worried looks with her husband. "Did he stop?"

"He stopped coming to the house." Bethia frowned miserably. "Father doesn't know that he followed me to the Royal Gallery Saturday."

"Why didn't you come to us?" Grady asked. "We could have helped you."

Bethia shrugged, her expression still wretched. "I figure the problem will resolve itself when I return to school. And well . . . he is Jewel's cousin."

"As are you." Jewel put a hand upon her shoulder. "And more dear to me than Douglas, though of course I have to put up with him now and again."

"I'll speak with him," Grady said. "Perhaps if a man explains the situation, he'll understand how it stands and give up." He turned to Mr. Birch, waiting three feet away and no doubt taking mental notes for retelling later. "Will you escort Miss Rayborn to the stage door?"

That exit led down a staircase into the narrow alleyway separating the Royal Court Theatre from the Metropolitan Underground Railway station. Ideal for making a quick getaway from amorous visitors, as some of the actors had already discovered.

"Of course, Mr. McGuire."

"Thank you!" Bethia said.

Jewel embraced her quickly, wished her pleasant journey tomorrow. She watched Mr. Birch and Bethia hasten in the direction from which they had just come, then turned again to her husband. "I'll go with you."

"Poor chap." Grady took Jewel's hand as they continued down the corridor. Just under the voices coming from the theatre, he said, "I would have followed you about like a love-sick puppy too, had you not fallen in love with me straightaway."

She laughed. "Just because it's true doesn't mean you shouldn't allow me some illusions, Grady. A woman likes to believe the man did all the pursuing."

"Oh, I pursued you," he said with a sidelong smile. "Make no mistake."

She squeezed his hand but released it when they reached the door leading into the lobby. It didn't seem fitting to advertise their contentment with each other in the face of unrequited love.

Douglas Pearce, clad in dark blue trousers, a short fawn-colored linen jacket, and cravat of colorful burgundy paisley, stood with hat in hand and his back propped against a post. Twenty-seven years of age, he was tall, at almost six feet, and handsome enough to catch the eye of most young women. But his shortcomings in the character department were etched permanently into his expression. He straightened, unfolded his arms, and looked past them.

"The old man said Miss Rayborn's still here."

"And good afternoon to you too, Douglas," Grady said pointedly.

"Afternoon, Grady, Jewel," Douglas said with hurried politeness. His hazel eyes slid past them toward the door again. "I need to speak with Miss Rayborn. Will you show me to her?"

"Sorry, old chap," Grady said. "I'm afraid we can't do that."

"And why not?"

Jewel sighed. "Douglas, she has a beau."

"A coachman's son," he said with the tone he would use to describe a serving of spoiled flounder.

"Yes," she replied. "And aren't you supposed to be at work?"

"They're not engaged," he replied, ignoring her question.

"I'm sure that will happen when he's home for good."

"Until such a time, she's fair game."

Grady stepped over to rest a beefy hand upon Douglas's shoulder. His frown did not dilute the compassion in his eyes. "Bethia isn't some grouse to be hunted, Douglas. She's allowed some say in the matter, and her heart is attached elsewhere."

Douglas's face clouded to the roots of his light brown hair. "That wasn't the impression I got at Covent Garden. We laughed over everything. It was obvious that she enjoyed my company."

"That doesn't mean she has romantic feelings for you," Jewel reasoned.

She may as well have spoken to a gatepost, for her cousin replied, "I *know* I can persuade her to change her mind about that Russell fellow . . . if you'll but allow me to speak with her."

"Can't you see? It'll do no earthly good." Pity came on the heels of Jewel's annoyance. "You're a handsome man, Douglas. There's a woman out there somewhere for you."

Her own words gave her pause. Would she wish Douglas upon any woman?

She would have to be foolish enough not to mind that he was expelled from King's College during his fresher year for cheating. And not quite bright enough to guess that he had procured his accounting position at the London main office of Sun Insurance Company because of Uncle Norman's influence. But conversely, strong enough to withstand Douglas's temper tantrums without crumbling and wise enough to encourage him to invest some of Grandfather Lorimer's legacy money for the times that he would probably be unemployed.

"Yes, find yourself a good woman and settle down," Grady said gently.

Douglas's jaw tightened. He shrugged Grady's hand from his shoulder. "I don't want just *any* woman! And it's no use hiding her from me. I'll go back there and find her myself if you refuse—"

"Douglas," Jewel interrupted. There was nothing to do but administer a dose of brutal truth. "We sent her out the side. She doesn't want to see you. I'm sorry, but that's how it—"

He straightened. "The side?"

"And there's no use trying to catch up with her. She's gone."

"We'll see!" He gave her a murderous look and dashed for the door, throwing over his shoulder, "I'll never forgive you for this, Jewel!"

"You're making a fool of yourself!" she shot back.

Grady patted her arm. "We tried, love. No use in getting upset over it." They walked to the door he had burst through. Douglas was sprinting toward the entrance to the Sloan Square underground railway station on their left.

"I shouldn't have blurted out what I did," Jewel said, standing back so that her husband could close the door. "Do you think we gave her enough time?"

Grady turned to her. "I believe so. Bethia's quick."

"Good thing Girton doesn't allow male callers." Jewel blew out an exasperated stream of breath. "This is Aunt Phyllis's fault. *And* Uncle Norman's."

"Indeed? But they live in Sheffield, do they not?"

"I'm speaking of how they reared my cousins. They denied them nothing, so they became little tyrants. Now they expect the whole world to indulge them the same way."

At least in Douglas's and his younger sister, Muriel's, cases, she amended to herself. Douglas's twin, Bernard, with a nice wife and infant daughter, was vicar of Holy Cross Church in a little town south of Sheffield proper and was proof that miracles still happened.

Grady smiled and touched her cheek. "Has anyone ever told you how beautiful you are when you're angry?"

It was impossible to enjoy a good stewing of temper with that man about, Jewel thought. She was aware that she would never be the beauty that her older sister, Catherine, and cousins Bethia and Muriel were. Men did not compose sonnets about women with sparsely lashed eyes behind wire spectacles. Her only assets, in her opinion, were a slender waist and generous bosom. She wrapped her arms about his neck and pecked his chin. "You have kind eyes, Grady McGuire."

"Not kind. Astute." The lines in his bulldog-like cheeks creased with his smile. Even after five years of marriage, it never ceased to amaze Jewel that two such plain people had found something so lovely in each other.

They were introduced at a benefit luncheon for Sedgwick School by Headmaster Hugh Sedgwick, Catherine's husband. Hugh and Grady were former classmates at Saint John's College and had even acted together in a couple of productions. Grady was, at that time, the stage manager for Sadler's Wells Theatre, and he invited Jewel to observe a dress rehearsal of *Little Lord Fauntleroy*. They were wed within six months, and three years later they were managing the Royal Court Theatre for the owners, Messrs. Cumberland and Fry.

Now that her parents had finally stopped blaming Grady for Jewel's abandoned plans for college, they had grown quite fond of him. She and Grady had no children as yet. At least no *infant* children, Jewel corrected mentally as her ears caught the increase in volume from the other side of the theatre door.

"You haven't an ounce of respect for those who have to work with you!"

Mrs. Steel's voice. Jewel did not have to guess to whom it was directed. She sighed at her husband. "I should see what's going on."

"And I'll get back to those matinee receipts," Grady said.

"Coward," she said with a loving smirk. Raised in a family where rows were commonplace, Grady could not bear to occupy the same room with disharmony. It was a wonder, Jewel thought, that he had offered to speak with Douglas.

"Yes." He smiled in guilty concession. "And grateful to have a wife so skilled in mediation."

They parted ways, and Jewel slipped into the theatre. The dispute onstage apparently centered about Richard Whitmore's breakfast.

"What on earth did you have, Mr. Whitmore?" Charlotte Steel scowled up at the leading actor, hands upon hips in a very unJuliet-like pose. Still, she was a beautiful woman, seeming far younger than twenty-eight, with a wealth of burnished auburn hair and pale blue eyes like chips of ice—startling and arresting between thick lashes.

"Sardines and onions?" she went on. "Could you not have spared a moment to clean your teeth before shouting your lines into my face?"

"If you'll run and fetch my toothbrush, old girl, I'll do that straightaway," Richard Whitmore replied, smirking down at her from his six-feet-four height, savoring the point just earned on the irritation scorecards he and Mrs. Steel kept.

At thirty-six, he was quite long in the tooth for the part of Romeo. Not that audiences would mind, for as many were drawn by his fame as from any love of drama. Still, the premature gray frosting his hair and beard would have to be dyed to stay within the bounds of credibility.

"Mrs. Steel . . . Mr. Whitmore . . . if you please!" Mr. Webb, the stage director, cajoled, wringing his hands. The recently hired actors standing nearby stared uncomfortably at their shoes. Those who had been around for a while studied their scripts with bored expressions while waiting for the tempest to pass.

Mrs. Steel wheeled upon Mr. Webb, pale blue eyes stormy. "Will you just stand there and allow him to insult me that way?"

"She takes offense at what *I* said?" Mr. Whitmore laid a hand upon his chest and quoted a line from the play to the invisible audience filling all three tiers and 642 seats. "Why, 'I am the very pink of courtesy.'"

Jewel sighed and hastened down the aisle. The frustration of dealing with giant egos notwithstanding, she loved everything about theatre: the thrill of witnessing the clumsy first readings of the playwright's lines gradually absorbed into an actor's personality and delivered with such naturalness as if the actor's mind were composing them; the transformation of canvas, lumber, and paint into scenes of distant places—of cloth and paste jewels into costumes of another era; the hush of an audience, all eyes fixed upon the stage, while thought of troubles and responsibilities, debts, disappointments, and heartaches were given a couple of hours' respite.

"You came to rehearsal in that state just to provoke me!" Mrs. Steel was saying.

"'E contrario,' Madame!" He faced the invisible audience again and quoted another line, causing several of the other actors to conceal smiles with their hands or by turning faces toward the backdrop. "Methinks 'thy head is as full of quarrels as an egg is full of meat.'"

"If you don't make him stop that, Mr. Webb, I shall leave!"

And because of the magic of theatre, Jewel thought wryly, come December, every occupant of every empty seat she passed would be convinced that the two bickering actors were passionately in love. That is, if she and Mr. Webb could prevent them from murdering each other beforehand.

Bethia, waiting just inside the stage exit, shook her head at the sounds of disharmony drifting her way through the wall. *Poor Jewel and Grady!* And here she was, adding to their burden with the Douglas Pearce situation.

This isn't your fault, she reminded herself. But believing that was another story. Why had she had tea with Douglas Pearce that day? Why had she not made it clear that she had no romantic affection for him when he first began appearing everywhere she went? And why had she not suspected he'd eventually show up at work?

It was dear old Mr. Birch who had insisted she wait until he determined that the coast was clear. After all, he had reasoned, there was no guarantee that someone as obviously unstable as Mr. Pearce would linger long enough to listen to Grady and Jewel.

The nerves in the back of her neck flinched when the doorknob started turning. But it was only Mr. Birch. "He hurried toward the underground station five minutes ago. It may be prudent to allow him another five, just to be certain."

"Yes, I'll do that. Thank you, Mr. Birch."

"Not at all, Miss Rayborn. At my age, a little intrigue is a welcome diversion." He leaned his aged head, studying her. "Did you say this young man is your cousin?"

"No," Bethia hastened to assure him. "He's *Jewel's* cousin."

"But so are you."

Bethia nodded. "Jewel's father, James Rayborn, is *my* father's younger brother. Uncle James is married to Aunt Virginia, and they have two daughters—my cousins Jewel and Catherine. It's Aunt Virginia's sister, Phyllis Pearce, who is the mother to Douglas Pearce and his siblings."

"Siblings. Oh dear. You mean there are others like him?"

The affected horror in Mr. Birch's voice made Bethia smile. For a second she was sorely tempted to share tidbits she had heard as a child about the infamous Pearce children—particularly the sister, Muriel. But however cathartic the sharing would be, loyalty to Jewel sealed Bethia's lips, except to thank Mr. Birch for watching out for her.

"We'll miss you up in the wardrobe room," he said warmly as they shook hands.

"I'll be back before you know it," she reminded him.

Two

*T*he most populous city in the world had humble beginnings—a settlement of thatched huts inhabited by Britains, a branch of the Celtic race. Roman invaders in 43 A.D. realized the military significance of the location on the River Thames and made it their headquarters, giving it the name Londinium. Over the centuries, London development advanced upon field and forest, absorbing the town of Westminster and villages such as Kensington and Mayfair and Chelsea, home to the Royal Court Theatre.

Three and a half miles north of the theatre's stone facade lay another of London's villages, quaint Hampstead. It was where Bethia Rayborn lived, in a house at 5 Cannonhall Road with her parents and nineteen-year-old brother, Danny, as well as her half-sister, Sarah, Sarah's husband, William Doyle, and their son, fifteen-year-old John.

Danny had left on Thursday past to begin his second year at the world-renowned medical school of the University of Edinburgh, and on this Tuesday morning of the fifth of October, Bethia was leaving for Girton College. She donned a traveling suit of blue-and-gray plaid cashmere, angled a blue French beret upon her head, and left with her parents for King's Cross Station.

They arrived an hour early, time enough for tea at one of the tables spilling out from one of the cafés under the arched train shed. Tea *and* watching people pass, at least for Bethia and her mother, Naomi. Her father, Daniel, scanned the brick walls and the myriad of posters touting the quality of such products as Pears Soap and Brook's Improved Patent Sewing Cotton. Bethia knew the purpose of his search—to find the clever and innovative Rowland's Macassar

Oil advertisements, which featured actual close-up photographs of men with disheveled hair and panicked expressions, over the caption, *What do you mean, we're out of Rowland's?*

Presently her father settled back into his chair, crossing his long legs at the knees. "Arnold Fox takes those photographs for Rowland's," he said, pointing at the latest poster with a trace of pride, for Arnold Fox was a fellow member of the British Camera Club.

"Does he, now?" Bethia said, exchanging knowing looks with her mother. "You've never mentioned that."

Her father looked at her through narrowed eyes. "Now you're mocking me, aren't you?"

"Just a bit, Father. Do you mind?"

"Not at all," he replied, smiling.

At length they stood on the platform, where the boarding whistle from the locomotive of the Great Northern Railway Express had induced a frenzy of farewells and gathering of luggage. Behind the engine waited six first-class passenger carriages, all smart and clean and yellow, with appropriate names on each door panel—*Queen Victoria, Prince of Wales, Venus, Mercury, Comet,* and *Star.* Father accompanied her to the door of the *Mercury,* where a woman and two girls, one old enough to be a college fresher, the other much younger, were stashing handbags and umbrellas over seats at the opposite window.

"Pardon me, is there a seat available?" Father said, just in case they were holding places for others.

We're expecting two more," the women said pleasantly. "My sister and niece. So there will still be one available."

All Bethia had with her were her umbrella and satchel, having sent her trunk ahead last week to avoid the commotion at Cambridge Station. Father placed these in the window seat facing forward. That was one of the nicest things about family, Bethia thought as they again joined her mother, out of the way of others. Everyone knew one another's preferences and needs, such as how riding backward gave her motion sickness.

"It seems all we do lately is put our children on trains," Father sighed.

At sixty-eight, Daniel Rayborn's hair and beard were completely gray, his posture still erect but eyes now dependent upon wire-rimmed spectacles. Bethia knew he was thinking of Danny, who had boarded the Flying Scotsman at this same station. She stood on tip-toe to kiss his lined cheek. "We'll be home again in two months," she reminded him. "That's hardly any time at all."

"You'll remember to dress warmly when the weather turns, now won't you?" Mother said.

"I will."

Bethia smiled as they pressed cheeks together. The habit of nur-turing was ingrained too deeply in Naomi Rayborn's psyche to expect her to lay it aside just because her children were practically adults.

Fifty-nine years had frosted Mother's strawberry-blonde hair with gray. But the bottle-blue eyes could still flash humor, and the voice that had soothed away Bethia's nightmares as a child would always endear home to her.

The second whistle sounded, followed by shrieks and giggles from the Mercury. Bethia glanced at the window. Another woman and girl of college age had joined the first three.

"It's going to be a long trip," Father said. "Too late to find another coach."

"I'm sure they'll settle down," Bethia said over another burst of giggles. She noticed the guard collecting tickets at the coach behind the locomotive. With two more quick embraces for her parents, she boarded.

"Good morning," she said to the women and three girls sharing her carriage.

"Good morning," all five replied in varying degrees of timbre.

Seconds later the guard appeared at the open window. "Tickets, please?"

"Thank you," said the women, passing their five tickets to Bethia in her window seat.

"You're welcome," Bethia said. After the guard closed the win-dow and was gone, she smiled at her mother and father through the glass. She did not turn away again until the train panted out of the station and the two were out of sight.

"Those were your grandparents?" the dark-haired woman seated beside her asked as the wheels beneath them gathered speed.

"My parents."

"Oh, I beg your pardon."

"It's a natural assumption," Bethia said, and smiled to show she took no offense. Years ago she had ceased bristling when people made such assumptions. Life was filled with good people who simply voiced their thoughts without pausing to consider if they were appropriate. And of truth, her parents *were* old enough to be grand-parents. "I'm very proud of them."

"And well you should be," the woman said hastily. "Please allow us to introduce ourselves. I'm Mrs. Jordan." She nodded at the girl in the center of the trio of girls. "And this is my daughter, Florence."

The other woman, two seats over from Bethia, had brown hair and spectacles just like Father's. She was leaning a bit to see past her sister. "And I'm Mrs. Linsell with my daughters Ursula and Mar-garet."

Ursula, at the window, was of college age like Florence. Margaret sat facing Bethia and appeared to be about nine.

"I'm Bethia Rayborn. I'm pleased to make your acquaintance."

"And we're pleased to make yours," Mrs. Jordan said. "May we be so bold as to ask if you're a Cambridge student?"

"I'm beginning my fourth year at Girton College."

"Girton!" Mrs. Linsell clasped her hands at her ample bosom. "Isn't that wonderful, girls?"

All three nodded. Florence said, "That's where we're enrolled."

Bethia smiled. "You made a wise choice. It's a fine school."

"We were impressed with our tour," Mrs. Linsell said. Concern dented the skin between her eyebrows. "But we're not quite certain of the arrival procedure. Will we be met at Cambridge Station?"

"Yes. Some of the assistant lecturers will be there, and usually Miss Jones, the vice-mistress. I'll be happy to lead you to them. And porters will be available to load your trunks onto the school wagon."

"Very kind of you, Miss Rayborn," Mrs. Jordan said. "What of transportation to the college?"

"I'm afraid there is none arranged," Bethia replied, "what with students arriving at scattered times. But you'll have no difficulty pro-curing a carriage. And don't worry about stopping for lunch. There will be sandwiches set out in the dining hall."

"Very good." Mrs. Jordan turned away to confer with her sister. While Bethia was not purposely eavesdropping, her ears caught the word *carriage* and her eyes caught the stricken looks the older girls were giving each other.

"Mother . . . we'll be fine," the one named Florence said.

Ursula bobbed her head. "*Please.*"

Mrs. Jordan gave the girls a doubtful look and turned again to Bethia. "We had assumed Girton would provide chaperones from the station on. You see, Miss Rayborn, the girls have asked us not to accompany them to school."

Mrs. Linsell, leaning forward again, said, "They wish to be independent young women. Having their mothers tagging along will make them feel less grown-up."

Bethia understood. She and most of her classmates would admit to having felt the same way when they were freshers.

"But they've never taken a cab without an escort. . . ."

"Mother, it's only three miles," Ursula whined.

"The cabbies have always been very helpful to the women students," Bethia assured the group. "But if it would put your minds at ease, your daughters and I could share one."

The older girls let out breaths in unison and gave their mothers hopeful looks.

"Why, that's most kind of you, Miss Rayborn," Mrs. Linsell said.

"Most kind," Mrs. Jordan echoed. "We'll not worry, with them in your capable hands. How can we ever thank you?"

"Really, it's nothing." Which wasn't quite so, for Bethia would now have to wait until the girls' trunks were secured on the school wagon. "I'm going the same way."

"Still, it's terribly good of you," Mrs. Linsell insisted. "What are you studying, Miss Rayborn?"

"History." Bethia looked at the older girls. "And you?"

Florence replied that she was interested in Natural Science, Ursula in Classics. "But I may switch to Mathematics next term, if I find I don't care for Classics," Ursula added, and shrugged. "Or I may just study both."

"Ursula has a wide range of interests," Mrs. Linsell said proudly, as her older daughter nodded. "She plays four musical instruments."

"And Florence enjoys tennis as much as science," said Mrs. Jordan. "She was awarded four trophies at Holland Park Academy."

"I won a medal for spelling last term," the young girl, Margaret, said timidly.

Her sister, Ursula, obviously embarrassed, gave Bethia an apologetic look. "It was only third place."

Bethia smiled at the younger girl, whose expression had crumpled. "I was never even good enough for third place. What's your secret?"

Margaret brightened. "As I write words for practice, I divide them into syllables. They're much easier to learn if you break them down."

"I'll be sure to try that."

"This is your sister's special day," Mrs. Linsell reminded her younger daughter. "Miss Rayborn, what are the library hours? Ursula is a voracious reader and will wish to spend a lot of time there."

"As will Florence," Mrs. Jordan chimed.

Bethia answered that question and several more. When there was enough of a pause to where she would not be acting rudely, she took Horatio Pater's *Studies in the History of the Renaissance* from her satchel. The women's boasting over their eldest daughters was becoming fatiguing. Thankfully they took the hint and began conversing among themselves again.

When the clicks of the rails beneath her became farther apart—signaling the approach of her destination—she closed her book to take in the familiar landmarks of Cambridgeshire. Fields and hedgerows, a half-timbered farmhouse with a grazing flock of gray sheep, the brown brick grammar school with red shutters, the white-haired man rising from the bench in front of his stone cottage to wave at the train, pipe in his other hand and Irish Setter at his feet. Bethia returned his wave, as she had done for the past three years.

Presently, movement ceased with a great hissing of steam. A hush fell over the fivesome as the coach rocked back upon its tracks. Bethia packed her book into her satchel and took hold of the umbrella wedged between her seat and the wall. The door opened, a smiling guard touched the beak of his cap and moved on.

"Well, this is it," Bethia said to Ursula and Florence.

"This is it," Margaret echoed wistfully.

Bethia gave the younger girl another smile and stepped out onto the busy platform, standing aside for the others to exit. As the group moved several feet from the train, the mothers reminded their daughters to shake Miss Jones's hand.

"But only after she offers hers," Mrs. Linsell said.

Mrs. Jordan nodded. "Give a firm grip, mind you, but not like a man's."

"Miss Rayborn?"

Bethia turned, unwittingly, and met Douglas Pearce's sheepish smile. Her umbrella clattered to the platform.

No! This could not be happening! She accepted the umbrella from Margaret's hand with face burning, too rattled to thank the girl.

"For a minute I wasn't certain it was you." Mr. Pearce's hazel eyes gave her an appraising look. "The hat suits you. You look like a French girl."

"You shouldn't have followed me, Mr. Pearce," Bethia said, as softly as the chatter of the crowd would allow, but with enough force in her tone to press her point. She was finished being nice, because that just did not seem to work. "Do you not have a job?"

"You left me no choice, don't you see? Jewel wouldn't allow me to see you yesterday, and your brother-in-law refused to fetch you to the telephone this morning."

"At my request," Bethia informed him.

"Who is he, Mother?" Margaret asked.

"Sh-h-h."

Bethia glanced at the faces beside her. Self-consciously the women and two older girls looked down at the platform. But they did not move away. The air was heavy with expectation—Mr. Pearce expecting her to say something to justify his appearance, the women perhaps hoping for some gossip to go along with their tea this afternoon.

"Miss Rayborn?" he said.

The voice grated upon Bethia's nerves like fingernails upon blackboard. How could she have ever found that voice pleasant, even warm, the day they had shared tea at Covent Garden? Had he no other interests besides *her*? Whatever in the world had he done with his life before that chance meeting?

". . . could speak somewhere privately?" he was saying.

Reluctantly Bethia moved closer, in order to be heard over the chatter of the crowd. "Good day, Mr. Pearce. Please go back to London. We have to leave now."

She was turning to usher the mothers and daughters toward the school authorities, when her upper arm was caught in a firm grip.

"Does it please you to torment me? I can neither sleep nor work for thinking of you!"

"Mr. Pearce, please let go," she said, trying to pull away. Others upon the platform were stopping to gape at them.

"Can't you see? Are you *that* stupid?" He held fast, digging his fingers into flesh even through her coat. "If that coachman's son loved you, he wouldn't have gone off to Italy!"

"Leave go of the lady at once!" said a male voice.

"Or we'll make you regret it!" said another.

The grip upon her arm released. Bethia mumbled thanks to her rescuers—one college-aged, the other an older man—but was too mortified to meet their eyes. She turned away, gave Mrs. Jordan an apologetic look, and hastened down the platform, ignoring curious stares, weaving her way around people and luggage carts, and fearing being seized again.

"You led me on, Miss Rayborn!" she heard from behind. "You trifled with my affections! What do you do, carve men's hearts in the handle of your hairbrush?"

Don't cry, Bethia willed herself. She made her way to the row of hired cabs, meeting no one's eyes, every nerve on alert. She hired a coach instead of a carriage so that she could hide behind drawn curtains, and instructed the driver not to stop, should anyone short of a policeman wave him down.

$\mathcal{N}$ot until Bethia stepped down from the coach could she breathe more easily, though her hands still trembled, and humiliation still clung to her like moss to a stone. Girton College stretched before her like a biblical city of refuge, its monotonous main block enhanced by the more recent round terra-cotta brick towers with conical roofs and rising windows. The two-and-a-half miles to the center of Cambridge may as well have been a million to any young man—even those with closer family ties than distant-cousin-by-marriage—who dared trespass these gates without permission of the headmistress.

Miss Welsh stood with notebook in hand beneath the clock at the main entrance, where headmistresses had greeted incoming students since the college moved from Hitchin twenty-four years ago.

"Of course you may telephone your parents," she told Bethia after an exchange of pleasantries. "And do wish them my best."

"Thank you, Miss Welsh."

Bethia went on inside to the reading room, set umbrella and satchel in a chair, and lifted the earpiece to the telephone mounted upon the wall.

"Number five Cannonhall Road in Hampstead, London," she said to the operator.

She had once teased her mother, labeling her as old-fashioned for marveling that persons could converse from opposite ends of England as if they were next door. But when a maternal "Bethia?" came through the earpiece, Bethia did not take that technology for granted. She needed to hear her parents' voices, even though she could not reveal to them just why.

"Two of those girls you saw in my coach were new Girton students," she said into the mouthpiece. "I was able to give them some advice about what to do when they arrived."

"Lovely," her mother said. "Then you had no difficulties."

"I did some reading," Bethia said evasively.

She spoke with her father next, and managed to sidestep his query about her journey. When she turned the knob to her upstairs apartment door and pushed it open, she felt the weight of someone on the other side.

"Oh dear me, Miss Rayborn!" gasped chambermaid Anna Fisher, hand to her chest.

Bethia had to wait for her own heart to cease pounding. For a split second her imagination had conjured up the image of Mr. Pearce, waiting behind the door.

"Are you all right?" Anna said. She was a couple of years younger than Bethia's twenty, ruddy-faced and freckled, with hair the color of copper.

"I'm just jumpy. Did I hurt you?"

"You only frightened me out of a year's growth. But I expect I've enough to spare."

Bethia could not help but smile at the maid's playful exaggeration. She stepped on into the room and dropped her umbrella into its stand, her satchel into the damask-upholstered chair near the door. Coals hissed in the grate. Pulling off her gloves, she said, "Mmm . . . toasty. Thank you."

The girl looked pleased. "I just now added more. Is that one of those French hats?"

"It's called a beret." Bethia took it off and handed it over for her to inspect. Bit by bit, the scene at the railway station was becoming a distasteful but distant memory. "I don't think there's anything more welcoming than a fire in the grate."

"Except food, to my way of thinking." Anna said. She set the beret upon the study table and stepped over to help Bethia out of her coat. "You should see the spread downstairs."

"Sandwiches, you mean?"

"Hardly," Anna chuckled. "There's boiled prawns, every sort of cheese, and figs the size of my uncle Ralph's nose. Miss Copage, who graduated this summer—only it's Lady Sherwood now, as she's married to a duke in Lincolnshire—ordered it as thanks for all her fond memories of the place, so says Miss Jones."

"What a thoughtful gesture."

"She even had some sent back to the kitchen for us servants too," the girl said, patting her stomach. "We sampled at it all morning, and still there's enough left for lunch. *And* Harold's roasting venison for mum's birthday supper tonight. Mrs. Jones said I can take off early. They'll have to carry me here in a wheelbarrow in the mornin'."

"It's good of you and your brother to do that. I hope your mother has a wonderful celebration."

"Thank you, Miss Rayborn." Anna took three steps toward the door but then turned and said, "Dear me, I almost forgot . . . you've had a letter waiting on the chimneypiece for days and days."

The envelope was propped up against the sea-green bisque vase Guy had won at Bartholomew Fair seven years ago, when he was but sixteen and Bethia was days away from turning fourteen. She smiled at the memory, as crystal clear in her mind as if it were yesterday.

"You've won yourself a pretty to give to your favorite girl!" the huckster at the darts counter had bellowed, which should have brought a blush to Guy's cheeks, especially with her parents and Danny in hearing distance. But instead, Guy had solemnly handed the vase to her, as if offering his heart. She accepted it in the same spirit, and their longtime childhood friendship took on a new dimension.

Noting the Bond Street address in the left corner of the envelope, Bethia slid a fingernail beneath the flap.

Dearest Lilly, she read. It was Guy's pet name for her, derived from Lilliputian, one of the tiny inhabitants of an island in *Gulliver's Travels.*

> When you read this I will have been in Bologna for three weeks. As for now, I have just returned from supper with you and your family at Hampstead, and your sweet face will be the last I see as the train leaves Waterloo Station tomorrow.
> Already I miss you!
> This will be short, for it is past eleven o'clock and, typically,

I have put off finishing my packing until the last minute. I just want to wish you a fulfilling Michaelmas Term. Don't spend all your time at study, for despite your insistence to the contrary, I am positive that it says somewhere in the Scriptures that a wife must not be brighter than her husband.

Bethia smiled. Guy would never know how much she needed to hear from him today, even if the letter was written weeks ago. She folded it up and put it away in the drawer of her small walnut davenport. Then she looked about the apartment, reacquainting herself. Everything was freshly dusted, the windowpanes clean, the nap of the rugs bristly from a recent beating.

In the bedroom, a glance in her wardrobe and stocking drawer revealed that Anna had already unpacked her trunk and sent it up to the attic. Bethia tipped the servants well at the end of every academic year, still, those like Anna went far beyond the second mile. Obviously Norma Copage had grateful memories of the same treatment. As Mother said occasionally, gratitude was the icing on the cake of life. Bethia thought of the spread waiting downstairs. Or *the prawns on the tray of life*.

She was not quite hungry yet, despite Anna's glowing descriptions. The thought of facing Ursula and Florence further quelled her appetite. She pulled out the chair at the davenport and filled her pen. She would answer Guy's letter first. She asked how his studies were progressing, and described stopping in to bid farewell to his parents yesterday morning on the way to the theatre.

Your mother was hurrying your sisters to dress for school, but made time to give me four lovely embroidered handkerchiefs. And your father spoke of plans to hire another clerk.

Guy's parents, Stanley and Penny Russell, had been servants at the Hampstead house for years, until they fulfilled a dream by investing their savings in a saddle-and-tack shop on Bond Street when the owner wished to retire.

This place is growing noisier by the minute, Bethia continued writing, as laughter drifted from down the corridor. It was such a relief to converse with him, if only on paper. After all, the bond between her and Guy had been forged from her earliest memory. Perhaps it was because that same sensitivity he had toward music allowed him a keener sense of what people felt in their hearts.

She made no mention of Douglas Pearce's attempts at courtship, nor had she in the two letters she had written since that Wednesday in Covent Garden. To be offered the scholarship was a great honor, and Guy needed to concentrate on his music. Mr. Pearce would be on his way back to London now—surely he had boarded the train again for its return.

This time the thought of food stirred a bit of interest in her stomach. And she could not hide from Ursula and Florence for the rest of the year. Capping her pen, she went to the bathroom to wash her hands and went downstairs. The voices from the dining hall were even more animated than the usual first-day chatter. Bethia discovered that Anna's glowing description had not done justice to the spread of food taking up almost every inch of the serving table. Besides the prawns, figs, and cheeses were artichokes *à l'Italienne* and pickled tongue, baked pears and eggs *à la tripe,* dishes of almonds and raisins, large Spanish olives, and three kinds of cakes. Bethia filled a plate with a bit of each and went over to one of the tables where freshers were collected.

"I'm glad you made it," she said to Ursula and Florence.

The two gave her cautious smiles and thanked her. Bethia did not ask if their mothers had allowed them to ride from Cambridge themselves. She had a feeling that, after the scene at the railway station, the women had walked them to Girton's front door.

The discomforting obligation over, Bethia joined a group of fourth-year students. Her classmates greeted her as if pleased to see her. But they addressed each other with far more intimacy, and some related visits to one another's homes over the summer and referred to letters they had exchanged.

Unfortunately, one consequence of juggling her studies with her theatre costuming responsibilities was that the school friendships formed during Bethia's freshman year had atrophied from lack of nourishment. Instead of a few intimate friends, she had several warm acquaintances. She realized she had only herself to blame and wished the situation were different. Still she seldom grieved over it. When would she find the time?

So why did a wave of sadness sweep through her as she peeled a shrimp and listened to the banter? It hovered briefly at the back of her mind and then took a step through the gauze curtain of conscious thought, becoming a mental photograph of the torment in Douglas Pearce's hazel eyes. Would he have been so persistent if, instead of hiding from him and refusing his calls, she had gently explained from the first that she felt nothing beyond friendship? How would *she* feel if Guy did not care for her in return?

You could have been more sympathetic, she said to herself, *instead of worrying over what others were thinking.* Her appetite deserted her again, but she finished her plate before excusing herself. A heady aroma met her nose as she opened the door to her sitting room. At the center of the study table, a bouquet of hothouse roses fanned out from the vase Guy had won for her.

Mother and father . . . Guy . . . Sarah and William? flitted through her mind. But she picked up the note propped against the vase with some trepidation.

Dearest Miss Rayborn,

I beg your forgiveness a thousand times over for startling you, and most particularly for those unkind things I said. Please understand the source of my pain. You have become as essential to my well-being as sunshine to these roses. If you would but grant me the opportunity, some little scraps of your time, I am certain that one day you will feel the same love for me that my tormented heart feels for you.

With everlasting devotion,
Douglas Pearce

She tore up the note and threw it into the wastepaper basket. In an instant the aroma had changed from pleasant to cloying, nauseating.

A soft tapping sounded at the door, still ajar. "Miss Rayborn?"

"Come in, Anna."

"Aren't they lovely?" the girl breathed. "A delivery boy from Thornton Gardens brought them by while you were downstairs. I was about to go down and fetch you, but then I thought you might like to be surprised."

"I was surprised," Bethia said dully.

"I put a piece of willow bark in the water to make them last longer." Anna leaned her head. "Is something wrong, Miss Rayborn?"

"No . . . yes. They're from a man who won't leave me alone."

"Oh . . ." A hand went to the servant's cheek. But dreaminess mingled with the concern in her green eyes. "It's quite romantic, isn't it? Does he say he loves you?"

"Yes." Bethia rubbed her temple. "It's not romantic when you don't care for the other person and he won't stop."

"Oh, no it isn't," Anna amended quickly, even though the dreaminess had not quite left her expression.

Not able to bear the thought of even touching the roses, Bethia was just about to ask Anna to take them and throw them out. But the enormity of the waste struck her. She could not stop Douglas's infatuation by destroying flowers that someone else might appreciate. "Do you think your mother would like them?"

Anna's eyes widened. "You mean that, Miss Rayborn?"

"Yes. Say that they're from *you,* mind you . . . for they're yours to give. It'll mean more to her that way."

"But the vase . . ."

"Surely Mrs. Bancroft will lend you one," Bethia said, rising again to hold open the door. For now, all she wanted was to have the flowers out of her sight. As the scent lingered in the air, Bethia swept up a couple of loose petals and threw them away. She remembered the nudging of her conscience on the stairs, and moved aside the unfinished letter to Guy to start another.

> Dear Mr. Pearce,
>
>   Thank you for the roses. I must confess to giving them away, for to keep them would mean that our relationship exceeds the limits of friendship. While the feelings you profess are flattering, they cannot be reciprocated; not now, nor in the future. Please do not send me any more flowers or letters. I regret exceedingly any pain I have caused you, and wish you well.

She placed the envelope in the outgoing-mail basket in the reading room with a great sense of having a load lifted from her shoulders. This would bring about the end of it. She was positive.

But even indirectly, Mr. Pearce still caused her distress, for she answered a knock a half hour later to find Anna standing in the corridor with face splotched and eyes watery, the vase cradled in her arms.

"Anna?"

"I dropped it!"

Bethia led the sobbing girl inside by the elbow. Between gulps of breath, Anna explained how she had successfully transferred the roses into a vase the housekeeper lent her and was on her way to return this one when she tripped upon the staircase.

"But it doesn't seem damaged," Bethia said, taking it from her arms. When she turned it over, she spotted the triangular crack where the curved side met the base.

"I'll buy you another," Anna said with wavering voice.

Bethia hurried into her bedroom, the vase secure in the crook of her arm. She brought back a handkerchief to press into the girl's hand.

"It was cheap. That's why it cracked." There was no constructive purpose in adding that its sentimental value far outweighed its monetary value. She set it back in its usual place on the chimneypiece, turning it just so. "You can't even see it now."

"But it won't hold water."

"I'll bring another from home." Bethia smiled. "We've dozens."

The misery did not leave Anna's expression. She pressed her lips together. "I scorched your blouse last term, and now I've gone and ruined something again. And this morning I tore some lace on Miss Mead's curtain. I *try* to do good work, but I'm clumsy as a cow!"

"Now, that's just not so." Resting a hand upon the girl's trembling shoulder, Bethia said, "Every student here wishes she had you assigned to her room."

The girl blew her nose into the handkerchief, her red-rimmed eyes giving Bethia a look of hopefulness mingled with disbelief. "You're not just saying that?"

"Cross my heart." Bethia gave her a little sideways embrace. "It's only a vase. Please put this out of your mind and enjoy your mother's birthday."

---

Four

*I*n the year 1677, a twelve-year-old girl named Mary Davies was wed to twenty-one-year-old Sir Thomas Grosvenor, bringing to the union, as her dowry, some three hundred acres of damp and substandard farmland west of London. For over one hundred and fifty years the land lay undeveloped and useless, until an entrepreneur named Thomas Cubitt persuaded the Grosvenor descendants of its potential. In 1830, on their behalf, Cubitt began developing the former Mary Davies' marshland into what became one of the most desirable neighborhoods in London.

Belgravia, an area bounded by Hyde Park, the gardens of Buckingham Palace, Sloane Square, and South Kensington, was the most aristocratic of these neighborhoods. And it was in Belgravia in June 1888 that another child bride took her vows on the arm of her much-older intended. The ceremony was conducted in the groom's house on Belgrave Square. It was a smallish affair attended by only the handful of family members and friends not outraged that sixteen-year-old Muriel Pearce was marrying barely divorced Lord Sidney Holt, twenty years her senior.

The bride and groom had met when Muriel was fourteen and accompanying her mother on a Christmas shopping foray into London from their home in Sheffield. As fate would have it, Lord Holt was visiting his mother, Harriet Godfrey, at the same time Muriel and her mother paid a call to Mrs. Godfrey in their former neighborhood of Belgravia.

This was actually Muriel's and Lord Holt's second meeting, but they did not count the time when she was eight and he saved her from dashing out into the street during a garden party—though they had enjoyed relating the incident to each other every so often over the course of their six-year marriage.

The two would have been well into their ninth year as husband and wife, had not Lord Holt's own shotgun misfired three years ago during a pheasant hunt on his Northamptonshire estate. Fortunately, he had directed his solicitor to draft a new will shortly after the honeymoon. Lord Holt had accumulated great wealth, hardly dented by the fifty-thousand-pound divorce settlement to the former Lady Holt, Milly Turner, who now shared a house in Chelsea with her friend Peggy Somerset, a chemist for the Hassall Commission. Muriel Holt's future was secure, as well as that of her daughter, Georgiana, born five months after her father's untimely accident.

The peerage of Belgravia held its collective breath in the waning days of the present Lady Holt's first year in mourning. Surely the young widow would not mourn beyond the societal set-in-stone minimum of twelve months and a day. Surely she would shed the black silk and crepe for the Parisian fashions and fine jewelry that had adorned her marvelous figure before her husband's passing. Certainly other men would begin calling. Some would be opportunists seeking fortune. Others would be enchanted by her violet eyes and ash-blonde and golden waves, such as in the paintings of angels by the old masters.

Whatever their reasons for ignoring the fact that she had contributed to the dissolution of Lord Holt's first marriage, the actions of these gentlemen callers would generate fresh gossip, the essential ingredient in every Belgravia party, soirée, and high tea.

But Lady Holt surprised them all by continuing to wear black another six months, then the half-mourning pinstripe-black for another six, followed by gray for still another six. When, after two-and-a-half years, she put aside the widow's weeds and began appearing in public—an evening at the Royal Opera House, lunch at the Savoy, shopping at Harrods—it was usually on the arm of her brother, Douglas Pearce. Those gentlemen callers, who shot out of the gates like thoroughbreds at the Derby when the word spread that Lady Holt was officially out of mourning, were not even shown into the hall of the Belgrave Square home.

"M'Lady is out" would say whichever servant happened to answer the door.

Often "out" simply happened to be out in the garden, where last summer she had discovered a fondness for digging in the soil. Why should she allow gentlemen to court her when courtship inevitably led to marriage? The six years with Sidney were more than enough.

It wasn't that she had not loved him. But after the initial breathy and wondrous first months, she had discovered that being kept upon a pedestal was wearying, as was having a constant companion whose happiness on any given day depended upon her mood at the time. And now with years to reflect upon it, she quite regretted having stepped out of childhood and into marriage so abruptly.

Not even to her mother had she confessed the rush of relief that had accompanied the news of Sidney's death. It was guilt over feeling thusly that had prolonged her mourning. Clothing herself in somber black and gray was surely due penance for the mornings she woke feeling giddy that her days were her own again. Why would she wish to surrender this newfound freedom?

There was a second, just as important, reason she had no desire to remarry. While her family was far from poor, thanks to an inheritance from Grandfather Lorimer, she grew up aware of a certain nervousness toward money in the house—Father grumbling at Mother about overspending, at her brothers every time a ball shattered a window; Mother scolding a parlourmaid for forgetting to extinguish the lamps when the family left the dining room, instructing the cook to trim costs by using margarine instead of butter in the servants' hall.

And then to marry Sidney, who recorded in his ledger virtually every penny they spent!

She enjoyed being wealthy enough to indulge her every material desire without considering the cost or having to ask anyone's permission. Horrid was the thought of another having access to her fortune, even if it was only to comment upon how she spent it. Better to shower her affections upon her wardrobe, decorating her house, pottering in her garden. These demanded nothing of her that she was not willing to give.

On Monday, the eleventh of October, she was on her knees by the east wall, transplanting annuals for the coming winter, when she heard female voices from Mrs. Beckingham's garden.

"How do you keep your eucalyptus so healthy, Maude?"

"Ramsey covers the trunk with fleece in winter, and every spring he prunes a third of the branches."

"A third?"

"He says you want some young foliage mixed in with your old."

Another voice said, "I hope you're paying Ramsey well, or I may steal him from you."

That remark prompted matronly giggles and Muriel to think, *How simple life is for the easily amused.*

Heaven forbid the Belgravia Literature Appreciation Society would invite *her* to join them. Milly had been a member, and Sidney had once said that his first wife was not nearly so avid a reader as Muriel was. *She probably poisoned them against me before she left.*

The only group to extend any sort of invitation to her was the National Union of Women's Suffrage Society, of which her neighbor three doors to the east, Mrs. Fiske, was a member. Muriel had accompanied Mrs. Fiske to a meeting in the Holland Park home of a Mrs. Millicent Fawcett, but the women gathered had frightened her with talk of carrying signs and stopping traffic outside Parliament. She thought it would be rather nice to be allowed to vote, but at the risk of going to jail? She would just as soon pass.

". . . still does, unfortunately," drifted over the wall. Mrs. Beckingham's voice.

"One would think she would have moved off to be with her people by now."

"Perhaps *they* don't want her either" was said, prompting another round of giggles.

"Did anyone see her in that purple gown at the opera last week?"

Muriel held her trowel motionless and cocked her head. *She* had worn a purple, or rather amethyst-colored satin when Douglas escorted her to the Tuesday evening performance of Puccini's *La Bohème.*

"Are you sure it was a gown? I think she put on a petticoat and dipped herself in paint."

"Perhaps she was stomping grapes for wine and got carried away?"

More giggles and a "Sh-h-h . . . her gardener's looking."

That was enough. Stabbing the ground with her trowel, Muriel rose. The top of the brick wall stopped just at her shoulders, so she could easily see the five women standing near the eucalyptus. They had not yet noticed her.

"Oh, Mrs. Beckingham?"

Five faces turned as one.

"You may wish to speak with your grandsons about using your garden for a water closet. I realize they're young, but you know how difficult it is to break a habit the longer it goes on."

"How dare you!" her neighbor exclaimed with a hand to her pearl-throttled throat.

Muriel smiled her sweetest. "But then again, it probably keeps the bugs away from your eucalyptus bark. Perhaps you could send them over here? My Himalayan birch is prone to algae."

"The cheek of you!" one of the other women said, giving Muriel the malignant look worn by most of the others. Muriel shrugged and dropped to her knees again, while on the other side she could hear sounds of hustling inside, and then a door slamming.

So much for book chat, when you can gossip about your neighbor. She was congratulating herself for the insects remark when she heard footsteps in the drying grass, then the voice of her daughter's nanny.

"M'Lady?"

Muriel continued gingerly pulling the geranium's fragile root tendrils from the soil, while her left hand held the bulk of the plant. "Yes, Tucker?"

"May I have a word with you?"

"Where is Georgiana?"

"Taking her nap, m'Lady. I asked Joyce to watch her."

Joyce was the chambermaid, who had her own work to do while Nanny Tucker was out here neglecting hers. But Muriel restrained herself from scolding, saying instead, "Here, push that closer."

The nursemaid bent down and, with a faint grunt, pushed the clay pot toward her. Muriel made a well in the soil with her gardening trowel, then dropped the bulk of roots and soil into it. Gardener Abe Watterson, mulching the base of the birch while whistling what sounded like a hybrid of "And the Band Played On" and "On the Beautiful Blue Danube," would later transport the pot and others to the greenhouse. Muriel shoved her spade into the dirt and got to her feet.

"Now, what is it?" she said, wiping hands upon her gardening smock. Nanny Tucker was a good six inches taller than Muriel's five-foot-five, so she still had to look up.

"I've a letter from my brother Robert in New York, m'Lady."

Excitement shone from Valarie Tucker's amber eyes, while the tremble of her lips betrayed some dread. Both displays of emotion gave Muriel an uneasy feeling. Was she about to give notice?

Were she any other servant, Muriel would have reminded her that the housekeeper Mrs. Burles handled all employment matters. As long as the household ran smoothly, Muriel could give a tinker's curse who dished her soup or made her bed. But the nursery was another matter. Having had a succession of nursemaids herself during childhood, Muriel wished her daughter to have more stability in her life. Besides, Georgiana was very fond of her nanny, so said Mrs. Burles.

"And . . . ?" Muriel said, holding her breath.

"He sent me passage money to join him." She hesitated. "I'll be giving notice to Mrs. Burles today. I can stay another fortnight, and then—"

"New York?" Muriel interrupted while her thoughts raced for a way to repair the situation, make the girl change her mind. "Why on earth would you want to go there?"

The nursemaid took in a deep breath. "Because our family's been in service for as far back as I can recall, Lady Holt. We never had the money for higher schooling, so that's practically all that's available to us here. There's a position for me at the sweets factory where he's been working, as soon as I can get there."

"And you consider factory work a notch above service?"

Raising her chin, Nanny Tucker replied, "Robert's been made manager. And Mr. Hirshfield—the owner—gives his employees a share of the profits, above wages. Robert says there's a real future in this. He says the sweet they make has caught on so big in New York that they're making plans to market it in other states by spring."

"Well, what kind of sweet?" Muriel asked, stalling for time.

"I'm not sure, m'Lady," the nursemaid confessed. Her eyes

shifted downward self-consciously. "Robert says it's called Tootsie Roll."

With great restraint Muriel held back a smile. One thing she had gleaned from her late husband's absorption with the stock exchange was that products with silly names were usually a flash in the pan and rarely stayed on the market once the novelty wore out. But she could not afford to offend Tucker. There had to be a way to convince her to stay. Muriel chose the method she deemed most effective.

"I'll raise your wages if you'll reconsider."

The nursemaid's eyebrows quirked, but any temptation that may have entered her head did not stay long enough to take root. "I miss my brother, Lady Holt. His wife, Nell, my nieces and nephews . . ."

"I'll *double* them. With whole Sundays off."

"They're all the family I've got."

"Triple! That's more than Mrs. Burles makes!"

"I'm sorry."

Muriel studied the girl's face, bemused. All her life she had assumed that the chief desire of those with little money was to acquire more. And all her life she had known that, by pleading and bargaining, she could make anyone do just about anything. To have both notions challenged was so unsettling she had to struggle to maintain composure.

Another strategy popped into her mind. She seized it with great relief.

"Have you given no thought to Georgiana? How abandoned she'll feel? She already has no father."

In truth, Muriel doubted that Georgiana, who would be three in February, even realized what a father was, much less that she had lost one. But it was an effective argument, for the nanny's eyes lustered.

Muriel pressed while she had the advantage. "Just stay until she's off to school, Tucker. Four years—perhaps only three. Then you could go off to the States with a nice little nest egg and the knowledge that you did what was best for a child who loves you."

Identical tears quivered in Valarie Tucker's bottom lashes as she drew in a deep breath. "I love Miss Georgiana," she whispered.

Muriel could smell victory but again restrained a smile. "Of course you do."

The nursemaid drew in another breath, sniffed. "And that's why

I came to you first, m'Lady. I've already thought about what this will do to Miss Georgiana, but . . . begging your pardon, there's something you can do to ease the pain."

The stupid girl's still going through with it? Muriel thought, teeth clinched. She relaxed her jaw and said with forced calmness, "I beg you . . . Valarie . . ."

"If you would only take more time with her, m'Lady," Tucker barreled on as if determined to get the words out before she could be silenced. "Surely you've noticed how her little face brightens every time you visit the—"

"That's hardly any of your—"

"A stroll now and again, perhaps if you read to her at . . ."

White-hot anger flashed in Muriel's head. It was bad enough that this servant would refuse her heartfelt pleas, but then to presume to lecture her on how to rear her own daughter?

". . . would gain more than you can—"

"That'll be quite enough," Muriel said tightly.

The nursemaid's face clouded. "I only want what's best for her."

"Obviously not, if you're deserting her."

Ignoring the servant's stammering protests, Muriel turned her face toward the far corner of the garden, where Mr. Watterson was pretending to be totally absorbed with his mulching. "Watterson!" she called, not caring if the neighbors heard. "Fetch Ham."

"M'Lady, I—"

"You've said quite enough, Tucker," Muriel said, holding up a silencing hand. "You'll have your trunk packed in ten minutes or you can carry it downstairs yourself. And when your *Tootsie Roll* factory goes under, you can remember how you turned up your nose at good wages."

Tears coursed down Tucker's flaming cheeks, dropping onto the bodice of her white apron. "Money's not everything, Lady Holt."

"Yes? Funny how it's those who haven't any who always say that."

With hands trembling she turned her back upon the nursemaid and resumed potting her geraniums, pausing only to bark out orders to coachman Ham Sherwin when he came hurrying over from the mews. "Help Tucker carry her trunk downstairs."

"Yes, m'Lady," said the coachman. "I'll just bring the carriage around and—"

"No! Just leave it on the porch. The little twit can hire a cab."

"Yes, m'Lady," he said after a fraction of a second.

Mrs. Burles ventured into the garden shortly afterward. Muriel waved her trowel at her. "Not now!"

The housekeeper stared at her for a moment and turned for the house again. It was when Muriel heard the commotion of the trunk being carried out front, the parting rings of horse hooves against cobblestones, that her eyes began stinging. She wiped them on the hem of her smock, blew her nose. Even with no one to notice, for Watterson had resumed his humming and raking, she felt humiliated. She had not even wept at Sidney's funeral, and yet a mere servant's snooty remark could reduce her to tears.

Mother, she thought, shoving her trowel into the dirt. She got up on one knee and then reconsidered. Mother's consolations would be comforting, but then would soon shift into recriminations over Muriel and Georgiana having not come up to Sheffield to visit since Easter. Her mother was practically housebound with severe rheumatism, and had not visited London since she stayed with Muriel during the latter weeks of her pregnancy and the early weeks of Georgiana's infancy.

It wasn't that Muriel felt no pity for her, but she wished her mother could understand how difficult it was to travel with an infant child, nanny, and all the trappings. If only she would accept her assurance that they would visit often once Georgiana was old enough. The guilt every telephone call induced made the lapses between them longer and longer.

Work was the remedy, mindless attention to the task at hand, allowing the cool October breezes to refresh her face and dry her tears. She lost all track of time, but looked up and noticed the shadow of the Acacia tree had swallowed much of the garden when Mrs. Burles stepped tentatively outdoors again.

"Lady Holt?" the housekeeper said, plump hands clasped. She was forty-seven years old, with grayish-brown eyes, and salmon-colored hair pulled into a topknot. "Miss Georgiana is weeping for Nanny Tucker and will not be consoled."

Muriel pulled off her gloves, chiding herself. *What were you thinking, running her off without a replacement?*

"Who's tending her now?"

"Evelyn, your Ladyship."

Evelyn was Muriel's lady's maid and as dull as shucked oysters. The only reason Muriel kept her on was that she soaked up magazines such as *World of Fashion* and *Godey's Lady's Book* like a sponge. Georgiana required a clever nanny, Muriel thought, such as Valarie Tucker, or she would grow up to be dull as well.

Brushing soil from her chin, Muriel said, "Well, send Joyce out for a new doll."

"A doll, your Ladyship?"

"Or something that winds up and makes music. That will cheer her. And telephone the agency, have them send some suitable replacements as soon as possible."

"Yes, your Ladyship." The housekeeper hesitated. "Would your Ladyship care to interview them?"

Muriel shook her head and knelt down again to her geraniums. "I'll speak with those you consider most promising, but there is no sense in my weeding through the whole lot when you're perfectly capable."

The nursery situation preyed so heavily upon Muriel's mind that she was snappish with the servants the rest of the day and scolded Evelyn for laying out a nightgown with the same broken button Muriel had brought to her attention days ago. As she lay in bed, Muriel wondered if the doll had helped Georgiana cope with the loss of her nanny. Whoever had the house built sixty years ago, had ordered an extra layer of flooring between the bedchamber and nursery floors. It was convenient when Georgiana was an infant and would have disturbed Muriel's sleep, but now Muriel had no idea if her daughter was still weeping inconsolably or fast asleep.

I should check, she thought, reconsidering her decision not to go upstairs for the usual good-night kiss, for fear of upsetting Georgiana anew. After all, wouldn't breaking the bedtime routine be just as disturbing? She wrestled with the dilemma awhile longer, then sat up and rang for Mrs. Burles. The housekeeper knocked and entered presently, graying hair in papers and the sash to her wrapper tied clumsily at her waist.

"You rang, your Ladyship?"

"Sorry to wake you, Mrs. Burles," Muriel said with an apologetic little grimace to prove it.

"I was reading, your Ladyship."

"Well, that's good. Who's with Georgiana?"

"Joyce, your Ladyship."

Muriel gave her the little grimace again.

"Would your Ladyship wish for me to look in on Miss Georgiana?"

"Please, Mrs. Burles."

She returned minutes later and reported that the child was sound asleep. That burden lifted from her mind, Muriel was able to lie back on her pillows and do the same. Hopefully by this time tomorrow, they would have hired a new nursemaid and her life would continue down its fairly unruffled path.

$\mathcal{I}$n spite of not wishing to be involved in the bulk of the interview process, Muriel could not resist taking a peek in the corridor outside Mrs. Burles's office the following morning. Applicants filled the seats brought in from the servants' hall, their spines erect, white-gloved hands folded in laps, and expressions hopeful. To Muriel's relief, at least a couple of the applicants appeared young, well-groomed, and intelligent looking. Thus she was stunned when, presently, Mrs. Burles accompanied a plain-faced woman of about forty into the sitting room.

"Your Ladyship, may I introduce Leah Prescott?"

Muriel took in the small, raisin-colored eyes and barely existent chin line, the mousy brown hair coiled at the collar of a faded black gown. What was Mrs. Burles trying to do? Frighten Georgiana?

"She's brought a letter of recommendation, your Ladyship," the housekeeper said with hurried voice, as if anticipating Muriel's misgivings. She stepped over to the sofa to hand Muriel an envelope. "From Mrs. Godfrey."

Harriet Godfrey, Sidney's mother, had moved to the Northamptonshire estate with her husband and son Edgar seventeen months ago, after Edgar was diagnosed with something called multiple sclerosis. Muriel charged them no rent, because after all, they were her late husband's family. And the situation worked to her advantage, for Henry Godfrey managed the property quite nicely.

But how could they have known she was in need of a nursemaid, Muriel wondered, with Nanny Tucker gone less than twenty-four hours?

She motioned toward the writing table. Mrs. Burles hastened to take the silver letter opener and bring it to her. As she unfolded the page, Muriel marveled again at how someone with such uneven penmanship had ever become a successful author of children's books. Sidney's mother had never learned to type and surely frustrated her editors to no end.

Dear Muriel, it read, with a blot causing the *u* to resemble an *a*.

> I hope this finds you keeping well. Thank you for sending the photographs. Georgiana is losing her infant looks and becoming quite the little lady. Please give her a kiss from her grandparents.
>
> Edgar's situation is the same, though we are encouraged that his appetite has improved since we hired a cook skilled in cooking for invalids. He spends much of his time sketching, in spite of the tremors, and shows the same talent our dear Sidney had.

The *had* was smudged. Muriel could not tell if poor penmanship or maternal sentiment had caused it. She read on as the two women stood waiting.

> If you possibly have any vacancy in your household, please consider Leah Prescott, the bearer of this letter. Her father, a pig farmer and one of your tenants, passed on a fortnight ago, and she is hoping to find employment in London. Miss Prescott is highly spoken of by the tenants on the estate for her years of selfless devotion to the eight younger siblings she reared to adulthood when their mother died in childbirth. While she did not have the advantage of formal education beyond grammar school, she has read every book in the Brigstock library, according to Miss Cook, the vicar's daughter.

Brigstock was the nearest village to the estate. Muriel lowered the page. "You weren't aware we had a vacancy?" she asked.

"I was not, your Ladyship."

While the woman's soft voice was not refined by Belgravian standards, she had not replaced the *was* with *were* in the Northamptonshire common vernacular that used to grate against Muriel's ears whenever she and Sidney visited the estate. The word *not*, however, came past her lips as two syllables.

"What would you have done, had we turned you away?"

Leah Prescott nodded. "Mrs. Godfrey kindly supplied me a general letter, should it be necessary."

The answer barely registered, for Muriel's mind was racing ahead to a novel concept. While she attended St. Peter's only on the obligatory high days, she did believe in God. She even prayed on occasion, such as when the lift stopped between floors at Harrod's last summer, holding her and other shoppers entombed for a quarter of an hour. But she had not thought to pray for a nanny for Georgiana. Had God, who knew everything, decided to set events in motion to fill this need before she became even aware that there *was* a need?

This was too radical to grasp in one sitting. But it brought on a sense of being special, almost privileged, and she resolved quietly to attend church more often.

Her mind returning to the task of interviewing, she asked, "Why did you come here first?"

"Mrs. Godfrey advised that I should." The woman opened her mouth again as if to say more, but then closed it, the small eyes measuring Muriel as if wondering how much was safe to confide.

This sparked a flicker of annoyance in Muriel. "Well, go on."

Again the hesitancy in the dark eyes. "I am glad yours was first, your Ladyship, for I prayed on the train that I would find a nurse-maid position, as I'm very fond of children."

Muriel's warm sense of entitlement evaporated, leaving an after-taste of resentment. Was God instead answering the prayer of this pig farmer's daughter? *But only if I hire her,* she reminded herself. She was tempted to dismiss her forthright, until the notion occurred to her that it may not be wise to defy God so directly. She had gotten away with a lot in her life, she realized, with no punishment. What if this was the final straw, in God's eyes?

Just wait, she said to herself. With a motion of the hand to include both women, she said, "Mrs. Burles has others to interview. If you wish, you may wait downstairs until she's finished."

An hour and a half later, Mrs. Burles knocked softly on the sitting room door. Muriel put aside the October issue of *Gardener's Magazine* she had been trying to read.

"Are you finished?"

"Yes, your Ladyship," the housekeeper said.

"And?"

"Miss Prescott seems the most qualified, what with the recommendation from Mrs. Godfrey and all. While she's had no experience as a nursemaid for hire, well, rearing all those children . . ."

Muriel pursed her lips for a fraction. "She's old. And homely."

"She's but forty, your Ladyship," Mrs. Burles said respectfully. "And aren't those things in your favor? She's not likely to go running off chasing some dream or to have suitors calling. And she doesn't have to serve notice to another employer."

Those arguments made sense, and combined with the punishment-from-God factor, disposed Muriel to consider Leah Prescott more seriously. "Well, bring her up here again."

This time the applicant proved her homespun education by reading eloquently from an article on fertilizers in Muriel's magazine and multiplying a pair of six-digit numbers in half the time it took Muriel to check the answer with pencil and paper.

"You'll be expected to wear uniforms," Muriel said, just in case the woman planned to wear that rag of a gown every day. Mourning her father or not, this was a household where things were done certain ways.

Leah Prescott blushed but did not lower her small dark eyes. "My father had debts, Lady Holt. I spent most of what was left to me on train fare."

Muriel looked at Mrs. Burles, wondering what that possibly would have to do with the uniform requirement.

The housekeeper nodded knowingly. "*Lady Holt* supplies the uniforms, Miss Prescott."

"Measure her and have Fenton's send some over," Muriel instructed. Fenton's was where the servants' uniforms had been purchased while Sidney was alive and pinching pennies to invest in the stock exchange. Now that he was gone, Muriel had one of her own dressmaker's assistants sew their uniforms, for she was particular about even the most minute details of her house, and servants were as noticed as the furnishings. But this was an emergency. "And have Doctor Lear over to examine her before you send her up to the nursery."

Leah Prescott was staring at her with a bewildered expression.

"Well . . ?" Muriel said, more than ready to get out to her garden.

"I've been hired, then?"

Muriel could not help but smile at the woman's taut posture, a thin hand up to her prominent collarbones as if all the hope in the world rested upon the reply.

"Yes. Providing Doctor Lear says you've no infectious diseases."

"Oh, I'm as healthy as a horse, Lady Holt. You'll see."

"If that's so, your wages will start at two pounds monthly and includes your meals and bed. You may have every other Sunday off, providing one of the others is available to mind Georgiana."

That afternoon Mrs. Burles stepped out into the garden to inform Muriel that Doctor Lear had indeed pronounced Leah Prescott healthy, if a bit undernourished.

"Well, good. It's settled," Muriel said.

"Not quite, your Ladyship. Nanny Prescott asked about Miss Georgiana's schedule."

"Schedule?"

"Meals, bedtime, and such?" the housekeeper supplied. "Having never been employed as a nursemaid before . . ."

Muriel waved the trowel in her hand dismissively. "Well, surely she's bright enough to figure something out herself. One doesn't put a child to bed at midnight or feed her supper in the mornings."

"Yes, your Ladyship. I'll inform her so." The housekeeper hesitated. "And . . ."

"What is it now, Mrs. Burles?"

"She wishes to know how often she should consult with your Ladyship."

"Over what?"

"How best to rear Miss Georgiana, she says."

The doubts Muriel entertained upon first meeting Leah Prescott returned. Was this how she reared her siblings, asking advice before every step? She thought back to her own nursemaids. None had seemed to struggle with the particulars of the position.

She blew out a long breath. This was a transition time, she reminded herself. Every newly employed servant in the house had probably needed a few days to adjust to the routine. Fortunately, Mrs. Burles shielded Muriel from most of those growing pains.

"Inform Prescott that she has full authority over the nursery, but if she ever strikes Georgiana she will be dismissed."

That was everything in a nutshell, Muriel thought.

Wednesday afternoon Mrs. Burles reported to Muriel that Georgiana already displayed signs of becoming somewhat attached to the new nanny, and that, given a few more days, surely the child would be just as fond of her as she was of Tucker.

Muriel received the news with relief, not even aware of how taut her nerves were over the situation until they began relaxing again. But just to be certain, she took to the staircase a half hour earlier than usual Thursday evening for the good-night kiss. On the third-storey landing, her ears detected faint strains of music intermingled with the rain pelting the roof and thunder rattling the windowpanes.

She was rather proud of the nursery, for it was a paradise of whimsy she had taken charge of decorating herself. Framed Kate Greenaway prints of children in quaint clothing hung from walls adorned with William Morris wallpaper of alternating pink, gold, and pale green stripes. The fireplace was surrounded by pretty tiles decorated with fairy-tale characters; a vast mauve and floral carpet covered most of the floor; four small bentwood chairs were arranged about a round table and child-sized dishes of a Royal Doulton tea set. A rocking horse dominated one corner, a three-storey doll house another, and white shelves displayed still more dolls and toys.

Muriel paused in the doorway. Nanny Prescott sat with her back to her on the low stool before the half-size pianoforte the Godfreys had given Georgiana on Christmas past. Muriel could see her daughter's flaxen curls just above Prescott's left shoulder. While the nanny's right hand fingered the keys, she sang, her voice steady and reassuring against the storm outside.

> ". . . and like the pretty plow-boy
> she'll whistle and sing,
> And at night she will return
> to her own nest again. . . ."

It was exactly what the position called for, someone who would be tender toward her child, and Muriel congratulated herself upon making the right choice. So why the lump in the pit of her chest?

She decided the ordeal with Tucker and its aftermath had drained more energy from her than she had supposed. Some hot chocolate would revive her spirits. And the bedtime kiss would only disturb

Georgiana if she happened to be asleep there against her nanny's shoulder.

Down a flight into the morning room she went. It had been Sidney's favorite refuge in the house, and now it was her favorite as well, since she had replaced the stuffy, heavy old furniture with the floral motifs, flowing swirls, and sensuous curves of Art Nouveau. Grandmother Pearce's collection of blue-and-white dishes was arranged on the wall over the mantelpiece, and the childhood dolls, which had survived Muriel's brothers, stared with glassy eyes from a tall mahogany case. Propped upon an easel in a corner was a canvas in oils, partially complete, of a bowl of fruit. The fruit that had served as her model had long ago grown soft and been discarded when Muriel's interest transferred from painting to gardening. But she had vowed to finish one day, hence she would not allow the servants to put the easel away.

The only older piece of furniture Muriel kept in the room was Sidney's comfortable single-ended mahogany-framed sofa, but only after having the tobacco-smelling red brocade upholstery and padding removed and replaced with China-blue velvet. After ringing for hot chocolate, she settled herself at the end of that sofa with stocking feet tucked up beneath her skirt and opened Bram Stoker's *Dracula* to where a ribbon bookmark rested in chapter four. Presently a draft of air from the corridor accompanied Joyce into the room. The parlourmaid placed the silver tray bearing cup and saucer and linen napkin on a tea table pushed close to Muriel.

"Will there be anything else, m'Lady?" Joyce asked after stoking the fire. She had coiled auburn hair, and seemed shorter than her medium height because of shoulders rounded from years of scrubbing floors.

Muriel took a sip from the cup and returned it to the saucer with a click. "Nothing more."

By the time Joyce returned to add a shuttle of coal to the fire and take the tray, the storm had ceased and only inky blackness was visible past the windowpanes. "Shall I close the curtains, m'Lady?"

"Yes," Muriel replied with eyes still on the page. She was halfway through another sentence when the soft squeak of hinges and another draft of chill air gave her second thought. She looked over her shoulder at Joyce, halfway through the doorway. "Leave the door open."

That meant the fire would not warm as efficiently, but Muriel was comfortable for the present, and a knitted afghan was folded within arm's reach. The Gothic horrors she enjoyed, such as Stevenson's *The Strange Case of Dr. Jekyll and Mr. Hyde* and Wells's *The Island of Dr. Moreau* usually gave her no more than a delicious mild scare, which she could put into perspective by reminding herself that the stories were made up. But *Dracula* was a little too intense to be reading alone, even though she could no more bear to save it for a less gloomy morning than fly.

> *For a moment or two I could see nothing, as the shadow of a cloud obscured St. Mary's Church and all around it. Then as the cloud passed I could see the ruins of the abbey coming into view. . . .*

"Muriel, I—"

"Ahgh!" She jumped at the touch on her shoulder. The book flew from her lap to the carpet with a thump. By that time, Muriel's mind had registered to whom the voice belonged.

"Douglas!" she exclaimed, twisting over the sofa back to slap his arm.

"Sorry," he said, but grinning like an eight-year-old who had just pulled a chair from beneath a schoolmate.

Before she could slap him again, his smile dipped into a trembling frown, and his eyes filled. Muriel stared at him for a second then groaned. "For mercy's sake, Douglas . . . not *her* again."

Her brother went around the sofa, dropped onto the other end. "I got a letter from her today. She said she gave away the roses I sent her and that we can't be anything more than friends."

"Well then, you have your answer." Muriel's feet touched the carpet briefly as she leaned down for her book. "She's proved she's not worth a minute of your time. Why can't you just forget her?"

"Forget her!" A sob tore from his throat. "Could you have stopped loving Sidney at will?"

"That's different. Sidney loved me in return." She drew in an exasperated breath. "Douglas, Mother always told us how Bethia's Hampstead clan has this bizarre affinity for servants. Her father married a cook, her half sister a stable boy. They're low-class people who happened to come into money and now think they're better than the rest of us. Why would you wish to associate with anyone from that lot?"

"The heart doesn't think about such things," he said with all the pathos of a lovelorn poet. "It only knows that it loves."

"Oh, spare me the sentimental rubbish," Muriel groaned.

They had had variations of the same argument for the past three weeks. She knew how this one would end, even if she reasoned with him until blue in the face. Reaching for the bell cord, she said, "Some cake would make you feel—"

"I don't want any cake! I'm older than you, in case you've forgotten, and you don't have to treat me like a little boy!"

"Sorry," she said, lowering her hand.

His hazel eyes filled with worry. "I shouldn't have followed her to Cambridge."

"You don't say?"

The sarcasm in Muriel's voice was lost on her brother, for he nodded thoughtfully and said, "I should have given her a little time. She would have begun to miss me . . . I just know it."

"Mm-hmm." Muriel reached again for the bell cord. *All this agony over a cook's daughter.*

"I said I don't want cake!" Douglas snapped.

"It's for *me*!" she snapped back.

𝒪ne week progressed and then another, with Douglas Pearce occupying less and less space in Bethia's mind as she immersed herself into the routine of lecture, study, letters home and to Guy, and forays to Fitzwilliam Museum to fill a new sketchbook with eighteenth-century costumes. *Lady Audley's Secret* was scheduled at the Royal Court for April, after *Romeo and Juliet* and a four-week run of *The Runaway* by an American touring group. It was not too soon to be thinking about wardrobe, to be prepared to purchase fabrics during Christmas vacation.

On Sunday the seventeenth, Bethia dressed in a skirt and short jacket of camel-colored moss cloth to accompany a group of thirteen students on the short walk up Cambridge Road. Heavy on her mind was the ten-page composition she had completed last night on the British Reformation. Should she have included Poynings' Law?

How could you have overlooked that? she admonished herself, for even though the legislative supremacy Henry VII had established in Ireland had nothing *directly* to do with the Reformation, it later enabled his son Henry VIII to impose the Reformation on that country.

But since Henry VII's actions predated his son's reign, she could not simply tack the material onto the end. Nor could she insert it at the beginning, for she had already numbered the pages. Not wanting to mark through the page numbers and have Dr. Becker deduct points for sloppiness, she would have to copy again the ten pages sitting on her study table.

Surely it's good enough as it stands.

Good enough. Her mind might as well have replaced the words with *inferior*, for the feelings they evoked, and she knew what she would be doing after lunch.

Twelfth-century Saint Andrew's was a squat, solid structure of light brown stone, with Gothic perpendicular windows and a handsome clock tower. Lime trees shaded the lane leading through the churchyard to the south entrance. In the nave, Bethia reluctantly pushed aside all thought of the composition. As Father had once said, allowing one's mind to mull over schoolwork during a worship service was just as irreverent as bringing along textbooks.

The Fisher family filled its usual back pew to the right of the aisle. Anna turned to send a quick smile. Bethia smiled back and moved on up with her schoolmates to fill a pew on the left side. The stanzas of opening hymn, "Come Thou Fount of Every Blessing" mingled in soprano and alto, tenor and bass voices, most harmonious, some disharmonious, some high and childish—the blend surely as pleasing to God's ears as a patch of discordant wildflowers to an artist's eyes.

Three minutes into the litany, Bethia was gripped with a faint nausea. *My shoes,* she thought, wiggling her toes in the summer doeskin slippers. Because she had lost track of time while reading over her composition this morning, she had dressed in haste, which meant no time for the tedious ordeal of lacing boots with a buttonhook. Had not Mother warned her a dozen times that chilled feet could bring on a cold, or worse? But surely the fifty-degree temperature outside was not enough to cause illness unless she were to pad about barefoot.

"That it may please thee to bless and keep the magistrates, giving them grace to execute justice, and to maintain truth," Vicar Groves read aloud.

You haven't time to be ill, Bethia thought as a chill snaked down her back. But at least this was Sunday, when a simple meal of soup and sandwiches would be available to those students not taking lunch in Cambridge. All her life Bethia had heard their cook, Trudy, declare that no scientist would ever invent a medicine more effective than a bowl of hot soup.

Bethia had to smile. Her mind was so filled with the adages of family and servants that it was a wonder she had room for any original thoughts. Realizing that the congregation was halfway through the response, she opened her mouth to join in.

". . . to hear us, good Lord."

Another shiver caught her shoulders. That voice, from close behind. Oddly familiar, yet she could not recall ever hearing it in Saint Andrew's.

She swallowed. *He wouldn't.*

". . . to bless and keep all they people," Vicar Groves was reading.

This time Bethia held her breath, listened.

"We beseech thee to hear us, good Lord."

There could be no mistaking that voice. Bethia pressed the palms of her gloved hands together.

"That it may please thee to give to all nations unity, peace, and concord," the vicar read on.

At her left Hannah Middleton, a fourth-year student with curly brown hair, looked at her during the congregational response and mouthed *Are you all right?*

"We beseech thee to hear us, good Lord."

Bethia gave a slight nod, but felt Hannah's eyes linger upon her for another second.

Leave now, Bethia thought, face rigidly aimed toward the pulpit as she felt a pair of hazel eyes upon her back. But one could not simply slip out from the middle of a pew without disturbing the worship service.

You wouldn't be the first to leave, she reminded herself. Nature's promptings could not always be ignored. A discomforting mental picture came to mind. What would stop Douglas Pearce from leaving as well, from stalking her through the empty churchyard? Not that she feared any physical injury—though she could recall Father's admonition the first time she left for Girton, that the infamous Jack the Ripper's victims had probably thought his appearance harmless enough. What she feared most was another scene.

There was safety in numbers. She sat still as Lot's wife, listening to her own breathing, while the nerves on the back of her neck threatened to creep out of her skin. For all she could absorb of the sermon, Vicar Groves might as well have been reading Shakespeare. After what seemed like hours, pews creaked and the soles of shoes shuffled as the congregation rose for the benediction.

". . . We stand to bless thee, ere our worship cease,
And still our hearts to wait thy word of peace.
A-men."

Center of the group, center of the group. Bethia's mind repeated the phrase like a mantra as she filed out of the pew with the rest of the students. Her eyes did not leave the back of Hannah's herring-bone jacket all the way down the aisle. On the churchyard path, and against her better judgment, she glanced to the side and spotted Douglas Pearce's tormented face as he stood beside a lime tree with bowler hat clutched in hands. She looked away again quickly.

No scene. Please, Father, don't let him cause a scene.

Conversation swirling about her in reverential tones provided a tenuous element of safety while the group strolled down Cambridge Road. The scene on Cambridge platform notwithstanding, she could only hope that Mr. Pearce would be too intimidated to insinuate himself into her company with so many witnesses about—not only the Girton group, but others making their way home.

She fought the urge to glance over her shoulder as they passed through the safety of Girton's gates. In the entrance hall, her heart still hammered against her rib cage, but at least she no longer had to fear turning around and seeing him. *Thank you, thank you, thank you, Father!*

"Did you finish your history composition?" Hannah asked as they followed the rest of the group toward the water closet past the cloak room to freshen up for lunch.

"I'm not sure," Bethia replied, grateful to have a subject to distract her mind from Douglas Pearce. "And you?"

"I have to copy a final draft from my notes." Hannah covered a yawn. "But why aren't you sure?"

"I thought I was finished last night. But I neglected to mention Poynings' Law."

"Hmm. Can't you tack it onto the end?"

"It wouldn't fit chronologically."

"It's just a composition," Hannah reminded her. "You're not painting the Sistine Chapel."

"That's a relief. My pen won't write upside down."

The quip was not even funny, Bethia realized even as she spoke it, but the fact that it made Hannah laugh lightened her dark mood. "I'll give it another look," she said.

But first she would have some soup, even though she suspected now that it was Mr. Pearce's voice and not her shoes that had caused her chills. She was halfway through a bowl of vegetable beef soup when Miss Fleet, the assistant lecturer on duty, hastened to the table with hands fluttering.

"Long distance, Miss Rayborn! Your brother!"

It's not Danny.

Bethia knew so even as she pushed out her chair, even as she smiled when one of the girls piped, "Is he very handsome, Bethia?"

But then, there was that minuscule chance that it was indeed Danny. Notorious for hating to write letters, he telephoned her once or twice from Edinburgh every term, and it *was* always on a Sunday afternoon.

"Hello?" she said into the mouthpiece in the reading room. *Please be Danny.*

Silence. Every nerve in Bethia's body bristled.

"Danny, are you there?" she asked, just in case he had become distracted while waiting for her to come to the telephone. She would count to five before hanging up, she decided, then she would ring her brother herself.

"You gave away the roses. Are daisies more to your liking?"

Bethia's heart lurched.

"Or would you prefer violets? I'm not sure what else is available this time of year."

Hang up, she urged herself. But then, would she feel his eyes upon her every Sunday henceforth? Perhaps her letter had not clarified her feelings strongly enough.

"Mr. Pearce . . ." She filled her lungs, grateful to have the reading room to herself, but lowering her voice just in case someone loitered within earshot in the corridor. "I *beg* you to leave me alone."

"You're angry because I startled you at church. But I didn't cause another scene, did I? I just had to see your face. Can you understand? I haven't even a photograph of—"

Just say it, Bethia thought.

"Mr. Pearce, I'm very sorry, but my feelings do not extend beyond friendship." The *friendship* part had to be forced through her lips, but she had to allow him at least some small dignity.

"You hardly know me." His words rushed out as if he feared she would hang up. "How can you decide against me so rashly, after only an hour at Covent Garden? It takes time to get to know someone."

Any more time with you and I'll scream, she thought. His own logic gave her an idea. "You hardly know *me* as well, Mr. Pearce. You can't decide you love someone in an hour's time."

"I didn't intend . . ." His voice developed an edge. "I treat you better than your stable boy does. Has *he* ever sent flowers?"

Bethia stepped closer to the mouthpiece. "Mr. Pearce, if you mention Guy again, I will be forced to hang up."

Another silence, and then his voice softened. "Have you no pity?"

"I do pity you. But . . . I'm afraid that's all I feel, Mr. Pearce."

She could hear a sniff.

"I'm so sorry," she said. "But one day you'll . . ."

The edge returned to his voice. "Miss Rayborn, please spare me the assurance that I'll find someone else."

All she could think to say was another "I'm sorry."

"Not as sorry as you'll be if you marry that stable boy! You don't deserve to be hap—"

She replaced the receiver and leaned against the wall until her pulse ceased racing. When she could walk toward the dining hall again, albeit with knees that felt like rubber, relief and guilt tugged at her from opposite corners. If only she had declined to have tea with him that day! But how could she have known that he would cast her in the lead role of the drama he was constructing in his own mind?

"How was your brother?" asked Eugenia Milner, another fourth-year student.

"It wasn't him after all," Bethia replied and filled the brief space of curious silence by lifting her spoon and saying, "The soup's quite good today, isn't it?"

When she returned to her sitting room a quarter of an hour later, Cynthia Wood, the school servant who assumed Anna's duties on Sundays, was pouring coal from a shuttle to her fire. Bethia thanked her and sat down at her study table. The fruit of last night's labors—ten completed pages—lay in a precise stack beside pen and ink, blot-

ter, and another stack of twenty or so pages of notes. Now she wel-
comed the task, for it would take her mind off the day's disturbing
events. So effectively did she succeed in pushing Mr. Pearce from her
thoughts, that by half past four the twelve pages of her new composition were finished.

Nap, she thought, rubbing word-weary eyes. But first she would
clean off her table. She was dropping her pages of notes, along with
the original flawed composition, into the wastepaper basket when
someone knocked at her door.

"Come in?"

Bethia's neighbor on the sitting room side, third-year student
Elizabeth Norman, stuck her head into the room. She had accompanied the larger group of students to services and lunch in Cambridge. "I brought back some éclairs. Come join us!"

Of habit, Bethia opened her mouth to decline gracefully. In Elizabeth's eyes she caught a disturbing look of resignation. *This is your
last year,* Bethia reminded herself. *Will your only college memories be
of lectures and books and costume sketches?*

"Thank you, that sounds lovely," she said, stifling a yawn.

Hannah was among the five other students in Elizabeth's sitting
room. "Finished?" she asked, passing the bakery carton.

"Just now." Bethia scooped out an éclair. "And you?"

"The same." Hannah covered a yawn. "We'll sleep like stones
tonight, won't we?"

But that was not to be, in Bethia's case, for when she returned to
her room, the Bartholomew Fair vase sat in the center of the study
table, overspilling with daisies. Her dismay turned to horror when
she discovered the finger of water arching out from the base to pud-
dle about her composition.

"No!" she cried. She grabbed the stack and quickly began peel-
ing pages from the top to lie out on the dry end of the table. All but
the first three were ruined, water blurring the edges deeper and
deeper, until the final page was a mass of pale blue scribbles.

Because of the ink on her fingertips, she used her knuckles to rub
her burning eyes. The envelope propped against the base was ironi-
cally dry, *Miss Rayborn* penned in Mr. Pearce's all-too-familiar block
script. She snatched it up and threw it into the wastepaper basket,
then turned the vase upside down to shake the daisies into it as well.

She was wiping water from the table with a towel when she thought of the original composition in the basket. Perfect or not, she was at the point where she would rather turn that one in than have to recopy the final pages of her revised one. With held breath she pushed aside wet stems and dug for the papers. They were legible enough to copy but not to turn in, for water had soaked the bottom right corners about two inches into the script. Woodenly she pulled out the chair and filled her fountain pen. If she worked through supper, perhaps she would be able to go to bed at a decent hour.

But first, she would write a letter. Chest on fire, lips pressed together tight, she unscrewed the jar of ink and refilled her pen.

Dear Mr. Pearce,

I discarded your letter, unread, and will do the same with future letters. The daisies are in the wastepaper basket. Any other flowers you send me will be tossed there as well.

If you telephone me, I will hang up the second I hear your wretched voice.

If I see you in church, I will ask the vicar to escort me back to school.

If you approach me in the railway station or in the village, I will go to the police.

A courtship between us is out of the question, even if you were the last man in England. If you have any pride, any decency, you will cease attempting to contact me.

With utmost contempt,
Bethia Rayborn

So cathartic was the act of committing her frustration to paper, that the words flowed as fast as her pen could form them. She addressed the envelope in care of Sun Insurance Company, London, and before she could change her mind, went downstairs to the reading room and added the envelope to a stack in the wicker basket.

It was during Miss Stauton's Monday morning lecture on Margaret of Denmark's conquest of Sweden that Bethia wished she had toned the letter down a bit. *You wouldn't kick a wounded animal in the street,* her conscience prodded. She could have expressed her sentiment just as firmly without resorting to cruelty. After lecture she hastened to the reading room. The mail basket contained only two envelopes, neither one hers.

Should she write again, explaining to Mr. Pearce her state of mind at the time the first one was penned? With cordial firmness she would add that her feelings had not changed, lest she give him false hopes.

The mere idea of doing so brought on such queasiness that she decided to let the situation rest as it was. He would despise her, but having experienced the effects of his professed love, perhaps that was preferable.

Seven

*T*hree little maids from school are we. . . ."

"Sh-h-h!" Muriel hissed, leaning closer upon Douglas's arm while feeling the stares of other patrons leaving the Savoy Theatre's production of *The Mikado.*

But that only encouraged him to sing more loudly. He had a rather nice baritone, identical to Bernard's. Only Bernard was more inclined toward hymns than Gilbert and Sullivan ditties.

"Pert as a school-girl well can be. . . ."

"Douglas!" But this time Muriel's stomach cramped from suppressed laughter. "Everyone's looking!"

"Filled to the brim with girlish glee, Three little maids from school!"

"Drunken sot!" was muttered from Muriel's right.

She wheeled on the speaker, an older gentleman with a young woman attached to his elbow. "My brother's a war hero with a bullet in his head," she said to the startled couple. "And I'll thank you for some compassion!"

"I-I beg your pardon!" the gentleman stammered.

"What did she say?" came another male voice from Douglas's other side.

"He's a war hero," still another male voice replied.

"How tragic," a feminine voice murmured.

Muriel dared not look at Douglas for fear they would both burst out laughing and spoil it all. Fortunately, they had reached the coach. Once Ham had closed the door behind them, waves of mirth struck them both so savagely that Muriel had to hold her sides.

"A *war hero?*" Douglas chuckled, top hat balanced upon his knees as the coach trundled past the queue of carriages on the gaslit Strand.

"It was the first thing that came to mind," Muriel confessed, wiping her cheeks with a handkerchief.

One week had passed since Douglas showed up in her morning room wringing his hands. This evening it was as if Bethia Rayborn had never existed. They had entertained each other with reminiscings of childhood antics over a fine meal at Gatti's and later smiled at each other in fifth-row theatre seats over Gilbert and Sullivan's clever lyrics.

He's over her, Muriel thought. She reached across for her brother's hand and felt safe enough to say, "I'm proud of you."

Douglas returned her smile. "But I wasn't *really* a war hero, you know."

Muriel laughed again. "I'm speaking of you-know-who. You've not mentioned her all evening."

Even in the dim light she could see the cloud that fell over his face. She groaned inwardly, chiding herself. *Why did you have to go and upset the applecart!*

She let out a relieved breath when he said, "You were right. She's not worthy of my affection."

"Good for you!" Muriel said, squeezing his hand.

But her brother's return to the Land of Common Sense was not to last. Two evenings later, she was lying against her pillows with her well-worn copy of Mary Shelley's *Frankenstein* when a soft knocking sounded.

"Lady Holt?"

"Yes?" Muriel lowered the book. "What is it?"

Joyce opened the door and stuck in her head. "Begging your pardon, m'Lady, but your brother, Mr. Pearce, is here."

"What does he want?"

The parlourmaid hesitated. "I don't know, m'Lady. But he seems in an awful state."

Muriel closed her eyes, blew out a breath. "Tell him I'm asleep."

"Yes, m'Lady."

"No, wait," Muriel said as the door was closing. She sighed again. "I'll be down in a minute."

She shrugged into her dressing gown and slippers, grumbling to herself at how much better her life would be without family. When she entered the sitting room, Douglas jumped up from the sofa and took a crumpled envelope from his coat pocket.

"Read this!"

Muriel yawned. "Must I?"

He was still waving it at her. With still a third sigh, she took it from him and sat on the sofa. She looked up at him. "I can't read with you standing over me blocking the light."

When he dropped into the cushions, Muriel pulled out the crumpled page. The words were as cruel as any she had ever read. She clenched her teeth together and thought, *How dare you!*

"She says she couldn't love me if I were the last man in England!" Douglas cried. "She signed it *with utmost contempt!*"

There was something odd about the letter, on second look.

"Why does she mention daisies?" Muriel asked. "I thought you sent roses. And what is this about church? And the telephone?"

His expression turned sheepish. "Well . . ."

"You didn't go up there again, did you?" Muriel asked, lowering the page.

"Sunday past."

"Douglas."

Quickly and defensively he said, "I just wanted another look at her. That was all. I didn't tell you because I knew you would lecture me. And besides, I *thought* I was getting over her."

"Well, it would certainly help if you burned this bit of poison." She thrust the page at him. "And stayed away from trains, don't you think? Where were your brains?"

He took a deep wounded breath, then another, eyes closed. When he opened them again there was a calmness about him that was disturbing in its rapid onset. Pocketing the letter, he said, "I had my fortune read yesterday, Muriel. I wish you could have been there. She knew everything about me."

"She whom?"

"Madame Aldona."

The laugh Muriel attempted to squelch came out of her nostrils in a snort. Her brother's face went pink, and he gave her an injured look, to which she shook her head helplessly with a hand over her own mouth. When she could trust herself to speak, she moved her hand and said, "You don't mean that place with the big hand for a signboard."

Nestled among the fruit stalls and flower stalls of Covent Garden, the shop was good for an elbow nudge and grin, with its yellowed hand-lettered sign in the window:

> *Madame Aldona*
> *Dry Herbs inside*
> *Charms for Bad Luck go Away*
> *Read Palm only 3 s.*
> *Welcome*

For years the price of the reading had been two shillings, but several months ago that was crossed out with the three-shilling price inked beside the old one. Muriel supposed even gypsies who could tell the future had to keep up with the rising cost of living.

"If you've never been, you've no right to criticize," her brother said with chin raised. "Madame Aldona knew I was suffering from a broken heart before I even said a word."

"Anyone could look at you and see that."

Ignoring her comment, he held out his left palm and pointed with the index finger of his right hand. "That long line running diagonally is my happiness line. Can you see those three broken sections branching out from it?"

Muriel humored him and leaned forward. "I suppose."

"It means the three efforts I've made toward happiness have failed. Can you see? The letters to Miss Rayborn, the flowers, and the visits. How could Madame Aldona have known that?"

"But wouldn't the telephone call count as four?"

He opened his mouth a second before any sound came out. "A telephone call is the same as a visit."

You gullible boy, Muriel thought, even though at twenty-seven he was three years her senior. By some quirk of nature, she possessed more common sense than both brothers combined. "It doesn't matter how she knew that, Douglas. *You* knew that too, before you handed over your three shillings. So what good did it—"

He waved away her lecture and held out the palm again. "The line here. See?"

"The happiness line?" Muriel asked.

"No."

"Well, I don't see another where you're pointing."

He closed the gap between his thumb and index finger, forming a crease which branched from the one he termed the happiness line. "Now you see it. It's my love line."

"And . . . ?"

"The love line is only visible when I take action—moving my thumb—and then it connects to the happiness line here. Which means that by my taking drastic action, I can make Bethia mine."

Frustration was sliding rapidly into boredom. Muriel let out a weary sigh. "So you're going to go back up to Girton and wiggle your thumb at her?"

Douglas snorted this time, but out of impatience and not amusement. "You can be so dense sometimes, Muriel. Moving the thumb is *symbolic*."

"And I suppose she informed you what sort of drastic action it represents?"

"She said the opportunity would present itself to me by the end of the day. And sure enough, less than an hour after I returned to the office, Mr. Rowley called me in and gave me the sack."

Muriel's eyes widened. *"What?"*

"He said he had run out of warnings over my missing so much work." Douglas shrugged. "I was distressed too, especially knowing how steamed Father would be over it. I was beginning to doubt Madame Aldona, when Randall Adams approached as I was cleaning out my desk—he's the co-worker I've mentioned."

"The one who cracks his knuckles?"

"It's just a nervous tick. But listen! He's going to Canada!"

Muriel gave him an odd look. "Whatever for?"

"To look for gold in the Klondike."

"What's a Klondike?"

"Do you never read newspapers? It's in northwestern Canada. Prospectors are raking in millions." He leaned closer with arm hooked over the back of the sofa, hazel eyes intense. "Randall and I are leaving next Friday. We can be in New York in six days, Alberta in nine—"

For a fraction of a second Muriel was struck with an unsettling *déjà vu,* as if she had lived through this scene before. *Nanny Tucker and the sweets factory,* she realized.

". . . purchase equipment, settle in for winter and be prepared when the spring thaws—"

"Douglas! You get sniffles when you sleep with a *window* open!"

"We'll bring our warmest clothes, of course."

"You get a *nosebleed* in a bumpy carriage!"

"Not lately, I haven't," he said in a miffed tone.

"This is insane. You're as loony as King George."

He drew up his shoulders, jaw taut. "That was the only drastic action suggested to me yesterday, and so I'm positive it was what Madame Aldona read in my palm."

"And exactly how would this help you win Bethia Rayborn's affections?"

"She'll have lots of time to think about how she mistreated me when she learns I'm gone. And it'll be worth any hardship to see the look on her face when I return with my fortune."

Delicately Muriel unraveled his plan, pointing out that if great wealth mattered to Bethia, she would not love a coachman's son, that Douglas could return with *no* fortune, that it would be cruel to worry Mother in her state of declining health.

"I *have* to do this," he said.

Muriel was not so delicate when pulling apart the final strand, but then, she had to extinguish his every thought of this foolish escapade, lest they have this conversation over and over for weeks to come.

"Think, Douglas," she said. "Just forget 'Madame Three Shillings'. If Bethia and that coachman's boy both graduate in June, they'll probably marry soon afterward."

"That's a risk I have to take," he replied. "But I don't think it will happen."

Muriel blinked at him. "And why wouldn't it?"

"Because it wasn't in my palm. Besides, didn't you say that if I would stop pursuing her, she may realize she has some affection for me?"

"That was before you stalked her to Girton."

"I didn't *stalk*—" He took in a deep breath, leaned forward again. "She has feelings for me, Muriel. She may not even realize that yet, with her mind filled with that Russell fellow, but a man can tell. Madame Aldona could tell, and she's never even *met* her. When Bethia learns what I've done, she'll regret not giving me the chance to court her. I'm convinced she'll wait."

And I'm convinced there's a Father Christmas. Muriel knew she should press on, but when had he taken her advice over the course of this whole ridiculous infatuation? It would be just as effective to argue with the mantel clock ticking away minutes that she would rather spend in bed.

But then one more idea occurred to her. She twisted to reach for the candlestick telephone on the table.

"What are you doing?" Douglas asked anxiously as she lifted the earpiece.

"I wish to place a call to Gleadless," she said into the mouthpiece, ignoring her brother's frantic waving hands. "Holy Cross vicarage."

Douglas's face was buried in his arms against the back of the sofa by the time a sleepy-sounding "Vicar Pearce speaking" connected with Muriel's left ear.

"Bernard?" she said.

"Muriel?"

"Sorry to ring you so late. It's just that—"

"Is Georgiana all right?" he said anxiously.

"Oh, fine," she replied. And then, realizing she had barreled past the necessary pleasantries, she said, "How are Agatha and Sally?"

"They're well, thank you. Sally *finally* has a tooth! And Agatha's mother says the later they appear, the stronger they'll be."

"Indeed?" Muriel said, vaguely recalling the same reverence in Nanny Tucker's voice upon announcing Georgiana's first tooth. "Yes, she'll be grateful for strong teeth. We have a problem here, Bernard. You need to speak with Douglas, get him to explain to you his plan to go to Canada."

Without waiting for a reply, she shoved the telephone and earpiece at Douglas. "Come on now."

Douglas raised his face, sighed, and took the telephone from her. "That wasn't fair, Muriel."

Muriel gave him a long-suffering frown, passed the cord over her head, and got to her feet. Being captive audience to the melodrama once was quite enough. She paused in the doorway until satisfied that Douglas was indeed describing his plan to his twin, then went on down the corridor to the water closet. When she returned, Douglas was replacing the receiver with a *click,* his face crimson.

"Well?" Muriel said, sitting again beside him.

"I'm not going," he said with voice flat.

Muriel leaned to pat his sleeve. "You're making a wise decision."

"Yes."

"Shall I have Joyce make some hot chocolate?"

"No." He shook his head and got to his feet. "I'm tired. I'm going home."

Home was the flat he leased in Bloomsbury. "That's a good idea," Muriel said, rising with him. "A good night's sleep, and you'll feel better about all this in the morning."

"Mm-hmm." He accepted her kiss on the cheek, his eyes as dull as his voice, and left the room with a backward wave from the doorway.

When he arrived to escort her to *A Happy Pair* at Trafalgar Theatre three days later, he seemed almost his old self and made no mention of Canada nor Klondike gold. And when she asked about his looking for another job, he replied that he had contacted some people.

But on Friday the twenty-ninth, Muriel was planting Orange Emperor tulip bulbs when Mrs. Burles entered the garden from the house with a telegram. "It's from Bristol, your Ladyship."

"Bristol?" She knew no one in Bristol. Still, she held up her soiled gloves as an excuse. She shared her mother's superstition that telegrams inevitably contained bad news. "You read it."

The housekeeper nodded gravely, cleared her throat.

"Departing on SS *Baltic* within hour. Please inform family. Return September, earlier if enough gold."

Muriel pulled off her gloves, muttering, "That foolish boy!"

"I beg your pardon, m'Lady?"

She did not reply but hastened into the house.

"This is an emergency," she said into the telephone mouthpiece. "To whom do I speak in Bristol concerning a ship leaving?"

"The Port Authority, madam," came the tinny reply.

"Well, get them on the line!"

She fidgeted, winding the cord about her fingers while waiting for the operator to make the connection.

"Good morning." a man drawled presently. "Office of the Port Authority. Mr. Starling at your service."

"I wish to speak with someone connected with the SS *Baltic*."

"Hmm. That would be the Cunard Line. But you'll have to telephone them direc—"

Muriel broke the connection, jiggled the bar a couple of times. When the operator's voice came through the line again, Muriel gave her the information and insisted she hurry.

"Why, yes. The ship left an hour ago," a man from the Cunard Line informed her.

"Please bring it back. I need to speak with my brother. His name is Doug—"

"Madam, that is quite impossible."

"You don't understand. This is an emergency!"

A pause, and then, "What sort of emergency, Madam?"

"He's going off to Canada to impress a silly girl who doesn't deserve to walk on the same side of the street as he does. He'll get himself killed."

Frantic worry had pushed the words past her lips. Too late Muriel realized she should have invented something more drastic. A death in the family, perhaps. "Please. You must bring him back and allow me to speak with him."

An infuriating chuckle came over the line. "Now, now, Madam. Do calm yourself. People go to Canada all the time. Your brother will surely return after he's had his adventure."

Simmering, Muriel questioned the legitimacy of the man's birth and broke the connection during his outraged reply. She lifted the earpiece again to telephone her parents. But as soon as the operator's voice came through the line, she realized that Mother would be hysterical—too much for Muriel's frayed nerves.

"Connect me with Vicar Bernard Pearce at Holy Cross vicarage in Gleadless." While waiting for her brother's voice on the line, she thought, *Well, you'll be happy now, Bethia. Won't you?*

Eight

*O*n Sunday, the thirty-first of October, Bethia's parents, along with Sarah and William and their son, John, came up from London to celebrate her birthday, which would actually fall on the following day. After services at St. Andrew's, they took lunch at the Carlton Hotel on Regent Street in Cambridge, where Bethia's father handed her a small satin-covered box. She raised the lid. On a pillow of velvet lay a gold ring, beset with tiny turquoises spiraling into a small oval.

"Oh my . . ." she breathed, taking it out and sliding it effortlessly down the third finger of her right hand.

"There are twenty-one stones, dear," Mother said.

"For twenty-one years." Father's eyes misted behind his spectacles.

"You'll notice she didn't hesitate to choose the *right* hand," William said. "Are we saving the left for something special, Bethia?"

Bethia made a face at her brother-in-law, but she loved him dearly. As head of the Hassall Commission, William inspected cases of adulterated foods and harmful or useless medicines. The eight-year-old scar running vertically up his square jar was a souvenir from an entrepreneur who took exception with being ordered to cease marketing the identical formula in half-pint jars labeled *Wright's Miracle Wrinkle Cream* and in quarts labeled *Wright's Miracle Wallpaper Stripper.*

"Don't embarrass her, William," Mother scolded.

"I'm not embarrassed," Bethia said while holding up her hand for all to see. In truth, she had a strong and lovely premonition that

Guy would be offering her an engagement ring for Christmas.

"Good for you, Bethia," Sarah said.

Bethia smiled at her. At forty-one, Sarah still looked as delicate as a Dresden figurine, with large green eyes and corn-silk hair. Biologically they were half sisters, sharing the same father. But the "half" never entered Bethia's thinking. Still, Sarah's childhood had been radically different from her own sheltered one.

It had started out in a typical, almost tranquil way—with University professor Daniel Rayborn and his first wife, Deborah, anticipating the birth of their first child. But when Sarah was born with a fingerless left hand, Deborah's sanity deteriorated to the point where she believed the deformity was punishment from God. Two years later she jumped into the River Thames with Sarah in her arms, leading the police and a distraught Daniel to believe both had perished. But an eel fisherman had pulled Sarah from the water, and later, turned her over to a Methodist orphanage in the slums of Drury Lane.

Then, at age thirteen, Sarah's life took another abrupt twist when a private investigator believed her to be the illegitimate grandchild of wealthy—and lonely—Dorothea Blake. In one day, Sarah went from an orphanage to a Mayfair mansion. When Mrs. Blake later discovered that her *real* granddaughter died shortly after birth, she kept the news to herself, for she loved Sarah, as did the whole household, especially the cook, Naomi Doyle, and her nephew William, stable boy turned Oxford scholar.

In still another twist, Uncle James applied for the position of a tutor in Mrs. Blake's home, and was stunned by Sarah's crippled left hand and the resemblance she bore to his brother's late wife. He went to Daniel with the news and helped him find proof that Sarah was his daughter. With his typical consideration for others, Daniel decided against barging into Sarah's life with the news right away, but instead applied for the position as her tutor.

The two formed an affectionate teacher-student bond. And Daniel and Naomi fell in love, later to marry. When an opportunistic curate, Ethan Knight, courted Sarah for the wealth she would inherit, Daniel revealed his own identity in order to expose Ethan's true nature. Sarah was overjoyed to learn that her tutor was her father and that she had an "instant" extended family consisting of

Uncle James, Aunt Virginia, and their daughters, Catherine and Jewel. Her joy was tempered with sadness, however, when her beloved Mrs. Blake passed on, leaving Sarah her fortune as well as Blake Shipping Company. As Sarah was coming out of mourning, she realized that she loved William and told him so.

The lesson being, Father had said more than once over the years, that a person must never give up hope that God can turn ashes to gold. Had he himself continued down a path of self-destruction by alcohol after losing his first family, he would have never been reunited with Sarah or met Mother. Hence, Bethia and Danny would never have been born. And Sarah could possibly be married to Ethan Knight instead of William Doyle, thereby canceling out John's existence.

"This is from us," Sarah was saying as she handed Bethia another small box. "We have to confess some collusion—I was with Naomi and Father when they bought your ring."

The box contained ear wires of the same turquoise stones. The food had not yet arrived, so Bethia excused herself for the lady's lounge to remove her gold pair and exchange them for the new ones.

"Very nice," fifteen-year-old John said when she brushed back her hair with her fingers for all to see.

"Thank you, John," she said, touched by so simple a compliment, for her nephew could not have cared less about feminine baubles. Sports of every variety were his passion, and over his relatively short life-span he had broken both arms, his right foot, and a finger.

The food arrived and commanded their attention for a few minutes—William and John squeezing lemon slices on their veal cutlets, Mother asking for tartar mustard for her baked cod, Father dousing his stewed mutton kidneys with mushroom ketchup, Sarah and Bethia dousing fried whitings with malt vinegar.

"Mr. Pearce hasn't attempted to contact you up here, has he?" Father asked at length.

"I believe he's forgotten all about me," Bethia replied, not directly answering his question. She hoped her reply to be the truth, for two weeks had passed since Douglas had appeared in church, and she had received no more telephone calls or letters.

"I'm relieved," Mother said.

"So am I." Sarah shook her head. "He seemed rather unstable."

"Small wonder," William said while sprinkling salt upon his green beans. "Was he the one who once kicked Mr. Duffy?"

"That was his twin, Bernard."

"Why would anyone kick Mr. Duffy?" John asked with the same outrage as if learning that someone had kicked the elderly Queen. Mr. Duffy, gone to heaven some five years ago, was more than a gardener—he was a gentle giant whose perpetual good mood infected everyone about him for the better. His widow, Claire, became the housekeeper when Mrs. Bacon retired on a pension.

"Because Mr. Duffy stopped his sister, Muriel, from feeding green tomatoes to a horse," William replied.

John's gray eyes widened. "Aren't they poisonous to horses?"

"Lethally so, in most cases."

"Then, why . . . ?"

"Because she's Muriel," Bethia said quickly. "And may we please change the subject?"

"Good idea." William nodded and asked Father if he had collected any more noteworthy research on the book he was writing about the Peasants' Revolt of 1381. Bethia gave her brother-in-law a grateful smile. The subject of Kentish rebels was far more agreeable than that of the Pearce family.

She was quite relieved as still more weeks went by without sight of letter or flowers from Douglas. When he did not appear out of nowhere at London's King's Cross Station on the tenth of December, the end of Michaelmas Term, she breathed another prayer of gratitude. Without the fear of him lurking behind every pillar or post, she would be able to enjoy the Christmas season.

Her optimism was dented a bit the following afternoon when Mr. Whitmore and Mr. Birch stepped out from behind the dressing screen in the Royal Court's wardrobe room.

"Oh dear," she said, fingertips up to her chin.

The actor, clad in brocade shirt, velvet cloak, padded short breeches and tights, turned to look in the cheval glass. "What is it, Miss Rayborn?"

Bethia glanced at the seamstresses. Miss Lidstone sent her a perplexed nod. Mrs. Hamby, sewing a sash at a machine, ceased pumping the treadle to gape at Mr. Whitmore. Mr. Birch, on hand to help the male actors into their costumes, merely shrugged and said, "He looks fine to me."

But he looked anything but fine, for Mr. Whitmore had gained some weight during the two months Bethia had been away at school. In fact, his shirt strained at its buttons. And four other completed Romeo costumes lay on the table, waiting to be fitted.

The actor cleared his throat. "Well?"

"I'm afraid we'll have to let out some seams, Mr. Whitmore."

Not only that, but she'd need to find some way to alter all five costumes to conceal the problem. The critics would have apoplexy over a Romeo with a paunch. *This isn't a disaster,* Bethia thought with more wishfulness than sincerity. Fittings had to be completed by the eighteenth, when full dress rehearsal was scheduled, and after which the theatre would shut down for eight days. With Danny arriving home this evening and Guy on the twenty-first, Bethia wanted more than anything to conclude her work on the *Romeo and Juliet* costumes as soon as possible.

"That hardly seems necessary," Mr. Whitmore said, raising arms to peer down at his bulging shirt. "And by the way, this purple suits my complexion. Do you agree, Mr. Birch?"

"Suits you very well, sir," the head attendant replied, but with an odd glint in his gray eyes.

A corner of Richard Whitmore's mouth twitched.

Folding her arms, Bethia said, "Mr. Whitmore . . ."

The actor unbuttoned his straining shirt enough to reach in and pull out a cushion of gold velvet. "Well now, how did this get here?"

Bethia laughed with the others, too relieved to be angry, and besides, the humor of it was a welcome relief to the strain of the day. Actors were not the most patient lot when it came to standing still for fittings.

"You should be ashamed of yourself, Mr. Whitmore," scolded Miss Lidstone, who at fifty-three was more than twice Bethia's age. Her face had sharp features, especially a long pointed nose, and she wore a gown of torturous pink that clashed with her ginger-colored hair. She stepped up to plop a flatcap upon the actor's soon-to-be-dyed locks. "Worrying us that way."

"Oh, but I am, Miss Lidstone," he said, and sent an unrepentant wink at Bethia.

"Mrs. Steel is late, ha-ha," Mrs. Hamby said with a glance at the wall clock at half-past two. She was an attractive woman, tall and broad shouldered, aged twenty-nine with thick brown hair. But the nervous laugh trailing the end of almost every sentence made her company a bit taxing in close quarters. Bethia thought it would be a kindness if someone would take her in hand and draw her attention to the habit she probably was unaware that she had. Someone with more fortitude than herself, she thought wryly, which was probably why the habit persisted. Everyone hoped someone else would act.

"We'll just fill in with others," Bethia said. This was not a problem, for the utility actors tended to show up early, and several were milling about the corridor. She and the seamstresses began fitting twenty-two-year-old Corrie Walters, flush with excitement over her first speaking part as Juliet's nurse. While she had a feminine face with high cheekbones, full lips, and turned-up nose, her boylike figure required padding in strategic places.

"We're taking the stuffing out of one actor and putting it in another," Miss Lidstone quipped as Bethia began fastening a girdle about Corrie's waist. The ruffled muslin attached gave the actress instant hips.

"I beg your pardon?" Miss Walters asked, holding arms raised.

"Mr. Whitmore," Bethia explained. "He wore a pil—"

The door opened, and Mrs. Steel breezed into the room. "Sorry I'm late," she said, pulling off gloves. "I had an appointment with my dressmaker."

Mrs. Hamby let out a nervous twitter. Bethia shook her head at her and fastened another hook to the girdle. "We're almost finished here, Mrs. Steel," she said pleasantly.

"I'm in rather a hurry," Mrs. Steel said.

"Then we'll work faster. Do please have a seat." To Miss Lidstone, Bethia said, "Will you hand me that chemise?"

The seamstress did so, but with a cautious glance toward Mrs. Steel, who was still standing, arms akimbo now.

"Please . . . I don't mind waiting," Miss Walters said.

Bethia was opening her mouth to explain that they only needed three more minutes at most, when she caught the pleading in Miss Walters's expression. She breathed a silent sigh. How easy it was to take for granted the security afforded her by her prosperous family. While she strove to get on with everyone she met, it was simply because it was her nature to do so, and not out of any peril to her livelihood. But Miss Walters could ill afford to get on the wrong side of a lead actress.

She turned to Mrs. Steel. "Very well. Miss Walters is willing to wait."

"Oh, never mind," Mrs. Steel said abruptly, moving over to the drafting table and the open tin of shortbread Mrs. Hamby had brought in this morning. "Are these for sharing? I've not had lunch and feel a bit light-headed."

Mrs. Hamby's head bobbed. "Please, help yourself, ha-ha."

By six o'clock the fittings scheduled for the day were finished. Bethia, followed by the seamstresses, descended the staircase on leaden feet. On the ground floor, Jewel stepped out of the office. "I'm glad I caught you," she said over the pleasant strains of Tchaikovsky's *Romeo and Juliet* from the orchestra in the rehearsal room. "Everyone is pleased with their costumes so far. Thank you for all of your hard work."

Mrs. Hamby twittered and Miss Lidstone tried, unsuccessfully, not to appear *too* pleased. Bethia smiled, amazed at how effectively a compliment could cure fatigue. After a round of good-byes, she was turning to accompany the seamstresses on toward the lobby when her cousin said, "Can you stay a minute longer, Bethia?"

"Of course."

"Grady's meeting with the printers," Jewel said, steering her to the greenroom, where actors and actresses waited during a performance for the callboy to stick his head through the doorway and give notice of who was required onstage. Five sofas and several upholstered chairs were set about, and a long mirror was propped in a corner. Hanging upon serene mauve walls were framed photographs of past performances, as well as a poster titled *Rules During Performance.*

1. Any performer not present in the greenroom at the time

announced in the playbills shall forfeit eight shillings.

2. Any performer who keeps the stage waiting after having been called shall forfeit three shillings.

3. Any performer standing in the wings in sight of the audience shall forfeit two shillings.

4. Any performer who steps onstage in a state of intoxication shall forfeit two pounds.

5. Any performer absent from a performance with no advance notice shall forfeit five pounds.

"I appreciate how you diffused the situation with Mrs. Steel," Jewel said, closing the door.

Bethia wasn't surprised that she knew. Grady had once said, half jokingly, that a person could whisper something in an empty room at the Royal Court and see it printed it in the *Times* the following morning.

"It wasn't really much of a situation," she replied. "And Mrs. Hamby's shortbread helped more than anything."

"I'll be sure to thank her" Jewel was saying, while worry lingered in the green eyes behind the lenses. "That's actually not why I stopped you. Let's sit for a minute, shall we?"

"Is something wrong?" Bethia asked as they took places at either end of the nearest sofa.

Jewel blew out a long breath. "Have you received any recent letters from Douglas?"

The quickening of pulse, the faint wave of nausea surprised Bethia. After two months of no contact, she had assumed that the mere mention of Mr. Pearce's name could not affect her in any adverse way.

"Bethia?"

Bethia focused her attention upon her cousin again. "No, not since mid-October."

"Tell me of the last time you heard from him."

Jewel would not ask out of idle curiosity, Bethia reminded herself. "He surprised me at church, telephoned afterward pretending to be Danny, and then sent flowers after I begged him not to." Her pulse raced from the memory. She swallowed. "I'm afraid I overreacted. I sent him a harsh letter."

Jewel's expression suggested she already knew of the letter. "He drove you to it, Bethia. Never forget that."

"But I could have phrased it more . . ." The weight of her cousin's second statement struck Bethia. A chill passed through her. "What is it, Jewel? He hasn't gone and—"

"No, not that." Jewel rested her hand upon Bethia's arm and leaned forward. "You'll forgive me for keeping this from you while you were at school. Grady agreed with me that it was best, with all you have on your shoulders. But Douglas left for Canada in early November."

Bethia's relief turned into panic. "Canada? Because of me? My letter?"

Jewel shook her head. "Because he hasn't the sense God gave a goose, and some palm reader took advantage of that. But frankly, yes, his infatuation with you is what's fueling this nonsense. He figures to come back with a fortune in Klondike gold to make you reconsider."

Klondike. Newspapers were filled with accounts of the gold rush, focusing on the hardships the miners were going through more than the fortunes carried back to England. Fatigue returned with a vengeance. She probed her temples with her fingers. *You could have telephoned Jewel or William for help. Why did you have to write such a letter?*

"Stop that, Bethia," Jewel admonished gently. "I know what you're thinking. You're not responsible for this foolishness. But we felt you should be informed now that you're back in town and could conceivably cross paths with Muriel."

"She blames me," Bethia said in a flat voice.

"If she does, that doesn't mean she has a valid reason. You have to understand my mother's side of the family, Bethia. They quarrel like blue jays, but let one suffer a perceived snub, and the rest fall into rank behind him. It matters not one whit if that person is right or wrong, it only matters that he's a Pearce."

"I wonder why they're like that," Danny said in the parlour of the Cannonhall Road house that evening. He had declared his intention to savor every minute of his first evening home, and so Bethia and John obliged him after the older Rayborns and Doyles had gone to bed. They sat at a table near the fireplace, with the boys taking turns stoking the fire or adding more coals.

Bethia clicked a black wooden domino in place. The conversation with Jewel still preyed upon her mind, and she had poured out the story to her brother and nephew. "Family loyalty is admirable, but only up to a reasonable point."

"What reasonable point?"

"When it makes a person *willfully* blind toward an injustice perpetrated on someone outside the family," Bethia replied. "If I knew either of you were purposely hurting someone else, I couldn't in good conscience take your side."

"You couldn't?" John picked up a domino from the semicircle facing him, put it back, and then placed another next to the one Bethia had just played. "I'd take your side no matter what."

Bethia smiled at the boy. "But you wouldn't be helping me, by shielding me from the consequences of my actions."

"And what if she murdered someone?" Danny asked. He was tall and gangly and freckled, with strawberry-blonde hair shot with brown and auburn. His big hands and long fingers befitted a pianist and future surgeon, and a pair of oversized feet kept him from losing his balance.

"Bethia wouldn't do that."

"Just for the sake of academics, what if she did?"

"I would encourage her to turn herself in," John replied. "But I couldn't do it myself. And you?"

Studying Bethia's face with an appraising eye, Danny replied, "That depends. Would there be a reward?"

"It's obvious who loves me the most," Bethia said with an affectionate smirk.

He wagged a long finger at her. "Ah, but didn't you just declare that you wouldn't want to be shielded from the consequences of your actions? Would you begrudge your brother a little profit at the same time?"

"Frankly, yes." Bethia nodded toward the five dominos still facing him. "And we'll have to nudge each other awake in church tomorrow if you won't take your turn."

"Sorry." He placed a domino beside the one John had played, connecting the *threes*. "Must be all the haggis I ate."

"Pass," Bethia said when none of her numbers matched the dominoes at either end.

John clicked a domino into place. "Haggis?"

"Quite popular in Scotland." Enjoying the effect the description would have on his nephew, Danny said, "It's the lungs, heart, and liver of a sheep, chopped and mixed with oats and onions, then boiled in its stomach."

"That's disgusting." John pruned up his face as if he'd actually tasted the dish. "I'm never going to Scotland."

"They don't exactly tie you down and force you to eat it, you know," Danny said. "And besides, why is eating a sheep organ any less appealing than eating its muscle?"

"Really Danny, that's enough," Bethia said, taking pity on John and feeling just a bit queasy herself.

John nodded. "Vegetarianism is suddenly making a lot more sense to me."

That sentiment was discarded with John's first whiff of the bacon being served from the sideboard at breakfast. True to Bethia's prediction, her mind was sluggish, though her brother and nephew, who had opted for another game of dominoes, looked even worse for the wear. But she was lucid enough to count her blessings during services at Christ Church: the Christmas season was here, she was home with family, she was on her way to completing her final year of college, she had a challenging and interesting career . . . *and Guy comes home in nine days!*

Only one thing put a damper on her joy. Though now an ocean away, Douglas Pearce still held her in his obsessive grip, for how could she rest easily until he returned? *Please keep him safe,* she added to her prayer.

---

Nine

*T*hirty-two actors had been fitted by Tuesday noon, including utility actors playing nonspeaking parts such as Citizens of the Watch and guests to the Capulet Ball. Once all the costumes for *Romeo and Juliet* were ready, Bethia began drafting patterns and purchasing cloth for *Lady Audley's Secret*, scheduled to open the first of April.

She worked long hours and was finished by Friday the seventeenth of December, when she met her mother and Sarah downstairs to watch the dress rehearsal of *Romeo and Juliet*. It was sheer joy to see the costumes come to life on the stage. But as much as she enjoyed her job, it would be a relief to have some time away from the theatre. Mrs. Hamby and Miss Lidstone would do the sewing for the next play's costumes over the next three months, and she would be back again in late March for final fittings.

On Monday the twentieth, she and Danny set out to purchase Christmas gifts for family and servants. John did not press to come along, having already taken care of his list in one hour in a bookshop last week. His absence was just one less ant in an anthill of shoppers at Harrods, attracted by the convenience of several departments under one roof, and the option of having their purchases wrapped and delivered.

The four and a half acre, seven-storey emporium started in a small way when, in 1849, tea merchant Henry Charles Harrod opened a small grocer's shop lit by paraffin lights. At the time, Brompton Road was just a poor street, lined with costers' stalls on Saturday nights. Two other shops were added soon after, and within a few years the whole of the shops between Hans Crescent and Queen's Gardens had been absorbed.

"Bethia, this way!" Danny said, beckoning her over to the camera counter on the ground floor.

"The Lancaster Instantograph Compact," the shop assistant said, smiling. He was exceedingly handsome, with neatly trimmed side-whiskers and blue eyes framed by thick dark lashes. "We just got them in last week, and this is the last one."

"For Father," Danny said unnecessarily, for both had grown up having every important event documented by their father's lens.

Bethia eyed the polished mahogany and brass of the camera in the shop assistant's hands. "You know how he is. He'll scold if you spend too much."

"It could be from both of us. It's much lighter than his old one. Better for his back."

"Allow me to demonstrate the changing box," the still-smiling shop assistant said with a snap and a click of a sliding door which, he explained, allowed glass plates to be transferred between storage box and plate holders.

"You mean he wouldn't have to find a darkroom between shots?" Bethia asked.

"Actually, he may take up to a dozen photographs at a time. Most convenient for picnics, strolls in the park, and the like." He cleared his throat. "I take lunch in half an hour. Fine day for a stroll, isn't it, Miss?"

"It's forty degrees outside," Danny growled. "And she has a beau."

The man's face reddened. "I certainly didn't mean—"

"We'll take the camera, thank you," Bethia said, touching her brother's sleeve. On the way to the lift, when they were well out of earshot from the counter, she gave him a sidelong look. "What's gotten into you?"

"Into me? He was flirting with you."

"No he wasn't."

"Fine day for a stroll, Miss," Danny imitated, batting his lashes. "I take lunch in half an hour. And what do you call that?"

"He didn't actually *ask* me out for a stroll."

Danny sighed. "He was testing the waters, Bethia. If you would have giggled and encouraged him, he would have asked quick as you could say John Bull. That's how men are."

"I never *giggle*," Bethia countered. "And I *know* how men are. I happen to work with them, remember?"

"But you don't notice how they court because you've been engaged to Guy since you were nine."

That made her smile. "Nine, Danny?"

"Very well . . . ten."

She laughed and took his arm. "Well, he seemed harmless enough."

"Guy?"

"No, the camera man."

"You thought Douglas Pearce was harmless."

"*Touché*. But seriously, I'll give you notice whenever I need a knight in shining armour."

When her brother looked a little hurt, she wished she had held her tongue. "You're a dear, though."

"Enough flattery," he said, mugging a face at her. "Let's go up to the perfumery, and you can advise me on Mother and Sarah. Unless you'd like to go back and chat with your new beau."

Bethia laughed again. "To the perfumery."

On the second floor she looked to the right and noticed a woman descending the last steps of the arched staircase. She was stunning, with ash-blonde and golden waves cascading over the shoulder of a toffee-colored cloak, and large violet eyes set in a finely chiseled face. Bethia recognized Muriel, having crossed paths with her a few times during their childhoods and from the benefit concert for Sedgwick School at the Royal Court last Christmas. The somber gray gown of half-mourning she had worn on that occasion had only enhanced her natural beauty.

If she had only not met Muriel's eyes, Bethia could have continued on. But too late for that, for Muriel was staring directly at her.

"Oh dear," Bethia said through stiff lips.

"What is it?" Danny said, looking about.

Muriel was too close now for Bethia to explain.

"Lady Holt," she said, taking a step to the right. "How long has it been?"

To Bethia's relief, Muriel took the hand she extended. But her smile was absent of warmth. "I believe a year, Bethia."

A jumble of thoughts flooded Bethia's mind. *I'm so sorry about your brother . . . I wish I hadn't written that letter . . . I wish I had never gone near Covent Garden that day . . . I pray every day he isn't killed over there.*

But what did one say in such a situation, with shoppers streaming by, her brother now at her side, and a pair of violet eyes regarding her coolly?

"I . . . wonder if you remember my brother, Danny?" she said. Anything to pretend that this was a pleasant social encounter. They were actors, delivering lines far removed from their actual thoughts.

Muriel offered Danny her hand, gave him a smile only a degree warmer. "I hear you're studying medicine."

"Yes, Lady Holt," he replied, taking her hand while stepping a little closer to Bethia, whether consciously or not.

"We need good doctors. My mother's doctor is an imbecile, but she refuses to see anyone else."

"I'm sorry," Bethia said as Muriel withdrew her hand from Danny's and slid her gaze over to her again. "Will her health allow her to come down for Christmas?"

"No. Georgiana and her nanny and I leave for Sheffield tomorrow. Of course it will be a somber celebration without Douglas."

Bethia was opening her mouth to stammer an apology when her arm felt the gentle nudge of Danny's elbow.

"We've detained you too long from your shopping, Lady Holt," her brother said respectfully. "And we've still several names left on our lists."

Muriel obviously caught his meaning, but she was not about to be swayed from delivering her innuendoes. In a pleasant tone, as if she were commenting upon the evergreen wreaths adorning Harrods' walls, she said pointedly, "How lovely that your brother accompanies you shopping. I would give anything if mine were here to do the same."

Danny flushed to the roots of his strawberry-blonde hair. "It's not my sister's fault he's not here, if that's what you're implying."

"Danny—" Bethia started.

"He's a grown man," Danny went on. "He's responsible for his own actions."

The violet eyes narrowed. "A woman's cruelty can drive any man to desperate behavior. Good day, Mr. Rayborn . . . Miss Rayborn."

She walked toward the mirror-lined archway leading to the perfumery.

Danny shook his head. "She goes for the throat, doesn't she?"

"Yes," Bethia replied, feeling more like she had been punched in the stomach.

"Why don't we go back downstairs and look for William's gift?"

"Let's just go home." All joy had been leached from the day, and she longed for nothing more than to take a nap.

"You can't allow her to do that to you. And besides, when will we get another chance to shop?"

"Very well," Bethia sighed. As they walked toward the lift, she realized she was grateful for one thing out of the encounter.

"Thank you," she said.

Danny slanted her a knowing look, as if it was on the tip of his tongue to remind her of her "knight in shining armour" statement. But he smiled instead. "You're welcome."

Fortunately, Muriel did not even appear in Bethia's vigilant peripheral vision as they continued shopping and then lunched in the restaurant. They hired a hansom cab, having sent coachman Hiram Wyatt back home that morning, for it would have been inconsiderate to ask him to wait with the horses in the cold for such an undetermined amount of time.

A thought occurred to Bethia on the way home. "Please don't mention to anyone what happened."

"Very well," her brother agreed. "But why? Mother and Father know Douglas is in Canada."

That was so, for Aunt Virginia had mentioned the fact in a letter.

"They don't know Muriel blames me. I haven't wanted to worry them with all this business. And Guy has enough on his shoulders, keeping up his scholarship." She shook her head. "I have to agree with Muriel. I also would give anything if Douglas were Christmas shopping in London."

The following morning she waited with her parents and the Russell family, Stanley and Penny and their two daughters, at Waterloo Station for the train from Portsmouth. Twenty-three-year-old Guy

Russell stepped out of the second-class coach with violin case in hand, his sapphire-blue eyes sharp with excitement and dark hair sprouting out in all directions. The presence of parents on either side abashed both Bethia and Guy so that they merely pressed cheeks. But later, while everyone was having tea and scones in the cozy parlour above Russell Saddle and Tack, Guy asked Bethia's father if they might go downstairs.

"A quarter hour, then we'll join you," Father said after a glance at his watch. "We'll have to be getting on by then anyway."

"I'll go with you," eleven-year-old Sharon said, rising from an ottoman.

"No, you may stay here," said her mother.

"They want to be alone," Lottie explained. Her sage look befitted her seventeen years and the worldly wisdom of a fresher studying voice at the Royal Academy of Music on Hanover Square.

Sharon's crumpled face brightened when Guy pulled her long brown braid. "Save your strength for Christmas shopping, Pet. I'll need you and Lottie to advise me."

Bethia and Guy held hands on the narrow staircase, even though Guy had to walk ahead of her. The aroma of leather and voices of shop clerk Mr. Neale and a patron wafted through the curtain dividing the shop from the hall at the foot of the staircase.

"I can't believe we're finally together," Guy whispered, taking Bethia in his arms.

"I can't believe it either," she whispered back.

Absence made the kiss they shared even sweeter than their first one. Light-headed afterward, Bethia rested her cheek against his shoulder and savored the strength of his arms about her.

"What do you eat while I'm away?" he asked.

She moved her head to give him an odd look. "I beg your pardon?"

He smiled and brushed a stray tendril of hair from her cheek. "You grow prettier and prettier. It must be something in your food."

"You look nice too." She touched the lapel of his brown wool coat. "Another new suit?"

"Almost new. I had it made in October. I hated to spend the money, but the professors already know I'm on scholarship. Some are quite snobbish. They cater shamelessly to the wealthier students."

Bethia wondered if that was the reason he discouraged his parents from visiting him at University, for they poured more money into the shop and into educating their girls than into their wardrobes. Immediately she shamed herself for the thought. Guy was not like that.

She frowned at the thought of any University professor looking down upon him. "I despise snobbery."

Too soon, footsteps sounded above.

"I'll come out to the house tomorrow," he murmured into her hair.

As loathe as she was to part again, Bethia understood that he needed to spend his first day home with his parents and sisters. Back in Hampstead she busied herself with helping Mother, Sarah, and their housekeeper, Claire Duffy, fill small baskets with candies and nuts, and glaze gingerbread figures for the tree Danny and John brought home from Epping Forrest.

Wednesday morning, Guy came over in spite of the icy rain slickening the streets. The servants who were part of his life in his earlier years greeted him as an old friend—Avis, who was still Sarah's lady's maid, Claire, Trudy, Susan, and Jack Woodley, the gardener.

Hiram, the coachman, invited him to look about the apartment above the stables where Guy's family had lived for most of his life. Guy smiled, but replied, "No, thank you."

Bethia was not surprised. It was one thing she could not quite understand about Guy, for she had never felt shame over her mother having been a cook for several years, even a scullery maid before that. Honest work was honest work. But she supposed she would feel the same way if her family had served *his* instead of the other way around.

After all greetings were exchanged, she and Guy slipped into the sitting room. They sat upon the sofa nearest the fireplace, hands clasped and her head nestled against his shoulder.

"After graduation I'll audition for the Royal Opera House," he said. It was known in musician circles that the London opera orchestras attracted the best metropolitan instrumental talent. "If I'm accepted—"

"*If?*" Bethia said. "That's a foregone conclusion."

He squeezed her hand. "Isn't there a fable about counting chickens before they hatch? As I was saying, *if* I'm accepted, the wages won't be outstanding during the first six months or so. But after I've proven myself, I should be able to earn a good living."

"You will," Bethia said, for she had never known Guy to fail at anything he set his mind upon. The scholarship was proof of that, for he was the first non-Italian recipient in the history of the University of Bologna's music department.

Turning to face her, he took both her hands in his. "Lilly . . ."

"What is it?" she asked, startled by his grim expression.

"I was hoping to have enough saved for a ring by now. I haven't."

It was not an easy thing for Bethia to hear. Ever since romance infused itself into their friendship, she and Guy had simply taken for granted that they would marry one day. They had waited so long. Even if an engagement ring would not bring their marriage any closer chronologically, it would be a milepost along the way, a reminder that one day they would be husband and wife.

"I don't want an extravagant ring, Guy."

He made no comment on that. They had discussed the matter at length, each time ending in a standoff. To Bethia it was the sentiment forged into the ring that mattered, not the costliness of the metal nor size of the gemstone.

But for Guy, a modest ring would remind people of his roots in servitude. Just like cheap clothing.

"As painful as it is for me to say this," he went on, "it's best we put off our formal engagement a bit longer anyway. Merely having a ring isn't enough. I want to ask for your hand when I can prove to your father that I can support you."

The perfect sense of what he said somewhat pierced the cloud of disappointment enveloping her. If she were a man, she told herself, she would feel exactly the same. Pride may have been a factor, but so was practicality. Birds did not start families until their nests were secure—a point Father would be certain to make, were Guy to ask for her hand before he was in a stable financial position. And Father would not count her wages at the Royal Court as a strong enough financial foundation for a marriage.

"I'll make it up to you," Guy said, blue eyes begging understanding. "When I'm a successful musician, you'll have a fine house, with every luxury you have here."

She was opening her mouth to say that luxury was not important, but he put a finger to her lips. "Please don't try to talk me out of that dream, Bethia. You deserve the best."

"I already have the best," she corrected.

"I wish that were so," he said. His eyebrows raised. "You do understand?"

"Yes. I understand."

He released her hands and dug into his waistcoat pocket. "I realize it's not appropriate for me to give you any jewelry until we're formally engaged, but surely your family won't protest a little something from your unofficial fiancé."

Bethia opened the narrow velvet-covered box he put into her hands. A pear-shaped stone of a variety of colors—yellow, brown, blue, gray, and white—was attached to a delicate silver chain.

"It's barite," Guy said. "Not expensive, but it's mined in Bologna."

"It's lovely," Bethia said, touching the stone. And she was able to put aside the final dregs of disappointment by reminding herself that mileposts came in many forms.

Thursday evening, Guy and his family, along with other friends and neighbors, arrived at 5 Cannonhall Road for the annual Christmas party. Jewel and Catherine and their families were up in Sheffield with Uncle James and Aunt Virginia, but Peggy Somerset and Milly Holt, former schoolmates of Catherine's, accepted the invitations. After trips to the refreshment tables began lessening in frequency, Sarah rounded up all musicians present. Guests sang carols to the accompaniment of Guy and Peggy on violins, Danny on piano, and neighbor Mr. Brooker on the dulcimer. The celebration continued well into the night, and as they left, everyone agreed that it had been a wonderful party.

Christmas morning dawned tinged with chilly anticipation, even though there were no little ones in the house to squeal over treasures in stockings. After breakfast the family walked to Christ Church, the nave so bedecked with holly that even members of the congregation seemed to be sprouting it. Gift exchanging occupied the space of afternoon before lunch, which was purposely late because of the abundance at breakfast. The parlour was fragrant with perfume as Mother and Sarah passed around bottles of Coronis and Violette de Parme for everyone to sniff. After the expected admonitions over the expense of his camera, Father arranged everyone for a photograph.

Just as everyone was gathering their gifts to put away and Mother was salvaging paper and ribbons for next year, William surprised everyone by bringing in one more gift, for Sarah—a Berliner Gramophone. Smiling, he turned the crank at the side and stepped back. A needle began moving across a cylinder, and through the large horn floated the somewhat brittle sounds of an orchestra. Soon a man's nasal tenor began singing "The Fountain in the Park";

> "While strolling in the park one day,
> In the merry month of May . . ."

They played it, and another cylinder with "Love's Old Sweet Song," over and over, and then again after lunch for Guy when he arrived with an apple spice cake his mother had baked. He visited with her family in the parlour, posed with her for her father's camera, and then he and Bethia bundled up for a stroll toward Hampstead Heath, where children were already trying out new bicycles and roller skates.

"When will you leave for school?" Guy asked.

"Next Saturday," Bethia replied, her hand resting upon the crook of his arm. One week away. And he would be leaving in four days.

"It's hardly fair," he said. "You're always the one seeing me off and meeting me."

"Your trip takes longer. You can't help that."

"You're too good for me, you know."

"That's what Father says."

He looked at her, crestfallen. "Really?"

"No, not really," she said and squeezed his arm. "He adores you, as we all do."

Guy gave her a relieved smile. "He paid for my piano and violin lessons as a boy. I'll never forget that. You have a remarkable family."

"As do you," Bethia reminded him.

"Yes." He nodded. "But Mother's not happy about Easter break."

"She'll miss you." So would Bethia. His scholarship obligated him to embark on a fund-raising tour with the University orchestra for six weeks during his final year. But she wouldn't wish it any other way, for this was a marvelous opportunity for him to see Europe.

"Just promise me one thing," she said.

He lifted an eyebrow. "That I won't set my cap for some French girl?"

"No," she said, smiling at the notion, for he never even seemed to notice other women in that sort of way. "That when you're in Spain, you'll stay away from the bulls."

"What bulls?"

"The bulls they let loose in the streets."

"Why would you think that would even cross my mind?" he asked.

"Because Mr. Whitmore ran with them when he was your age."

"The actor?"

Bethia nodded. "He said he only planned to watch from a window, but that some group madness comes over hundreds of men who otherwise wouldn't think of doing such a thing."

Sapphire eyes merry, he said, "Then I give you my word that I'll keep my distance from any Spanish bulls. Besides, I believe that happens sometime in July, when I'll be safely back here at your side."

Ten

By the time Royal Court Theatre's *Romeo and Juliet* went into its fourth week of production in late January 1898, performances were sold out, and the drama critics in such publications as the *Strand Magazine* and the *Times* had written laudatory columns, including no less than George Bernard Shaw's comments in *Saturday Review:*

> . . . the sparks between Mr. Whitmore and the beautiful Mrs. Steel are almost palatable, the costuming magnificently authentic; the settings are works of art, and the acting is so flawless that the lines float out to us as effortlessly as flower petals on breezes.

It was the break Jewel and her husband, Grady, had worked and prayed for. They woke smiling every morning and went to bed smiling every night. Messrs. Cumberland and Fry threw a huge party for cast and crew in the ballroom of the Hotel Rembrandt. Congratulations were traded like marbles in a schoolyard: the backstage crew and utility actors for the bonuses adding weight to their purses, the lead actors for what the superior reviews would do for their careers.

And then, during another sellout performance on the twenty-fifth of January, Charlotte Steel leaned over the balcony—a timber-and-papier-mâché structure that could not be discerned from authentic stone in the limelights—and threw up on Richard Whitmore's upturned face.

The curtain closed upon a cast no less stunned than the audience. In the greenroom, a coffee cup and magazine were pulled out of understudy Daphne Lloyd's hands, and the creases fluffed out of her gown. However much Mr. Whitmore simmered as Jewel bathed his face and hair with a wet towel, he was too professional to cause a scene that might be heard over the six-piece orchestra's replaying Bach's Italian Concerto in F Major from the Capulet Ball scene. When the curtain opened again to sympathetic applause, Richard Whitmore's performance was as brilliant as ever, in spite of the fact that he reeked, and Miss Lloyd carried her part as Juliet admirably, considering that the opportunity had literally dropped upon her from above.

Newspaper critics made no mention of this the following day, but with London boasting thirty-six theatres, that was not surprising. On the twenty-seventh the *Times* critic alluded to the spectacle with delicacy, expressing his wishes for Mrs. Steel's full recovery from whichever ailment had stricken her.

Only, Mrs. Steel would not be recovering for at least another five months, she informed Jewel and Grady with face glowing as they visited her bedside in Mayfair. And even then, she had doubts about returning to the stage. The replacement of a leading actress in a sellout production could not be ignored by the critics for long, and the reviews descended into lukewarmness, each lamenting, in a variation of words, the same observation—that the spark between Romeo and Juliet had fizzled like coals doused with water.

Ticket sales began declining, so that by the seventh of February's performance, eighteen percent of the seats were empty. A fog of gloom crept backstage and settled in every crevice and corner. Jewel and Grady explored the feasibility of returning the competent-but-bland Miss Lloyd back to her minor role as Juliet's nurse. But with only three weeks remaining in production, the chances of engaging a *known* actress as Juliet's replacement were slim to nonexistent.

Still, Jewel made some discreet calls, such as to Mabel Love, who was due to start *The Musketeers* at Her Majesty's Theatre in nine weeks.

"I'm not a quick study," the beautiful Miss Love confessed over tea in the parlour of her St. John's Wood town house on the eighth of February. "And I'm afraid I've never played Juliet. Your production would be over before I learned my lines."

When Jewel returned to the Royal Court, cleaners Mrs. Shore, Mrs. Ainsley, and Mr. Ryder were loitering in the corridor just outside the office. Jewel thought nothing of it, for they had the right to take pause from their hard work now and again—but when they mumbled hurried greetings and scattered, she sent a suspicious look toward the office door. It opened when she was but two feet away, and she had to step back to keep from smashing into Mr. Birch.

"I just brought coffee to calm them," said the old man.

Jewel did not have to ask who belonged to the other part of *them*. "Thank you, Mr. Birch."

Two men turned flushed faces toward her as she entered an office redolent of coffee and filled with an almost palatable tension. Hands wrapped about his coffee cup as if it were a walnut he were trying to crush, Mr. Whitmore sat in the chair facing Grady's desk. "That woman is destroying my career."

Jewel closed the door, catching a whiff of something besides coffee. She intercepted her husband's grim little nod and said to the actor, "Mr. Whitmore, that's simply not true. The receipts are still healthy enough."

"And gin will ruin your career quicker than any actress will, Whitmore," Grady said gently.

"What do you expect?" Mr. Whitmore exclaimed, handsome face flushing a deeper crimson beneath his dyed dark brown hair. "I have to play against a zombie every night! I never thought I would miss Charlotte Steel, but I would kiss every corn on her big feet if she would but return!"

"Mr. Whitmore, please." Jewel could picture the three cleaners slipping again into the corridor and Mr. Birch cocking his ears. "Three weeks—that's all we have left. Just bear with us."

He uncurled a hand from the cup to shake a finger at her. "I've offers from other theatres, you know. I'll not go down with this leaky ship! You find a decent leading lady for *Lady Audley's Secret*, or—"

"We'll find one." Grady came around his desk and clapped a hand upon the man's shoulder. "But for now, we've barely four hours until curtain. No sense getting out in traffic just to turn around again. Have a nap in your dressing room, and I'll send you up a proper supper in a bit."

For a second it seemed the actor would refuse. Jewel held her breath. She let it out again when he nodded.

Sending a message with his eyes, Grady said, "Jewel, will you make sure the stove is lit in Mr. Whitmore's room?"

"Certainly," Jewel replied.

"That's not necessary," Mr. Whitmore said, making motions to rise, but Grady's hand held him in place.

"We wouldn't want you to catch a chill, old chap," Grady was saying as Jewel hastened into the corridor.

On her way to the staircase she spotted Mrs. Ainsley through the open doorway to the greenroom, ostensibly dusting chairs.

"Come with me," Jewel said, motioning.

Dressing rooms lined both sides of the corridor above ground floor. Leading actors and actresses had their own, and others were shared, depending upon how many characters were necessary in a production. Jewel opened the door to Mr. Whitmore's room and turned to the cleaning woman.

"Please light the stove while I look about."

Mrs. Ainsley nodded knowingly. "I'd check under his cot first if I was you."

The half-filled bottle turned up in one of Romeo's short leather boots. "I would appreciate it if you'd keep this to yourself," Jewel said as she concealed it in the folds of her skirt, should she happen upon Mr. Whitmore in the corridor.

"Mum's the word, Mrs. McGuire," Mrs. Ainsley replied, brushing soot from her hands while her eyes betrayed her eagerness to rejoin her co-workers.

"Really, Mrs. Ainsley, this is important." But as she had neither the time nor legal right to tie a gag around the woman's mouth, Jewel left her and hastened to the water closet to pour out the gin. She met Grady and the actor on the staircase, the two men flattening themselves against the stone wall so that she could pass.

"I shouldn't have brought Mrs. Ainsley up there with me," Jewel fretted when her husband returned to the office. "It'll be all over London."

Grady rubbed her back and soothed, "It wouldn't have made any difference. Everyone could see what condition he was in before you even arrived."

"Will he sober up by performance time? We can't have two understudies in lead roles."

"He'll sober up. You forget, I'm an old hand at this, with my father and brothers so fond of their cups."

That reassured Jewel a little. Until she recalled her earlier errand. "Miss Love declined the part. I offered her twice Mrs. Steel's wages."

"Ah, I figured as much," Grady said. "Not much we can do, with three weeks left. But look on the bright side—we'll have the whole month of March to plan ahead.

The stage was to be consigned to a New York touring group and their production of *The Runaway*, allowing the Royal Court performers to devote all of March to rehearsals of *Lady Audley's Secret*.

With the aid of the nap, supper, and several cups of coffee, Richard Whitmore recovered before curtain. Grady was relieved not to be forced to impose the two-pound fine, for in Mr. Whitmore's state of mind, the actor could very well walk out of the production. And then the Royal Court may as well close its doors for the rest of February.

"We dropped to twenty-one percent vacancy last night," Grady said the following morning after counting the receipts. He ran a hand through his reddish hair and nodded toward the *Times* folded upon his desk. "And Shaw's column raked us over the coals."

Now it was Jewel's turn to comfort him. She rose from her desk and stood behind him to massage his broad shoulders, digging her fingertips into knotted muscles. He groaned appreciatively, moved his neck from side to side. "That feels good. Ah, Jewel, in times such as this, your love is all that's keeping me from leaping into the Thames."

Flattered as Jewel was by the compliment, this was a bit disturbing to hear. Grady was not the sort even to joke about suicide. "Surely that's not the only restraint."

"Well, that and the fact that I can't swim."

She laughed, grateful that even this latest discouragement could not douse the spark of humor at the core of his personality. Still kneading muscles, she said, "Let's leave all this today. We'll find a matinee at another theatre."

"Sorry, love. Another theatre is the last place I want to be right now."

Jewel leaned close to his ear. "We could just go back home, then."

Her husband turned his head enough so that she could see the light in his gray eyes. "Yes?"

A knock sounded at the door.

"Wonderful timing," Grady muttered.

"We'll send whoever it is away," Jewel said, then went to answer. Her sister stood there, one hand holding a parcel wrapped in pink paper and ribbons, the other holding the hand of four-year-old Nicholas.

"Catherine! Nicholas!" Jewel exclaimed. "What a pleasant surprise!"

"It's good to see you too." Her sister deposited the parcel on a chair, while Nicholas made a beeline for Grady and the peppermints all three Sedgwick children knew they could expect.

"Well, I'm not sure I have any . . ." Grady was saying in a teasing tone to the sound of a desk drawer opening, while Jewel and Catherine smiled and embraced.

"Are the other boys in school?" Jewel asked. She could never quite keep straight when the terms began and ended. Eight-year-old Hughie and seven-year-old Miles attended Sedgwick School, which their father had founded and where he acted as headmaster. Catherine had taught there for the first five years of their marriage.

"They are."

"Here, give me your coat."

"We can't stay." Catherine went over to peck Grady's cheek and shook her head at Nicholas for taking two handfuls of peppermints. At thirty-five, she could still turn heads, with her stunning gray-green eyes set in an oval face and a wealth of chestnut-colored hair. "Have you forgotten what day it is?"

"Forgotten?" But before her sister could reply, the significance of the pink parcel sank in. Jewel hurried over to her desk, took her handbag from a drawer. "Georgiana's birthday! I'm so glad you stopped by. . . . I'll just have to buy something on the way."

"Jewel, we're not going. I came to ask you to take our gift over."

"Not going?"

"I thought I could, for Georgiana's sake. But I just can't."

Jewel nodded understanding. Milly Holt was one of Catherine's best friends. It mattered little that, now that the trauma of infidelity and divorce were distant memories, Milly was happier than she ever was when married to Lord Holt. Friendship was friendship.

Were it not for Lord Holt's untimely demise, Jewel thought, she herself would still have nothing to do with Muriel. Neither she nor her family members had attended the wedding, which had caused hard feelings from Aunt Phyllis's side of the family. But at Lord Holt's funeral, attended by all of Jewel's family, Jewel and Muriel had embraced and declared they would again be as close as they were as children.

Catherine, not able to go that far, had decided that she would *tolerate* Muriel's company when necessary for family harmony. But she would never set foot in the house where Milly had lived with Lord Holt.

"I'll be happy to take your gift by," Jewel said, and for curiosity's sake, asked, "What is it?"

"A doll. She probably has hundreds, but with boys, I seldom have an excuse to shop for one. I'll write your names on the card as well, if you like."

"No, thank you. There's a toy shop just across the Square." Jewel nodded in her nephew's direction and mouthed, *Shall I take Nicholas?*

Her sister shook her head. "Thank you, but we're on our way to Oxford Street to buy shoes."

"Boots," Nicholas corrected, a lump in each cheek.

"Boots," Catherine said.

"I'll walk you out." Jewel planted a quick kiss on Grady's bulldog-like jowl on her way to the coatrack. "You'll see to your own lunch?"

"Of course," Grady said. "And take your time."

She said farewell to her sister and nephew in front of the underground station.

"Sorry to burden you with this," Catherine said, handing Jewel the parcel.

"It's no burden. I planned to go anyway."

Her older sister hesitated. "You must think me terribly stuffy."

"I would *never* think that." Jewel embraced her again. "You have the right to choose your friends."

Sloan Square, once a village green where boys played cricket, was now where shop assistants and accounting clerks took their sack lunches on pleasant days. Today the Square was empty, save the newly planted plane trees with young boughs quivering in the February breezes. Jewel crossed the Square to W. H. Cremer's and scanned the shelves in a panic. What was appropriate for a three-year-old? Another doll? If only she had asked Catherine's advice!

"They enjoy picture books at that age," the young woman behind the counter suggested and produced three she said were very popular: Henry Anelay's *A Child's Picture Alphabet*, Christina Rosetti's *Sing-Song*, and George Routledge's *Tiny Tales in One Syllable*.

"Yes, thank you," Jewel said.

"Would you like these wrapped?"

Jewel looked at her watch. "No, thank you. A bag will be fine."

A bundle under each arm, she stepped out onto the pavement and headed toward a hansom stand, for Victoria Station, the nearest underground railway stop near Belgrave Square, would still be a walk of several blocks. The two-bedroom Kensington flat she and Grady leased had no mews, and they saw no need to waste money on horses, a driver, and coach, as well as a rented stable, when one could get anywhere in London via underground railway, omnibus, or hansom cab.

After a twenty-minute ride she stepped down in front of a familiar mauve stucco house and paid the driver. There were no signs of life, no chaperoned children ringing the doorbell.

Joyce answered Jewel's ring and took her hat, coat, and gloves.

"Are there no guests?" Jewel whispered.

The parlourmaid gave her a somber nod. "Not a soul but you, Mrs. McGuire."

In the parlour Muriel was pacing the carpet. She had dressed to the nines, in a double-breasted short jacket of teal green velour, with jet buttons, and a skirt of black woolen sateen. Behind her, treats of all sorts were arranged in silver trays around a beautiful but forlorn-looking white birthday cake at the center of a table.

Jewel laid the parcels on the arm of a chair just in time, for Muriel advanced and fell into her arms. "Oh, Jewel . . . no one's coming!"

"There, there, now." Jewel patted her cousin's heaving back.

"Perhaps everyone else had plans."

"Every child in the neighborhood?" Muriel said bitterly. "I sent out sixteen invitations, three weeks ago. Their mothers don't want to be seen here. I know what they think of me, but I didn't think they would hold it against a three-year-old! I could just spit in their faces!"

Painful as it was to admit to herself, Jewel could understand the neighbors' reluctance to involve themselves with Muriel. After contributing to the breakup of Lord Holt's six-year marriage, she had moved into Belgrave Square naïvely confident that the same respect and acceptance Milly had earned would be automatically transferred to herself.

"Why don't you move?" Jewel said. "You certainly have the means to live anywhere you wish."

"Allow them to run me off?" Muriel stepped back and gave a violent shake of her head. "I'll not give them that satisfaction. I lived in this same neighborhood when I was a girl, remember. I've as much right to live here as they have."

"That's like cutting off your nose to spite your face, you know."

"It's my nose to cut off, if I wish," Muriel sniffed, snatching a napkin from the table to wipe her eyes.

Tenacious to a fault, Jewel thought, including in that description Douglas's obsessive pursuit of Bethia. Changing to a happier subject seemed the best thing to do, and fortunately, one was available just upstairs.

"When may I see the birthday girl? I brought her some gifts." She hesitated. "And Catherine sent something."

Muriel's expression darkened. "She's not coming?"

"You have to understand . . ."

Her cousin muttered something Jewel could not discern but at length shrugged and said, "What did you bring?"

"Picture books."

"Books?" Muriel said skeptically. "She's only three."

Jewel restrained herself from rolling her eyes at her cousin. There were times that they may as well be nine years old again and arguing over such things as whether to roller skate or dress up their dolls. "Mother was reading to me when I was three. She'll love them."

"If you say so," Muriel said, reaching for the bell cord.

$\mathcal{G}$eorgiana's nanny ushered the girl through the doorway.

"Why, aren't you a little princess!" Jewel exclaimed, holding out her arms. And indeed, she did look fetching in her dusty-rose velvet gown, trimmed with cream-colored lace. She showed promise of becoming as strikingly beautiful as her mother, with her late father's blue eyes and dimpled chin, and Muriel's blonde curls and heart-shaped face.

"My dressmaker ordered the fabric from Paris," Muriel said with a wave of dismissal for the nanny. "But I wish her birthday were a few months later. Spring fabrics are so much prettier."

Jewel lifted the girl to balance her upon one hip. "And how old are you today?"

Georgiana hesitated. "Free year old."

"You're not a baby anymore, are you?"

This time Georgiana did not have to think. She shook her blonde curls. "I not a baby."

"Well, would you like to see your presents?"

"Want to see them," she replied, craning her neck to peer over Jewel's shoulder.

The doll held her interest for all of ten seconds, but she clapped her little hands at the books. "Read to me?" she said, holding out *A Child's Picture Alphabet*. Jewel obliged, taking the girl in her lap on the sofa.

> "A begins Apple, so juicy and sweet,
> That, when ripe in Autumn, we all like to eat. . . ."

Meanwhile Muriel drifted from sofa to chair to sofa again, occasionally going to the window to peer into the street and mutter such things as "I'll make them sorry."

". . . Z begins Zenith, the sky overhead,
Where shines the pale moon as we lie in our bed."

"Read another?" Georgiana asked, helping Jewel close the book.
"But of course, dear."

"Nanny will read to you, Georgiana," Muriel said, reaching for the bell cord. She turned to Jewel. "Let's you and I take lunch at the Savoy."

Jewel's eyes moved from the girl upon her lap to the spread upon the tablecloth. "But it's her—"

"Prescott will tend to her. The servants may have the rest of the food." Muriel's violet eyes were desperate. "If we don't leave here now, I'll lose my mind."

When Nanny Prescott returned, she did not seem surprised at Muriel's instruction to fix up a tray to carry up to the nursery with the child. Jewel kissed little Georgiana's cheek, and when nanny and child were gone, she went to the telephone. "I must tell Grady where he can reach me. We had a little . . . problem yesterday."

"What sort of problem?" Muriel asked.

Jewel shook her head, for the operator was speaking. Grady came on the line and said that he and Mr. Webb were just about to step out to Giovanni's, the Italian cafe on the Square, and that he had spoken via telephone to a sober and relatively serene Richard Whitmore just minutes ago.

"But why are you leaving Georgiana's party?" Grady asked.

"Yes, it's cold, but I brought my coat," Jewel replied, glancing up at Muriel. It was hers and Grady's secret code, which meant "I'll explain later." There were variants of the code, such as "Yes, it's raining, but I brought my umbrella" or "Yes, it's hot, but I'm wearing light clothes." Any abrupt reference to the weather served.

"Ah, I see," Grady said. "Well, have a good time."

In the coach on the way up Piccadilly Street, Jewel asked how the new nanny was working out.

"Fine," Muriel replied, pulling a string from the hem of one glove. "And you know . . . I'm actually *glad* she's so homely, now that I've grown used to her looks."

"Why is that?" Jewel asked. Not that she had found the nanny particularly homely. She would be the *last* person to paste that label upon anyone else.

"Because Georgiana's old enough to learn not to set too much stock in appearances. Mother had her faults, but she did teach the boys and me that one shouldn't judge a book by its cover."

Whether Aunt Phyllis had done such a thing or had not was debatable in Jewel's mind, for over the years she had witnessed Muriel's and her brothers' derogatory and sometimes blatant comments about someone's protruding teeth or poor complexion or wide girth. "Well, she seems competent."

Muriel waved a gloved hand. "Enough of that. What sort of problem are you having at the office? Has it to do with Mr. Shaw's column?"

"You read it too," Jewel said flatly.

"Seems as if Daphne Lloyd is bringing down the whole production."

"That's not so, Muriel. No production rests upon the shoulders of one person alone."

"Hmm." Muriel's rosebud lips pursed thoughtfully. "Yet, the costumes and sets and rest of the cast are the same the critics were raving over just weeks ago, before she replaced Charlotte Steel."

"Well, yes," Jewel had to concede.

"Mrs. Steel is obviously more popular than I realized."

"It was her vitality that endeared her to everyone." Jewel gave her a dry smile. "Except to Mr. Whitmore. They both have such forceful personalities that putting them in the same room was like fire and kerosene. But it worked onstage."

"Why don't you order Miss Lloyd to put more vitality into her role?"

"We've suggested it." Jewel sighed. "And she makes the attempt. But changing one's personality isn't like changing a gown. She's certainly competent, and every bit as beautiful as Mrs. Steel. But she hasn't her strong personality. And when Mr. Whitmore compensates for Miss Lloyd's . . . well . . . blandness . . . his acting seems overdone, artificial. He realizes it too and is a bear to be about lately."

"Hmm. Can't you replace her with someone with more experience?"

"It's too late into the production for that." Jewel swiped a hand across the window. The granite columns, colored pillars, and terraced balconies of the Savoy Hotel loomed through the hole in the condensation. She turned to her cousin and took her hand. "Forgive me. Here you are, needing some cheering, and I'm burdening you with our problems."

"I asked you what was wrong, remember?" Muriel said. "It takes my mind off my own problems. And besides, it's interesting. How many people are privy to the goings-on of a theatre?"

Jewel had to laugh. "You'd be surprised."

The Savoy's maître d' led them to a table in the center of the vast dining room. Jewel, following Muriel, noticed how many admiring glances her cousin attracted from men, and not a few envious ones from women.

"You said there are only three weeks left in this production," Muriel said after the server had taken their orders. She took off her gloves, and the diamonds of her engagement and wedding rings caught light from the chandelier. "What will you do next?"

Jewel puzzled over the interest in her cousin's violet eyes. Muriel usually grew impatient within five minutes when any subject of conversation did not directly involve herself. It was a relief to pour out her troubles to someone not connected with the Royal Court. And she had no worry about the information going any farther. For all her faults, Muriel was discreet.

"Fortunately, a New York touring company is bringing *The Runaway* for March, so we'll be able to concentrate fully on rehearsals for *Lady Audley's Secret*."

"Indeed? And will Miss Lloyd be assigned the lead?"

"Sh-h-h." Jewel glanced over at the nearest table. Two elderly men and a young man were involved in a friendly but animated debate over whether the artist Aubrey Beardsley had talent.

Still, she lowered her voice. "We're making some inquiries."

"With whom?"

Jewel shook her head, for negotiations with lead actresses were conducted in strictest confidence, even though so far nothing had come of them. "And we've posted a casting call notice in the *Stage* for two weeks from today. Miss Lloyd is most welcome to read for the part, if she desires."

"But she'll probably be demoted to a minor role," Muriel said with a knowing little smile.

"Now, I didn't say that."

She was relieved when the server, a man of about forty, chose that time to arrive with bowls of hare soup and tea, for she was in danger of sharing information not already common knowledge in Sloan Square. With amusement she watched the server try to avoid staring at Muriel as he ground pepper into her soup.

"What's it like?" Jewel asked.

Muriel dropped a sugar cube into her cup with a tiny splash. "I haven't tasted it yet."

"No, not the tea. Having men admire you everywhere you go."

"You have Grady. Why would you want that?"

"Everyone wants to be admired," Jewel replied, picking up her soup spoon. "But yes, Grady's admiration counts the most."

"I don't attract as much attention as you think," Muriel said.

And at that moment as if to prove her wrong, a gentleman appeared at the table. His auburn hair was wavy, like the late Lord Holt's, his top lip was almost hidden by a full mustache, and he wore a finely cut woolen frock coat with raspberry checked cravat. "I beg your pardon, ladies," he said, but addressing Muriel. "If you'll permit me to introduce myself. . . . My name is Alan Slater. Have I the pleasure of addressing Lady Holt?"

Muriel eyed him for a fraction of a second, shook her head, and replied, "I'm afraid you're mistaken."

"I was so certain. Lord Holt, God rest his soul, was a fellow member of the Brooke's Club. He and Lady Holt shared a booth with me at the Derby five years ago, and the resemblance is—"

"They say everyone has a twin. My name is Nelly Grimshaw. Perhaps you've heard of my husband, Jack Grimshaw, the boxer?"

His expression was doubtful. "Ah, I'm afraid I haven't."

She picked up her soup spoon and held it poised over her bowl, sending the message that she had had enough of Mr. Slater's company.

"I beg your pardon," he said and walked away.

"That was cruel, Muriel," Jewel said when the man was out of earshot. Still, she felt guilty for the effort it took to refrain from smiling.

Her cousin took a spoonful of soup. "You take that risk when you approach people who are minding their own business."

"Have you heard from Douglas?" Jewel asked, changing the subject.

"Last Wednesday, Mother and Father, Bernard, and I received letters he had posted in December. He and Mr. Adams are in a town called Edmonton or Edwardton or some such, waiting for spring. He asked to borrow some money, so I sent a cheque. I wish now that I'd sent railway and steamer tickets instead. If he runs out of money, he would have no choice but to come home, yes?"

"I suppose. Poor Douglas."

A frown tugged at the corners of Muriel's lips. "I realize you take issue whenever I criticize your father's side of the family, but I strongly resent Bethia for driving him to this."

"That's simply not true." Jewel shook her head. "He hounded her to death, even though he knew she has a beau."

"I hardly think a few letters constitutes hounding."

"Good heavens, Muriel!" Over Muriel's shoulder Jewel noticed three women turn heads in her direction. She lowered the volume but not the emotion of her voice. "He followed her to Girton!"

Her cousin frowned. "Yes, that was stupid. But she *could* have used more tact in informing him she wasn't interested."

"How could she have been any more tactful?"

"Oh, I can think of one way—by *not* sending him a snooty letter saying she couldn't love him if he were the last man in England. And signing it 'with utmost contempt!' Who does she think she is?"

Jewel sucked air through her teeth and counted silently to five. "I'll have you know that Bethia regrets writing the letter. She was most upset when I informed her he'd left his job and gone off to Canada. And almost every time we speak, she asks if I've heard how he's faring."

"How good of her." Muriel smirked.

"You're only looking at this from Douglas's side."

"And why shouldn't I? He happens to be my brother."

This merry-go-round just isn't going to stop, Jewel thought. "Muriel, are you sure some of your animosity toward Bethia isn't because her family didn't attend your wedding?"

"Not at all," Muriel replied at once, then belied her statement by following with, "Sidney warned me that they would ignore the invitation, that they thought themselves better than him, even though William Doyle used to clean his boots at Oxford."

"*We* ignored the invitation too," Jewel reminded her.

"But *you* attended the funeral. They didn't even send a note of condolence."

Jewel placed her linen napkin beside her half-finished bowl and reached for her handbag on the empty chair. She would return to the theatre, where at least she was *paid* for mediating petty complaints.

"You're not leaving, are you?" Muriel said, eyes widening.

"I think it's best."

"Please don't be angry, Jewel." Her expression grew contrite. "With Douglas away, you're the only friend I have."

"I'm not angry. Just frustrated. Bethia's my cousin too."

Muriel reached across the table and touched her hand. "I'll not mention it again—I promise."

An uneasy truce presided while they chatted of safer things such as one of the servants finding an ear wire Muriel had lost on a flagstone in the garden and Jewel's housemaid having to borrow the neighbor's cat when a mouse took up territory in the kitchen. The server returned with entrees—roast pigeon with stewed celery *à la crème* for Muriel and scalloped oysters with German carrots for Jewel.

Using knife and fork to carve a bit of breast, Muriel said, "I'd like to see for myself if Miss Lloyd is really as awful as you—"

Jewel's pulse jumped. "I never said she was awful."

"Oh, very well," Muriel said with rolled eyes. "Just leave me a ticket at the call box tonight."

"Wouldn't you prefer tomorrow?"

"Tomorrow?"

Of the things Jewel could not understand about Muriel, her casualness toward motherhood was paramount. "I just assumed . . . Georgiana's birthday . . ."

Looking slightly offended, Muriel said, "She'll be in bed by that time."

"Of course."

Her cousin sighed. "But perhaps tomorrow will be better after all."

"We'll put you in Lord Brandon's box. He's in the country and has no guests coming in. I'll even join you after I've counted noses in the greenroom." And to ease the reproach still lingering in her cousin's expression, Jewel added, "Just promise me you won't throw tomatoes at Miss Lloyd."

"Don't worry," Muriel said, finally smiling. "I happen to know a lot about tomatoes. They aren't in season."

Twelve

*M*uriel rose late the following morning, having read from H. G. Wells's *War of the Worlds* until midnight, then lying awake listening to her own heart thump as house noises became malevolent Martians. At half past twelve, she finally rang for Joyce to sit just inside her bedchamber. Even then, she had to bury her head under her covers with just a space for breathing, before she was able to drift into fitful slumber.

No more scary stories at night, she promised herself at breakfast, knowing she would break that resolve within the week.

Downstairs, she pulled boots on over her slippers, a knit cap over her head, and a cardigan over a fresh gardening smock. Frigid February air stung her nose in the garden. "Good mornin', m'Lady," Watterson said, shovel clanking against the bed of the barrow as he pushed a load of bark toward the ligustrum. He had been a boxer in his youth, so said Mrs. Burles, and had the misshapen nose to prove it.

Muriel nodded and stepped farther along the path, surveying the direction from which the gardener had come. He would finish mulching well before evening. The tender plants were secure in the greenhouse, lily bulbs were in the ground waiting for summer flowering, the rose of Sharon shrubs had been pruned. The only task remaining for the next fortnight or so was the application of a winter wash of tar oil to the plum and birch trees. That she would leave to Watterson, for the chore was messy, and besides, why should she pay him for idling?

She was bored to tears and had no idea what to do with herself.

She went back inside, removed smock, cardigan, cap, and boots. In the morning room she took Douglas's letter from her writing desk and dropped upon the sofa.

My dear Sister,

As I write this, Christmas is but ten days away. Yours will have long passed by the time this reaches you. How I wish I were there to celebrate with all of you! I do hope you thought to give Georgiana something from her uncle.

Randall and I are sharing a room in a lodging house in Edmonton, Alberta, for the winter. We, and many others, were prevented from pushing on to Dawson City by a snowstorm and now must stay until late March or early April. In the meantime we are gathering supplies, which our landlord allows us to store in the cellar, for a fee. A list of recommended necessities is posted in most mercantile shops. We will purchase horses at the very last minute, to save on stabling and feed money. The list is endless, but I will give you some examples:

2 axes, 3 shovels, 3 picks
3 gold pans
1 whip saw, 1 hand saw
1 frying pan, 1 baking pan
1 granite kettle, 4 granite cups
2 large cooking spoons, 4 each of knives, forks, and spoons
hammer, wire nails
canvas tent, mosquito netting
oiled canvas sheet to lay under blanket
2 heavy pocket knives
candles, matches, and soap
200 feet oakum rope
sheet-iron stove with reflector for baking
4 woolen blankets each
2 sleeping bags made of oiled canvas and lined with wool
rubber boots
1 rifle, 2 Colt revolvers and 4 boxes of ammunition for each

I am not mentioning the firearms in Mother and Father's letter for obvious reasons. We are also laying a store of warm clothing, medicines, and food—for example, they recommend 250 pounds of smoked bacon!

This leads me to an embarrassing request. Because we did not anticipate having to purchase so many supplies, I am running a

*little short on money and fear we will not have enough for some
decent packhorses. If you would kindly send your dear brother a
cheque for two hundred pounds, I will repay you when I bring back
my fortune.*

*It is difficult to wait for the snow to melt. One can only play so
many games of Commerce, and Randall sulks when he loses. Bernard will be happy to know I have started attending a little Presbyterian chapel across the street. The choir is quite good for its size
and was in need of a baritone, so I allowed myself to be pressed into
service. But I am looking forward to pressing on to the Klondike.
More and more of late, I go through a whole day forgetting to
grieve for Miss Rayborn's lack of esteem for me. I do believe, dear
Muriel, that this will be the adventure of my life.*

If you don't get yourself killed, Muriel thought, wiping her eyes.

A soft knock sounded. She folded the letter. "Yes?"

Mrs. Burles entered the room to stand just inside the doorway.
"May I speak with your Ladyship?"

"What is it?"

"It's about Nanny Prescott." The housekeeper's expression grew
a little uncertain.

"Must I drag it out of you, Mrs. Burles?" Muriel said. "What has
she done?"

"Sorry, your Ladyship. It's just that we're all fond of her, and
she's very kind to Miss Georgiana, but she's gone and boxed up most
of the toys and put them in the attic."

The housekeeper's report sounded so ludicrous that Muriel had
to allow it to run through her mind again before she had the wits to
respond.

"Well, make her take them back down."

"She reminded me that you gave her full authority over the nursery and said that Miss Georgiana has too many toys for her own
good."

"Too many for . . ." But what was she doing, sitting there par-
roting everything Mrs. Burles said? Muriel sighed and got to her feet.

"Shall I tell her you—"

"No," Muriel replied. "I'll speak with her."

Leah Prescott sat on the edge of the day-nursery rocking chair.
Georgiana, clad in little coat and boots, stood before her, submitting

to having the strings to a knit cap tied beneath her dimpled chin.

"There you are, a wee Laplander," Prescott was saying.

"Laplan?"

"It's a place far up north."

Georgiana turned her face toward the doorway and brightened. "Mummy, we go to Laplan."

"Well, just to the Square," the nanny said, smiling and rising. "Good morning, Lady Holt."

"Good morning." Muriel entered the room. She had expected the day nursery to be bare, but there were several toys about—Georgiana's dollhouse, a heap of building blocks, and others. Still, Prescott had overextended her authority. Calmly, for her daughter's sake, she said, "Why did you put away Georgiana's other toys?"

Prescott nodded. "Forgive me, m'Lady. I realized after speaking with Mrs. Burles that I should have asked first. It's just that, with the new birthday gifts, Miss Georgiana had so many about that she couldn't enjoy them."

"We put horsy in a box," Georgiana said, too absorbed in pulling on her mittens to be distressed.

That did not matter. They were *Georgiana's* things, not Prescott's. "I fail to see your logic," Muriel said. "Explain."

With an uncertain look at Georgiana, as if she feared the discussion would cause her to demand her toys, Prescott replied with soft voice, "She didn't know how to sit and play with *one,* m'Lady. She would run from one to another to another and eventually became bored with the whole lot."

"She's three years old," Muriel reminded her. "What do you expect?"

"But—"

"You'll get those toys down before bedtime. Do you understand?"

It seemed for a second that the nanny would protest. But she eventually nodded. "Yes, m'Lady."

"We go now?" Georgiana asked, proudly holding up her mittened hands for their approval.

She was so fetching that Muriel smiled. But she had to ask Prescott, "Isn't it too cold for a walk?"

"We go out to snatch a bit of sunlight every day weather allows, and Miss Georgiana has suffered no ill effects. But if m'Lady would rather we didn't . . ."

An accusing little voice, which sounded remarkably like Nanny Tucker's, spoke in Muriel's mind, saying that any good mother would be aware of her daughter's activities, including walks in the Square. But how could she have known, Muriel thought, when it seemed only yesterday that Georgiana was a red-faced infant being carried, or pushed in a pram?

"It not too cold, Mummy," Georgiana said desperately.

Muriel eyed Prescott's face for any sign of disrespect or, worse, judgment upon her mothering abilities. When she detected neither, she replied, "Oh, very well."

Georgiana clapped her hands. "Laplan!"

"Not quite so far, I'm afraid, Miss Georgiana," the nanny said. She looked up again at Muriel, hesitated, and asked, "Perhaps m'Lady would care to join us?"

"Some other time," Muriel said automatically. "I've too much to do."

Instead of just hearing the voice this time, Muriel could see Nanny Tucker's face with her mind's eye. *I do so spend enough time with my daughter!* Focusing her attention upon Nanny Prescott again, she said, "But I suppose I could spare a little time . . . just today."

Traffic was scant on Belgrave Street, still Muriel carried Georgiana across until she could safely lower her to the weathered grass of the Square. The walk started off well, Muriel holding her daughter's small hand with Prescott following just closely enough to be available if needed. Every now and again, Georgiana would look up at her with wonder in her little face. Smoke rose from chimney pots of houses on all four sides. Muriel hoped some of her neighbors were witnessing how little their snubbing of Georgiana's party yesterday had affected them.

"Moke," Georgiana said, pointing.

"What is it, darling?"

"Moke in your mouth."

Muriel understood and blew out a stream of vapory breath, which made Georgiana laugh.

"It's coming from your mouth too," Muriel said. "Blow out and see."

Her little face screwed up in concentration as she pushed out her lips in a circle, but nothing happened.

Muriel demonstrated pulling in a deep breath, blowing it out. "Try again."

This time the girl blew out a faint but definite stream of vapor, and they both laughed. Never mind yesterday's disaster of a birthday party—today was fresh and clean, and Muriel wished it could stretch out like this forever.

"You'll be taking a walk this same time tomorrow afternoon?" she impulsively asked Prescott over her shoulder.

The nanny smiled. "If it doesn't rain, m'Lady."

"Perhaps I'll join you again."

———————

"O gentle Romeo!
If thou dost love, pronounce it faithfully:
Or if thou think'st I am too quickly won,
I'll frown and be perverse and say thee nay. . . ."

"Is she taking quinine?" Muriel leaned to whisper. "*I* could do better than that."

Jewel put a finger to her lips.

From their vantage point in box six, Muriel could see the reason for the worry and resignation in her cousin's face. Less than three-quarters of the Royal Court's seats were filled, and from the three-pence upper-galley seats drifted the low hum of conversation, then laughter when a Cockney voice called out, "Come on, love . . . say it like yer means it!"

Muriel had to suppress a smile. Faint ripples came from even the upper-class seats below. Richard Whitmore broke character only long enough to send a tight-lipped glance up into the galley, which silenced the laughter and voices, for he was still quite popular even among those of the rougher sort.

The effect upon Miss Lloyd was negligible; she went on stoically delivering her lines.

"This bud of love, by summer's ripening breath,

May prove a beauteous flower when next we meet. . . ."

"Opium," Muriel could not resist speculating. "Have you checked her dressing room for a pipe?"

Her cousin looked at her, pressed her lips together, and nodded.

———————

It was as her clock was softly chiming four that Muriel roused to drink from the carafe on her bedside table, not bothering with the glass. As she settled again into her pillows, she willed herself to gather up the fragments of the pleasant dream the clock had interrupted. She was onstage at the Royal Court, dressed as Juliet, addressing Richard Whitmore's Romeo with every emotion drawn from every part of her being.

> *"Of all the days that's in the week*
> *I dearly love but one day—*
> *And that's the day that comes betwixt*
> *A Saturday and Monday. . . ."*

Which was actually from "Sally in Our Alley," a poem by Henry Carey she had memorized in grammar school, for her dream self was not acquainted with Shakespeare's lines. But Romeo and the audience approved; she could tell by the smiling faces from the front row . . . Jewel and Grady, Mother and Father, Douglas and Bernard. Even Sidney was there, face flush with pride, and their Belgravia neighbors, faces flush with sheepish envy.

> *"For then I'm dressed all in my best*
> *To walk abroad with Sally;*
> *She is the darling of my heart,*
> *And she lives in our alley. . . ."*

When she woke in the morning, the glow from all that approval clung to her for a little while, until reality set in again and caused it to dissipate. What would it be like to be an actress, she wondered as she brushed her teeth. To see one's name above a theatre marquee and eventually become a household name, like Sarah Bernhardt, Charlotte Steel, Ellen Terry. To stand under lights, every eye in a huge auditorium on *her*.

And Jewel had said the Royal Court would be holding auditions for *Lady Audley's Secret* in two weeks. Wouldn't it be something if she were to show up as well?

You're insane, she said to herself, bristles working on the hard-to-reach space between her lower back teeth on the right side. *You're not an actress.*

But who *were* actresses but ordinary people who discovered they had talent? They weren't Martians. They weren't born onstage—they'd had to make that first step, attend that first audition at some point in their lives.

She was certainly attractive enough. She didn't consider herself vain, but mirrors did not lie. *And you have experience,* she realized while rinsing her mouth with water. Had she not acted the part of a grieving widow flawlessly during the two-and-a-half years of her mourning? What could she lose by auditioning, except suffer a little embarrassment if she were rejected? Acting was now considered a respectable profession; some actors such as Henry Irving and Charles Wyndham had achieved knighthood.

The notion continued popping into her mind all morning, like a dresser drawer sliding open on its tracks in spite of her efforts to keep it shut.

"What would you think of my auditioning for a play?" she asked Evelyn, while the latter fastened the buttons running up the back of Muriel's Wedgwood-blue silk gown.

Muriel wasn't in the habit of sharing secrets with her lady's maid, but her closest confidant was across the ocean, probably wrapped in bearskins huddled by a fireplace, and her second-closest confidant was one of the people who could make this notion happen, so this wasn't time to discuss a half-baked idea with Jewel and regret it later. The idea should be discussed with someone whose opinion did not matter, so that Muriel could sort it out in her mind with no fear of losing face.

"A play, m'Lady?" Evelyn said with the same inflection she would have used had Muriel asked if she should go to a hospital and perform surgery today. "Begging your pardon, but they only allow actresses to be in plays."

"Yes, that's so," Muriel said and repeated her earlier thoughts.

"But actresses are just people like you and me. They're not Martians, you know."

Evelyn came around to fasten the four buttons on either of Muriel's cuffs. "I'm not acquainted with any Martians, m'Lady."

"Well, no one is, Evelyn. They're creatures from Mars."

"Oh." The expression in her gray eyes faded a bit. "Yes, I expect not, m'Lady."

Muriel joined Nanny Prescott and Georgiana on their afternoon walk and had as lovely a time as yesterday, though she had to work a little harder to keep her thoughts in the moment and not onstage at the Royal Court.

This is ridiculous, she said to herself in the morning room after lunch, when she could not even concentrate fully on the pages of *War of the Worlds.*

"I beg your pardon, m'Lady," Joyce said at the door. "Telephone for you. It's Mrs. Pearce."

Muriel closed her book, went to the parlour, and picked up the body of the candlestick telephone with one hand, the earpiece with the other. "Hello, Mother?" she said, sinking into the cushions of the sofa. "How good to hear from you. How are you keeping?"

"The same" came her mother's peevish voice. "Did Georgiana's dress arrive?"

Muriel winced. She had intended to telephone her mother to thank her for the lovely royal blue velvet and lace dress and put Georgiana on the line to do the same.

"I'm sorry, Mother. I meant to call, but I've been quite busy these past two days, with the party and everything. . . ."

"Too busy to spare your mother two minutes? I devoted my whole life to my children, and you hardly ever come up to see us, and Douglas went traipsing off to Canada. Bernard is the only one who appreciates me."

That stung. Ever since Bernard chose the ministry and requested a parish near where their parents resided, he had become the perfect son. How easy it was for Mother to forget such things as his setting his bed on fire while sneaking Father's pipe upstairs for a smoke or causing Douglas to break an arm by daring him to jump from a tree limb with an open umbrella.

Don't argue or you'll never get off the telephone, Muriel thought.

"The dress is lovely. Georgiana looks like a princess in it." Or at least she would when Muriel's dressmaker took up the seams a bit. "How is Father?"

"Spending too many hours at the office, as usual," Mother replied, still peevish. "Agatha and Sally spent yesterday with me."

Muriel breathed a quiet sigh. Agatha was perfect Bernard's perfect wife. But at least she took some of the pressure off Muriel to travel up to Sheffield every other week.

"Agatha's doctor confirmed she's going to have another baby," Mother continued. "Heaven knows how she'll manage two so close in age."

"Indeed?" At least Muriel smiled, for she loved her brother in spite of his irritating goodness and knew how much he doted upon Sally. "Do congratulate them for me."

"Oh dear," Mother fretted. "Bernard wanted to be the one to give you the news."

"What news?" Muriel said. "I can't recall a word of what you were just saying."

They shared a rare laugh, and then Muriel promised to bring Georgiana up for Easter. She had no sooner replaced the telephone onto the table when it rang again. Thinking it was her mother, Muriel did not wait for one of the servants to hasten in.

"Mother?" she said into the mouthpiece.

It was Bernard, almost giddy. "I've the most marvelous news!"

"You won at the horses?" Muriel feigned a guess.

"As if!" he chuckled. "We're going to have another baby!"

She said she was happy for him and asked how Agatha was feeling. He replied that she was hale and healthy, which did not surprise Muriel, for in keeping with her perfection, Bernard's wife had sailed through her first pregnancy with none of the nausea that had kept Muriel practically bedridden for nine months.

"I pray she continues feeling as well as last time," he said as if reading her thoughts. His voice became tender. "Poor Muriel. You had such a difficult time of it, and so soon after Sidney . . ."

"All that's over. I'm fine now," Muriel said, and because the compassion in his voice touched her and made her feel closer to him than she had in a long time, she added, "I'd like to ask your advice."

"But of course."

"I've this notion. . . ." She waved a hand as if he could see her. "Silly, actually, to audition for a part in a play at Jewel's theatre. I can't stop thinking of it."

After a pause, he replied, "I was hoping you were going to ask me to help you choose a church."

"Georgiana is too young to sit through a service," she replied, already beginning to regret bringing up the subject. "We'll go when she's older."

"I hope you mean that."

"Yes, absolutely. But about auditioning . . . ?"

"I believe it's a healthy thing to push oneself toward new experiences, as long as they're morally sound. But, as you said, Georgiana's still young. She needs you."

"My child is not lacking for attention," Muriel said defensively. "In fact, we take strolls in the Square together."

"She'll lack attention if you have to devote long hours to the theatre." A sigh, then, "Muriel, you asked for my advice and here it is. Wait a few years. You don't appreciate how privileged you are, even as a widow. Many women in my parish have to spend twelve hours a day at factory work and can only dream of being able to rear their own children."

Muriel blinked salt tears from her eyes, touched by his words and the concern in his voice. "Yes, of course," she said, and the issue was settled in her mind and she was at peace.

For at least the remainder of the afternoon.

The night was a different story, for again she could picture herself on stage, soaking up adulation from every seat in the theatre.

———

Over toast with quince jam and a cheese omelet the following morning, she decided it couldn't hurt anything to *read* the play, if only to understand the performance better when it eventually came to the Royal Court. *With an experienced lead actress, of course.*

Impulsively she rose from the small table in the morning room, where she customarily took breakfast, to ring the bell cord. She heard footsteps on the service stairs, and Joyce entered the room seconds later.

"You rang, m'Lady?"

"Yes. Send Ham to the bookstore for me."

"Very well, m'Lady. What is it he should buy?"

Muriel hesitated. Was she imagining amusement in the parlour-maid's eyes? Had Evelyn, curse her dull soul, mentioned yesterday's scrap of conversation? She could just imagine the servants in the kitchen, sharing a chuckle over her brief delusion of grandeur.

They're only servants, she reminded herself.

But servants talked to other servants, and back-door gossip bounced about the Square like a tennis ball.

Raising her chin, Muriel said, "Never mind. Have him bring the coach around in ten minutes."

*H*atchards, London's oldest book shop, was located at 187 Piccadilly, in one of the old residential houses converted into businesses. A somber, almost ecclesiastical atmosphere permeated the place, with its oak floors that creaked in certain spots, and nooks and crannies and heaps of shelves all fitted with books. Most of the assistants were very old men with beards or side-whiskers, so dignified and scholarly that they could have been University dons who sold books as a hobby.

"Ah, Lady Holt," said one of the rare younger assistants, a Mr. Humphreys, who shared her taste for Gothic horror and science fiction. "I've saved a copy of *War of the Worlds* for you."

"Thank you, but I'm already halfway through it," she said, and when he looked a little disappointed that she had not purchased it from Hatchards, she added, "I sent my coachman in last week. He apparently did not inform you it was for me."

That lightened his expression. "And are you enjoying it?"

"Yes, but it gives me nightmares," she confessed.

Mr. Humphreys chuckled, in a dignified way befitting his station. "I'm afraid we've nothing new in that category you haven't read." He lowered his voice. "Nothing new that is worthy of your attention, I should clarify. Some of these recent ghost stories are no better than penny dreadfuls—with better covers."

"Hmm. What a shame." Muriel looked about in all directions, not really seeing the books moving in front of her eyes.

"But if you would care to see some . . ."

"I suppose not. I'll stop by in another week or so."

"Very good, Lady Holt," he said with a small inclination of the head. He accompanied her to the door, but before Muriel reached it she turned, as if struck by afterthought.

"While I'm here . . . have you a copy of *Lady Audley's Secret*? The play, not the novel." And because she thought she detected the same amusement in his eyes she had suspected in Joyce's, she added, "It's for my cousin. She's a manager of Royal Court Theatre. With her husband."

"Ah, a gift," he said, excused himself, and emerged from one of the dim corners with a booklet in hand. "Shall I wrap it for you?"

"Yes," Muriel replied. "After all, it is a gift."

Lady Audley was the role any actress would give her last shilling to play, Muriel thought, flipping through the pages in the seclusion of the morning room. For according to Jewel, London audiences loved those Becky Sharps and Heathcliffs they scowled at, more than the Amelia Sedleys and Edgar Lintons for whom they wept. Here on the pages was a beautiful bigamous heroine who deserts her child, murders one husband, and contemplates poisoning another. Of course that plum would go to a lead actress, probably as the result of those negotiations Jewel was so tight-lipped about.

The utility parts in the play were those of servants and country-women. Many were nonspeaking. Were she to confess to Jewel her growing-by-the-hour desire to audition, it would be one of those parts her cousin would advise—after she picked herself up from the carpet from laughing.

Jewel wouldn't do that. Still, it would be harder for her cousin to take her seriously. What was the saying Father used to explain why the insurance agents under his supervision underwrote more policies to people *outside* their own neighborhoods? *Familiarity breeds contempt.*

"I need advice," she muttered. But not from Bernard, not this time. *As if I would neglect my own daughter!* she thought. After mulling the matter over, she had an idea where to find it.

"You rang, your Ladyship?" Mrs. Burles asked.

"Yes. Have Ham bring the coach around again."

The housekeeper stood just inside the doorway, staring at her indecisively.

"Well?" Muriel said.

"Begging your pardon again, your Ladyship, but his half-day began after lunch, and he mentioned going to visit an aunt."

Muriel was opening her mouth to snap that he could visit his aunt tomorrow just as well as today, when she realized this was all for the best. It was one thing for the servants to know she went to a bookstore, for that was a frequent occurrence. But a call upon Charlotte Steel would set their tongues wagging for certain.

"Would your Ladyship wish me to speak with him?" Mrs. Burles said hesitantly. "Perhaps he could wait . . ."

"Certainly not." Muriel smiled to herself, enveloped in a rare feeling of confidence that everything would fall into place as it should. "Just telephone for a cab in half an hour. A coach, not a hansom, mind you."

After lunch she had Evelyn help her into a gown of cinnamon-colored sateen that brought out the gold in her hair. She added a black velvet belt with wide inverted V to accent her tiny waist and full bosom. One look in the mirror and she shed the belt, recalling how when pregnant with Georgiana, she had despised every woman with a figure. Better not to rouse any jealousy in Mrs. Steel.

"Are you familiar with Mayfair?" Muriel asked the cabby, who wore the ubiquitous black frock coat and top hat. "I wish to call upon the actress Mrs. Charlotte Steel."

"I know where to find the house," he said, holding open the door. He reined the team to a stop next to a cab stand on Old Bond Street, and through the window Muriel watched him converse with a hansom cabby. Seconds later they were moving again, and eventually they stopped in front of a white-columned stucco house on Grosvenor Street.

"Wait here," Muriel instructed the coachman—just in case.

The butler who answered Muriel's ring read her card with the respect due the title before her name and the hauteur of one who had held many such cards in his hand. "I'm afraid Mrs. Steel is not receiving guests at this time, Lady Holt."

"Of course, I understand," she said, careful to maintain dignity in her voice, for as she reminded herself, this was just a whim and she could change her mind at any time. "Will you inform Mrs. Steel that I was introduced to her at the opening night party for *Over the Garden Wall* and that Mrs. McGuire is my cousin? If she could spare me five minutes, I would be most grateful."

"Very well, Lady Holt," he said with an elegant little inclination of the head. Still holding her card, he took her coat, led her to a parlour, and asked her to wait. A man her father's age was repairing the inner workings of a long-case clock, his open leather tool satchel resting upon the back of a chair. After a polite nod he did not look in her direction, but Muriel was glad he was there, for watching him work distracted her from the voice in her head saying she should go home now while she still possessed a shred of dignity.

The butler returned and escorted her up a flight of stairs to a drawing room furnished in the Rococo Revival style, inspired by eighteenth century France with its serpentine backs and curved legs on delicately upholstered walnut sofas and chairs. Charlotte Steel reclined upon a sofa, head propped upon pillows at one end, slipper-clad feet propped upon a pillow at the other. She was still beautiful, in a pale sort of way, with her shining auburn hair draped over one shoulder. If she was showing yet, it was impossible to tell for the loose, faded green plaid flannel dressing gown she wore.

"My husband's," Mrs. Steel explained after Muriel reintroduced herself. She raised a sleeve to show a frayed hem. "I won't allow it to be thrown away. It's the most comfortable garment in the house, and I need comfort at this time. Do have a seat, Lady Holt."

"I'm grateful you agreed to see me," Muriel said once seated stiffly in a pale blue damask-upholstered chair with her reticule in her lap. Not certain yet if Mrs. Steel would hold her to her five minutes, she would have rather skipped the preliminaries, but that simply could not be done. "How is your health, Mrs. Steel?"

Mrs. Steel smiled. None of the acidity for which she was famous was evident in her wan face, but then Richard Whitmore was not in the room. "I'm much better in the afternoons. So you chose a good time. What may I do for you?"

Relieved to be getting down to business, Muriel replied, "This is embarrassing to come out and say, but I'm considering auditioning for a part at the Royal Court."

The actress stared at her, but as there seemed neither amusement nor mockery in her expression, Muriel was able to relax the tiniest bit.

"You've the looks for the stage," Mrs. Steel said at length. "But have you any acting experience?"

"None whatsoever." Mentioning the bit about playing the grieving widow did not seem a good idea. "But I feel certain in my heart I could do it."

A wry little smile quirked the actress's pale cheeks. "You and every other Londoner. It's not as easy as it appears."

"No . . . of course . . ."

"Why did you come to *me*, Lady Holt?"

Muriel drew in a deep breath. "I realize the limitations of your condition, Mrs. Steel. But if you could manage to tutor me for an audition in less than two weeks, I would pay you five hundred pounds."

The actress's eyebrows lifted. After a space of two seconds, she said, "What makes you assume I need money?"

"I don't assume that in the least, Mrs. Steel. But I've nothing to lose by asking, and it could be that you would enjoy the challenge."

Mrs. Steel seemed to mull this over. "What part are you interested in reading?"

"Lady Audley," Muriel replied, and the revelation took her as much by surprise as it obviously did Mrs. Steel. But why go to all the expense, effort, and potential humiliation for anything less?

"Impossible," the actress said.

"I'm willing to take that risk."

"Being related to the McGuires will not give you an edge, if that's what you're hoping. There are too many other employees dependent upon them."

Muriel shook her head. "I realize that. In fact, it will probably work against me."

"Then why not look up auditions in another theatre?"

The thought had not entered Muriel's mind. But she shook her head. "This isn't something I'm forced to do to survive. If I don't succeed, I'll know it wasn't meant to be. And I can't imagine working for anyone but Jewel and Grady."

Mrs. Steel slanted a sage look at her. "Can you imagine paying a *thousand* pounds . . . in advance?"

Do you really want to do this? Muriel asked herself. She did. "I have a cheque in my bag."

"With no guarantee that you'll win the part?"

"No guarantee."

"Very well." Mrs. Steel motioned toward a writing table near the window. "You'll find a pen in the drawer."

Every afternoon following, Ham delivered Muriel to Grosvenor Street, with the exception of Friday, his afternoon off, when she took another cab. She had ceased caring whether or not her servants had guessed the nature of these calls, though she did not discuss them even with Mrs. Burles.

For the audition, Mrs. Steel chose the part in Act I, Scene I, where Lady Audley's first husband, George Talboys, reappears in her life. It is one of the more difficult parts, she explained, because it begins with a soliloquy where Lady Audley explains how she happened to marry again while George was in India.

"I chose this part after ringing Mrs. McGuire and—"

"You spoke with Jewel?" Muriel said with a leap of pulse. She had not yet informed Jewel and Grady of her plan. For a reason she could not fathom, just the idea of doing so caused a queasiness in the pit of her stomach.

"I didn't mention *you.* I simply asked how everyone was getting on. But with some strategic questions, I learned that the actor assisting with the auditions will be Mansel Robbs and that he has already been assigned the part of George Talboys."

"Assisting?" Muriel asked.

"I forget how green you are," Mrs. Steel said. "He will be onstage with script in hand, ready to assume any supporting role needed—male or female."

"Hmm," Muriel said with a little nod, though she had not a clue where this was leading and hoped Mrs. Steel would explain before she was forced to ask.

"You see, even though Mr. Webb—he's the stage director—will announce every act and scene for the McGuires' benefit, every actress who steps out onstage will first have to show Mr. Robbs the actual spot in the script where she is to begin. Only after he finds his place can she assume the role of Lady Audley."

"Hmm."

Mrs. Steel rolled her eyes. "Just hear me out and you'll understand. I happen to know that Mr. Robbs is a perfectionist and will probably have memorized his entire part by then. You should assume that he has and step from the wings as Lady Audley, not taking time to fumble with the script. If you begin immediately with the soliloquy, he'll have time to recall his lines and know where to step in."

"And if he hasn't memorized them?" Muriel asked.

"Then you'll look ridiculous. But when you only have a slim chance, you have to take the greater risk to gain an edge. And if I were you, I would learn as much of the scene that follows yours as possible. One never knows."

She also taught Muriel correct deportment onstage.

"Don't lock your knees together like that," she said as Muriel practiced standing sideways to the pretend audience to address George.

Muriel looked down at her skirt. "How can you tell?"

"Because you're as stiff as a palace guard. Advance the leg that's farthest from the audience out ahead of the other, about the length of your foot."

When Muriel complied, the actress nodded. "There. Much more natural and graceful."

Even her entry was practiced, with the doorway to the drawing room representing the divider between wings and stage.

"Your entry is your first and therefore most valuable impression," Mrs. Steel said. "Novices tend to lunge out from the wings when their names are called. You must take a moment to step back several feet. Take a deep breath, then another, until you *become* Lady Audley. Begin your walk from there, and mind that your steps are firm and decided."

Muriel spent the mornings striving to commit her part so deeply to memory that the line between her own thoughts and the words in the script became blurred. She even performed her daily routines, such as rubbing glycerin into her skin and stirring sugar into her tea, as if she were Lady Audley. Three days of intermittent rain showers beginning on the fifteenth assuaged her guilt somewhat over not having time to join her daughter on the daily walks. She still managed to get up to the nursery at bedtime and sat in the day-nursery rocking chair two mornings, studying lines as Georgiana and her nanny played with blocks or arranged furniture in the doll house.

"Read the book to me, Mama?" her daughter said one of those mornings, propping elbows on Muriel's knees.

"I'm afraid this isn't a proper story for you, dear," Muriel replied, running fingers through her daughter's curls. *After the audition you'll have more time,* she reminded herself and was guiltily relieved when Georgiana took one of her books over to Nanny Prescott.

She was stepping down from the coach in front of her house after another lesson on the eighteenth when Mrs. Fiske from three doors down happened to be passing on the pavement. "Will there be war, do you think?" the older woman asked after an exchange of pleasantries.

"War?" Muriel sent a panicked glance toward the house. "With whom?"

"Between Spain and the States. The battleship *Maine* was sunk in Havana, and over two hundred sailors were killed. Have you not seen the newspapers?"

"Ah, I've been rather busy. My daughter and all." Relief swamped Muriel. She had no idea where Havana was, but Spain and the United States were not England, so there was no risk to her family. At least from any *war,* she amended, thinking of Douglas.

Jewel telephoned an hour later, asked, "How are you keeping?"

"Fine, thank you." And so that her cousin would not be added to the list of those who thought her ill informed, Muriel added, "Isn't it a pity about those sailors?"

"Yes, a pity," Jewel said at length. She mentioned the possibility of war, just as Mrs. Fiske had, but then thankfully changed the subject. "Sorry, but I can't speak long. We're meeting with Mr. Cumberland and Mr. Fry in a bit."

"Oh dear," Muriel said. "Are you in trouble?"

"I don't think so. They've been in the business long enough to know there are ups and downs. But listen—Mother and Father will be arriving in town tonight. Why don't you and Georgiana join us for lunch at Catherine's tomorrow?"

Muriel was quite fond of Aunt Virginia and Uncle James, who were much calmer than her own parents. And she was a little relieved that Catherine would see fit to have her in her home—even if it was Jewel who did the inviting. But she could not afford to miss one day of her acting lessons. "I've a wretched cold. Must be the rain."

"Have you informed the McGuires yet?" Mrs. Steel asked on the twenty-first.

"I've not," Muriel confessed.

"You fear that just knowing they have misgivings will destroy your confidence in yourself." The actress smiled at Muriel's astounded look. "I've worn your shoes, dear. I didn't even inform my parents of my first audition at sixteen."

"That's reassuring."

"Yet I didn't have to *face* them at the theatre. How will you feel having the McGuires there appraising you professionally?"

Muriel thought it over. "I'll remind myself that I'm Lady Audley and that she's never met them."

"Good for you! And as it's Mr. Webb who'll arrange the order of the readings, you'll probably not even see them until you step out onstage. The houselights will be low, so it will be easy to pretend they're not there."

"Do you think I have a chance?" Muriel asked.

"Honestly?"

"Yes, please."

Mrs. Steel gave her a droll little smile. "Frankly . . . only if every experienced actress is struck by lightning between now and Tuesday."

Disappointment thickened Muriel's throat. "I'm that bad?"

"Actually, you're quite good. But hoping you have a chance will only make you too tense to be natural. Just go out there and put on a good performance, but only for the sake of the performance. That is my final advice to you."

Fourteen

*M*r. Webb was a birdlike man, with a high-beaked nose and red hair winging out from a peak at the forehead. He even walked like a bird, leaning forward with elbows protruding in back and feet splayed outward. Comical as were his mannerisms, he took his position as stage director seriously, running a tight theatrical ship. Actresses reading for parts were not permitted to loiter in the wings, but were required to stay in the greenroom until summoned by Lewis, the script boy, in alphabetical order, no matter what their range of experience.

The *known* actresses, with whom Jewel had consulted privately during the previous weeks, would not have been asked to audition should any have accepted the part. But none had, thus, Jewel and Grady sat in the third row in the auditorium, quietly comparing notes.

At least Daphne Lloyd would not be auditioning, though she was to continue playing the part of Juliet for the final week of production. Only yesterday she had informed Jewel that her heart wasn't in acting, that she planned to return to Newnham College after Easter break to resume her studies in mathematics.

"Ellen Brand," Mr. Webb announced from the stage. "Reading from act two, scene one."

Jewel knew the play practically by heart. This would be the scene where Luke, the blackmailer, confronts Lady Audley. A young actress with brown hair hurried to center stage, where Mansel Robbs waited. Miss Brand consulted with him briefly in whispers; he shuffled pages in his script, nodded, then began reading.

"It wouldn't do for us to be enemies; at least I don't think it would answer your purpose." Mr. Robbs held out his hand menacingly. "Come, tip up!"

Shrinking back a bit, Miss Brand asked, "What money do you expect?"

"Her voice is too high," Jewel whispered.

Grady nodded.

"A hundred pounds will do now," Mr. Robbs quoted without looking at the script.

A calculating look crossed Miss Brand's face. "I shall bring it to your house; I have not so much with me."

"But her voice carries well," Jewel whispered again. "She *could* make a good Phoebe, do you think?" She had already assigned that part to Corrie Walters, who was doing a fine job as Juliet's nurse, but the role still had a lot of stage time and thus needed an understudy.

"How can I get rid of that man?" Miss Brand was saying, delivering the soliloquy that followed George's exit. "Shall a boor, a drunkard, a ruffian, hold me in his grasp ready to crush me when he pleases?"

"I think so if *you* think so," Grady whispered. He enjoyed the auditions, giving his input, but the ultimate casting decisions he left in Jewel's hands. Just as she left the accounting in his.

But for the moment, it was far too soon to tell. Jewel scribbled Miss Brand's name in her notebook, with *Phoebe?* beside it.

"How do I know," Miss Brand continued, staring out into the empty balcony seats, "even if I bribe him into silence, that in some drunken moment he may—"

"Thank you, Miss Brand," Jewel said when the actress paused for breath. With thirty-seven other hopefuls waiting in the greenroom, she would have to hurry the process along. And of truth, a cook didn't have to consume a whole pot of soup to know if it was fit for the dinner table. "Please see that Mr. Webb has an address where you may be reached."

The actress, obviously familiar with auditions, did not look crushed, but nodded and exited the stage. Taking her place on the boards was a Nadia Cooper, who had acted in utility parts at the Royal Court until two years ago, when she was offered a more substantial role in *The Promise of May* at the Alhambra.

"Oh, let the dear girl go on, I can forgive her . . . we shall know each other better by and by. Still, it is unpleasant for me to be aware that my affection for your dear daughter is not reciprocated."

"Not bad," Jewel whispered to Grady, who raised eyebrows and nodded. Not *outstanding*, but they were still in the early letters of that alphabet.

"She would have to wear a wig," Grady whispered, for the Lady Audley character was blonde, and Miss Cooper a brunette.

She would agree to balance a waterpot on her head for this part, Jewel thought and smiled up toward the stage. "Thank you, Miss Cooper." She did not have to remind those with whom she had worked before to leave their telephone numbers or addresses. The actress gave her and Grady a little wave and exited.

By the time they were halfway through the alphabet, Jewel was cautiously hopeful. True, the theatre no longer had the draw of Charlotte Steel, but Richard Whitmore was still quite popular and, when teamed with a skilled actress, would shine again. It was just the matter of finding one who could produce that spark, that chemistry.

"Miss Esther Newman," Mr. Webb announced. "From act two, scene one."

"I bumped into her on my way in," Jewel whispered as a blonde actress stepped from the wings. "She was understudy for one of the *King Lear* daughters at the Lyceum."

"Right hair color," Grady whispered back.

Miss Newman took center stage, clasped a fist to her bosom and began. "Closer and closer around me seems to draw the circle, which threatens to bind me within its folds! Shall I . . ."

She paused, screwed up her forehead, bit her lip.

"Yield to his menaces," Mr. Robbs whispered, looking up from his script.

"Shall I yield to his menaces and leave rank, wealth, and . . ."

She floundered, sent Jewel and Grady an apologetic look, then held up a silencing hand just as Mr. Robbs was opening his mouth to supply her with the words.

". . . position? No! My motto has, hitherto, been death or victory; and . . ."

"To that end I am fixed," Mr. Robbs whispered after two seconds of silence.

"Thank you, Miss Newman," Jewel said up to the stage. "Please leave your address with Mr. Webb." She only said the latter out of compassion, for leaving out the customary request would humiliate the actress further.

Miss Newman stared out at her, opened her mouth, closed it, opened it again, and sniffed. "I *knew* this part this morning," she said with wavering voice. "Ask anyone left in the greenroom—I recited it—" she sniffed again, continued— "just before I came on. It's just that I've never auditioned for such an important part. I tossed and turned last night, and my nerves are a mess."

"But of course they are, dear," Jewel said. "Mr. Webb, will you have someone fetch Miss Newman a cup of tea in the rehearsal room?"

"And then . . . *sniff* . . . may I be allowed to try again? Please?"

"Very well," Jewel replied.

"Oh, *thank you!*"

Mr. Webb called offstage to Mr. Birch as the actress exited.

"She's young. She'll learn from this," Jewel reminded her husband.

Grady nodded, looking on the verge of tears himself. He had watched tears flow onstage for years but never could bear to see a woman cry in earnest. But he would not try to talk her into reconsidering Miss Newman, even should her second audition turn out to be flawless. The livelihoods of too many people were at stake to be taking a gamble with lead actors with fragile nerves.

"Muriel Pearce," Mr. Webb announced. "Act one, scene one."

Jewel looked up at the stage again. Was this a joke? Yet Mr. Webb was not the jesting sort, and besides, those in the company who knew of her cousin knew her as Lady Holt.

It was neither Lady Holt nor Muriel who strolled from the wing as if taking a turn in the park a second later but Lady Audley, it seemed. Jewel realized her mouth was as open as a rain barrel and closed it. In a stroke of genius, Muriel did not break character to show Mr. Robbs where to turn in his script, but addressed him as if he were George Talboys, Lady Audley's first husband.

"I tell you, not one letter reached my hands; I thought myself deserted, and determined to make reprisals on you; I changed my name; I entered the family of a gentleman as governess to his daughters. . . ."

She looked simply stunning, in a gown of deep amethyst serge to enhance her violet eyes, the skirt elaborately trimmed with bands of black braid. Her hat, of black straw, was trimmed with black feathers, and her magnificent ash-blonde and golden waves, caught in a simple comb, rippled all the way to her narrow waist.

". . . and now I have gained the summit of my ambition, do you think I will be cast down by you, George Talboys? No! I will conquer you or I will die!"

Mansel Robbs watched as if transfixed, the script forgotten in his hand. But upon this cue his face fell into animation, and he took a step toward her.

"And what means will you take to conquer me? What power will you employ to silence me?"

Muriel stared back at him while the tiniest of smiles curved beneath calculating eyes. "The power of gold."

Jewel turned to whisper to her husband, but Grady was staring at the pair with a look of a child seeing his first Christmas tree.

"Gold!" Mr. Robbs spat. "Gold purchased by your falsehood!"

"We can't even think of it," Jewel leaned to whisper.

Grady blinked at her. "Definitely not," he whispered back. But his uncertain expression belied his words.

They turned faces toward the stage again. Mr. Webb gaped at the scene from his stool. The performance went on, Jewel determining that she would stop it after the next line, and then the next, until that determination melded into a curiosity over how much of this part her cousin knew.

"Listen to me. I have fought too hard for my position to yield it up tamely." Muriel went on. Not once did she acknowledge Jewel's or Grady's presence, no nervous looks. She seemed completely at ease, as if she had tread the boards all her life.

She's Lady Audley, Jewel realized. *A woman with a past.* No wonder the part fit her so well. Only, Muriel had not murdered anyone. At least not to her knowledge.

The scene reached its natural conclusion five minutes later, where Lady Audley pushes her former husband down a well as he stoops to draw her some water.

"Dead men tell no tales."

Every actress Jewel had ever seen play this part exclaimed the closing lines as they were written in the script, with great gusto. Muriel simply stared down at Mansel Robbs, lying on the boards to represent the well, and murmured them in a thoughtful voice that carried easily past Jewel's ears.

"I am free."

Stunned silence filled the vast empty auditorium. Mr. Webb began applauding, and Mansel Robbs rose to bow at Muriel. Muriel did not even seem to see them, for still in character, she looked furtively over her shoulder, as Lady Audley would have done, and slipped into the wings.

"Jewel?" Grady said.

"She has no experience," Jewel said, to reassure herself as well as him that what they were both thinking was unthinkable. "No one's ever heard of her." At least no one outside Belgravia.

"They will," he said. "She's a natural talent, Jewel. How many of those are we privileged to come across?"

Jewel could not deny that. In her moments on stage, Muriel had *defined* Lady Audley. "Auditions are only halfway over," she reminded him. She just *knew* someone better would step from the wings any minute.

"We're not promising you the part," Jewel said in the office later, shrugging out of Muriel's third embrace. *Heaven help us. How did we get into this?*

She went on, her voice firm. "*If* any of our previous negotiations take a turn for the better before rehearsals begin, you could *possibly* become understudy for whomever we engage."

"Yes, I understand," Muriel said, violet eyes glowing like twin jewels.

"During rehearsals we work long hours," Grady warned.

She went over to embrace him. "I'm willing."

He smiled over her shoulder at Jewel, eased back a bit and sobered again. "And what of your little daughter?"

Muriel paused, as if the question had not occurred to her. "She has a good nanny. I'll make time to be with her."

"And there is one more matter which concerns me." Jewel

folded her arms, for Muriel appeared on the verge of lunging at her again. "What about your hard feelings against Bethia?"

"I love the whole world today, Jewel!" Muriel exclaimed, glowing.

"It's not today I'm worried about. What about when Bethia is here? I'll not have her mistreated."

"No hard feelings," Muriel promised. Prevented from embracing Jewel, she hugged herself.

"Now, run on," Jewel said, clamping a gentle but insistent hand upon her cousin's shoulder. "We've tons of work here."

"When will you . . ."

"Soon, I expect. We've still some people to ring."

Jewel made a beeline for the telephone when the door closed. Grady folded his arms and watched, propped against her desk, his expression more maddeningly peaceful than in weeks.

"Mrs. Patrick Campbell please."

She did not have to give the operator an address, for one would have to live in a monastery not to have heard of one of London's most popular actresses.

"Is the Berlin engagement still on?" Jewel asked once connected, after the conclusion of pleasantries. That was the reason Mrs. Campbell had given for turning down the part of Lady Audley, that she would be playing Ophelia in *Hamlet*. But she had reckoned there was no harm in asking.

"Why, yes," Mrs. Campbell replied. "As a matter of fact, we're in the midst of packing."

"I see."

"You've still not found a lead?" the actress said sympathetically.

Jewel turned her back to her husband's serene little smile. "I'm not quite sure."

———

The Americans made themselves at home, bringing endless cups of coffee up to dressing rooms, borrowing hairpins and ribbons from Mrs. Adams, the hairdresser, and running up to the wardrobe room to ask for the repair of occasional ripped hem and torn bit of lace. But they were good-natured and delighted to be performing in London. And *The Runaway* drew good crowds. The twenty percent from ticket sales was welcome, Jewel said when Bethia arrived for Easter break, but even more profitable was the fact that people were getting used to attending the Royal Court again. Hopefully next month these same audiences would be curious about the newly discovered lead actress—one with a title, at that—whose portrait, with Richard Whitmore's, was plastered on signposts all over London.

"Now, raise your arms to shoulder level, please?" Bethia said to that same actress in the wardrobe room during final fittings on the afternoon of the twenty-fifth of March.

Muriel complied, and Bethia stepped back a bit. The belted waist still stayed in place, very important, for it was distracting to have costumes riding up onstage.

"Thank you, Lady Holt," Bethia said. "You may lower them."

She had known her as Muriel since childhood but addressed her by title because everyone else did so, and she did not wish to take away from any of the respect due her. And Muriel had not corrected her.

"You're welcome," Muriel said in the polite, chilly voice she assumed for Bethia and the theatre servants.

Bethia took the pearl-gray gown for the last scene from the dressing table and handed it over to Mrs. Hamby, who was waiting to assist Muriel behind the dressing screen.

"This is the last costume, Lady Holt," she said.

She did not allow her voice to slip into obsequiousness. Perhaps she could be tempted if she had a starving family depending upon her wages. But that was not the case, and she had done a lot of thinking and praying while at school the past term. While she regretted, more than anything, the impulsive and cruel letter she had sent Douglas Pearce, she had not purchased the ticket that sent him off to Canada. Cycling regrets through her mind over and over until her head ached did not change the situation one iota.

Which was not to say that she always stuck with that conviction, for guilt swept away had a habit of creeping back in.

The door opened a bit, allowing in the notes of the American orchestra tuning up for the matinee that would begin in a half hour. Richard Whitmore stuck his head through the opening. "Are we about finished here?"

"Not quite," Bethia said and added good-naturedly, "and please remember to knock whenever the door is closed, Mr. Whitmore."

"Sorry!" He raised eyebrows toward the screen, where only the tops of one blonde and one brunette head were visible. "I was just wondering if Lady Holt would care to join me for lunch afterwards."

Miss Lidstone ceased basting gold braid onto a hat and sent Bethia a sage look. Most of the males in the company, even some of the Americans, were smitten by Muriel. She took their attentions in stride, as if simply her due, but did not seem to return them in any degree.

"Thank you, but I'm afraid I shall be busy all afternoon" came from behind the screen.

Mr. Whitmore cleared his throat. "Tomorrow after rehearsal? Or for breakfast before?"

"No, thank you," Muriel replied. "Mrs. Hamby, will you fasten this?"

"Very well," Mr. Whitmore said, flashing Bethia and Miss Lidstone a smile.

He may be a first-rate actor, Bethia thought, but he could not cover the disappointment in his olive-green eyes before the door closed.

Muriel came from behind the screen, adjusting the collar to her pearl-gray satin. She rolled her eyes at Bethia. "Men!"

Bethia smiled, and for the fraction of a second they could have been any two good friends. But then polite aloofness resumed itself on Muriel's face, and she held out an arm.

"This cuff binds my wrist. The button should be moved."

Bethia joined Jewel and Grady for a late lunch at Giovanni's, where they talked each other into trying a new item penned at the bottom of the menu. The pizza pie, a dish of cheeses, tomatoes, and meat baked upon bread, was delicious, if messy, for the cheese pulled apart in elastic strings.

"How is Muriel behaving toward you?" Jewel asked as her knife sawed the tip from a wedge upon her plate.

"Or should we say . . . *is* Muriel behaving toward you?" Grady asked.

"Muriel and I get on fine, so don't worry." While the warmth of those few short seconds in the wardrobe room would be nice to have on a consistent basis, she could live with polite civility.

She smiled at the relief in both expressions. They were taking a huge gamble, casting a novice in a lead part. Their positions were probably on the line, as well as the fate of the company. As unnatural as it felt to hope that Muriel would be a great success, Bethia sent up a silent prayer for that very thing while Jewel and Grady complimented Mr. Giovanni on his new dish.

———————

On the evening of the second of April, Muriel stepped out in front of the toughest audience in the world, London theatregoers. While she had a sense that the theatre was filled to capacity, she did not allow her eyes to dwell on any particular section for affirmation. She was Lady Audley, and Lady Audley's sight was reserved for the characters who made up her own world. Indeed, she so effectively blocked out those in the seats that when the cast was called out for final bows, minor characters first, it was only then that she became intimidated.

"I'm shaking," she confessed to Richard Whitmore as they stood in the wings.

"You'll do fine," he said over another round of applause.

He took her hand when it was their turn. They hastened out together as the cast divided to make room for them. They bowed, and the audience roared approval. People began rising from their seats. They bowed again, then Mr. Whitmore let go of her hand and took a step backward. Muriel found herself standing out there in front of everyone, drinking in the adulation, the shouts of "bravo!"

The shaking ceased. This was better than her dream.

"Thank you for helping me through it," she said to Mr. Whitmore during the opening night party afterward.

His face lit up pathetically, like a pup praised for fetching a stick. "I could give you more tips over lunch tomorrow."

"No, thank you," Muriel said. "I'll be busy."

"Read it to me again," Muriel's mother said over the telephone one week later.

Gladly Muriel complied, holding out the ninth of April's *Satur-*

day Review in front of her. She probably could have quoted Mr. Shaw's column by now, but every word was a feast for her eyes.

> "The surprise of the season is neophyte Lady Holt's portrayal of the infamous Lady Audley at Royal Court. Deftly and gracefully she weaves her web of lies, schemes, and manipulations, while we sit in horror until we remind ourselves with a rush of relief that this is theatre and those same characters whose lives she destroys will be safely in their beds tonight and up and treading the boards again tomorrow evening."

She had to read it again for her father, and when her mother took the telephone again, she asked Muriel to send them a copy and one for Bernard as well.

"I just wish I felt well enough to travel down there and watch you."

Uh-oh. Muriel recognized the little tremor in her mother's voice. She would not allow anyone, even her own mother, to make her sad today. Agree and divert, that was the tactic. Breezily she said, "Next time I'm up, I'll put on your very own show. You should see the flowers people have been sending, Mother. Roses. They were crowding my dressing room so we sent most here."

But her mother was not to be diverted this time. "I suppose we'll see you even less now."

"Nonsense, Mother. This is just a hobby. I expect I'll tire of it after playing Lady Audley. And remember, when Georgiana's old enough, we'll come up once a month or so."

"That would be nice," Mother said wistfully but with just enough disbelief in her voice to annoy Muriel.

"We'll make absolute pests of ourselves," Muriel went on. "Oh dear, I hear the doorbell. Just some of the neighborhood ladies, I'm sure, trying to persuade me again to join their literature discussion group. As if I have the time!"

After hurried farewells Muriel put down the telephone and rang for Joyce.

"Send Ham out for three more copies of *Saturday Review*," she said to the parlourmaid. She would save a copy for Douglas as well.

"Very well, m—"

"Wait . . . four copies. Have him leave one at Mrs. Beckingham's door."

"Her door, m'Lady?"

"I don't recall stuttering."

The parlourmaid lowered her head. "Sorry, m'Lady."

Muriel let out a sigh, reminding herself that patience was a virtue and that a great leading actress could afford to be gracious. And so she explained, "It's little thoughtful gestures that make for good neighbors."

Fifteen

*T*wo hundred miles north of London, in the city of York, two men stood facing each other on the seventh of May. One was tall and dark, the other fair and of medium height. The only physical characteristic they shared beyond the obvious two arms, two legs, and so forth, was the hatred in their expressions.

"If you have courage enough to fight me, I'll meet you in any country!" Noah Carey, the taller man challenged. "I'll fight you here in London . . . or, if you're afraid of that, I'll go over to France, or to America, if that will suit you better!"

Jude Nicholls' hands curled into fists at his sides. "Nothing of the kind will suit me at all. I want nothing to do with you."

"Then you're a coward!"

"Perhaps I am! But your saying so will not make me one!"

"You're a coward, and a liar, and a blackguard!" Noah withdrew the pistol from his pocket, eliciting some satisfying gasps from out in the darkness. The actors of York Theatre Royal held the audience in the palms of their hands this evening—most gratifying for the closing performance of Anthony Trollope's *Can You Forgive Her?*

Jude, cast in the role of John Grey, took a step backward. "Does that mean you're going to . . . murder me?"

"I mean that you should not leave this room alive," Noah replied, face twisted as if the fictitious George Vavasor's tormented thoughts ran through his own mind, "unless you promise to meet me and fight it out!"

"Is there any more beautiful sight than a standing ovation?" Jude, still very much alive, asked in the dressing closet they shared a half hour later.

"I can think of one, offhand," Noah replied, wiping away the charcoal shadings from beneath his eyes with a damp face flannel.

"I stand corrected." Jude paused from unfastening the buttons to the costume shirt, his head angled thoughtfully. "But then again . . . Olivia *was* out there as well."

"Very well then," Noah conceded. "There is no more beautiful sight than a standing ovation—provided Olivia is in the front row."

Dropping the flannel back into the washbowl, he picked up his white shirt from the back of the chair and gave Jude a sidelong smile. They had been fast friends since their early preparatory school days at age nine. "Truthfully, I thought my heart would burst out of my chest. But I'm happier for you. A fitting birthday gift, yes?"

"Absolutely!"

Their mutual love for theatre began ten years ago at Oxford, when they dared each other to audition for roles in Corpus Christi College's production of Sophocles' *Philoctetes*. After University the acting experiences were limited, as the majority of productions booked for York's Theatre Royal were from touring companies. For years they had spoken of making a go of it in London, the crown jewel of acting, with its thirty-six major theatres.

But certain ties bound them both to Yorkshire. Whether or not Olivia could be persuaded to uproot once they were wed, Noah could not leave his mother. Five years ago the ninth Earl of Danby had died of a high fever after being caught out on his horse during a sudden winter rainstorm. As his mother's only child to have survived infancy, he could not bear to heap more loss upon her shoulders.

The ties that bound Jude were woven more with strands of guilt than responsibility, more the pity. Jude seemed better suited to be a bank clerk or schoolmaster, with his hair the color of dust and features perfectly proportioned to his oval face so that none stood out as remarkable. His bland appearance served him well onstage, for he was a chameleon, who molded himself to suit every setting.

Unfortunately, Sir Thaddeus Nicholls maintained that acting was frivolous foolishness and barely tolerated the few weeks a year his son spent on the York stage. Jude's father was the proudest man Noah had ever met. He was proud of his name, of his race, of his pedigree, proud of his unstained honor, his large fortune, and his devout Presbyterianism—the result of a great-great-grandfather's marriage to a Scottish woman. As the river Esk gathered force and strength from every tributary, so Sir Thaddeus made every gift that God and his ancestry had bestowed upon him tributary to his pride.

For over three hundred years, since Henry VIII rewarded an ancestor with buildings and six hundred acres seized from a monastery outside Stockton, ten miles northeast of York, the Nicholls, like the Careys, had lived off the labors of their tenant sheep farmers. It mattered not one whit that Jude stood to inherit the estate only if all four elder brothers were to meet with fatalities. The church or the army were the only options acceptable for any younger brother not content with the life of an idle gentleman. Jude could discern no calling from God for the former and was too infatuated with acting to consider the latter.

The old man could at least come watch a performance before he passes judgment, Noah thought grimly as he unfastened shirt buttons.

". . . only regret it, if I don't."

Noah raised his chin. "Sorry . . . regret what?"

Jude drew a breath, as if his words had been so weighty that he had to draw upon some reserve fuel to repeat them. "I've decided to go to London."

"London? When?"

"Perhaps the day after tomorrow."

"For how long?"

"However long it takes."

Surprise, concern, and even envy tugged at Noah's insides. "When did you decide this?"

Jude gave him a sheepish smile. "During the ovation."

"During the . . ?" Noah shook his head. "You can't make such an important decision just because of an emotional moment, Jude."

"You of all people should know that it wasn't a notion that flew into my head from nowhere. We're twenty-seven years old, Noah. Time is running out."

The sentiment could have come from Noah's own mind. Still, someone had to ask the difficult questions, for Jude's sake. Sir Thaddeus was not a man to be crossed. He would be sure to cut off Jude's allowance and possibly even strike him from his will.

"How will you support yourself?"

Jude lifted his white shirt from the back of a chair and shrugged into it. A casual movement, but his jaw was tense. "I've been saving a bit here and there against the day I'd have the nerve. If I run out of money, I'll sweep streets, clean chimneys—whatever it takes, until I start getting parts."

The conviction in his friend's voice brought a lump to Noah's throat. He busied himself with pulling on his own shirt, turning his head to blink away the threatening tears.

"Noah?"

Noah turned again, met Jude's searching look.

"I would have thought you of all people would be happy for me," Jude said.

"I'm happy for you. I just don't want you to be disappointed."

"But don't you see? If I don't even give it a try, the disappointment will come when I'm old and it's too late to do anything about it. This way, at least there's a chance that I *won't* be disappointed."

Put that way, it made perfect sense. Wouldn't he do the same in Jude's position?

Jude gave him a sad smile. "I just wish you were coming with me, big fellow."

Crossing the tiny room in three steps, Noah clapped a hand upon his shoulder. "I'll revel in your successes from up here. At least one of us will be keeping the dream alive."

"Thank you, Noah."

"When will you inform your family?"

"In the morning," Jude replied with a feigned shudder.

"Would you like me to go with you?" Oddly enough, Sir Thaddeus was somewhat fond of Noah, or at least respected his title and that the acreage surrounding Carey Park was half again the size of the Nicholls estate.

Jude shook his head. "Thank you. But I have to do this myself."

A banging and rattling of hinges brought the conversation to a halt. The door swung open and Cole Siddons, who played the part of Mr. Cheesacre, thrust his bearded head inside. Sending Noah a glance laden with meaning, he said, "Can you two schoolboys possibly finish preening yourselves within this century? The party started hours ago!"

The door thundered shut, and Noah and Jude exchanged grins. "Hours ago," Jude said.

"No doubt it seemed like hours to him. Patience isn't Cole's forte." Hastening to fasten the remaining shirt buttons, Noah gave himself a mental kick for dawdling. But then, what was he to do when his friend dropped such news? Continue on as if he had commented upon the weather? He looped his silk cravat about his collar. "Guess we should hurry before he has an apoplexy."

"I think I'll pass on the party and get on home. I'll need a good night's sleep behind me when I face Father."

Don't overreact, Noah thought. "Well, at least stop in for a minute. This may be the last time you see everyone together."

"Of course." Jude nodded. "I didn't even think of that."

The corridor outside the rehearsal room was alive with the conversation, laughter, and piano music typical for closing night, when actors and other theatre employees, patrons, and family gathered to celebrate a good run. Noah stepped through the open doorway, sent a quick smile across the room to Olivia, chatting with stage manager, Mr. Brown, and his wife, and then turned so that he could watch Jude's face.

"Ladies and gentlemen, if you please!" Mr. Brown clapped hands, causing an expectant hush to fall over the room and heads to turn their way.

"Now . . . what's this all about?" Jude asked, eyeing the long cake inscribed with *Happy Birthday Jude* and skillfully decorated with the iced forms of Comedy and Tragedy. Those who had been in the corridor skirted into the room behind him.

"We'll give you twenty-seven guesses!" someone said.

More laughter, and the pianist struck up a chord. No Nicholls face was among the fifty or so presently singing "For He's a Jolly Good Fellow!" even though Noah had sent a note out to Jude's house two days ago. But then, that was no surprise. After the song Noah watched his friend receive handshakes and embraces, claps on the back, and wishes for many happy returns. Unlike himself, bashful to the point of being standoffish until he knew someone well, Jude never met a stranger. If his sense of humor was somewhat warped, at least there was not an ounce of cruelty in it. If anyone deserved a chance, he did.

Later that night, on his knees, Noah prayed. *Please make it happen for him, Father.*

Soft knocking woke him the following morning, followed by the creaking of door hinges. Bernice, the chambermaid, stepped into the room with coffeepot on a tray.

"Mornin', Lord Carey!"

"Good morning, Bernice," Noah mumbled, blinking the dregs of night from his eyes. Because the quickest way to Danby was via the North Eastern Railway for fifty miles and then another twelve on horseback, he leased a suite in the Hotel Lady Anne Middleton's on Skeldergate Street during the run of a play. Two other actors stayed at the same hotel, and the chambermaids there knew not to disturb them before ten on mornings after a performance.

"Shall I bring your breakfast next?" She was a thickset, dark-haired woman of twenty or so, married to one of the waiters in the restaurant downstairs.

"No, thank you. I'm meeting someone for early lunch."

"Will you be checking out today?"

"Yes." Noah eased himself up against his pillows, sliding over so that she could place the tray on the side of his bed. "But I'll not leave York for another two hours or so, if you'd like to put off packing until you've made your morning rounds."

"That's very thoughtful of you, Lord Carey. How was the play?"

"We had a standing ovation."

"Is that a good thing?" she asked doubtfully while pouring coffee. He laughed, taking the cup from her hands. "If you would have used your tickets, you could have found out for yourself. What did you do . . . sell them?"

"Listen to you, m'Lord!" she said. "I gave them to my brother Lucas. He fancies hisself a poet, and I knew he and his Mary would enjoy the outing more."

"Well, I'll give you four to *The Importance of Being Earnest* if you'll promise to go."

"I will. Very kind of you, Lord Carey. I can't wait to ring Lucas."

"Well, you've plenty of time. It's not until December first."

That was the way of provincial theatres; local productions were outnumbered greatly by touring companies staging such productions as a London company's *The Corsican Brothers* and a Russian opera company's *Boris Godunov*. In the seven-month interim, most of the local actors continued with their daily occupations such as bank clerking and giving art lessons and selling shoes. Noah considered himself most fortunate in that Olivia, whom he was to marry on the second of August, had no objections to his joining the others for rehearsals after they returned from a three-month honeymoon in Greece.

Enough light filtered through the drapes to allow Bernice to lay a fire in the hearth. Noah sipped his coffee, savoring the warmth spreading through him. When Bernice took the tray, he settled back beneath the covers to doze while fire broke the late-morning chill.

He was actually an early riser of habit, for that had been the routine since his boyhood, when he and Mother and Father would breakfast in the morning room. As he plowed the Star Safety Razor through the lather on his face at the washstand a half hour later, he wondered if Jude had yet broken the news to the Nicholls family.

His first order of the day was to go down to the lobby and ring his mother.

"Well, how did it go?" Mother said over the telephone. She had attended the play twice during its run, so he had not pressured her to come into York last night.

"We had a standing ovation."

"But of course you did. You're an excellent actor."

He could picture the smile on her plump face, and teased, "Well, there were *others* up there onstage with me, you know. And you're not exactly my harshest critic."

"That doesn't make you any less excellent. When are you coming home?"

"I'll catch the two-thirty train. Olivia's joining me for early lunch." He raked his fingers through his dark hair, pushing it back from his forehead. His George Vavasor character called for long locks that became increasingly more disheveled as his state of mind grew more agitated. "I'll try to squeeze in time for a haircut."

"I'm sure Mrs. Moss would still be willing."

Noah smiled. The housekeeper's two sons, who worked on the

estate, appeared to have stepped out of fifteenth-century portraits with their cropped hair. "I'm a bit old for the bowl-over-the-head look, don't you think?"

"Very well, you ancient thing. Give Olivia my love. I'll send Vernon to meet your train this afternoon."

"Wait."

He had figured he would have time to break the news to her in person, but it was conceivable that Sir Thaddeus would send Jude packing. "Will you keep Vernon handy to fetch Jude from the station in case he rings?"

"Of course."

He had been poised to explain, but her tone suggested an inkling of already having grasped the reason behind his request. She was perceptive in that way.

"Was Jude surprised, or was that just acting?" Olivia Ryce asked from across the small table in the hotel restaurant, after she had folded her hands for silent prayer.

"He didn't have a clue." Noah smiled. "Thank you for ordering the cake. It was delicious."

"That's because Mrs. Bromley baked it. I wanted it to be special."

"How kind of her. I'll give her the money we would have spent at the bakery."

Olivia smiled. "She didn't buy any of the ingredients herself, silly. And Papa wouldn't hear of your repaying him."

"Still, the amount of work . . ."

"I'm sure she was happy to do it." Reverting back to the subject at hand, Olivia said, "And Jude is determined to leave for London?"

"He is. I just pray his father will surprise me and be understanding about it."

"I'm afraid that's a lost cause. Papa says he's the most overbearing person he's ever met." She pressed a finger to her smile. As the daughter of a physician, she was not supposed to be repeating gossip about his patients. "You're to forget you heard that."

He winked at her. "My lips are sealed."

The waiter brought their favorite dish, identical servings of *Lobster à la mode Française*—lobster meat cut into small squares, sim-

mered in cream and seasonings, returned to the cleaned shell, covered with bread crumbs and melted butter, then browned before a
fire.

Olivia picked up her fork with her slender fingers, causing the
one-carat pear-shaped diamond in her engagement ring to catch
light from the chandelier. "Whenever Jude decides to leave, make
certain he knows I expect him to stop by the house first. We'll have
a basket ready. Heaven knows his father won't give him money for
decent meals on the trip."

"That's very kind of you. But wouldn't you like to see him off
with me?"

"No. Best friends should say their farewells without the distraction of a third party."

"You're not exactly a—"

She shook her head. "That's how it should be, Noah."

"Thank you, Olivia." He smiled across at her again as his chest
filled with pride that he would be married to such a thoughtful,
beautiful creature in just three months. What could he have done
that God should favor him so?

In jest he accused her of marrying him just to rid herself of the
name that was the bane of her grammar school days. It had not mattered to her schoolmates that "Ryce" was a noble Anglo-Saxon
name meaning "powerful." They only cared that they could make
her blush by tacking *pudding* onto the end.

In some ways they could have passed for siblings or cousins, for
they had in common hair the color of ink, high foreheads, and eyes
so brown that the irises seemed to meld into the pupils. Yet there
were enough differences to prevent local gossips from speculating
some sort of hidden kinship. The Careys were tall and strapping—
one aunt on his father's side an inch shy of six feet—whereas Olivia
had inherited her father's small frame; Noah's nose was gloriously
Roman, and Olivia's was as small and dainty as a gumdrop.

Funny how acting before an audience of hundreds barely caused
him a flicker of nervousness, but in the first weeks of their courtship,
he had felt awkward in her company, as if he were a lumbering giant
and she a china doll. One step out of place could crush her dainty
foot, a careless motion of the arm might knock her to the ground.
Mercifully, none of that had happened, though he did manage to

knock a beaker of lemonade into her lap at the White Hart Inn last September. She took the mishap with good grace, assuring him that accidents happened to everyone. That was when he first realized he loved her, and he proposed marriage three months later.

He realized she was staring across at him expectantly.

"Forgive me, darling," he said. "Did you say something?"

She gave him an indulgent smile, which did not mask the concern in her eyes. "I asked if you wished you were going with him."

"To London? And leave the most beautiful woman in the world?"

"That's not an answer, Noah."

He had not realized that when the words left his mouth. He thought for several seconds, while concern deepened in her expression. How easy it would be to assure her that no such thought had passed through his mind. But they had determined they would have a marriage based upon Christian principles such as truthfulness. Shouldn't a betrothal be based upon that same foundation?

Leaning forward, he reached across the table to touch the back of her hand. "I confess to a little pang of envy when he first broke the news, Olivia. We've spoken of London for years, you see. But I can honestly say that I'm happy with the life God has given me here."

"What if Jude is a smashing success?"

"I pray he will be."

"Will you resent me?"

"Never." Noah shook his head for emphasis. "Give me fifty years to prove it to you."

Her expression smoothed. "That'll be lovely. Fifty years together."

"Lovely," he echoed, smiling into her brown eyes.

They finished their meals—at least Noah did. Mrs. Ryce had taught her four girls that they would never have weight problems if they left roughly a fourth of their food upon their plates, which meant enough to feed another person went to the ash can. It seemed wasteful to Noah, but he assumed it was a standard practice for most females old enough to watch their figures, even though his mother never left food upon her plate.

A hired coach and a trio of hansom cabs waited outside for restaurant and hotel customers. Noah guided her to the coach, and they held hands from Skeldergate to Nunnery Lane. He was helping her to the pavement in front of the Ryces' three-storey town house when a Maltese came bounding from next door with white coat rippling.

"*Chaucer!* Go away!" Olivia shooed.

"I thought they fixed the gate," Noah said over high-pitched barks.

"He figures out a way to open it."

At least Chaucer had never bitten either of them. Olivia had assured Noah that the animal was as tame as a lamb whenever *he* wasn't present. Which did not increase Noah's fondness for the animal. He walked Olivia to the door and then went back to the coach with the dog barking and snapping at his heels.

After his usual barber on North Street trimmed his dark hair, Noah hired a coach to carry him back to the hotel for his trunk, then on to York Station. The fifty-mile journey took an hour and a half, what with stops in such towns as Haxby, Grambe, and Pickering. Vernon Thatcher, the Careys' coachman, met him at Sleights Station with the wagon and team of two horses, the easiest way to transport the trunk over the highs and lows of the twelve-mile lane.

"Mr. Nicholls is at the house," Vernon said as the two hefted the trunk into the wagon bed. Auburn-haired, he was the only person at Carey Hall taller than Noah, and by a good three inches.

"For how long?" Noah asked.

"A couple of hours. The smithy's boy drove him."

"How did he look?" Noah asked, knowing the coachman was intelligent enough to discern that he was asking of Jude and not fifteen-year-old Aaron Jenkins, who earned extra money carrying people from the station in his father's wagon.

"Not too good, m'Lord."

Once when Noah was a boy playing near his mother in the garden, she beckoned him over to where she was planting crocus bulbs. "This is north Yorkshire," she said, pressing the fingers and thumb of her right hand into the moist soil, ink-black from sulfur streams. She pointed to the mound below the imprints and said it was the Glaisdal Moor, running east to west.

"See where my fingers were? They're the dales, and the high

spaces between them are moors. My thumb imprint represents Wes-terdale, and then there is Danby-dale, Little Fryup, Great Fryup, and Glaisdale. Do you know where we live?"

Obediently Noah had pointed to the impression made by the first finger. "Danby-dale."

"Very good," she'd said. "Only, the land isn't as smooth as these imprints."

Already Noah knew this, from riding about on the front of his father's saddle and surveying neat fields divided by drystone walls, the copses of gnarled and ancient trees. High on either side of those dales towered the brown moorland banks, carpeted with purple heather in late summer.

Carey Hall, four storeys of gritstone weathered into a gray-and-mossy coloring, high gables, slate-tiled roofs, and mullioned windows, was built by the fifth Earl of Danby, Noah's great-great-great-great-grandfather. The first Earl of Danby, Andrew Carey, was given his title by King Charles II in 1668, as reward for impoverishing himself in his support of the ill-fated Charles I in the war against the Roundheads. In the following year the Earl of Danby was granted the goods, chattels, and debts of all felons in the manor and forests of Danby.

Later Careys were not so colorful but made good livings from wool and the rents of tenant farmers. Noah did not take that living for granted, for it afforded him the opportunity to act upon the York stage. Uncle Bertram, his mother's younger brother as well as his father's bailiff of sixteen years, ran the estate with his usual competence, and Mother did the bookkeeping. Noah's absence was hardly a ripple in the goings-on, though he helped out whenever in residence.

Inside, Mrs. Moss eyed his fresh haircut with faint disapproval in her expression and informed him that his friend was in the conservatory with m'Lady. Noah found them sharing a marble bench.

"I saw tears in your father's eyes that time you were in the hospital for pleurisy," his mother was saying, hand resting upon Jude's shoulder. Emily Carey was perfectly cast in her maternal role, plump and graying, with small hands and soft green eyes. "He does love you."

Jude's face wore crimson splotches. "He has a fine way of show-ing it."

"Jude . . . forgive me. . . ." Noah said, advancing and lowering himself upon one knee before them. "I should have gotten here earlier."

His friend made a feeble attempt at a smile. "It's done me good to speak with Lady Danby."

"And your father . . . ?"

"He says if I leave for London, I'm not to come back."

To fit in with his schoolmates during his fresher year at college, Noah had picked up the habit of swearing. That is, until a curse word slipped through his lips in the presence of his father, whose look of quiet disappointment caused him to cease immediately. He had not been tempted to take up the habit again until just that moment, when he had to swallow the oath that rose in his throat.

"I'm sorry," he said instead, trading looks with his mother. "What will you do?"

"I'm leaving for London. Tomorrow."

"Well, this is your home now," Noah said.

Jude turned his face away to blink watery eyes.

Noah's mother's eyes teared as well. "I'm sure this wouldn't have happened if your mother had lived, Jude," she said. "Mothers often bring out a softer side to fathers."

But Jude wouldn't know, for his mother had died shortly after bringing him into the world. Another reason, Noah and his own mother privately speculated, that the man was so hard on his young-est child.

"I would have liked to have seen a softer side of him." Jude wiped his eyes. "Just once. But I thank you. Both of you. You've always been the family I've always wished I had."

"We're the family you *have*," Noah's mother said.

"Did she say lunch?" Jude said, hefting the basket appreciably the following morning at York Station. "There must be enough here for a week. You'll thank Olivia again for me, won't you? And the Ryces' cook?"

"I will." Noah pretended not to notice the searching glances Jude sent toward different ends of the platform now and again. He dipped into his coat pocket and brought out the five crisp twenty-pound notes he had just withdrawn from his account. "To help you get started."

"I can't," Jude said, taking a step back.

"Please don't disappoint me." Noah pressed it into his hand.

Jude looked down at it. "A loan, then."

"Very well. You may pay me back when you're a roaring success."

Precisely at one minute before nine, a shrill whistle that seemed to issue from the bowels of the earth pierced the air from the south, and in an instant the engine appeared, smoking and snorting like Beowulf's dragon. Another twinge of envy shot through Noah. He admonished himself for it. He was a grown man with commitments. Too old to behave as a child in a sweetshop, unable to appreciate the one treat his halfpenny would purchase for longing for the whole display.

Sixteen

With no role to play other than his own, Noah fell back into a routine of sorts. He began memorizing the part of John Worthing, whom he would play in Oscar Wilde's *The Importance of Being Earnest*. He played cribbage with his mother, started reading Fielding's *The Journal of a Voyage to Lisbon* as well as the book of Isaiah, and fished for pike and bream in the pond. He also helped out with chores about the estate, such as docking lambs' tails and repairing a tenant farmer's chimney. He rather enjoyed manual labor, finding that it relieved as much tension as it had once generated when he was a boy grumbling to himself over how Father refused to allow him to idle away school holidays.

He went into York to see Olivia twice, spending the night in the Hotel Lady Anne Middleton's. On the fourteenth of May, he also visited his tailor on Stonebow to be fitted for the black suit he would wear at his wedding. Rain early in the following week and the subsequent muddy roads prevented him from seeing Olivia again until Friday the twentieth, when he donned top hat and tailcoat and hired a hansom to deliver him to Nunnery Lane. He was to have dinner with her family before escorting her to see *The Corsican Brothers*.

"Yip-yip-yip-yip!" Like a blonde comet, Chaucer streaked from the neighbor's garden as Noah stepped down to the pavement. "Yip-yip-yip-yip!"

"Get away, you loathsome little cur!" Noah growled, resisting the urge to deliver a stout kick. The dog nipped at his heels all the way along the short path and up the steps.

"Good evenin', Lord Carey," said Joan, the parlourmaid, stepping back to allow him inside. She shooed at the animal on the other side of the threshold. "Go home, Chaucer!"

"Do they feed him?" Noah asked after she slammed the door. He handed her his hat. "Because he's determined to make a meal of my ankles."

The maid smiled appreciatively. She was younger than Noah, nineteen or so, with dimpled cheeks and brown hair caught up in a comb behind her lace cap. "I think he's insane, if you ask me, m'Lord."

Noah pulled off his gloves. "Can that be possible?" He knew it to be so with sheep, for his father had once had to shoot a ram after it continually charged a stone wall until its head was bloody. But if Joan knew the answer to that question, he was not to hear it, for Olivia entered the hall, lovely in a moss-green brocade gown, her dark hair cascading in ringlets from a modest tiara.

"Noah!" she said, smiling as the servant slipped away with his hat and gloves.

"You take my breath away, Olivia," Noah said, touching her cheek. He would have leaned down for a kiss, but the parlour door opened and Mrs. Ryce approached cooing greetings. They moved into the parlour, where Olivia, her mother, and four sisters, ranging in age from eleven to sixteen, fluttered about him. He did not mind and rather enjoyed being the center of attention. Presently Doctor Ryce joined them. He was a smallish man, reticent in social situations, content to allow the women of his household to do the talking.

They sat down to a dinner of roast ribs of beef, braised ham and spinach, Yorkshire pudding, peas, potatoes, and stewed rhubarb. The bread pudding, Noah's favorite dessert, was not up to Mrs. Bromley's usual standard, but then, the price of sugar was rising dramatically because last month's onset of the Spanish-American War made future shipments uncertain. Olivia's smile was all the sweetness Noah desired.

The Ryces' coachman, Alan Stern, delivered Noah and Olivia to the Royal York Theatre, where they settled into front-row orchestra seats. Just ahead were the railings to the pit. Musicians below were softly tuning instruments.

"You don't mind my not renting a box, do you?" It was not that

Noah couldn't afford it. As in most theatres, the boxes in Theatre Royal did not allow full view of the stage, which in Noah's opinion defeated the whole purpose of attending theatre. The most distractions he and his fellow actors had experienced while onstage had not come from the galley, but from those swells in the boxes discussing where they should dine afterward and gossiping about those in other boxes.

She met his eyes and smiled. "No, of course not."

He took her gloved hand in his as the curtain began rising to Franck's Symphony in D Minor. Within seconds he was caught up in Dion Boucicault's adaptation of telepathic twins separated at birth. He absorbed the play on two levels, enjoying the story while studying every facial expression, the inflection of every line, hoping for ways to improve his own techniques—or things to avoid. He appreciated how the actor playing Mario Franchi curled his fingers about the lapel of his coat when angered, but did not approve of how the actress playing Isabelle Gravini pontificated her lines.

When the last bows had been taken and the final curtain closed, Noah and Olivia joined the exodus of patrons moving toward the lobby with rustlings of silks and murmurs of conversation. Alan was waiting with team and coach. The hour was half-past eleven, and a sort of drowsy quietness had settled upon the town once they were clear of the theatre area.

"Did you enjoy the performance?" Noah asked.

"Yes," she replied. "But the actress playing Isabelle was surely an understudy."

"I believe that's so," Noah agreed. He hoped that one of her fellow actors would pay her a kindness and suggest she speak more naturally onstage, for the sake of her career. That thought led him to imagining what it would be like to be involved in the London theatre world, if only part of a touring company.

"Less than three months," Olivia purred, resting her head against his shoulder.

He winced, stabbed with guilt. *What an infant you are,* he said to himself. He was perfectly aware that were he in London this very evening, he would be pining away for Olivia and the great future he had before him in Yorkshire.

"Is your gown almost finished?" he asked.

She sighed. "The seamstresses have *finally* gotten to the train."

"Oh dear. They deserted you, did they?" He couldn't resist.

Turning her head enough to look askew at him, she said, "Deserted me? Why would they? I just said they're working on the train."

That brought to mind another joke, of seamstresses shoveling coal into an engine, but he kept it to himself. Olivia's sense of humor did not extend to things vastly important to her, such as her wedding gown. "Yes, you did," he replied.

"Appliquéing lace patterns to ten feet of satin is meticulous work, but Mrs. Burton assures me it'll be finished in time. By the way, James and Lilith wish to host a garden party in our honor on the sixteenth of July."

When he gave her a blank look, she said, "My cousin on Father's side and his wife. You met at the house at Christmas."

"Ah yes. A pleasant couple."

He would be years learning the names of all of Olivia's relations. But he was glad that their children would have a large extended family, what with his own abundance of uncles and aunts and cousins on his mother's side.

"The invitation includes your mother, of course." She hesitated. "And I would appreciate it if you didn't wear that green cravat you're so fond of."

"You don't like it?"

"Frankly, it looks as if you dribbled pea soup down your neck. The blue one you wore to the cast party suits your complexion. And your yellow paisley is attractive."

"Yes, attractive," Noah murmured, enjoying the scent of her perfume.

"You're not even listening, are you?"

"No green cravat." He shifted in the seat to put an arm about her shoulders. "I'll dress to the nines. But we're almost at your house. . . ."

She smiled and raised her chin. He kissed the tip of her nose, then her eyes, and finally, her soft mouth. Too soon they were stopped outside 8 Nunnery Lane, where light burned from the parlour window. Noah could hear Alan climbing down from the box.

"Oh dear." Olivia's hands fanned her face. "Mother will notice my cheeks." Mrs. Ryce waited up for Olivia when she and Noah had a late theatre night, saying she would not be able to sleep soundly until all her daughters were safely abed.

"Surely she suspects we kiss."

"Sh-h-h!" She put a silencing finger to his lips as the coach's door opened.

"I'll deliver your Lordship to the hotel when you're ready," the coachman said as Noah stepped to the pavement behind Olivia.

"Thank you, Alan. I shan't be long." Fortunately, the neighbor's Maltese spent nights inside, so they were able to walk to the front door unhindered. Gently Noah knocked. Because Doctor Ryce kept addictive agents such as morphine and quinine in his cupboard, the doors had to be locked at night. But within seconds, the knob turned with a hollow *click* and the door swung inward.

Mrs. Ryce, clad in dressing gown and holding a book closed with forefinger as her marker, smiled sleepily at them. "And how was the play?"

"Nice," Olivia replied, kissing her cheek.

"Even without Noah in a role?"

"Well, of course, that would have made it better."

"Careful now, you'll make me vain," Noah said.

Mrs. Ryce chuckled, bade him good evening and excused herself after a pointed "You'll be up soon, Olivia?"

"Yes, Mother."

Noah and Olivia stood smiling at each other until Mrs. Ryce's footsteps on the stairs faded sufficiently. Then they moved as if drawn together by a string. His arms went about her. They kissed, and her perfume was sweet. Until his nostrils inhaled a faint whiff of something else.

"What's wrong, Noah?" she asked as his arms loosened about her.

"I'm afraid . . ." Sniffing, he raised his right boot to peer underneath, then his left. "Uh-oh."

"Chaucer!" Olivia said, stepping back.

Noah could not remove his left boot without sitting, so he angled it so that his weight rested upon the heel. He looked about the marble flooring for other telltale signs. Fortunately, there were few.

"Is that . . ." she asked.

Blackwell

"It is. Will you find me some cleaning rags?"

"Cleaning—"

"But check your shoes first."

She raised the hem of her gown just enough to inspect both shoes, then the hem itself. "I think I'm all right. But I don't know where to find rags, Noah."

"Then a towel, please. I'll replace it. Do wet it good and rub some soap on it."

Olivia turned and left the entrance hall, only to reappear seconds later. "I rang for Joan."

"Are you serious?" Noah glanced at his watch. "Olivia, it's after midnight."

"Well, we can't very well have everyone tracking it about in the morning."

"But I can have it clean in five minutes. You didn't have to wake her."

He remembered that Vernon kept some rags beneath the box in the family coach so that passengers could clean their shoes on muddy days before entering. Would a coach used in the city have the same? He turned on his heel, walking on the side of his left boot and avoiding suspicious areas, and took hold of the doorknob.

"Where are you going?" Olivia asked.

"Send her back upstairs," Noah said over his shoulder. "And please get a beaker of water and some soap."

"Shall I take care of it, your Lordship?" Alan said, handing down a frayed flour sack.

"Just stay where you are. We don't need more tracks." Noah shook his head, muttered, "Vile little creature!"

"At least he's not a Great Dane, eh, m'Lord?"

Noah had to grin. "If he were, you'd be down here too."

With the coachman's soft chuckling at his back, Noah walked circumspectly to the side of the dark walkway leading to the front steps, hoping for no more surprises. Inside, Olivia stood with arms folded. And hands empty.

"The water, Olivia?"

She stared back as if he had lost his faculties. "Noah. Just think for a minute. I cannot stand by and allow you to stoop to that level. You're an *earl*, for heaven's sake."

"You're making a mountain out of a molehill, Olivia," he replied. "I can't see the sense in hauling someone out of bed for a two-minute chore."

Her cheeks flushed. "Carey Hall has four times the servants we have. Do you do all their work for them?"

The whole argument was getting more and more ludicrous. He could have cleaned the floor, stolen another kiss, and been on his way home if she had just brought him a towel. Flopping the rag over his shoulder, he began easing out of his left boot. He supposed he would have to go for the water himself. "Our servants work. But we don't mistreat them."

"*Mistreat*? And what of our coachman out there? You don't mind his losing sleep."

"It's not the same. Your father insisted, and besides, you know I tip him well." Noah got down on one knee. "Olivia, for the last time, will you get some water and soap? Or must I hop through the—"

He sensed a presence and looked toward the arched doorway to the side of the staircase. Joan, clad in gingham wrapper, pillow-matted brown hair wound into a hasty knot, gaped at them.

"You rang for me, Miss?" she asked with sleep-thickened voice.

Olivia looked at Noah, then back at the parlourmaid. She raised her chin a fraction and said in a tone that was civil but devoid of warmth, "I accidentally pulled the cord, Joan. Now, go back up to your bed."

But the maid caught sight of the rags in Noah's hand. Her puffy eyes widened. "Please, Lord Carey . . . you ain't supposed to be doin' that."

"We'll take care of it," Noah said. "Go on upstairs."

———

"You've a letter from Jude," Noah's mother said three days later as she stepped onto the terrace.

"Yes?" Noah laid *The Strange Case of Dr. Jekyll and Mr. Hyde* on the flagstones beneath his wicker chair without bothering to mark his page. It was a relief to have something to think about other than the incident at Olivia's house. As he tore open the envelope, his mother eased her plump figure into another chair.

Hello, Big Fellow! the letter began. Noah smiled and gave the first paragraph a cursory skim. His eye latched on to what he had hoped to see. "He has a part!"

Mother clasped her hands. "Wonderful! Where?"

"I'll read it to you."

"You don't have to . . ."

"He won't mind. I'll just skip over the part about the drunken rows."

He could feel her smile without even looking up. They both knew Jude was as moral as they came, in spite of his father's certainty that he was on the road to perdition.

"I would have telephoned you, but my landlord refuses to allow us to make long-distance calls. Too many actors have skipped out without settling their bills, he says. After auditioning for *The Magistrate* at Jury Lane and *Henry V* at the Garrick and *H.M.S. Pinafore* at the Savoy, I have finally landed a part! Me! On the London stage! I celebrated by having a steak at a genuine restaurant and wish you were here to celebrate with me.

"A utility part, mind you, a guard in Shelly's *The Cenci* at Daly's Theatre off Leicester Square. But it's a start. When a woman on the omnibus upbraided me for acting fresh this afternoon, I realized I had been grinning at everyone like a Buddha statue.

"I can just picture his face," Noah said, and continued.

"Forgive me for ranting on about myself! How are all of you keeping? Very well, I hope. Please give Lady Carey and Olivia my love. More good news! Because the play opens the sixth of August, I shall be able to come up for the wedding. Only overnight, for dress rehearsal is the fifth, but I am overjoyed at still being able to serve as best man."

"Ronald will be disappointed," Mother said.

Noah smiled. His cousin, Uncle Bertram's eldest son, had dropped several hints that he would be only too willing to serve as a substitute.

"You and Olivia will make a splendid couple, and I am not just writing that in the hopes you'll name one of your children after me. Preferably a boy."

The latter part made Mother chuckle, but it only caused a tug of sadness in Noah's chest. He lowered the letter, finished save the closing, and looked at her.

"Were you ever disappointed in Father?"

"Yes," she replied without blinking. There was a hint of awareness in her expression, as if she had sensed this had something to do with his lethargy of the past three days. Her quick reply was surprising and a little disturbing to hear, for Noah considered his parents' marriage the best he had ever witnessed.

"How so?"

"Your father was a good man. But it took him years to learn to say 'I love you.' The Careys didn't express affection verbally, and it was as bread and butter to my family. I needed to hear it."

"But you knew he loved you. He just wasn't in the habit of saying it."

"When you care enough about people, you change your habits." A faraway look passed over her softly lined face, and then she smiled. "And he eventually did, for which I'm thankful. What's troubling you, son? Did you and Olivia have words?"

He shrugged. "A minor disagreement."

For, as disagreements went, it would probably be considered tame—Olivia weeping as he cleaned the floor and him feeling like a boor for making her cry. They had apologized, kissed, and made up, and when he telephoned her the following morning he was relieved to find her in good spirits, enthusing over a cashmere shawl an aunt had brought by for her trousseau.

"It's normal even for people in love to have disagreements," his mother said. "You shouldn't feel disappointed over the fact that Olivia has some opinions you don't share."

"I wouldn't want her to share all of my opinions," Noah protested. Otherwise, he may as well marry himself, the only person with whom he agreed one hundred percent of the time. *Or at least ninety percent of the time,* he thought. He would hope, however, that he and his future wife would share the same *values.*

But since the little scene in the Ryces' foyer, other scenes had trickled through his mind, incidents he was apparently too love struck to pay much heed when they had occurred.

Such as when he knocked the lemonade into her lap last September. Once she recovered from the shock, Olivia had smiled and assured him that accidents happened. Now his mind's eye focused upon the server hurrying over with towels. She was a nervous young woman, obviously new at her position, but she worked diligently at mopping Olivia's lap, blaming herself for overfilling the beaker. Olivia had ignored the girl, even seemed irritated at her for taking so long. It was Noah who had thanked her afterward and insisted that the mishap was not her fault.

And it was *he* who had thanked Mr. Jakes, one of the tenant farmers, for taking time away from his chores to repair Olivia's broken bootheel when she took a misstep between two stones during a stroll on the estate. Olivia had fussed over her own ripped stocking and gave scant notice to the man's good deed.

It wasn't that Olivia lacked gratitude, Noah reminded himself. One reason he delighted in giving her gifts was to witness her reaction to them, how her face lit up and her arms went about his neck. And she had sent Jude a note of thanks for agreeing to escort her sister Constance to a soirée, as well as thanked Mother effusively for passing down Grandmother Carey's jade bracelet to her, even though they weren't yet married.

Jude's family is wealthy, raced across Noah's mind. He banished the thought, but it was followed by another. *So are we.*

This was beneath him, he told himself. Olivia was a decent Christian woman, the epitome of virtue. And *he* certainly wasn't perfect.

And what about her thoughtfulness? As he seized upon that sterling quality, he also remembered that her thoughtful deeds seldom seemed to cost her any of her own effort, such as the lunch she had Mrs. Bromley pack for Jude.

His mother was still watching him. Noah sighed and got to his feet. "Sorry I'm such poor company, Mother. I think I'll walk down to the pond."

She nodded. "But may I ask you one more question?"

"Of course."

"Are you sure these misgivings you're having over Olivia have nothing to do with Jude's being in London?"

"Why, no. Not at all." He lowered himself into the chair again. "Why would you ask that?"

"Sometimes our own motives hide from us, Noah. Could you

possibly be looking for an excuse to call off your engagement and join him?'"

"The thought hasn't even crossed my mind."

He was certain that he would be as keenly disappointed over the way Olivia had acted toward her parlourmaid Friday evening if Jude were still in Yorkshire, or in Timbuktu. All this required was for Olivia and him to sit down and discuss the matter, once he got over these doldrums.

Or perhaps it would be best to wait until after they were married. He would take her hands and delicately, carefully, confess his concern. And just as Father had learned to say "I love you," she would learn to be more considerate of those not in her social class.

That made him more optimistic. "I still love her, Mother."

She studied his face. "Enough to give up your dream of London, son?"

"There's no comparison." He was sure of it. "And besides, I wouldn't go to London even if we weren't marrying."

"Because of me," his mother said, a little sadly.

"No, Mother." He got to his feet again, went behind her, and leaned to kiss the top of her graying head. "Because this is where I belong."

Seventeen

*N*oah's stroll was brief because once he reached the pond he was struck with the longing to see Olivia again. He went to the parlour and picked up the telephone. Joan, the Ryces' parlourmaid, answered, and presently Olivia's voice came through the line.

"Noah, darling . . . how wonderful to hear your voice."

"And I, yours," he said, flooded with shame for ever doubting her goodness. "I just got a letter from Jude. He's found a part."

"Marvelous!"

"It's a small part. But it's a foot in the door. And he can come for the wedding."

"I'm so glad," she said. "When you write back, mention I'm praying he'll be a huge success."

More shame. Noah asked, "When may I see you again?"

"Well . . . I do have this enormous craving for lobster."

"I can be there at six."

"Oh dear. I've a fitting for my gown and will be tied up until seven."

With great reluctance he passed up the opportunity to make a joke.

"But you may come on to the house early," she continued. "Mother and my sisters will entertain you."

"I really should use that time to book my hotel room," he said quickly. However fond he was of her mother and sisters, an hour was a little too long to spend at the center of that much high-energy attention without Olivia.

"Shall I send Alan to the station for you?"

"No, thank you. I'll grab a cab."

Upstairs, he asked Rhodes to draw a bath and lay out some evening clothes. "But not the green cravat."

"Very good, sir," Rhodes replied. He was sixty or so, having served as Noah's father's valet since Noah was a boy, but seemed ageless, save the fringe of hair that crept lower and lower every year. "Top hat or bowler?"

"Bowler. We're just going for dinner."

Noah realized that he should inform his mother. While he could send a servant out to the garden, he wanted to reassure her that all was well between Olivia and him. He could hear the telephone ringing as he descended the staircase. When he reached the landing, one of the parlourmaids met him. "Telephone for you, m'Lord."

"Thank you, Rosemary."

In the privacy of the parlour, Noah picked up the telephone. "Hello?"

He fully expected it would be Olivia, calling to say the fitting was canceled and six o'clock would be fine. But another, vaguely familiar and almost inaudible, voice came through the line.

"Lord Carey?"

"Yes, speaking," he said, pressing the earpiece closer.

"It's me . . . Joan. From Doctor Ryce's?"

"Yes?" Though he strained to hear her, he caught the panic in the voice. His imagination at once conjured up an image of Olivia, ashen-faced and abed with some serious ailment or injury, the family gathered about her too distraught to telephone him. His pulse quickened. "I can barely hear you. What's wrong, Joan?"

A hesitation, and then in the same low voice, "You're a very kind man, Lord Carey. Mrs. Bromley says I oughtn't call, that I'll get us all sacked. But you ought to know something."

"Know what? Has something happened to Miss Ryce?"

Another hesitation. "I heard Miss Ryce say you're coming to town. You should go speak with Roberta Spear at the Saxon Arms. It's down from the station."

"Yes, I'm familiar with it." A two-storey stone hotel with shutters painted a shade of orange that assaulted the eyes. "But why should I speak with Miss—"

"Spear, your Lordship."

This wasn't making any sense. But he felt a great tug of relief that this did not involve some injury to Olivia. "What is this about, Joan?"

"I can't say any more, Lord."

"Wait. What—"

"I beg you . . . please don't tell Miss Olivia I called." Her words were so rushed that he had to strain even harder to hear them. "I'll be sacked."

"I still don't under—"

But the connection broke abruptly.

"Strange," Noah muttered, leaving the parlour.

His mother was in the morning room, arranging marigolds in a vase. "What did you say, dear?"

He opened his mouth and hesitated. No sense in troubling her over a situation he didn't yet understand himself. "I'm taking Olivia to dinner, Mother. May I bring you anything from town?"

"No, thank you." She smiled. "I'll send word out to Vernon. And I'll wrap some of these in paper for Olivia."

"She'd like that."

The doorman at the Saxon Arms motioned Noah to an armchair in the lobby. Presently the hotel manager came out from the dining room. He was about forty, with deep lines curving out like parentheses on the sides of his mouth.

"Good evening, I'm Mr. Pickering. How may I be of service, Lord . . . Carey?"

"Carey it is," Noah said, rising. "Did I interrupt your supper?"

"Not at all," the manager said as they shook hands. "I was just making sure preparations were in order."

His brows rose questioningly. Noah decided it was time to sink or swim.

"Have you a guest by the name of Miss Spear?" he asked. "I don't recall her given name."

"No, I'm quite sure we haven't."

"Would you mind checking your register?"

The man smiled. "We're a small establishment, Lord Carey. I know the names of our guests."

184 ᴁ Lawana Blackwell

Serves you right! Noah chided himself. Setting out like some Sherlock Holmes because of a vague telephone call. "Well, thank you for—"

"But we've a chambermaid by the name of Roberta Spear," Mr. Pickering said tactfully, as if fearful of giving the impression that someone with Noah's stature would be calling on a member of the cleaning staff.

The name clicked a light on in Noah's mind. "Is she here? May I see her?"

Mr. Pickering sent a glance toward the doorman, who was hovering just inside pretending not to listen, then cleared his throat. "I'm afraid our staff aren't allowed gentleman callers, Lord Carey."

Heat rose to Noah's cheeks. "It's not that sort of call, Mr. Pickering. I would just like to speak with her. Five minutes."

"But of course," the manager said at once. "You'll please forgive me . . . times being what they are. Would you care to wait in my office while I send for her?"

Mr. Pickering escorted him to a sofa and left, apologizing for the ledgers and stacks of papers upon his desk. "I like to get a head start on end-of-the-month receipts."

When the office door opened again, Noah rose as a woman about his own age entered. She wore the ubiquitous black gown with white apron and a lace cap atop her brown hair. Her complexion was marred by several smallpox scars.

"Miss Spear?" Noah said.

"Yes, Lord Carey?"

Odd that she knew his name. But then, of course, Mr. Pickering would have informed her who was waiting. Motioning to the far end of the sofa, he said, "Will you please have a seat."

She did so after a slight hesitation, folded work-reddened hands in her lap and waited, her hazel eyes timidly not quite meeting his.

"I received a puzzling call today from Joan at Doctor Ryce's house," he explained.

At mention of Doctor Ryce, a corner of her mouth tugged downward. "Joan?"

"She's the parlourmaid there. I'm sorry, I don't know her surname."

Miss Spear shook her head. "There weren't any Joan when I worked there."

"Were you the parlourmaid?"

"Up until August past. But I helped Mrs. Ryce and the daughters dress too, as they didn't have a lady's maid."

"Then Joan must have replaced you."

"Hmm," she said politely, as if she felt he was expecting an acknowledgment of some sort.

It was as if Noah were in a dream, where conversations made no sense. He still had no clue why he was here. What was he supposed to ask next?

A question popped into his mind. "Why do you suppose Joan would have asked me to speak with you?"

"I don't know, sir."

Well, this is a monumental waste of time. He didn't intend to get Joan in trouble, but he would certainly convey to her he did not appreciate her making mischief.

Yet, she had seemed truly fearful of losing her position. Why would she risk that over a prank?

If he asked enough questions, surely one would make the connection that was supposed to be made. "May I ask why you're no longer employed at the Ryces'?" he asked, gently, not wishing to embarrass her if she had been sacked for some incompetence.

A corner of her mouth flinched just a bit. "I found this job, sir."

He had touched a nerve, he realized. "Why did you leave there, Miss Spear?"

"I found this job," she repeated.

"But what prompted you to look?"

Caution mingled with fear in her expression. "I wanted to work in a hotel."

Noah hooked one knee over the other, trying to keep his voice from revealing his growing frustration. "Yes, but why did you wish to leave the Ryces' employment?"

It was as if a curtain had dropped between them. She sent a longing look toward the door. "I have to go back to work now."

"Can't you just tell me?"

"It weren't nothing," she replied, rising. "The Ryces were very good to me. But I wanted to work here."

Noah got to his feet as well and watched her walk across the small room. At the door she turned just enough to send him an apologetic look. "Good evenin', Lord Carey."

"Wait, please."

Not removing her hand from the knob, she looked at him again.

"I'm to marry Olivia Ryce in less than three months," he said. "If there's something I should know . . ."

"I can't help you, sir."

"Please?"

Their eyes locked for a second, two seconds. Her shoulders rose and fell with a long breath. "You wouldn't be trying to trick me into saying something that would get me in trouble, would you?"

He blinked. "Why should I wish to?"

"You ain't a lawyer?"

"Why, no." He shook his head.

She turned from the door, hand still upon the knob. "Doctor Ryce said if I went about spreading gossip over why I left, he would take me to court for . . ."

Her brow furrowed.

"Slander?" Noah supplied automatically, while his mind rebelled against the thought.

"That was the word. But Mrs. Bromley already knew. She was the cook."

"She still is. She must have been the one who spoke to Joan." *But of what?*

Panic filled the scarred face. "Please tell her to stop, sir! I can't afford to be sued!"

"Sued for what, Miss Spear?" Noah pressed, taking only one step closer for fear she would flee any second. "You have my word as a Christian and a gentleman—what you say to me will not leave this room."

After studying his face for a long second, she moved her hand from the knob. Noah stood still, lest he frighten her away.

"You won't think it's important," she said.

"Allow me to be the judge of that. Please?"

She bit her lip. At length she said, softly, "No one ever slapped my face before—not even my mother or father. I could bear bein' screamed at, mind you. Even here, sometimes a guest will have a fit of temper when he's in his cups. But if he ever put a hand on any of us, Mr. Pickering would show him the door."

"Did Doctor Ryce *slap* you?" Noah asked. It was difficult to imagine a man so soft-spoken and nurturing harming anyone, but judging by the emotion in Miss Spear's face, *something* had happened.

That's why Joan telephoned, he realized. If Doctor Ryce would mistreat a servant, he could possibly have done the same to his daughters. *If it's true, we'll find the vicar and marry tonight.* Hang the gown and cake. He would get Olivia out of that house.

"It was a accident, your Lordship," Miss Spear continued, drawing her arms about herself. "Scorchin' the dress. I was always careful with the iron. But I had such a beastly headache that I weren't thinkin' straight. I get them now and again, and powders only make me sick to my stomach."

"Wait." Noah shook his head, not comprehending. "Doctor Ryce slapped you for ruining a gown?"

She looked at him. "It was Miss Ryce who slapped me, your Lordship. She was awful fond of the blue sateen. The yoke had a sort of Chinese embroid—"

"*Olivia* Ryce?"

Miss Spear's ruddy hand automatically went to her left cheek. Noah could not help but compare it with Olivia's ivory white hands, so soft and delicate, with slender fingers and perfectly tapered pink nails. Hands that fit so neatly in his palm, making him feel strong and protective.

"Miss Spear," he said. "This is very important. Are you positive this occurred the way you remember it? After all, you *did* say you had a headache."

Her expression faded, as if she was resigned to the fact that he would take up for Olivia. Tears glistened in both eyes. "I didn't know there was a red mark on my cheek till Mrs. Bromley asked me about it later."

After needing a moment to digest this, Noah had to ask one more question. "Forgive me, Miss Spear. But could this have been in any way an accident?"

"It ain't a accident when someone calls you a stupid skivvy at the same time, sir."

If she were skilled enough as an actress to be fabricating the incident, Noah thought, she would be onstage somewhere instead of cleaning hotel rooms. He sighed. "Thank you for being forthright with me."

"I'm sorry, Lord Carey," she said softly.

"You've nothing to apologize for, Miss Spear," he said. "I asked you for the truth."

She hesitated. "You'll remember your promise?"

"I will." He realized he could pay back the courtesy she had paid him by giving her a bit more peace of mind. "And by the way . . . it's highly unlikely that Doctor Ryce would ever come after you for slander. It's not slander if it's the truth."

"Is that so, sir?" she said with faint hope in her tone.

"I would almost guarantee it." He would not embarrass her by adding that as she probably had few financial assets, Doctor Ryce would not wish to pay an attorney to pursue a matter that would hardly raise eyebrows among most of his friends and family.

"But in the scant possibility that he does," he went on, "you just write to me in care of Carey Hall in Danby-dale, and I'll hire you the best lawyer in York."

She closed her eyes briefly, and when she opened them her expression and posture eased as if a heavy load had been lifted from her shoulders. "Thank you, Lord Carey. You're a kind gentleman."

"Oh, I don't know," he shrugged, not quite certain of anything for the moment.

"You are. And if it helps . . . it was the only time Miss Ryce ever struck me. As I said, it *was* her favorite gown."

*H*e needed time alone to think. When Mr. Pickering said there was indeed a room available, Noah gave the doorman a crown to pay the waiting coachman and another one to collect his portmanteau.

"May I borrow your telephone?" he asked the manager. Thankfully, Mr. Pickering allowed him privacy in the office once again.

He asked for Doctor Ryce's home with hands a little shaky, even while knowing that one of the servants would answer and not Olivia or another family member.

"Doctor Ryce's residence."

Joan's voice. Noah cleared his throat, but the lump did not go away. "Joan, Lord Carey here. Will you relay to Miss Ryce that I'll not be able to come by after all?"

There was a brief silence followed by a stilted, hurried, "Yes, your Lordship. And good day to you as well."

He understood her haste. The Ryce family in the parlour, naturally ceasing conversation at the ring of the telephone. Had they not broken the connection quickly, someone, possibly Olivia, could have motioned for the telephone. Then what would he say? He was an actor, but he would not be able to pull off pretending nothing was wrong.

This was more than a matter of indifference to those less privileged, Noah thought, dully unbuttoning his coat in his chamber. This was blatant cruelty. And he was not foolish enough to imagine it could be uprooted by reasoning with her.

Nor did he even wish to try, he realized. Whether or not a person of Olivia's age could be taught compassion was not the question. He wanted a wife who already possessed that quality. He had loved an illusion. The illusion was crumbling. How could he ever feel the same about her?

God, please help me know what to do, he prayed.

———

Joan answered the door of the Ryce house in the morning. She wore the expression of one who had been dreading the present moment. "Good morning, Lord Carey."

"Good morning," he said, stepping over the threshold.

As she took his hat, her eyes begged, *Am I in trouble?*

Noah shook his head slightly, for the clicks of heels were growing louder.

Mrs. Ryce entered the hall trilling, "There you are, you naughty man! Olivia's beside herself, fearing you met with some mishap."

"Is that Noah?" came Olivia's voice from the landing above.

"Forgive me for last night," Noah said up to her.

"That depends on how believable your explanation will be," she teased, floating down the stairs in a rustle of sea-green silks.

"Heh-heh," Noah forced out through a stiff smile, because his soon-to-be-no-longer-mother-in-law-to-be was beaming at him, expecting it. He could no longer bear his own hypocrisy, the chatter so reeking of normalcy. "Olivia, may I speak with you?"

"I beg your pardon?"

"In private?" he said.

Both mother and daughter stared at him. He could hear Joan's soft retreating footsteps. After a second, Mrs. Ryce nodded toward the sitting-room door. "There's no one in there."

It seemed she would follow them, but she stopped short in the hall. Noah watched the two trade perplexed looks as Olivia closed the door. Olivia turned and moved toward him. Of habit, Noah's hands left his sides to take hers. But he lowered them again.

She noticed and looked hurt. "What is it, Noah?"

Tears burned his eyes. In spite of his righteous indignation in the coach, he discovered that he could not bring himself to deliver the speech his mind had composed in the wee hours. So he softened it by saying, "I'm terribly sorry, Olivia. But I think it might be wise to postpone the wedding for a while."

"Postpone? What do you mean?"

"I just need some time to think."

His conscience burned. He was acting cowardly. Time would not change his mind. It was wrong to parcel out the pain in small doses to avoid the discomfort of a scene.

"Time to think about what, Noah?" She rested a hand upon his sleeve. "You're not making any sense."

This was ten times more difficult than he had imagined. He took a deep breath, braced himself mentally. "I'm sorry, Olivia. We can't marry."

She gaped at him. "But why?"

"I'm sorry," he said for the third time, and he was, for having to hurt her. "I no longer feel the same way. I'll reimburse you for your gown and any other expenses. And please keep the ring."

"You won't give me a reason?" Tears lustering her eyes, she shook herself as if attempting to wake from a dream. "Is this because of Friday night?"

The promise he had made to Miss Spear was a weight upon his mind. And how could he reply that Friday night's incident was the loose pebble that escalated into an avalanche, without jeopardizing Joan's position? He sighed, frustrated, realizing the unfairness of giving Olivia only part of the whole reason. "It was a mistake to become engaged so soon after we met. We really don't know each other. My fault."

She dissolved into tears, and again, he had to restrain himself from embracing her, patting her shoulder, or touching her in any way that might dilute the message he had given her. It was tough enough to say the first time. He tried to give her his handkerchief, but she shook it away.

The door *whooshed* open, and her mother hurried into the room, giving Noah a stunned look as Olivia fell into her arms. Once she gathered the reason for her daughter's sobs, Mrs. Ryce called Noah a rakeshame, a libertine, and scoundrel, and when Doctor Ryce entered, he added some epithets of his own. Becky and Lydia, Olivia's youngest sisters, wandered wide-eyed into the room but were ordered out by their father. The confusion upon their faces was as painful to Noah as the anger and hurt on everyone else's, for it drove home to him that he would no longer be a part of this family's lives.

He left the house feeling as battered as if he had been beaten and more alone than he had felt since his father's death. In the hired coach on the way to York Station, he tugged lose his cravat from his collar and wiped his eyes and cheeks, blew his nose. No matter what she had done, what her parents had done, no matter that he no longer could make himself love her, he hated to be the cause of so much pain.

Back at home he could hear his mother in the parlour, playing whist with Uncle Bertram and Aunt May and their son Ronald. Ronald was describing a Lanchester motorcar he had seen in York this morning, and fortunately no one seemed to notice Noah pass by the open doorway.

"I wish we could get one," he heard on his way to the staircase. "Just think, no more baling hay and mucking out horse stables."

"Nonsense." Uncle Bertram's voice. "They're just a flash in the pan, I tell you. What will happen to all those automobiles when there's no more petrol in the ground?"

Upstairs, Rhodes helped Noah out of his Wellington boots and inquired as to the whereabouts of his hat.

"I forgot it," Noah said.

The elderly servant looked at his face and gave him a grim nod. Noah was certain he would sleep like a stone from exhaustion. But sleep mingled uneasily with wakeful memories of the scene in the Ryces' parlour, and he tossed and turned until he had to get out of bed and tuck his sheet back under the mattress.

He threw himself into physical activity over the remainder of the week, helping the estate workers dig stones to enlarge the barn. The sweat seeping out through his pores did not drain his body of the guilt-induced queasiness, but he did sleep most nights. When he broke the news to his mother, strolling with her in the garden, she wiped away tears. She was fond of Olivia and, he suspected, had already pinned some hopes upon having grandchildren.

"Why, Noah?" she asked.

"I discovered something of her character that I couldn't live with."

"How did you discover this?"

"I'm afraid I'm not at liberty to share that." He gave her a regretful look. "Not even with you, Mother. I gave my word to the person who informed me."

"Hmm." She started walking again, he with her. "Are you certain this person was truthful?"

"Quite sure. She took a risk by telling me."

"And did Olivia dispute her story?"

Noah sighed. "That's the hardest part. I couldn't bring it to her without breaking my promise."

"That hardly seems fair. Everyone should have a chance to defend himself . . . herself, when accused."

"I know, Mother. I've said that to myself a thousand times. But there is more compelling evidence to believe the story than to not. And even if it *isn't* true, it's brought on enough doubts to where I just can't marry her."

He held his breath for the argument certain to continue, but she simply shook her graying head. "What a shame. You got on so well together."

The fact that she would not press for any more details gave Noah more freedom to vent the feelings bottled up inside. "I had her on a pedestal. That was wrong of me. If I would have really allowed myself to get to know her, it wouldn't have progressed this far, and people wouldn't be hurt."

His mother looped her arm though his. "There's not a person alive without regrets. Not a *sane* person anyway. What can I do to help?"

"Would you consider hiring the Ryces' parlourmaid if she ever needs to leave her position?"

When his mother gave him a curious look, he shook his head.

"She's not the person I made the promise to. But she did do something for me, and I'd like to let her know she has another place if she wishes."

"Of course," she replied.

The following day Noah wrote to his late father's attorney and good friend, Mr. Gates, asking that he call on Doctor Ryce and ask the total expenditure the family had applied toward the wedding. Mr. Gates called upon Noah at Carey Hall on the last day in May with a letter from a Mr. Southworth, another York attorney, stating Olivia Ryce's intention to sue him for breach of contract.

"How much does she want?" Noah asked after Mother left them alone in the parlour with tea.

"Ten thousand pounds, if it goes to court."

Noah felt veins pop out against his collar. "*Ten* thousand?"

"Mr. Southworth was quite adamant."

"I don't *have* ten thousand pounds."

"I realize that, Lord Carey," Mr. Gates said, having administered Noah's father's will five years ago. The estate was bequeathed to Noah, but with a life-estate provision favoring his mother. As long as she lived, the income generated by wool sales and tenant farmer rents was hers to control.

It was not that Noah's father had not trusted him to care for his own mother, Mr. Gates had explained at the reading, for he had drafted the will when Noah was an infant. His legal firm had advised it, having witnessed enough horror stories of young men gambling away entire estates or bringing in a young wife who begrudged her mother-in-law every penny.

"I'll not borrow money from my mother," Noah seethed, building up steam.

The attorney's spectacle lenses magnified the gravity in his expression. "I'm compelled to inform you, Lord Carey, that unless you can provide witnesses to testify to any moral fault of Miss Ryce's, the verdict will probably go in her favor."

"I can't do that," Noah said.

"Not one witness? Are you absolutely certain?"

"Yes."

"Pity. Justice may be blind but judges aren't, and a heartbroken beautiful young woman on the stand is certain to evoke sympathy."

"You said *if* it goes to court," Noah said. "Does that mean the Ryces are open to the possibility of settling out of court?"

"They are. For four thousand pounds."

"Four thousand," Noah mused aloud. "After your bill, that will be almost to the penny what's left in my personal account." It was what remained of the five thousand his father had given him when he started at Oxford, so that Noah would not have to ask for pocket money.

"Indeed?" Mr. Gates's brows rose above tortoiseshell frames. "Did you happen to mention that account to your former fiancée?"

"Why, yes. I told her everything." In an instant, every nagging doubt Noah had suffered over whether he had done the right thing by breaking his engagement was silenced. He sighed, set his cup and saucer on a side table, and got to his feet. "Please excuse me for a minute. My cheques are upstairs."

"Just like that?" the attorney said when Noah returned. "I could try negotiating them down."

"I want this to be over. If that's what it takes to appease them, that's what it takes. I only ask that you have Doctor Ryce sign some sort of privacy agreement before you hand him the cheque. I'd rather not worry my mother over this."

"Very decent of you, I must say." Mr. Gates slipped the cheque into his satchel. "Oh, I almost forgot. . . ."

He brought out a flat shirt box tied with blue satin ribbon. "Apparently Miss Ryce is just as eager to put this unpleasantness behind her. She asked me to give you this."

"A gift?" Feelings assaulted Noah from all sides. Relief, that Olivia apparently did not despise him. Regret, that the engagement had ended for the reason he had to end it. Guilt, that he had pursued her like an infatuated schoolboy, glossing over her true character. And a fair bit of anger toward the Ryces for seizing this as an opportunity for financial profit.

But as soon as Noah held the box in his hands and felt its lightness, dark humor swept all other emotions away.

"Aren't you going to open it?" Mr. Gates said.

Noah gave him a dry smile. "Later."

Upstairs, he untied the ribbon and raised the lid.

"I'm afraid it's beyond repair, your Lordship," said Rhodes. The valet did not ask the circumstances surrounding the bowler hat that lay flat as a pewter platter, but his raised eyebrow plowed furrows in his forehead. "It's not even fitting for the charity box."

"I want to save it anyway," Noah said. After all, it was his diploma from the school of foolish actions. He only wished the tuition had not been so expensive.

During the days that followed, Noah felt as if he were a planet knocked out of its orbit by some giant asteroid. It was not that he grieved for Olivia, for all he had to do was imagine her slapping a servant or spending his four thousand pounds on silk dresses and, bit by bit, any lingering traces of affection seeped from his heart.

But now that courtship no longer dominated his time and emotions, now that marriage no longer waited in the foreseeable future, he realized how directionless his life was. He had no goal to set his sights upon other than improving his acting craft, and were he to become skilled enough to make Sir Henry Irving look like a boy in a church pageant, he would continue on as before, acting in York at every opportunity, helping out on the estate between times.

When Jude's second letter arrived on the sixth of June, Noah had to wipe his eyes every third line or so.

The eleven bedrooms are as tiny as biscuit tins and are occupied by struggling actors and musicians, Jude wrote of the Irving Street lodging house where he had secured a room on the third floor.

> Mr. Savill, the landlord, is a decent fellow as long as the rent is paid on time. Mrs. Savill is Prussian, and a fine cook, but no one dares ask her for second helpings if she appears in a sour mood. Her mother, Frau Roswalt, is a frail woman who floats about the place soundlessly. Though she is quite deaf, somehow ringing noises are painful to her ears, so she hangs up the telephone if there is no one to stop her. This makes everyone nervous, and we take turns at guard duty in the sitting room. But at 35s weekly, the rent is the most reasonable I have found—the food is good, the linens are changed every fortnight, and I can walk one block to Daly's Theatre on Leicester Square.

Noah read on of Jude's experiences at rehearsal, followed by:

> I may be prejudiced, Noah, but my fellow actors are tops, and I can feel in my heart that this production of *The Cenci* will be the one Londoners talk about for years to come. I only wish you and Olivia could be here in August for opening night, but then, I hear that Greece is rather nice as well.

"Well, I guess it's time to tell you, old friend," Noah murmured and went to his writing desk. He did not write the reason for the broken engagement, just that he and Olivia had gone their separate ways. He had no qualms against complaining to his best friend about the settlement, but later, in person, when they could talk long hours as before.

"Why don't you visit Jude when his play opens?" his mother suggested in the parlour after supper, when Uncle Bertram and Aunt May and Ronald had retired to their chambers. "It would do you a world of good."

It would do him more than a world of good, Noah thought. It would do him a universe of good. He dared not admit how near broke he was to her, for she would insist upon giving him money. However, a weekend and theatre ticket he could afford, with the forty-three pounds he had remaining.

Mid-June was the time for shearing, a chore Noah had lent assistance with since age twelve. The seventeenth began as a fine day, with sweet heather-laden breezes wafting in from the north. Sheep bleated in the pen and the male workers challenged each other over who would produce the most fleeces while the women gossiped outside the wool room, where fleeces were graded and packed.

The older sheep usually submitted peacefully, but the younger had to have their legs tied. That job fell to Noah. He was teamed with Mr. Anders, who was, at age fifty, one of the fastest workers. The process went along smoothly, Noah holding steady the animal, Mr. Anders's experienced fingers feeling close to the skin where the fleece was finest, then the clippers plowing through the wool as if powered by steam.

"Hold her steady, now!" Mr. Anders barked when a young ewe kicked loose of its restraint.

"Yes, sir!" Noah replied, grabbing the animal's leg. He may have been lord of the estate, but during shearing time, the shearers were the kings.

By sunset every joint in Noah's body ached, though he dared not share this information with Uncle Bertram, Mr. Anders, and the other older workers who complained about having to quit just as they hit their strides. After supper he took a good long soak in the bathtub, until the water chilled too much for comfort. He pulled on the clean nightshirt Rhodes had left on his bed and was stretched out across the mattress, propped on his elbows reading *The Drama:*

Addresses by Henry Irving, when a knock sounded at his door.

"Come in."

His mother entered, still in the blue poplin gown she had worn to supper. Noah noted the page number, closed the book, and sat up.

She smiled. "Tired?"

"Not as tired as the sheep are, I imagine. But I'll wager I'm more sore."

"Let's have a chat, shall we?"

"But of course." He got up and pulled on his dressing gown and shoved his feet into his slippers while she went over to the upholstered chair near his window. Noah took the chair from his writing desk and joined her.

"Am I in trouble?" he said jokingly, for once he became too old for bedtime stories, she almost never entered his room.

"Well, yes you are," she replied with a mock severe look. "Why didn't you tell me about the settlement?"

Heat spread in Noah's cheeks. "Mr. Gates . . . ?"

"You forget that your account and the estate's are in the same bank. And some bank clerks are more chatty than others."

"Well, I'm certainly going to . . ." he began, and realized there would be no point in changing banks. He could expect no income until rehearsals began in October, and even that would barely cover his hotel bill and expenses in the city. It was the love of acting, not high wages, that attracted local talent to provincial theatre.

". . . write a letter of complaint," he finished lamely.

His mother shook her head. "You'll do no such thing, dear. I'll not have someone sacked because of my inquisitiveness."

He had to allow that to soak in for a moment. "You mean you asked about my finances?"

"Let's just say I dropped some broad hints. I knew Mr. Gates would not have come all the way out here looking so grim if he was only collecting for a wedding gown."

"And so you interrogated our banker."

She gave him a sheepish look. "Well, yes. It was unforgivable of me. But do hear me out."

"Have I any choice?" he snapped and instantly regretted it. He could not sustain any anger at his mother for more than a few seconds. He blew out a long breath. "Sorry, Mother."

"I had it coming," she said with a little smile and sat back against the cushions, one elbow propped upon a chair arm. "Did you and Olivia ever discuss having children, Noah?"

What this had to do with the subject of chatty bankers he had not a clue but assumed she would meander her way back to it eventually. "Of course," he replied.

"Do you still want children one day?"

"Yes."

"Why?"

"Why do I want children?" He had never really asked himself that question, just knew he would like very much to be a father one day. But the answers came easily. "To watch them grow. Play games with them. Teach them the good things I've learned and hopefully to avoid the mistakes I've made."

Her green eyes glistened a bit in the lamplight. "I pray you experience all that. A parent never loses those feelings, son. You're just as much a delight to me as you were as a child."

"Thank you, Mother," he said, touched.

"*And* nothing would give me greater pleasure than seeing you achieve your dream. I want you to go to London now."

He shook his head. "I can wait until August. I would probably be in Jude's way now anyway."

"I'm not speaking of visiting Jude. I'm speaking of living there. Trying out for theatre. It's time, Noah."

When he could speak past the lump in his throat, he said, "I'll not leave you, Mother."

Whether he had spending money or not was a moot point. If the situation were different, Father still here for mother, he would walk to London if that was what it took. Sleep in doorways and, as Jude had once said, sweep streets until he landed a part.

"Then you'll break my heart," she said.

"That's unfair, Mother. I'll break your heart if I leave you here alone."

"But I'm *not* alone, Noah. This has been my home for fifty-three years. I have friends, family. And you'll come back for visits, unless you get so famous that you forget your roots."

"Never," he said. "Do you really mean this, Mother?"

"With all my heart."

Immediately Noah's mind started racing. His forty-three pounds would cover his railway fare and at least a couple of month's lodging and meals, perhaps even three. He would have to learn to economize, pinch pennies, but the notion of doing so loomed out in front of him as an adventure. How much more rewarding it would be, were he to gain success on the London stage, to be able to look back and know that he had paid his own dues. What a story he would have for fireside chats with his grandchildren!

And as for *The Importance of Being Earnest,* the Theatre Royal would have plenty of time to replace him before rehearsals. There would be no hard feelings there, for almost everyone in the company shared the same London dream.

". . . enough to start?"

Noah's mind rushed back to the present. "Forgive me, Mother. What were you saying?"

"I asked how much I should transfer into your account initially. Five hundred? A thousand?"

He rose from his chair and knelt by the side of hers so that he could take her soft hand and press it to his cheek. "Not one penny."

"But you—"

"I know it's available to me should I truly need it. But for the time being, I'd like to see if there is more to me than being a spoiled, rich brat."

She frowned miserably. "You'll starve. I just know it."

He shook his head. "I'm not *that* noble."

"Promise?"

"Absolutely," he replied. "And by the way, thank you for letting me go. I realize what a sacrifice this is for you."

"What sacrifice?" She smiled at him, tears still lingering in her eyes. "You've not exactly been a ray of sunshine lately."

Nineteen

*O*n the eighteenth of June, threatening dark clouds necessitated arranging chairs into rows in Girton College's Stanley Library for the commencement ceremony. The address was delivered by 1893 alumna Grace Chisholm Young, who had continued her education in mathematics in Germany and became, two years later, the first woman to receive a doctorate in any field in that country.

Guy's commencement from University of Bologna was held the same day, the address delivered by Bologna native Guglielmo Marconi, inventor of wireless telegraphy.

Both speakers stressed that education is a lifelong process and should not cease with the completion of formal schooling—so Bethia and Guy discovered when they compared experiences four evenings later in Hampstead. Inspiring speeches, and yet what the two remembered most of that momentous day was how each had wished the other there.

"We're pathetic," Guy said, arm around her waist as they stood on the terrace looking out at a sliver of moon.

"Pathetic," Bethia agreed.

"How about another kiss?"

Bethia looked over her shoulder toward the house, where their families were engaged in after-dinner chat in the parlour. She smiled at Guy. "They're probably beginning to wonder."

He sighed. "You're right."

"You give in too easily," Bethia said, closing her eyes and raising her chin.

Within nine days Guy had secured a seat in the Royal Opera House. During gaps between performances and rehearsals he planned to work in his father's shop as well as hire out to soirées, balls, and the like. Anything to better himself financially.

The whole time he was in Italy, Bethia had simply looked forward to his permanent return to London, not taking into account that he would have to spend most of his waking hours at work of one sort or another. But at least they would have Sunday afternoons together, after attending church with their families—Bethia's at Christ Church just down Cannonhall Road, and Guy's at St. Thomas's on Regent Street.

On the third of July, Bethia took the underground railway to meet Guy in Kensington for lunch at Jewel and Grady's. The McGuire apartment was one of six sharing the second storey of Shepherd's Gardens, a wide terra-cotta brick building on Albert Place. With the two practically living at the Royal Court and with no children romping through the apartment, Jewel and Grady employed a maid to clean twice weekly and deliver their laundry to and from the laundress. Any meals they took at home were ordered from the Red Lion Inn, such as today's boiled brisket of beef, with turnips and carrots and suet dumplings.

As Bethia helped Jewel wash up the dishes, the men delivered the serving tins back to the inn and returned with a chocolate cake. They sat in the den with tea and cake, and Grady read aloud the earliest accounts of a battle fought between the Americans and Spanish on San Juan Hill near Santiago, Cuba.

Though Jewel did mention that Mrs. Steel had delivered a healthy boy she and her husband named Michael, there was no further discussion of anything having to do with the Royal Court. Bethia knew that her cousin and Grady loved their jobs even more than she loved hers, but with such an intensity of their commitment, it was a relief to forget them for a few hours and discuss even such a morbid subject as war.

"Would you care for a little stroll?" Guy asked Bethia outside the apartment at ten of four.

"Certainly," Bethia said, slipping her hand through the crook of his arm. The light in his eyes compelled her to ask, "Where?"

"Some houses a customer mentioned to Father." He took a slip of paper from his pocket, unfolded it with his free fingers. "I haven't looked them over yet, but I thought we could do that together, if you like. It's not too early to keep an eye out. . . ."

She nudged his side. "You know I would."

They walked two blocks, turned and walked another to Abington Road, to a row of charming narrow two-storey, stone-brown stucco terrace houses with slate roofs and tiny front garden plots.

"Primrose Terrace," he said and stopped in front of one cast-iron railing. "I thought they would be bigger."

"They're lovely," Bethia said, touching the blunt spear of the railing. The Hampstead house was a fine one, but it wasn't *hers*. She could easily see herself building a life in a dollhouse such as this one with Guy.

"We could plant roses in the garden," she said. "No . . . flower boxes would have to do, and a few shrubs. The children should have room to play."

He shook his head. "We wouldn't be here long enough for that. I'm just thinking of our first year or so. Better than renting a flat that we can't resell when we move up."

"Yes, good idea," she said, knowing how useless it would be to insist that "moving up" was not high on her priority list. Surely he would not be so restless once they had turned it into a home, with their things set about and family portraits upon the wall. "And it would be nice to live so close to Jewel and Grady."

"Are you sure about this, Bethia?" he asked.

"I'm sure."

"The land agent—the customer in Father's shop—says construction is due to start any day on another row across the street, to be finished and put on the market in four or five months. I'll save every penny I make for a deposit. By Christmas, I ought to have something to show your father."

Bethia was saving her wages as well but refrained from saying so for the sake of his pride. As close as she and Guy were, the difference in their family incomes had acquired almost a presence of its own in their relationship. She understood that it was the dream of almost everyone alive to better himself financially, but Guy was driven. It was as if he could not accept himself as a man until he was able to shower her with the fine things that really did not matter to her.

". . . and enough for a nice ring," Guy went on. "I've got my eye on one in Prosser's, around the corner from the shop. A diamond, with—"

"I'd rather you put the money toward the house, Guy."

His jaw tightened. "I'll not ask your hand without a ring to put on it."

"And I'd like to have one." Bethia fished the chain with the barite gemstone from beneath her collar. "I've a great sentimental attachment to this. It would be lovely mounted on a gold band."

"I paid six hundred lire for that, Bethia," he said with a little grimace. "It's just a reminder of what it's like to be broke."

"It's a reminder of how you bought me a gift even *while* broke."

"That's less than five shillings, Bethia."

She shrugged. "My parents paid nothing for me. Does that mean I'm not valuable to them?"

Guy rolled his eyes. "You're being obstinate."

Raising fingers to his lips, Bethia said, "You can buy me that diamond for our tenth wedding anniversary."

"For our engagement," he mumbled through her fingers.

Even though she had one less iron in the fire now that her schooling was complete, Bethia was as busy as ever at the Royal Court, for costumes needed to be prepared for Tom Taylor's *The Ticket-of-Leave Man* before rehearsals started the following week.

"And why must I submit to this again?" Muriel Holt asked in her cool tone on the seventh of July, as Bethia wound the measuring ribbon about her slender waist. Naturally, Muriel was assigned the lead role of May Edwards in the coming production. During Bethia's absence, her popularity had grown to where audiences were still filling the theatre for *Lady Audley's Secret*. Prince Edward and Princess Alexandra had even attended on Saturday past.

The critics loved her as well, judging by the framed newspaper critiques Miss Lidstone said were hanging, framed, in Muriel's dressing room.

"Weight can fluctuate," Bethia explained. "Especially women's."

"Not mine."

"Then you're very fortunate, Lady Holt."

After affecting a sigh, Muriel said, "Not when you consider it's worry over my brother's safety that stifles my appetite. But then, you wouldn't know anything about that, would you, Miss Rayborn?"

Bethia became aware of the sudden silence of the sewing machine trestle beneath Mrs. Hamby's feet. *This isn't the time nor place,* she thought. But she could not ignore the accusation hovering in the air between them, unchallenged. Trying to keep her voice steady, even while her hands trembled, she said, "I pray for your brother's safety every day, Lady Holt."

"Indeed? I do wish you had considered his safety before you wrote that malicious letter."

Like a fish gasping in the bottom of a boat, Bethia struggled for words. Did Muriel really believe her so callous?

Muriel was staring, violet eyes challenging.

"How could I have known he would leave for Canada?" Bethia asked bleakly.

"You knew he was desperately in love with you, enough to do something rash!"

Miss Lidstone cleared her throat and approached, touching Bethia's hand that held the measuring ribbon. "Why don't I finish here, Miss Rayborn?" she said.

"Yes," Muriel said, raising her chin. "That would be more to my liking."

———————

Guy came up to Hampstead the following Sunday afternoon. After spending a half hour visiting with the family, Bethia and he took a walk on the Heath.

"Father says a highwayman named Jackson was hanged near this spot two centuries ago," she said when they reached the large elm near the road from Jack Straw's Castle. "He's collecting research for a book on the history of Hampstead."

"Why here?" Guy said. "I thought hangings were always out in the open."

"It's here that he killed a man."

The account had fascinated Bethia when her father related it, for she shared his interest in history. But she wished now she had not brought it up, for the fates of a hapless traveler and merciless robber were to her melancholy mood as fuel to a fire. She sighed. "Let's go back now."

Guy's sapphire eyes studied her face. "What's the matter, Lilly?"

The concern in his voice was all the prompting she needed to tell him everything, beginning with happening upon Douglas Pearce in Covent Garden.

"Why did you keep this from me?" Guy asked with arm wrapped about her shoulders while she leaned her head upon his chest.

"You were at school. I didn't want to worry you."

"Please, never do that again."

"But what could you have done?"

"I don't know," he admitted. "But *something*. We've confided in each other since we were children, Bethia. Please . . . promise me you'll never keep something important like this from me again."

Bethia nodded. "I promise."

"That's my Lilly," he said gently, squeezing her shoulders. "And I make you the same vow. Our marriage will be based upon total honesty."

Twenty

*T*he arched train shed of St. Pancras Station was a masterpiece of daring function—iron framework filled with glass and rising up a hundred feet to a pointed crown. *I'm here,* Noah thought with wonder while threading his way down the platform on the morning of the twelfth of July. The smell of coal smoke, the streams of humanity pouring past and sometimes jostling his arm with hurried apology, the scraps of conversation and piercing whistles—they were all perfume to his nostrils, music to his ears.

And then Jude, waving!

"So you made it!" his friend exclaimed.

Noah dropped the Gladstone bag from his right hand, the portmanteau from his left, and embraced his friend, clapping him on the back. "I thought you'd be in rehearsal!"

"The stage director appreciates my promptness. He gave me a couple of hours. So let's make haste."

Jude took up the portmanteau and led Noah toward the exit marked *Euston Road.* Over his shoulder he said above the noise, "I'm glad you packed light."

"Well, you said a trunk wouldn't fit in my room."

"It's even worse than that. The trombonist whose room you're getting, well, his touring company's departure is delayed ten days."

Noah slowed down on the pavement outside. "So where will I—"

"Do hurry, Noah. You've seen London before. And you're sharing my room for now."

Jude turned to plow ahead, and all Noah could do was follow to a hackney cab with room on the floor for the luggage. "Haymarket Theatre," Jude said to the driver and turned to Noah. "We would take the underground if time weren't the element."

"Haymarket? I thought we were going to the lodging house."

His friend smiled as the driver snapped the reins and the horse pulled out into the traffic. "There's a casting call for a half hour from now. They require four actors for Douglas Jerrold's *Black-ey'd Susan*. I'll drop your luggage off on my way back to work, and you'll have to find your own way there."

Excitement and panic surged through Noah's chest. "But I'm not prepared," he said, reaching back a hand to scratch his neck just below his collar.

Jude produced a worn playscript from his coat pocket. "I picked this up from a secondhand shop and marked the parts that are available. With so many, people will probably have to take turns using the theatre copies. You'll have time in the greenroom to acquaint yourself with it. I wrote the address of the lodging house on the back, by the way."

When Noah still gaped at him, at the playscript in his hand, Jude cuffed him on the upper arm. "May as well seize this opportunity, big fellow. There won't be another for a week or so."

"Yes, of course," Noah said and relaxed enough to say, "Thank you, Jude. It's good to be here with you."

"It's good to have you here." His friend gave him a cautious look. "You're not too torn up about . . . you know . . ."

"I'll live."

The hackney stopped in front of a beautiful white stone building with six gilt-topped white columns supporting a marquee with the words *Theatre Royal Haymarket*. After handing the driver a crown, which would surely cover both fares, Noah waved farewell to his protesting friend. *This isn't a dream. I'm actually going to set foot on a London stage before the day's end,* he thought while walking toward the only one of five arched doorways that was open. The stage doorman stood to the side and nodded somber entry to two men just ahead of Noah. Halfway fearing he would be turned away for being an impostor, Noah approached and stated his purpose.

"Good morning, sir. I'm here to audition?"

The man nodded affably. "Can't be too careful these days. Go on inside."

Every seat in the greenroom was filled. Noah scratched a persistent itch on his arm, took one of the chairs set out in the corridor, opened his playscript, and mentally blocked out his surroundings.

Or at least he made the attempt.

"I say, is that a copy of the script?" said the fellow who was seated at his right, a young man wearing white flannels. A straw boater hat was perched upon on knee.

Noah gave him a polite smile. "It is."

"I was told they were out. Where did you get it?"

"A friend bought it from a secondhand shop."

"I wish I'd thought of that." He motioned toward the greenroom. "They said copies will filter back from the stage as they're available."

"My friend warned me," Noah said. "But auditions generally move along. You should have a copy shortly."

"I see," the man said with defeated voice.

As Noah's eyes returned to the page, his neighbor leaned close enough so that their arms pressed together, and Noah caught a whiff of the macassar oil in his blonde hair.

"I say . . . you wouldn't mind if I read over your shoulder, would you?"

"Sorry," Noah said, easing himself to the left a bit. "I have to concentrate."

And that was proving more difficult. The itching struck again, this time between his shoulder blades. When it began in various places upon his body three days ago, he had chalked it up to anxiety and excitement over leaving Yorkshire. He had barely noticed it during the railway trip. But now, in the windowless and hot corridor, he had the compelling urge to get up and rub his back against a post.

A second later, his attempt to regain concentration was hindered again by a sigh and more pressure upon his arm. "I beg your pardon . . . would you consider selling it?"

"Sorry," Noah said again.

"I'll give you a fiver."

The amount raised Noah's eyebrows now that he had to watch his pennies. He reminded himself that he was down here to fulfill a dream, not scramble for the odd fivers. His neighbor mistook his hesitation for agreement and dug a purse from his coat pocket.

"I'm not interested," Noah insisted.

"Anyone else?" the young man said, holding it up for the half dozen others in corridor chairs.

But only two men had copies of the script and were, like Noah, not inclined to part with them. Noah took pity upon the young man and nodded toward the greenroom. "I'm sure you'll find someone in there to do business with you."

The man brightened, rose, and walked off. He returned seconds later, grinning, with a script in hand. "I say, what parts are open?"

You walked in here without even knowing? Noah stifled a sigh and showed him the markings Jude had made. "The admiral and Jacob Twig, Doggrass and Lieutenant Pike."

A bald man in shirt-sleeves exited the greenroom with notebook tucked in the crook of one arm. "My name is Mr. Kaye. When I approach you, be ready to state your name, address where you may be telephoned, and most recent stage experience."

He began across the corridor, so Noah concentrated again on the playscript and on *not* scratching. Presently Mr. Kaye crouched before his neighbor with a creaking of knees. "Your name, please?"

"Lord Cecil Bovey," the young man replied. "Our in-town address is 19 Park Lane. Perhaps you've heard of my father, the Duke of Chertsey? My family leases a box here every season."

"Mm-hmm," Mr. Kaye murmured, writing. "Experience?"

"Well . . . none, actually," Lord Bovey admitted and chuckled. "Unless you count playing a shepherd in the school Christmas pageant when I was ten. My mother said I was quite extraordinary."

Mr. Kaye raised weary-looking eyes from his notebook. "Acting lessons, perchance?"

"None. But I'd like to give acting a try."

"I beg your pardon?"

"I'd like to be an actor," the young lord repeated.

A little smile curled both corners of Mr. Kaye's mouth. "Wouldn't you, just?"

Lord Bovey returned his smile. "Why, yes, I would."

A man seated across the corridor snorted suppressed laughter, bringing a flush to Lord Bovey's fair cheeks. In spite of the irritant he had been, Noah felt pity for the young man.

And the humiliation was not over. Mr. Kaye straightened. "I'll make a deal with you, *your Lordship*."

"Why, thank you."

"There's a branch of Coutt's Bank down Haymarket, a stone's throw from here. Go down there, tell 'em you'd like to give accounting a try. If they hire you, come back here, and I'll escort you to stage myself."

Lord Bovey flushed deep crimson, rose from his chair. "You'll hear from my father before the day's over."

"I can hardly wait," Mr. Kaye said in a mocking tone.

The young man turned and stalked up the corridor. Over the laughter Mr. Kaye snorted, "That's the upper crust for you! Thinks his silver spoon is the only qualification he needs."

More laughter, and then he became businesslike again.

"Name, please?" he said to Noah.

It struck Noah that the title he had worn since infancy, so much a part of his life experience that he took it for granted, did not belong here. Perhaps later, when he had proved himself. And then, perhaps not. Was he any better a person than, say, Jude? What had he done to deserve *Lord* before his name other than been born? "Noah Carey," he replied.

The first role to be cast was that of Jacob Twig, the bailiff, and while not the lead, it was not a small part. When his name was called, Noah put his index finger into the playscript to mark his place and walked out onto the wing.

Stand tall, he reminded himself, taking a deep breath. He walked out to center stage, where the actor who would read the part of Mr. Doggrass waited. Blessed with a good memory, Noah felt his confidence build as he quoted two sentences at a time before having to glance down at the playscript.

"Yes; I was in the public-house when the Captain was brought in with that gash in his shoulder!"

Heat rose from the footlights and wafted down upon him from the battens. The trickle of sweat meandering down Noah's back signaled for the itching to strike full force.

"I stood beside his bed; it was steeped in blood. . . ."

He had to ignore it. He may be new to London, but he had

experience enough to ignore outside distractions and focus totally upon his part.

". . . when I looked on the Captain's blue lips and pale face . . ."

The itching made the sweating worse, and vice versa. But he was Jacob Twig, he reminded himself. Not the Noah Carey whose skin was on fire.

". . . I thought what poor creatures we are; then something whispered in my—"

"Thank you, that will be enough" came from the first row. "Mr. Black will show you out."

"Oh, but I'll be reading three other parts," Noah said, peering into the dimness.

"Sorry. We don't really have a place for you. Better luck next time."

"I say, Noah, stop thrashing about! I've rehearsals in the morning!"

"Sorry," Noah muttered, wondering if any night had ever been so long.

"It's time you saw a doctor!" Jude groused.

"If it's no better in a couple of days, I'll—"

"'To sleep!'" bellowed through the thin adjoining wall. "'Perchance to dream!'"

Noah and Jude both smothered chuckles, and then Noah attempted to lie still and ignore what felt like a dozen ants performing morris dances upon his skin. That, and cling to his side of the concave mattress to keep from rolling against Jude. *Three more days,* he reminded himself. He would have his own room and bed and could thrash about without robbing anyone else's sleep.

Most times during the day the itching was more tolerable, what with his excitement over living in London, pouring over the *Stage* and the *Era* to line up audition dates, touring the great city on foot and by omnibus. But at night there were no distractions, save Jude's occasional snoring and the laughter and music coming through the open window from the Hotel de Province next door.

Paying dues, Noah reminded himself. *Grandchildren on your knee at fireside, remember?*

A few seconds more of trying to ignore the itching, and he was praying, *I'm not quite sure I can afford these dues, Father. Please make this itching go away.*

"Sorry, old chum," he said to Jude in the morning after coming up from the kitchen with a pitcher of hot water to make it up to his long-suffering friend.

Because the one bathroom had to serve a dozen lodgers—thirteen until the trombonist left—the Savill family, and two servants, it was reserved only for a once-weekly tub bath. Pitchers and bowls in the rooms served for shaving, brushing teeth, and sponge bathing. Fortunately, three days ago Noah had discovered a public facility on Orange Street off Leicester Square, St. Martin's Baths, that charged only a tuppence for a cold bath in the evenings. Jude laughed at his fastidiousness, but Noah reckoned he would walk as much as possible and save his pennies rather than go about with oily hair. And now with this itch, he had more reason to want to scrub down completely.

"And *I'm* sorry for complaining," Jude said, lathering his face with a shaving brush. He gave Noah a worried look in the cracked wall mirror. "Are you positive you've not gotten lice somehow?"

"If I did, surely you'd have them by now." Noah eyed the worn blanket that served as a coverlet on the bed. "Don't they crawl?"

"I believe they hop," Jude replied, scratching his bare shoulder with his left hand. "Like jackrabbits."

Noah's eyes widened. "Why are you—"

His friend turned to raise innocent brows at him. "Beg pardon?"

"Jude!" Noah laughed, shaking his head.

"Seriously Noah," Jude said on the narrow staircase a few minutes later, "It's time you saw a doctor."

"It can wait until I've found a job."

"And what if it gets worse in the meantime? If you're worried over running out of money, I still have some of what you lent me when I—"

"No." Noah scratched above his right elbow through his sleeve. "But I appreciate the offer."

At the bottom of the staircase, they stood aside to allow room for Horace Fletcher, who had fallen in behind them on the first floor and tromped down the steps like a company of infantrymen without thought for those still asleep.

"Everyone on his floor is ready to hang him," Jude muttered as the utility actor disappeared through the dining room doorway. "And by the way, it's quite selfish of you . . . not taking some of your own money back for a doctor."

"How is that selfish? You're already sharing your room."

"For which Mr. Savill charges you full rent." Jude's nostrils flared the tiniest bit. "Why was it all right for me to accept money from you, but you can't take some of it back from me? Is it because your *Lordship* is too high and mighty to—"

"Jude . . ." Noah glanced toward the open dining room door. He had asked Jude not to spread word of his title.

His friend continued, but with voice lowered. ". . . take charity from—"

Noah clapped a hand upon his shoulder. "I'll take the money, Jude. And thank you!"

The dining room was as tiny as any of the other rooms, with four seats available at each of two square cloth-covered tables. But as the lodgers kept varied hours, Noah had yet to see anyone have to stand to eat. Meals were served à la carte, with Mrs. Savill or her kitchen maid, Eweretta, standing by for portion control. From eight until nine, there were rolls and butter, sausages, wedges of yellow cheese, and tea or coffee. Sundays were the only variation of that theme, with ham and potato pancakes and poached eggs.

According to Jude, Mrs. Savill had realized long ago that those in-house for lunch were often absent from supper and vice versa. So to lighten her load, she cooked a huge kettle of soup to serve for both meals with crusty brown bread and butter. And to economize, every odd day's soup contained no meat. There was goulash soup on Mondays, lentil soup on Tuesdays, oxtail soup on Wednesdays, potato soup on Thursdays, hunter's stew on Fridays, and bean soup on Saturdays. The only sweets were at tea time, which included such savories as warm apple strudel or plum cake, with no seconds allowed, though coffee and tea were plenteous. Sundays were non-soup days, and again, the same meal was served for lunch and supper. On Sunday past it was *sauerbraten* with dumplings and red cabbage, and Noah had no complaint, for it was delicious both times.

"Your turn to watch the telephone, Carey," said Lionel Rye at their table that morning. The older actor had played utility roles at a dozen theatres, but his passion was the novel he was writing, and many times during the day Noah could hear the tattoo of typewriter keys as he passed the second-floor landing. "I'll relieve you after lunch."

"Yes, very well," Noah said, buttering his roll. After breakfast he accompanied Jude upstairs to fetch stationery and stamp and a copy of the *Midsummer Night's Dream* playscript he had borrowed from an actor on the second floor. He accepted reluctantly the fiver Jude dug out of an old flat tobacco tin he kept stashed in the short space beneath an ancient wardrobe.

"There's a doctor on the north side of Coventry, before you get to Piccadilly Circus," Jude advised, taking up bowler hat and umbrella.

In the sitting room, which also served as hotel lobby, an amiable fellow named Basil Manning sat at an ancient piano, softly singing his tenor part in the chorus in *H.M.S. Pinafore* at the Savoy.

> "He polished up the handle of the big front door,
> He polished up that handle so care-full-ee,
> That now he is the Ruler of the Queen's Nav-ee!"

Piano notes became even softer as Mr. Manning turned to give him an apologetic look. "Are you about to study lines?"

"Not until I've written home," Noah said, folding himself onto the low and lumpy brown sofa. "And I can block you out. Please continue."

As he picked up an outdated issue of *Era* from the lamp table to use as a lap desk, he returned the smile of Frau Roswalt, sitting in the light of the window and darning stockings, for which lodgers paid her a halfpenny each. She looked fragile, with skeletal fingers pulling a needle through the wool, but according to Jude, she could reach and hang up the telephone on the adjacent wall in mid-ring. Mr. Savill simply shrugged whenever anyone complained, and with every lodger certain he was but one telephone call away from a job or better opportunity, guard duty was the only option.

With a novice's optimism, Noah had hoped his first letter home would bear good news. But he had failed to land a part in yet another casting call, held yesterday at the Gaiety Theatre on the Strand for a minor part in Henry Jones's *Heart of Hearts*.

Before I even opened my mouth, the stage director thanked me for coming and said I was too tall, Noah wrote while scratching his chest through his shirt.

Someone in the greenroom had warned that the lead actor was self-conscious over his height and wanted no one towering over him onstage. I shrank down in my clothes as much as possible without being obvious. But I'm much more optimistic about the audition Thursday at Marylebone Theatre for *A Midsummer Night's Dream*. You won't be embarrassed if I win the part of Bottom, will you?

He did not mention the itching. What would be the point of worrying her? After sealing the envelope and rising to drop it in the letter box, he studied the playscript until lunch, even though he had seen Shakespeare's play performed twice and read it three times over his lifetime. After lunch he set out on foot up Coventry Street, scanning the names upon bronze plaques outside doors. He found one inscribed with the incongruous name of *Amos Payne, Doctor of Medicine*.

"Step into my surgery and take off your coat and shirt," instructed the physician, who looked younger than Noah's twenty-seven years. He pressed his thumb into the rash upon Noah's upper arm. "Hmm. Not measles."

"I had them when I was an infant," Noah offered.

"Do you ever go out into rural areas?"

"Not since a week ago."

"A week ago?"

"I lived on a sheep farm in Yorkshire." Which was true, though he had started to say *estate* and changed his mind at the last second. The waiting room furniture and the desk inside the surgery looked expensive. His experience with Doctor Ryce had shaken his belief that all doctors chose their profession for altruistic reasons. He wished to give Doctor Payne no temptation to increase his bill.

"Hmm. That's it, then." The doctor backed up, folded his arms. "You've stumbled across some sort of poisonous plant. Some wild parsnip, probably."

"I can't recall doing so."

"You don't have to be in direct contact. Just being downwind from wild parsnip mixed in a pile of burning leaves can affect you."

Who burns leaves in July? Noah thought.

"Or petting a cat or dog whose fur rubbed against it," the doctor went on.

Noah nodded. In the course of visiting some of the tenants' cottages for farewells the Sunday afternoon before leaving, he had held Mrs. Gale's cat after the animal jumped up in his lap.

When he admitted such to Doctor Payne, the doctor smiled and said, "Lanolin will take care of the problem."

Thank you, Father! Noah prayed.

"But it may take several days," Doctor Payne went on, "with such a severe case as yours. Be patient."

"I can be patient," Noah said.

The examination and large jar of lanolin amounted to a reasonable twelve shillings and sixpence, causing Noah to feel guilty over his misgivings. Stepping over the threshold and out again onto the pavement of Coventry Street, he decided that he would deliver the good doctor a couple of theatre tickets as soon as he landed a part. And he was positive one waited just around the corner, now that the itching was on its way to being a thing of the past.

Twenty-One

*A*nd you say acting has been your dream ever since you were a child?" asked the reporter for the Arts section of the *London Chronicle* in Muriel's parlour on the afternoon of the twentieth of July. Mr. Fines's dark hair was heavily oiled and divided by a precision part above the beginning of his left eyebrow. The pencil in his long fingers made curious swirls and loops upon his notebook page, symbols he had explained to Muriel as "shorthand."

"Yes," Muriel replied, allowing sentiment to soften her voice. "My parents took me to see *The Countess Cathleen* when I was nine. I was smitten! Afterward I gathered my little playfellows into the garden, where we staged our own production for parents and servants. Naturally I played the part of the countess."

Mr. Fines was smiling as the pencil moved. It paused a second later, and he looked up. "Are you quite sure it was *The Countess Cathleen,* Lady Holt? Yeats only wrote it six or seven years ago."

Muriel rolled her eyes prettily. "Well, it couldn't have been that, then, could it have?"

The reporter chuckled. "The actual play doesn't really mat—"

"It was *Hamlet,*" Muriel corrected with no fear of contradiction, for she reckoned Shakespeare had been dead for at least a hundred years. "And I pretended to be Ophelia."

The pencil began moving again, stopped. "Yet you never gave serious thought to auditioning until only months ago. Why is that, Lady Holt?"

Staring off dreamily into the space just above the reporter's shoulder, Muriel mustered a melancholy little smile. "I married

young and put my aside my dream to devote my life to my late husband. And then I had an infant child to tend." She straightened in
her chair. "But I have no regrets for any of that, Mr. Fines."

"No, of course not." When Mr. Fines's pencil ceased moving, he
looked up and said, after a brief hesitation, "The interaction between
you and Mr. Whitmore onstage is quite remarkable and, as I'm sure
you're aware, has sparked rumors of romance. Would there be any
truth . . . ?"

"Absolutely not," Muriel replied stiffly. How many times must
she hear that question?

"Forgive me, Lady Holt, but I'm compelled to ask."

"Yes, I understand," she said, voice softening. It would not
behoove her to offend a writer for the *Chronicle*. "It's just that I still
miss my husband."

Now it was Mr. Fine's voice that softened. "Do you?"

Muriel closed her eyes for a second, opened them. "Every time I
step out onstage, Mr. Fines, I imagine Lord Holt is there in the front
row, smiling, encouraging me on. It's for him that I perform."

The reporter was staring at her as if caught up in the same vision.
He cleared his throat, scribbled some more marks on the page, and
smiled. "May I take a photograph, Lady Holt? You with your daughter, perhaps?"

"But of course." Muriel had anticipated this request and had
instructed Prescott to give Georgiana her after-lunch nap earlier so
that she would be awake. She rather liked it that most reporters rel-
ished the poignancy of her situation—beautiful young widow balancing a stage career and motherhood. She nodded at Joyce, who stood
just inside the door in case she was needed, and the servant left.
While they waited, Mr. Fines explored the room for the best lighting
angle, finally asking permission to close a curtain. Muriel had just
settled into the chair he had positioned in front of the curtain when
Prescott and Georgiana came through the doorway.

"Mummy," the child said, letting go of her nanny's hand and
hurrying over to Muriel with only a passing glance at Mr. Fines. She
looked like an angel in the white lawn-and-lace dress, chosen by
Muriel earlier so that there would be well-defined contrast between
it and her own sage-green gown in the sepia tones of a magazine
photograph.

"Good afternoon, Georgiana," Muriel said, lifting her daughter. "Did Mother's girl have a good nap?"

Georgiana wrinkled her little nose. "I not like nap. I want to go Laplan. Mummy go to Laplan?"

"Not now, darling." She held her daughter by the waist and turned her to sit facing away from her. "Let's be a good girl and look at the nice gentleman."

Mr. Fines was smiling as he opened up a tripod and camera. "Laplan? Is that from a storybook?"

"She actually refers to Belgrave Square. That's where we take our daily stroll."

Muriel glanced at Prescott, standing now where Joyce had stood. The fact that the nursemaid was so obviously trying to keep judgment from her expression irritated her. So she had spoken before thinking; *anyone* could stumble momentarily in the presence of a reporter who would be putting her words into newsprint before the week was out. Unfortunately, it was too late to amend her words to *weekly* stroll.

Even weekly would be an exaggeration, Muriel realized with a little pang as Mr. Fines stepped forward to position her chin. How long had it been? Rehearsals for *The Ticket-of-Leave Man* consumed early afternoons, and then she had to squeeze in a nap. And as far as tucking Georgiana in at night, how could she manage that when she had to be at the theatre six nights weekly?

You're going to have to spend more time with her, she admonished herself. She'd start tomorrow, for the interview and photographs were taking up this afternoon, and she had to have an early supper before leaving for the theatre to have her makeup applied and hair arranged. Tomorrow she would shorten her nap by a half hour and go up to the nursery and play with Georgiana, or perhaps she'd take the walk with her in the Square.

"Now, let's smile pretty, shall we?" Mr. Fines said from behind his cloth, more to Georgiana than to Muriel.

"Smile, Georgiana," Muriel said through stretched lips.

After a meal of stewed veal sweetbreads with mushrooms and boiled asparagus—enough to ensure against her stomach growling onstage yet not enough to induce lethargy—she went upstairs to brush her teeth and collect her handbag.

"Good evening, Mrs. Beckingham!" she called breezily on her way from her front door to the waiting coach.

Her neighbor, climbing her steps with a parcel-bearing maid following, turned her head just enough to send Muriel a sour look. The maid did likewise. Muriel smiled and waved, delighted to have scored two hits with one arrow and secure in the knowledge that her reception at the Royal Court would be much warmer.

Actors and actresses, attendants and musicians ceased gossiping in corridors to smile and send her admiring looks; Grady grinned and waved a receipt ledger at her; Dorothy, the makeup girl, said it was a shame that stage lighting made it necessary to cover such fine skin with greasepaint; Jewel brought a jar of peppermints to her dressing room; Gillian, the hairdresser, wished that every actress's hair was as naturally curly, and Mrs. Allgood, the women's dresser, wished that for just one day in her life she could have as feminine a figure; Amanda Hill, understudy for the roles of Lady Audley and Alice Audley, asked for advice on how to laugh naturally in the scene with Robert Audley.

But the reception that really mattered, which made all others pale by comparison, still awaited her. It was for that one she prepared, while others in the greenroom chatted softly or, in Mr. Whitmore's case, sent her wistful glances. She fixed her eyes upon the door, practicing the deep-breathing exercises Charlotte Steel had taught her.

Presently Lewis, the callboy, stuck his blonde head into the room. "Lady Audley and Sir Michael!"

"Well, shall we?" Mr. Whitmore said, rising and crooking his elbow. He wore a blue velveteen coat, flowered waistcoat, cord breeches, and gaiters. His hair was frosted completely gray. Muriel smiled and extended her hand. She could bestow upon him the attention he craved, for he was now the wealthy and gullible Sir Michael, and she his young wife, Lady Audley.

They were met with roaring applause as they strolled arm in arm from the wings onto a set constructed to resemble a lime-tree walk with an ancient hall in the distance.

"Come along, come along, my dear Sir Michael, you shall have no rest today," Muriel said, quoting her lines, drinking in the applause but not allowing it to penetrate the identity she was to wear for the next two hours. "I'll take you all over the park and grounds, to see all the festivities I've arranged in honor of my dear husband, my pet—my treasure, my only joy!"

Richard Whitmore smiled as she reached up to pat his cheek. "Bless you, my dear, bless you! What a happy old man you make me!"

Only after the last bows were taken and the final curtain closed did she allow herself to become Muriel Holt again.

"Please do something with these," she said to the cleaning staff of the bouquets of roses that were beginning to crowd her dressing room.

"No, thank you," she said to Richard Whitmore's suggestion of a late supper in a café open for theatre staff until the wee hours.

"Certainly," she said to the dozen or so tenacious members of the audience waiting at the stage door, asking to have their playbills inscribed.

"Sorry," she said to the beggar holding out a battered hat as Ham escorted her to the coach.

Traces of clear starry sky were visible between tree boughs of Sloan Square and the rooftops of King's Road. Muriel stared out the coach windows and wondered what grand or noble thing she had done that God would favor her so. If only Douglas were home, her life would be perfect.

And it seemed that God had heard that thought and decided to grant it as well, for Mrs. Burles met her at the door and said, "Master Pearce is waiting in the parlour, your Ladyship."

"My brother?" Muriel said with hand over her racing heart.

"Yes, your Ladyship."

Muriel hurried into the room. But it was Bernard rising from the sofa. She could tell them apart even when they were children, and it was easier now, with Bernard a bit stouter. His expression was grim, and his hazel eyes, so like Douglas's, looked weary.

"Mother?" Muriel said as a knot formed in her throat. "Father?"

He shook his head. "They received a letter from a Bishop Bompas yesterday. He's the administrator for an Anglican mission and hospital in a mining town called Caribou Crossing. Douglas passed on there five weeks ago."

"H-how?"

Her brother came to her, opened up his arms. "Pneumonia."

They wept together, Bernard quietly and Muriel leaning against his chest while one sob after another tore from the pit of her stomach until her weakened limbs could no longer support her weight. At length Bernard led her to a chair and knelt beside her.

"The letter says Douglas made his peace with God during his final days," Bernard said gently. "That gives me great comfort, Muriel."

"I'd rather have Douglas than comfort," Muriel rasped.

The soles of Bethia's ankle boots barely met the pavement of Duke Street. She would have whistled if women were not frowned upon for doing so in public.

In her experience of designing costumes for the Royal Court, she had never procured the complete range of fabrics needed without shopping all over London. But she had caught Spencer, Turner & Boldero just as the shelves had been restocked and found everything she needed. She could not wait to inform Jewel and the seamstresses. And Grady, who cared little for costumes, would be pleased to learn that the establishment had offered a ten percent discount in the hopes that Bethia would visit them first the next time.

She turned left onto Oxford Street, toward Oxford Circus Underground Station, and was still so deep in happy thoughts that she nearly collided with a gentleman stepping out from a shop.

"I beg your—" she began, her portfolio jostled from beneath her arm.

"My fault," the gentleman said gallantly, dropping to one knee to retrieve the sketches fanning out onto the pavement. When he looked up at her, Bethia's heart leapt to her throat.

"You're back!" Not only had he returned safely from the gold fields, but apparently the trek had been beneficial to him, for his face had fleshed out somewhat.

Bethia had not realized how heavy the weight of guilt had rested upon her shoulders until that instant, when it was lifted. She would have embraced Douglas but for the fear of re-igniting his infatuation with her.

The hazel eyes were completely devoid of recognition as he handed over her sketches. "I beg your pardon?"

It was only then that Bethia noticed the clerical collar. She had not seen Bernard Pearce since she was a young child, but Jewel had informed her that he was a vicar near Sheffield. He was staring at her, and she was compelled to explain herself, as the weight of guilt again settled upon her shoulders.

"I thought you were Douglas Pearce. But you're his brother, aren't you?"

"And you are . . . ?" he said taking her extended hand.

"Bethia Rayborn. Catherine and Jewel's—"

"Cousin," Reverend Pearce finished, nodding. If it were possible, he seemed older than his twin, for his face was haggard, with shadows beneath his eyes. He still held Bethia's hand, as if not realizing he was doing so. "I'm afraid Douglas has passed on, Miss Rayborn. I was just turning in the obituary for the newspapers."

Her wits abandoning her, Bethia looked at the door Bernard had come through just before their paths met. *Jay's Mourning Warehouse, est. 1841* was stenciled in dignified block letters upon the door glass. She had known of such establishments that catered to the needs of the bereaved, for Mother and Sarah had accompanied Claire Duffy to such a place to help her make arrangements when Mr. Duffy passed on.

The street noises, colors, snatches of conversation of people streaming past, Mr. Pearce mouthing something, his Douglas-like face washed with concern for *her,* her knees buckling. The next thing of which she was aware was an arm about her shoulders, leading her through the door she had noticed a second ago. Inside the establishment, lamps set about on tables and stands, rolls and rolls of black and gray cloth created a somber, almost ethereal atmosphere. She was led to a dark green velvet settee; Reverend Pearce sat beside her while another gentleman in a black frock coat brought over a steaming cup.

"There, there now," Reverend Pearce was saying, pressing the cup into her hands, helping her hold it. "Drink this. It will make you feel better."

She took a sip. The tea was too heavily sugared, but the warmth helped bring her back to reality.

Enough to realize the horror of the situation. The man beside her had lost a brother, and here he was comforting her. Tears burned her eyes.

"I'm so sorry," she said, shaking her head. "He went there because of me."

Reverend Pearce took the cup from her hands and handed it to the frock-coated man, thanking him. The man nodded, went over to sit at a small desk and picked up a pen. Apparently, tears were not unusual in Jay's, for the patrons and other shop assistants hardly looked their way. Bethia fished a handkerchief from her bag, blew her nose, and turned her face toward Reverend Pearce again.

He ceased mopping his face with his own handkerchief and looked at her. "I loved my brother, Miss Rayborn. But he acted against the counsel of everyone in our family."

"You don't understand." Bethia sniffed. "I sent him a horrible letter."

"I know of the letter."

But of course, Muriel would have informed him. Bethia squeezed her eyes shut, rocking herself slightly. "I'm so sorry, Mr. Pearce. So sorry."

Her hand was once again enveloped by his. "Everyone has the potential of acting rashly when provoked, Miss Rayborn. I knew my brother's flaws. Do you suppose you were the first young woman he hounded?"

"What do you mean?"

He shook his head regretfully. "A neighbor's daughter in Shef-field—Iris Ravensworth was her name. Her father finally sent her to live with an aunt somewhere."

The pain so obvious in his kind face told Bethia that he was not fabricating this in an effort to lessen her guilt. He went on. "The reason I say *somewhere*, Miss Rayborn, is that Mr. Ravensworth refused to inform even our father where she was sent for fear of Douglas finding out. He was but seventeen."

He could produce one hundred such examples, and Bethia knew she would still regret writing that letter. But she did feel somewhat better. Better enough to know that it was wrong of her to take advantage of Reverend Pearce's state of bereavement for her own consolation. She was about to thank him for his kindness when his eyes assumed a faraway look and he began speaking again, softly, as if more to himself than to Bethia.

"I understand how his mind worked. Our parents indulged us to the point where we had no strength of character for dealing with refusal."

"And yet you became a minister," Bethia said, not certain if she should insinuate herself into his musings.

His smile was touched with more irony than sadness. "I actually chose the church because I thought it would be easier than selling insurance. Then I met God along the way."

"He changed you," Bethia said, chill bumps prickling her arms.

"God, and my wife, Agatha. She threatened to go back home to her parents until I grew up."

From somewhere in the ethereal recesses of Jay's Mourning Warehouse drifted the sonorous tones of Westminster chimes in a long-case clock. Mr. Pearce patted her hand. "Well, I've much to do. We're having a memorial Saturday."

Bethia took the hint and rose to her feet so that he would feel free to do likewise. But she had to ask. "How is Lady Holt?"

He got to his feet, hesitated. "Not well, I'm afraid."

She felt the sting of tears still again. How would she feel if something happened to Danny? *Poor Muriel.* "If only there were something I could do."

"Just pray for her. I telephoned Jewel and Catherine a little while ago. They're probably with her as we speak."

"Would you extend . . ." Bethia swallowed. Extend what? Her condolences to the family? Jewel and Catherine and Aunt Virginia would accept them, yes. But Muriel . . . probably never.

She had to try. "May I write to her?"

"Yes." He opened the door for her. "Do that, if you wish. It may help."

"Thank you for being so kind, Reverend Pearce," she said, offering her hand as they reached the pavement, wishing there was something she could do to lighten his burden, as he had so lightened hers.

He took her hand, patted it. "Ah, but it's no sacrifice to be kind to someone as gracious as yourself, Miss Rayborn."

Just as they were turning to go their separate ways, Bethia heard him speak her name.

"Miss Rayborn?"

"Yes?" she said, facing him again.

"I haven't thought about this in years, but . . . when I was a boy, your family had a gardener by the name of . . ."

"Mr. Duffy," Bethia supplied.

"That's it." He pursed his lips remorsefully. "I'm afraid I once kicked him in the shin, when he was only trying to protect our horses. Will you please convey to him how terribly sorry I am?"

She nodded. "I will."

"Or perhaps I should ring him."

"He doesn't really use the telephone. I'll deliver the message. You have enough on your shoulders right now."

Relief washed over his face. "Thank you, Miss Rayborn."

As Bethia walked toward the underground station, automatically circumventing lampposts and people, she prayed silently. *Forgive me for lying, Father.* There had been enough talk of death. She could not bear to add to it.

At Royal Court, Grady ceased packing papers into a satchel and came over to take her hands. "Will you sit down, Bethia? I'm afraid I have some sad news."

"I already know," she said as her throat tightened. "I happened upon Bernard."

"You're not to go blaming yourself for anything."

She did not have the strength to bear another discussion of the degree of her innocence in the tragedy. So she nodded and said, "Thank you, Grady."

He studied her face suspiciously. "Go on home, Bethia. I'll send word up to wardrobe."

"Thank you," she said again.

By the time she reached Hampstead, Aunt Virginia had telephoned with the news.

"Such a pity," Mother said.

That afternoon she took a walk down Cannonhall Road, to the churchyard of Christ Church. Fresh Michaelmas daisies fanned out in purple glory from a stone crock before Mr. Duffy's headstone.

"Hello, Mr. Duffy," Bethia said. "Reverend Pearce asks your forgiveness for his kicking you when he was a boy."

She was perfectly aware that the tenderhearted old man was nowhere near the churchyard. He was probably happily tending celestial gardens. But hopefully God, who heard everything, would pass the message on.

Twenty-Two

*T*o every thing there is a season, and a time to every purpose under the heaven: A time to be born, and a time to die . . .'"

Bernard's voice filled the nave of Holy Cross Chapel in the village of Gleadless, five miles south of Sheffield. Father's associates at Sun Insurance in Sheffield were there. Aunt Virginia and Uncle James, Catherine and Hugh and their three sons. Jewel and Grady. Christina Smith and Georgiana Crane, cousins-twice-removed on Mother's side, with their husbands and children.

Mr. Rowley, manager of Sun Insurance in London, with his wife.

Father had said it was decent of them to come, considering Mr. Rowley had been forced to give Douglas the sack for missing so much work. It was only for her father's sake that Muriel had not ordered the couple to leave; however, she had treated them with no more than icy civility, even when Mrs. Rowley gushed that she had enjoyed *Lady Audley's Secret* so much that she bought tickets for her grown children and their spouses.

"'. . . time to weep, and a time to laugh; a time to mourn, and a time to dance . . .'"

With typical British ingenuity, the mourning industry marketed black handkerchiefs that would not stand out against mourning clothes. Muriel watched her mother beside her, so frail and crooked, wipe her lined cheeks with one, watched her father blow his nose into another.

We don't even have a body to bury, Muriel thought. No grave to visit. He lay in ground that had never been home to him, surrounded by strangers.

After the memorial, people came to her parents' house. Servants passed around trays of little sandwiches and cakes. At length the men gathered in the sitting room, the women in the parlour. Both rooms were equally somber, but at least some of the men had the distraction of their cigarettes and pipes. And then the guests left, a few at a time, their relief to be doing so visible through the cracks of their somber veneers.

Through it all Muriel's parents moved about like sleepwalkers. Mother's doctor had given her a sedative this morning, but even Father's motions and speech were sluggish. Wednesday morning, Jewel, Catherine, and their families left again for London, and Uncle James left for the school of which he was headmaster outside Hathersage, though Aunt Virginia stayed on. Without the distraction of so many visitors, sadness pressed down upon the house and settled into the corners.

Only the children were spared—Georgiana, and Bernard's little Sally. Nanny Prescott and Agatha kept the two out in the garden as much as possible. Muriel envied their innocent ignorance of the tragedy.

Condolence letters arrived daily. Bernard and Aunt Virginia were the only ones to open them, though occasionally Mother would have one read aloud to her, then dissolve into tears. Muriel could not bring herself to read any, for what could anyone write that would make her grieve for Douglas any less? Bernard was mindful to inform her whenever a letter arrived from someone of her acquaintance, such as cast members from the Royal Court, Richard Whitmore, and even Charlotte Steel. Incredibly, there were even letters from some of Muriel's neighbors on Belgrave Square.

Thursday morning, Muriel pretended to sleep while listening to Aunt Virginia dress. She was grateful when her aunt crept out of the room they shared without attempting to rouse her. She would stall going downstairs for as long as possible. Wallowing in misery left very little energy for comforting her parents, and the thought of facing everyone at breakfast was too fatiguing. But it was impossible to drift back into sleep again, now that the torturous thoughts were stirred into activity, so she sat up against her pillows and worked on her lines from the playscript of *The Ticket-of-Leave Man*.

"Come in," she said a half hour later at the odd knocking that seemed to come from the bottom part of her door, as if from the toe of a shoe.

"Can't."

She pulled on her wrapper and crossed the room. Bernard stood in the corridor, balancing a tray upon each hand. He lowered one to show her a small pot of tea with cup and saucer and two thick slices of buttered toast resting upon a napkin. "Thought you might be hungry."

"You dear," she said, truly touched. She stood on tiptoe to kiss his cheek.

"Careful now," he said, but with a pleased smile.

Muriel took the tray. "Who's the other for?"

"Father." One hand free, Bernard reached into his coat pocket. His expression grew anxious. "This came yesterday. I wasn't sure if you were ready for it."

"Who is—?" Muriel noticed the Hampstead return address and shook her head. "Thank you for breakfast, Bernard. But I'm not interested in anything she has to say."

"Please, Muriel. What can it hurt to read it?"

"I can't believe you're *still* taking her side," Muriel said. She jostled the tray, causing a couple of drops of tea to leap from the spout. "He was your brother too. Your *twin*, for mercy's sake!"

"I miss him as much as you do," Bernard said with eyes reddening. "But I refuse to make a *saint* of him!"

At the sound in the corridor, Bernard turned, and Muriel looked over his shoulder. Father stood blinking at them, the suit he wore yesterday wrinkled as if he had slept in it.

"I heard voices?" he murmured.

"Just delivering some breakfast, Father," Bernard said.

Muriel softened her voice for her father's sake, took the envelope. "Thank you, Bernard."

But once Bernard stepped away, Muriel closed the door and tore up the envelope without breaking the seal. Bethia Rayborn could send a thousand pages, begging forgiveness on every line, but Muriel would never forgive her for the misery upon her parents' faces for as long as she lived.

"I want the stockings rolled, not folded," Muriel instructed her mother's maid, Florence, on Friday evening. Tomorrow would be one week since the memorial, and she, Georgiana, and Nanny Prescott would be leaving.

"Very good, Lady Holt."

Aunt Virginia was putting one of Muriel's hats into a box, while Mother sat in the corner chair. The two sisters hardly looked related; Aunt Virginia, softly rounded and energetic despite her gray hair, and Mother, thin and fretful. The only remnant of beauty remaining were Mother's dreamy brown eyes, but even now, pain and loss often dulled them to flatness.

"You don't plan to go right back to work, do you Muriel?" Aunt Virginia asked.

"I'm afraid so," Muriel replied.

"Can you not stay longer?" Mother came out of her lethargy long enough to ask.

Aunt Virginia nodded. "I'm sure Jewel and Grady appreciate your dedication. But they would understand if you took more time off."

"I'm needed there. *Lady Audley's Secret* closes next Saturday night. And we're in rehearsals for the next show."

She actually looked forward to all of it. Working all day, sleeping all night would allow very little time for gloomy thoughts. And she needed applause like an addict his opium.

"Jewel says Muriel's a big hit," Aunt Virginia said, trying to brighten Mother's mood.

"Yes?" Mother said, but her expression had faded again, and Muriel knew that her thoughts were a long way from the theatre.

An hour later, when the women were downstairs, Muriel thought over Aunt Virginia's words. While she grieved Douglas with all her heart, she could not help but wonder how the critics would react to her returning to the stage so soon after suffering another tragic loss. Words like *courage* and *dedication* popped into her mind, followed by a tremendous rush of guilt.

I'd give it all up if you could be back here, Douglas!

From out of the gloom another thought struck her. She had the power to avenge his death. Not in a huge way, but a little revenge was better than no revenge at all.

"I'm afraid I'll need to stay another week," Muriel said into the telephone mouthpiece Saturday morning. "Mother and Father are still having a difficult time of it. I should be here for them."

It was the absolute truth, she reminded herself, which eased her conscience over manipulating her cousin.

"We understand," Jewel's voice said over the line. "Stay as long as you need to."

Of course Jewel would say that. But Muriel knew her well and could hear the disappointment she was so carefully attempting to conceal.

"I suppose Miss Hill is delighted for this opportunity."

"I wouldn't say *delighted* . . ."

"Oh, you know what I mean," Muriel said. "How is she doing?"

There was a hesitation, then an overenthusiastic, "She's quite capable. She's learned a lot from watching you. Attendance hasn't fallen as dramatically as we had feared."

But it's fallen, nonetheless, Muriel thought, replacing the receiver. Her absence was felt. That was all she needed to know. By the time she sat out another week, Jewel and Grady would be even more committed to her staying on at the Royal Court.

And there would be one condition to that.

"She'll be away another week," Jewel said after hanging up the telephone. "Aunt Phyllis and Uncle Norman need her."

"I knew life was moving along too well for us," Grady muttered, tapping his pencil against the open receipt ledger on his desk.

"Grady . . ." she said with a reproachful look, shocked at this display of uncharacteristic coldheartedness. Especially considering how often he wiped tears during Douglas's memorial service.

"Forgive me, darling Jewel." He appeared perilously close to tears again and said with voice soft, "I don't know what came over me. You lost your cousin, and here I sit grousing over numbers."

How could she not forgive him? She gave him an understanding little smile. "It's your job to grouse over numbers."

"But not to the degree where they're all that matters."

"Well, we've people dependent upon us. It's not just *our* rent that's affected if we don't make a profit."

But it did seem as if God had decided that they had sailed along on favorable winds for long enough.

On a positive note, rehearsals for *The Ticket-of-Leave Man* were going on well. It was the story of Robert Brierly, framed and falsely imprisoned because a notorious underworld thief desires the love of his fiancée, May Edwards. After serving his time, Robert conceals his identity to gain employment at a bank, only to be blackmailed by the same underworld thief. Amanda Hill was gamely rehearsing Muriel's role as May Edwards, in addition to playing Lady Audley in the evenings. With Muriel such a quick study and perfectionist, Jewel had no worry over her cousin stepping up to the lead role once she returned.

"You know, we've just gotten spoiled," Jewel said. "We need these reminders of how vulnerable we are now and again, so we don't take our blessings for granted."

She remembered those words on the following Monday, the first of August, when they received another such reminder. Lewis, the callboy, burst into the office to inform them that Oscar Hicks, understudy for the lead role of Robert Brierly, had collapsed during rehearsals. Jewel waved Grady on and rang Doctor Ramsdell, whose office was on nearby Symons Street.

When she hurried to the stage, Grady and Richard Whitmore knelt on either side of the groaning man. Cast and crew stood about with helpless expressions or hovered over the trio with helpful suggestions.

"Hang in there, Mr. Hicks," Grady was saying.

"What is it?" Jewel asked.

Mr. Whitmore shook his head. "Don't know. He says he's been having pains in his abdomen."

By late afternoon Mr. Hicks was admitted to St. George's Hospital, where the source of the pains was determined to be gallstones. He underwent surgery the following morning.

"How is he?" Jewel asked when Grady returned.

"He was still feeling the effects of the ether when I left." Grady gave a little chuckle. "He addressed me as 'Mr. Whitmore' more than once. I was quite flattered, I must say."

"And the surgery?" Jewel said pointedly, her nerves frayed from begging the secretaries of the *Era* and the *Stage* to squeeze in last-minute casting call advertisements in their August issues.

"It went well, so says his surgeon." Grady paused, pursed his lips, and shook his head. "I've forgotten his name already. I hate that. He was a real decent fellow too. Didn't speak to us as if we were imbeciles."

"Well, we've missed the deadlines for the trade magazines."

"It was one of those long aristocratic names. Began with a *C*. That much I do remember."

Jewel closed her eyes and rubbed the space between her brows. She did not know if she preferred the Grady who worried or the Grady who occasionally strayed down irrelevant paths to refrain from worrying. "Have you heard a word I've said?"

"Heard you? Why, yes." Grady advanced to his own desk. His revolving chair squeaked with his weight. "Advertising wouldn't help anyway, dearest. By the time the papers hit the stands, we'll only have eight days until opening night. Not much time for rehearsals."

"Perhaps Mr. Hicks will have recovered by then?" Jewel said with faint hope. After all, she knew nothing of how long it took to recover from gallstone surgery.

Grady shook his head. "Two weeks in the hospital, another month at home, perhaps even two." He slapped a palm lightly upon his desk top. "*Cavendish!* That was his name."

This was not a disaster, Jewel reminded herself, picking up her pencil again and rotating it with her fingers. Not when one positioned this on a scale of possible disasters. A disaster would be the theatre burning down during a production, killing everyone inside. The Thames flooding and sweeping the building away, killing everyone inside. An earthquake . . .

"We'll post signs about town." Grady's voice broke her morbid train of thought. "Devote a day to auditions."

Jewel shuddered. While they could assume that most people who read the trade papers had a least a little stage experience, posted signs would also draw in people simply following a whim, figuring they had nothing to lose. Reminding herself that Muriel had followed a whim by auditioning simply reinforced that belief. Lightning did not strike the same place twice.

But what other choice had they? Lead roles required skilled understudy actors, and none of the utility actors in the company had

Richard Whitmore's height and stage presence.

She was about to mention all of this to Grady when he came to that conclusion himself. Rising from his desk again, he said, "No good, posting signs. Every petty thief in town would consider it an invitation to wander the corridors. I should give the cast a report on Mr. Hicks. Why don't you call about, love, see if anyone knows someone who's looking."

For an understudy role? Jewel thought, taking her address book again from the top drawer. No one ever *looked* for such a role. In an actor's eyes, that was the reward for not being *quite* as talented or famous as the lead. To understudy for a healthy lead actor meant staying in the background, playing utility parts such as crowd and bystander scenes, and when granted the lead during a matinee or odd night now and again, pretending not to hear the disappointed murmurings as he steps out on stage.

"No one so far," she said when Grady returned.

"Ah, well . . ." He showed her an Irving Street address scribbled in pencil on the back of a yellowed playbill for *The Foundling of the Forest*. "Mr. Rigby says there is a tall, good-looking fellow in his lodging house who has some experience on the York stage—and has been chasing down auditions."

"Hmm. If he's any good, why hasn't he found a job?"

"Apparently he's only been down here but for two, three weeks. What do you think . . . shall we give him a ring?"

By *we,* Jewel knew he meant *you.* She sighed and dropped the paper upon her desk. "I'm too hungry to think. Let's have lunch, then we'll telephone." By *we'll,* she meant *I'll.*

———

"Thank you," Noah said, pushing out his chair in the dining room. "That was delicious."

He was not overly fond of lentil soup, but today's batch contained bits of bacon. Mrs. Savill came over as if to pick up his empty bowl and spoon, but instead eyed him critically.

"Why do you scratch yourself, Mister Carey?"

He did not realize anyone had noticed. He had tried to be so discreet, even hiding his hands with the bloody whelps on the backs. But the itching was driving him mad, despite the fact that he felt like a basted Christmas goose from all the lanolin. Yesterday it had distracted him so during the audition at the Criterion Theatre for E. V. Seebohm's *Little Lord Fauntleroy* that he lost his place in the script not once, but twice.

"I'm sorry, I—"

"I cannot allow lice in my house."

Cheeks on fire, Noah glanced at the three other lodgers in the room. They had ceased spooning soup into their mouths to watch. "My head doesn't itch, Mrs. Savill. I've seen a doctor, and it's not lice, I assure—"

"We will see. You will come with me."

Like a little boy, he followed her into the kitchen, up a narrow flight of stairs, and into the tiny courtyard. Towels hung limply on the clothesline, and an herb garden sent out scents that would have been pleasant were he not so humiliated. The landlord's wife motioned toward the lone bench, and he sat and submitted to the further indignity of her digging fingers through his hair as if they were monkeys at the Zoological Garden.

"Be still!" she ordered.

"Sorry."

In the pursuit of steady employment and absorbed as he was by the itching, he had not taken note of the significance of today's date until that very moment. The second of August. What a far cry from waiting at Saint Thomas's altar for his bride to walk up the aisle.

Paying your dues, Noah reminded himself for the hundredth time. What choice had he if he wanted to stay? Besides, he was beginning to wonder if lice were the culprits after all.

"Hmph!" Mrs. Savill said finally, taking a step backward. "What does the doctor say?"

Noah blew out a breath. "That a poisonous plant caused it. But I'm treating it with lanolin, and it should be better with time."

"Lanolin?"

"It's a salve. It comes in a jar."

"Very well. You do that, and stop scratching or you have to leave. You frighten the others away."

"Yes . . . sorry."

"You want more soup?"

"No, thank you." He could not be dragged by his heels back

into that dining room. He would stay out here until he was certain the other three lodgers had finished. Opening the door for her, he said, "Will you tell the others I don't have lice?"

"I'll tell them."

Returning to the bench, he folded his arms, crossed his knees, and listened to the street noises. The pattering of an automobile engine reached his ears. He had seen three since arriving in London and ordinarily would have hurried to the front for a look.

Am I being punished, Father? he prayed beneath his breath. With the fact that this was his wedding date fresh upon his mind, he realized he could have handled the situation with Olivia with more tact, somehow. He did not regret not marrying her, but the anger and bewilderment upon her face, her family's faces, still made him cringe inside. He should have gone home and cooled off for several days after meeting with Miss Spear. Perhaps asked Miss Spear's permission to confide in Vicar Norris, ask his counsel. He could not even recall praying over the matter.

Perhaps, rather, his offense was not finding a church in London, he thought, scratching his arm through his sleeve. Or even accompanying Jude to the Presbyterian chapel just a block down Irving. God was a member of no denomination. The itching, which was his excuse, did not keep him away from casting calls, disasters that they were. Could he not spare an hour a week to worship, as he had since a child?

I'll do better, Father, he promised—even if he was never relieved of this condition and itched until his hands had to be tied to keep him from scratching off his skin. For it was wrong to try to bargain with the Almighty. But he could not stop himself from hoping that God would be pleased enough with his resolve to work a miracle this time.

An hour later, it was all he could do to keep from shedding his coat and shirt and rolling in the grass in Leicester Square like a dog with fleas. "That's the largest jar you have?" Noah asked in the Boot & Company Limited drugstore on Leicester Street.

The chemist cocked an eyebrow and grinned. "Have you been eating the stuff?"

"Heh-heh," Noah obliged, resisting the urge to reach over the counter and grab the man by the collar. He realized his reddened hand was resting upon the counter, in plain sight, and shifted it to his pocket.

"That's quite a rash you have there," the chemist said.

The sympathy on the man's bearded face disposed Noah to think more favorably of him. "It's driving me mad, quite frankly." He could only shudder at the thought of how much worse it would be, were he not faithfully applying the lanolin twice a day. He would be in Bedlam by now.

"Seen a doctor?"

"He's the one who recommended lanolin. He believes I came in contact with some sort of poisonous plant up in Yorkshire."

The chemist leaned forward to rest an elbow upon the counter. "Hmm."

"What is it?" Noah asked.

"When were you last in Yorkshire?"

Noah thought for a second. "Three weeks ago to the day."

"Well then, you should be better by now."

"I've wondered . . ."

"I've had patrons complain of soap allergy," the chemist said. "They use one brand for years and suddenly they're covered with a rash."

"We've used Swan Soap for as long as I can remember," Noah said. In fact, his mother had packed a half dozen cakes among his bath towels and face flannels.

"It's fine soap. We use it at home. But it was *Swan* my neighbor's cook was using when her skin broke out into rashes. I recommended she switch brands, and—" he raised himself to snap his fingers— "it cleared up within days."

Even though the man behind the counter did not have a diploma from the Royal Medical College on the wall of a posh waiting room, the authority in his voice and his gray hair made Noah take him just as seriously. Cautious optimism swept away the despair that had so plagued him for weeks.

"What brand would you recommend?" he asked.

The chemist smiled and produced a round cake wrapped in silver wax paper. *Peerless Erasmic Herb Soap* was written in script on the label, beside an etching of a young woman holding up a looking glass. In smaller block letters were the promising words *Recommended by the Medical Profession for Improving & Preserving the Complexion.*

Gladly, Noah dipped into his pocket for his purse. "I don't suppose I need continue the lanolin. . . ."

"Not unless you're fond of wasting your money," the chemist said, sweeping the jar into his palm. "It's the soap, young man. I'd wager my last shilling."

Outside again, paper bag clutched in one hand, the other discreetly scratching his ribs beneath his coat, Noah caught himself smiling in the reflected glass of a milliner's shop. *Thank you, Father!* This time he was going to get relief. He just knew it.

A short barrel-chested man about Noah's own age, with gray eyes sunk into bulldog-like cheeks, was leaving the lodging house. He glanced at Noah and reached back to stop the door from closing.

"Thank you," Noah said, catching the door with his free hand.

"You're welcome." But instead of standing aside, the man squinted up at him and said with a faint trace of Irish brogue, "Would you happen to be Noah Carey?"

In spite of his most recent spate of optimism, the first thought in Noah's mind was *Olivia.* Not satisfied with the money she had bled from him, she had hired a local attorney to try for more.

You're closer to Bedlam than you think, Noah chided himself, and dropped the bag into his coat pocket so that he could offer a hand. "I am. And you are . . . ?"

"Grady McGuire," the man replied, smile widening as they shook hands. "I'm from the Royal Court Theatre. Mrs. McGuire tried to telephone you, but the connection was broken each time. May we walk to that coffeehouse across the street for a chat?"

ill Mr. Hicks be allowed fruit when he leaves the hospital?" Jewel asked Mr. Birch, who, according to him, had endured so many surgeries that his skin resembled a patchwork quilt.

The head attendant paused from counting the playbills stacked upon Grady's desk to shake his aged head. "Not for weeks. Get him a wheel of mild cheese. Wensleydale, for example. But the family would appreciate the fruit."

"I believe I'll get a ham as well."

"A ham would be nice."

"I don't understand the logic of taking flowers to sick people," Jewel went on, ignoring the commonplace sounds of footfalls in the corridor. "Food is more practical."

"Quite so," Mr. Birch agreed. "And a basket of fruit is every bit as attractive as a—"

The door opened and Grady walked in, followed by a tall, strapping fellow with Roman nose, high forehead, and ink-black hair. "Jewel, may I introduce Mr. Carey?"

Mr. Birch had been around long enough to know that was his signal to excuse himself. He would probably eavesdrop through the greenroom wall, but since the whole cast and crew knew they were searching for a replacement for Mr. Hicks, Jewel was not overly concerned. The old fellow had but few thrills remaining to him.

"And may I introduce my wife, Mrs. McGuire," Grady continued as the door closed. "Will you have a seat, Mr. Carey?"

The actor gave Jewel a shy smile and folded himself into the chair facing Grady's desk. Grady pulled out his own chair.

"I've informed Mr. Carey that the opening is for Mr. Whitmore's understudy and will only be available until Mr. Hicks is able to return to work."

"It would be an honor to work with Mr. Whitmore during any length of time," Mr. Carey said, elbows resting upon chair arms. "I've read of his work in the *Strand*."

"And . . ." Grady said, his grin so wide that his jowls disappeared, "Mr. Carey has played the part of Robert Brierly in York!"

This was too good to be true. Cautiously, Jewel asked the actor, "Did Mr. McGuire inform you that the starting wage is three pounds weekly?"

He gave her a weary little smile. "At this point in my life, Mrs. McGuire, that seems a fortune."

The only hitch, Grady explained, was that Mr. Carey suffered a skin condition that was made intolerable by theatre lights.

Mr. Carey stared at the carpet, his cheeks flush.

"I said that he could read for us here in the office instead," Grady went on.

What were you thinking? Jewel sent her husband as puzzled a look as she dared without seeming rude to their visitor. She turned again to Mr. Carey.

"You do understand that we're not able to lower the lights during a performance. For the occasional evening or early morning scene, yes, but as a rule they burn full strength."

The actor raised his head again. He shifted in his chair. "Yes, I understand."

Regretfully, Jewel noticed his eyes were nice, a rich dark brown fringed by dark lashes. In fact, he had what they were always seeking: handsome face, imposing stature, and experience to boot. Perhaps down the road, if he recovered, they could find a part for him.

And then, perhaps not. Any fellow who would seek an audition and then declare that he could not work under stage lights had a problem that went deeper than the afflicted skin.

"But just today a chemist diagnosed the cause of my rashes," Mr. Carey continued. "I had developed an intolerance to soap. He informed me that switching brands will clear it up within days."

"Indeed?" Jewel had never heard of anyone not able to bear soap, but after a second's thought she recalled an actress who had

had to leave the profession a couple of years ago because even the smell of greasepaint broke her out into hives.

And Mr. Whitmore enjoyed excellent health, she reminded herself. He seldom put Mr. Hicks to use. Why, it could be weeks and weeks before Mr. Carey stepped out under the lights.

Jewel met her husband's hopeful look, smiled, and rose from her desk. "I'll get a couple of playscripts."

"How is Mr. Carey working out?" Grady asked when Jewel returned to the office on Friday during a break in rehearsals.

"You're a genius," she replied.

Grady beamed. "I like hearing you say that."

"And *I* like saying it."

Indeed, the understudy disaster had proved itself a tempest in a teapot. In spite of having already acted the role, for the past three days Mr. Carey had studiously observed rehearsals from the wing with playscript in hand. He arrived early, stayed late, and did not attempt to chat up the actresses or insinuate his presence in any way.

Of course part of the latter could be due to the wide berth that most members of the cast gave him. Jewel spared her husband the few rumblings that had met her ears, the fears that this newest cast member might have lice or even measles. Those would die of their own weight once Mr. Carey recovered.

Normalcy loomed promisingly on the horizon. Even though attendance would be weak for tonight's closing performance of *Lady Audley's Secret*, opening night for *The Ticket-of-Leave Man*—with Muriel back in the lead—was only eight days away. A promising start to the new season.

Which reminded Jewel. Bethia should be warned, hopefully to spare her any awkward moments.

"I believe I'll take Bethia to lunch," she said. "Will you stay here in case Muriel stops by? I'll bring yours back."

"But of course," said Grady, still glowing from her earlier compliment. He pushed his chair out from his desk. "I think I deserve a kiss before you leave, don't you?"

Jewel smiled and walked around his desk. A fraction of a second later, she was seated sideways upon her husband's knees.

"Someone could walk in," Jewel murmured after a nice long kiss, her head resting against his broad shoulder.

"I know," he replied, rubbing the small of her back. He sighed. "It's difficult sharing an office with a temptress. A lesser man would never be able to concentrate on his work."

"But then, you're a genius," she reminded him.

"A genius to marry you, love."

The wardrobe room was organized chaos, with some costumes hanging about on hooks and others draped over chairs and tabletops. Final fittings were scheduled for all of next week, in preparations for dress rehearsal on the twelfth of August. There were shadows under Bethia's eyes, her hair was gathered carelessly into a long scrap of fabric with frayed edges, and she wore a bandage about the finger she had gashed with a razor while letting out a seam yesterday.

"We've just some last-minute trim and buttons," Bethia informed Jewel as the two seamstresses sat at the drafting table, pulling needles and threads through a gown and a shirt.

"Have you had Mr. Carey up here?" Jewel asked.

"We've not had time. Hopefully Monday. But I spotted him in the wing, and it's fortunate that he appears to be the same size as Mr. Hicks. We may get by with altering what we have instead of having to make new costumes.

"There is no hurry," Jewel assured her. Understudy costumes were important but never top priority. "And he may be more comfortable in another three days."

Bethia nodded understanding. The seamstresses' heads bobbed likewise over their sewing. Jewel was not surprised that word of Mr. Carey's affliction had risen to the upper storeys.

"Come have some lunch with me," Jewel said after Bethia showed her the last finished costume, a peach-colored poplin gown for the character of Mrs. Willoughby.

"Oh, but we've too much to do."

"You can always spare the time to eat."

"But I brought—"

"Oh, go have some lunch," Miss Lidstone said, waving her on. "We'll give your sandwich to Lewis. He's always sniffing about for something to eat."

"Very well," Bethia said halfheartedly.

Jewel smiled and tugged on an end of the piece of trim, releasing the mop of Bethia's hair. She brushed the curls over her cousin's forehead with her fingers. "But first let's make you presentable."

They walked up the pavement to Capucine's, a bakery popular for its flaky meat pies as well as pastries. Because the time was barely past eleven, only one of the small round tables outside the bakery was occupied. Jewel shepherded Bethia to the one farthest out and ordered two pork pies and two cups of tea from the server.

"Are you all right, Bethia?" Jewel said, glad she had come up with the idea of spiriting her away from the theatre for a while.

Bethia pushed some of her hair back from her forehead. "Well, you know how final fittings are."

"But I've never seen you look so tired. Should we hire another seamstress, do you think?"

"Oh, no. I would be hard-pressed to find her something to do during slack times."

Jewel laughed. "What, exactly, is a slack time?"

That brought a smile to her cousin's face. The meat pies and tea arrived. Jewel cut the corner of her pie with a fork and became serious again.

"It's not just fittings, is it?"

"What do you mean?"

"You're thinking about Douglas."

Bethia did not reply, but the luster that came to her blue eyes was answer enough.

"What happened wasn't your fault, Bethia," Jewel said.

Her cousin pressed her lips together, nodded. "I accept that intellectually, Jewel. Most of the time. But my heart says otherwise."

"Then trust your intellect."

"I'm trying," Bethia said and mustered a smile. "Really, I am."

When they were halfway through their pies, Jewel could delay the inevitable no longer. "Muriel returns to town today."

"Poor Muriel." Bethia set down her fork. "Will she return to work?"

"She says she would like to."

"I'm not sure how I should behave when we're together," Bethia said, pushing away her plate a bit.

"That's understandable," Jewel said. "But I want you to know that I asked Bernard to speak with her when we were up there. He assured me he would inform her of some things in Douglas's past that the family kept from her at the time. She'll see how wrong it was to blame you."

Bethia blew out a breath, closed her eyes briefly. "Thank you, Jewel."

A roan horse was pulling away a hansom cab from the front of Royal Court Theatre when Jewel and Bethia drew near. It was not an unusual occurrence, and as Muriel's own coach and driver would have met her train and brought her by the theatre later, Jewel thought little of it. She and Bethia parted at the staircase inside, Bethia clutching the brown paper bag containing raspberry charlottes for the seamstresses and the remaining half of her pork pie for Lewis's bottomless pit.

Muriel was seated in the office, swathed in mourning clothes.

"Hello, Jewel."

"Muriel!" Jewel placed the bag containing Grady's two meat pies on a bare spot on his desk. Her cousin rose and allowed herself to be embraced.

"She's not even been home," Grady said.

"But where—?"

"I sent Georgiana and her nanny on to the house," Muriel said.

"You poor dear." Jewel held her cousin out by the shoulders. Through the black netting, Muriel's fair skin looked paler than ever. "You must be exhausted. Will you take some tea?"

"Tea would be nice," Muriel replied.

Mr. Birch appeared in the open doorway. "Shall I fetch some, Mrs. McGuire?"

"Yes, please," Jewel replied. With so many tea drinkers about, Mrs. Ainsley kept a couple of kettles simmering on the little stove behind the refreshment counter just before the lobby. They left the door open for Mr. Birch's return. As his footfalls faded, Jewel asked about the family.

"Mother drifts from chair to chair. Father has finally returned to work but rarely speaks. Bernard and your mother see to them as best as they can, but . . ." She shrugged. "It was good that I stayed that extra week after all."

Jewel had no idea what she meant by the 'after all'. Wasn't that the idea, to help out her parents? But then, Muriel was probably not thinking clearly.

Mr. Birch returned with a pot and three cups. Jewel took the sugar bowl and a spoon from the corner cupboard and served everyone. When the door closed behind the elderly man, Muriel took a sip, looked up, and said, "I'm afraid I have more bad news."

Jewel's cup froze halfway to her lips. She could not hear Grady hold his breath but knew he was doing so just by the rigid set of his shoulders.

"What is it, Muriel?" she said.

"It's Bethia Rayborn." Muriel pressed her lips into a line for a second. "I'm the last person to cause trouble, Jewel . . . Grady. And I appreciate all you've done for me. But I cannot continue being under the same roof as *her* every day. It's just too painful for me. I hope you'll understand."

All Jewel could do was stare.

"You can't mean that, Muriel," said Grady.

"It's not as if she needs money," Muriel said defensively, as if rattled by their silence. "You wouldn't be throwing her out into the streets. This is just her *hobby*, for heaven's sake."

Jewel sighed, set her cup on the desk, and rose to stand behind Grady's chair with hands upon his shoulders.

"I *don't* understand, Muriel."

"Nor I," Grady said softly. "Surely you've gotten over blaming her for Douglas."

"Didn't Bernard speak with you?" Jewel asked.

"Bernard." Muriel rolled her violet eyes. "He would have forgiven Napoleon. Bethia could have come to me, gone to you, done any number of things, but instead she sent that vile letter."

Deep breath, Jewel told herself, watching her cousin sip from her cup. "I'm sorry about Douglas, Muriel. I have fond memories of when we all played together as children. But he brought this upon himself."

"We're not discharging Bethia," Grady said.

Jewel nodded. "But if it would make you more comfortable, we'll ask her to leave the wardrobe room when you've appointments and have Miss Lidstone or Mrs. Hamby measure you from now on."

And it wouldn't break Bethia's heart, she thought, for word had reached her ears about Miss Lidstone having to take over the measuring once before because Muriel was being difficult. Bethia had not even complained but had replied when Jewel approached her about it, *"You're not to worry . . . I don't have to deal with her that often."*

Muriel raised her chin. "Then you'll have to find someone else for *The Ticket-of-Leave Man.*" A little bark of a laugh, then, "Perhaps you can persuade Daphne Lloyd to come back."

Faintly Jewel tasted blood and realized she had bitten the inside of her mouth. "You mentioned appreciation, Muriel. Is this how you show it? You've no idea of the gamble we took, putting you in a lead role. We could have lost our jobs for it."

After a sigh, Muriel replied, "Of course I'm grateful, Jewel. But you should also be grateful to me, don't you think? I filled your theatre again."

Jewel felt her husband's shoulders rise and fall. She knew what was coming. Grady was the most amiable, easygoing person she knew, but a difficult childhood had put something of a street fighter in him as well.

"We are grateful, Muriel," Grady said softly. "But we cannot allow extortion from anyone. Even you. If you walk out, you'll find no more stage work in London."

She gave him a wary look. "Perhaps you've not read my reviews, Grady McGuire."

"Perhaps *you've* not read the contract you signed for run-of-the-show. Petty vindictiveness is not an excuse for breaking it. We may be competitive with other theatres, but there is a certain code of honor we share. It comes down to this, Muriel. Do you wish to act or don't you?"

For what seemed like a full minute, the violet eyes stared across at him as if she were undecided if he were bluffing. And then Muriel lowered them, murmured, "I want to act."

Jewel circled around to her, took the cup from Muriel's hand, and set it on another one of the rare bare spots on Grady's desk. She put her arms about her cousin's shoulders. After a second, Muriel leaned her head against her as much as her hat would allow.

"You've suffered a great loss, darling Muriel," Jewel said, patting her shoulder. "Taking it out on Bethia . . . on *anyone,* won't bring Douglas back to us."

Eventually she heard a sigh, a small voice. "I know."

Darting a relieved glance at her husband, Jewel said, "Let me take you home."

"I have a cab waiting."

"Then I'll ride with you, keep you company."

"I don't want company, Jewel. I just want to go home and nap."

"Very well." Jewel helped her to her feet.

Grady, rising from his chair as well, said gently, "You'll forgive me for speaking so bluntly with you?"

"Yes, Grady," Muriel said, giving him a wan smile.

"Everything is fine between us now?"

Muriel nodded. "As long as you keep Bethia Rayborn away from me."

———

Keeping his vow to God, Noah walked to St. Andrew's with Jude on Sunday. "I'm just glad my father can't see me now," Noah said as he caught sight of worshipers ascending the three wide steps and entering the stone-front chapel. The Careys were as staunch Anglican as the Nicholls were Presbyterian.

"I suspect he can," Jude replied.

Noah sent a glance up toward the cloudless sky. Was his father frowning down on him from heaven, or was the concept of denominations as out of place there as the concept of greed? He hoped so.

"I was just as surprised to find myself coming here, the first time," Jude said. "But for the opposite reason. If Father thinks of me at all, he expects me to remain Presbyterian. It was very tempting to find something else, just to spite him."

"Why didn't you?"

His friend's casual shrug was contrary to the emotion in his voice. "When you've lost your family, you realize just how important your church is. The rituals I've grown up with add stability to my life now that it's changed so abruptly.

The service was comfortingly familiar, with its reading of the litany and singing of hymns. When the minister announced the theme of the sermon, trusting God, Noah imagined it had been written solely for him, until he glanced about at others in the congregation wearing absorbed expressions, also soaking in that hope for whatever their needs might be.

Still, he would gladly settle for a portion of that hope. He needed the reminder that God could be trusted with his future, what with the itching beneath his clothing causing his upper lip to bead with sweat. Mentally he latched on to the passage the minister read from Lamentations.

> "This I recall to my mind, therefore have I hope.
> It is of the Lord's mercies that we are not consumed,
> because his compassions fail not.
> They are new every morning: great is thy faithfulness."

It was a new and strange concept to grasp that perhaps his affliction was not some punishment for some sin—unconfessed or confessed—but was necessary in order that some plan for his life might be fulfilled. That perhaps, God actually felt compassion for him.

Back at the lodging house and after a lunch of bratwurst, sauerkraut, and fried potatoes, Noah went up to his room for a nap to supplement what scant sleep the itching had allowed last night. But between the tasks of pulling off his boots and turning his pillow, he took pen and paper from the top of his chest of drawers and wrote *His compassions fail not.*

He wedged the paper between shaving mirror and wall so that he could see the words every time he glanced in that direction. That would help keep discouragement at bay, he hoped. For the morbid thoughts would try to creep into his mind again. He was only human, and he was hurting.

Twenty-Four

O n Monday morning, Mr. Birch came around the dressing screen with a concerned expression.

"This doesn't look good."

Oh dear, Bethia thought. She traded puzzled looks with Mrs. Hamby. Wasn't the newest member of the cast supposed to be recovered by now?

"Mr. Carey?" she asked.

"One moment, please."

When he came around the screen, he was not wearing Robert Brierly's gray convict costume, but his own suit. "There is no sense in wasting your time. It's no better."

He did not seem to feel the need to explain what "it" was, because having had theatre experience, he would certainly know that any newcomer would be the focus of gossip and speculation until the newness wore off. From what Bethia's ears had picked up in the wardrobe room, corridors, or directly from Jewel, she knew that Mr. Carey had had lead roles in several York productions, that he now resided in a lodging house for struggling artists near Leicester Square, and that intolerance to soap caused him to stay in the shadows of the wing during rehearsal.

There were rumors as well, originating probably from Mr. Rigby, who resided in the same lodging house, that Mr. Carey came to London after being jilted at the altar by a fiancée. That spawned another rumor that he came here to forget the last tragic moments he spent at a fiancée's bedside. This led Bethia to believe—in the few occasions she had time to think about it—that both rumors were false, or one was false, or Mr. Carey was a lothario who had had two fiancées at the same time. Only, he didn't have the look of a lothario—however they were supposed to look.

At the moment, buttoning his coat in front of the dressing screen, he looked deflated, discouraged.

"Such a shame, Mr. Carey," she said.

He shrugged, made an effort at a smile.

"Have you been to a doctor?" Mr. Birch asked, holding out a pea green cravat toward him with two bony fingers, as if it might be contaminated.

"Almost three weeks ago."

Mrs. Hamby approached from her machine, stood a cautious three feet away. "Have you tried lanolin, Mr. Carey, ha-ha-ha?"

Looping the cravat through his collar, he gave her an uncertain look. "It didn't help."

"Now, I'm surprised," she went on. "It cleared up my nephew's nappy rash in two—"

"I hardly think your nephew's nappy rash is relevant to Mr. Carey's situation," Mr. Birch snapped. Mrs. Hamby's little laugh sometimes brought the worst out in people, Bethia noticed.

"Yes, well." Mr. Carey turned to Bethia. "Thank you, Miss . . ."

"Rayborn," she supplied. "You won't leave without speaking with the McGuires, will you?"

"I'll stop in the office on my way out."

As Mr. Carey walked toward the door, Mr. Birch glanced behind the screen. "Wait, Mr. Carey. Your playscript."

The understudy hesitated, looked back, and said, "I don't think I'll be needing it, thank you."

"There's the pity," said Mrs. Hamby when he was gone. She clamped shut her mouth before the laugh could escape, giving Mr. Birch a reproachful look as if he had taken something from her.

"Yes it is," Miss Lidstone said while tacking on a bit of lace to a gown sleeve. "And you wouldn't guess he had a problem from the look of his face."

"Except when he's twitching and frowning, ha-ha," said Mrs. Hamby. But with a sympathetic frown.

It was almost a relief to be leaving, Noah thought as he knocked upon the office door. He had become a social pariah, like one of the biblical lepers—unclean and unfit for decent society. That notion was reinforced by the wide berth that most members of the cast gave him whenever their paths happened to cross.

"Won't you change your mind?" Mr. McGuire asked after admitting him to the office. "Wait this out a bit longer?"

"We should have our doctor see you," said Mrs. McGuire.

Noah shook his head. "It won't help. But I thank you for giving me a chance. I hope you find another understudy soon."

"Ah, you're not to worry yourself over that, Mr. Carey." Mr. McGuire said, taking a metal box from a drawer. It rattled when he set it upon his desk. "We always manage."

"I'll not accept any money."

"You must, Mr. Carey." Mr. McGuire swung back the lid. "You worked hard."

Reluctantly Noah accepted the three pounds, one week's wages. He had a railway ticket to purchase, and his landlord could possibly ask for a penalty for breaking his lease with such short notice. He thanked them again and walked out of the office.

The lobby was empty. He cocked his head to listen for approaching footsteps, then turned to rub his back against one of the columns. The relief was intense, but he was aware that it would bring on more itching when he stopped.

He had come to this, he thought as he blinked burning eyes. Lord Carey, who had arrived in London confident with his stage experience, certain that theatres would open their collective arms to him with time, now reduced to scratching himself like a bear against a tree. And returning to Yorkshire as a failure.

"His compassions fail not," passed through his mind.

I'm trying to cling to that, Father, he prayed. *Please forgive my lack of faith by asking, but if you could just send some sign that you haven't forgotten me. . . .*

"My turn?" Mr. Graham, the actor cast as Mr. Gibson, the bill broker, took a hesitant step through the doorway.

"Do come in, Mr. Graham," Bethia said. He was the last of the men to be fitted because of a severe cold that had kept him at home last week. Tomorrow would be the women's turns, not because they were less important, but because the fine detailing of their costumes meant it took longer to sew them.

As Mr. Graham went behind the screen with Mr. Birch, Bethia inspected the hems of two gowns of plain brown linsey, a coarse fabric of wool and flax, that Muriel and understudy Amanda Hill would wear as the penniless May Edwards. She would not actually *see* it on Muriel until dress rehearsal, for she would have to slip from the wardrobe room before eleven tomorrow, when Muriel's fitting was scheduled.

"Does your grandson still build stained-glass windows?" Mr. Graham asked Mr. Birch behind the screen.

"The finest in London," Mr. Birch replied. "In fact, he has a waiting list. Are you in the market?"

"Not me, my Uncle Miles. But he lives in Wimbledon."

"That's not too far for Lucas. He's fitted windows as far as Chertsey."

"How does one . . . communicate with him?"

"With pencil and paper. He can read and write, same as any—"

Suddenly it was Miss Lidstone's voice Bethia was hearing, in her mind.

"And you wouldn't guess he had a problem from the look of his face."

Absently Bethia pressed the rough fabric between her fingers. Mr. Carey was well groomed, his face clean and hair shiny. And he was clean-shaven. One could hardly accomplish any of that without soap. Then, why was there no rash upon his face?

A vague memory drifted into her mind but popped like a soap bubble before she could grasp it. Something she had read. Or overheard? Or even dreamed? She strained to remember, then realized her best course was to relax, resume her work, and hope the memory would return with more clarity.

Mr. Graham stepped from behind the screen, Mr. Birch following. The actor's black suit fit well, save the legs of the trousers puddling about either side of his shoes.

"I thought I hemmed those, ha-ha," Mrs. Hamby said.

That's it! Bethia thought, and turned to the seamstresses. "Will you see to it now? I'll be back."

She hurried down the empty staircase, rapped upon the office door and turned the knob before hearing an invitation to enter. Jewel and Grady turned grim faces toward her; Jewel from her chair, Grady from where he stood propped against his desk with arms folded.

"Mr. Carey's gone?" Bethia asked, though the answer was obvious.

"Why, yes," Grady replied. "Just a moment ago."

She turned for the lobby, ignoring her cousin's "Bethia?" She would explain later. Outside she stood under the marquee and scanned the pavement both ways and Sloan Square across the street. With his height, Mr. Carey would be easy to spot, and she recalled he was wearing a gray suit. The fact that he would accept an understudy role and lived in a lodging house meant he was poor, so she was quite certain he had not caught a hansom. Which left the underground railway.

"I beg your pardon, Miss?" the booking clerk said from the ticket window. "You must purchase a ticket!"

"I'm not taking the train," she replied, hoping she had an honest face.

Fifty-one steps led down from the booking hall to the tracks. A half dozen steps were behind her when reason surfaced. Bethia paused, hand upon the railing, heart thumping. She could simply telephone the lodging house.

But then a man below her swayed briefly to the right, allowing her sight of Mr. Carey.

In for a penny, in for a pound, she thought, taking another step. Besides, she could not bear the thought of anyone suffering a minute longer than necessary the disappointment she had witnessed in the actor's expression.

She certainly couldn't yell to him like a fishwife, but he was too far a distance for him to hear her if she called to him in a civil tone, with chattering and the tromping and clicks of shoes and boots. The gap was widening, so she risked a loud-but-just-within-the-bounds-of-decorum "Excuse me! Mr. Carey?"

The result was a few curious looks in her direction. Mr. Carey continued on with no change in the set of his shoulders to indicate he had heard.

You're being foolish, she thought. She wasn't even certain her information would be helpful. She was wondering if she should just ring him later after all, when, eight steps below, a boy of about seven twisted to glance back at her, turned again, and put a hand to his mouth. "MISTER CAAA-REEE!"

"Jimmy!" the woman with him scolded, jerking his hand as people turned to look.

But it worked, for Mr. Carey was one of those who stopped and looked back at the boy with puzzled expression. Then he raised his eyes higher to meet Bethia's.

"Thank you!" Bethia said. The boy was apparently enjoying his spot in the center of attention too much to hear her, but the woman looked over her shoulder and, despite crimson cheeks, nodded.

Mr. Carey shifted to the banister on his left and began climbing the steps.

Thank God for little boys, Bethia thought.

What did you forget? Noah asked himself, trying to decipher the message in Miss Rayborn's expression. Had he not gotten the point across that he was quitting? Was she about to insist he come back and complete the fitting?

"Are you Mr. Carey?" the boy who had shouted asked as Noah drew near.

"Jimmy . . ." the woman holding the boy's hand said.

Despite the crushing disappointment, as well as the discomfort of having morris dancing ants frolicking beneath his clothes, Noah nodded and gave the boy an ironic smile. He had finally gained *some* recognition in London. Or at least *below* London.

The wardrobe mistress had returned to the top of the stairs and waited off to the side in the booking hall with hands clasped together.

"Miss Rayborn?" Noah said, joining her.

"Forgive me for calling you back," she said. "But I've some information that you may find helpful."

"If you're referring to an audition elsewhere . . ."

"No, of course not." She motioned toward a space less congested, between a letter box and sign reminding passengers to carry all parcels when departing the trains. "If you please?"

He supposed he had nothing to lose. Slipping hands into his trouser pockets, he said, "What is it, Miss Rayborn?"

"I've a book at home that I consult now and again," she replied. "*Textiles and Weaves.* There is a section that mentions an intolerance to wool, which causes one's skin to break out in rashes. And your *suit* is obviously wool."

He appreciated how she got immediately to the point. Even if the point was incorrect. "Wool isn't the problem, Miss Rayborn. I've been surrounded by sheep all my life. In fact, I sheered dozens just before I came down here, with no ill effect."

"The book says a person can develop the intolerance suddenly, and at any time in his life."

That rang too familiar to Noah's ears. "A chemist said the same of soap."

She did not look surprised, which surprised *him* until he remembered she was part of the theatre. Even the Royal Court's mice probably had learned of his supposed soap intolerance.

"I believed him and changed brands," Noah went on. "The only place I've seen any improvement at all is on my hands." But the bloody whelps on the backs were still healing, so he continued allowing them to rest in his pockets rather than repulse her.

"Do you wash your face and hair with soap?" Miss Rayborn asked. "Shave?"

"Well, yes."

She peered up at his cheeks, forehead. "Miss Lidstone's right. No trace of a rash there, Mr. Carey. Does your face itch?"

"Not at all." He thought a second. "It never has, actually."

"Your scalp?"

He shook his head.

"Then, how can it be soap?"

That sounded reasonable. And the rash all over his feet could be attributed to woolen stockings. Noah thought of his hands again. Why had they only broken out shortly *after* his visiting the doctor?

The answer came in a flash.

"Miss Rayborn, I think you may have something there."

"Yes?"

"My hands were fine until a doctor recommended rubbing lanolin into my skin. Naturally I got it all over my hands."

As her expression faded, Noah could almost hear the wheels of her mind turning, trying to make a connection. He smiled. "Lanolin is made from wool. Or rather, the oil in the follicle."

She was nodding now, eyes bright. "Yes, I've heard that, now that you mention it—probably from my brother-in-law. He—" She stopped and gave her head an abrupt shake. "But that doesn't matter, does it? Mr. Carey, it stands to reason that if you stop wearing wool, you'll recover, yes?"

His hopes had climbed that same staircase twice, only to tumble to the bottom. Yet, perhaps because of the belief in her blue eyes, he wanted to believe as well.

And that posed another problem. He passed a hand over his face, realized what he was doing, and shoved it back into his pocket. "How does a man go about avoiding wool, Miss Rayborn? I know next to nothing of cloth. My shirts are probably linen or silk. But coats, trousers . . . are they not always wool?"

After all, he was from Yorkshire. *Houses* would have been made of wool if it were practical.

Miss Rayborn shook her head. "There are some fabrics that serve just as well. Henrietta cloth, for example."

"Henry . . ."

"It's almost identical to fine cashmere, but it's made of silk. And Strasburg cloth, from cotton. We use them all the time up in wardrobe. They keep their shape better and are more comfortable under the lights."

Doubts began tugging at Noah's mind. How much money dared he invest to test her theory? London tailors were probably more expensive than those in York. What if he had a couple of suits made and nothing changed?

But what if she was the sign he had prayed for just minutes ago? What had he expected . . . writing in the sky?

"Miss Rayborn, do you know of a reasonably priced tailor?" he asked. "One who would make me a suit or two from one of the types of cloth you mentioned?"

She leaned her head thoughtfully. "A friend of my family owns a shop on Saville Row. But it would be a shame to go to that expense and discover that wool isn't the culprit after all, wouldn't it?"

"I see no other options before me. And it's worth the risk. May I have his name?"

Instead of replying, she said, "Mr. Carey, I believe I have a better idea. Will you walk back to the theatre with me?"

Noah glanced toward the arched doorway that led out to Sloan Square. "I've already tendered my resignation."

She slipped a hand into the crook of his arm, not in a flirtatious manner, but as she might if he were a brother or close acquaintance. "Trust me, the McGuires will be most happy to see you."

"The coat and two pairs of trousers we made for Mr. Hicks for *A Pair of Spectacles* are just sitting up in storage," Bethia said to Jewel and Grady, while Mr. Carey sat wearing the expression of a man who is not quite certain what is going on about him. "He hardly wore them, and it will be years before you run the play again, if at all."

"We'll lend them to Mr. Carey," said Grady, the first to catch on. He turned to the actor. "Can't hurt to stay on and wait this out for a few more days, yes?"

A slight glimmer of hope crept into Mr. Carey's brown eyes. "But what if I damage them . . . spill something . . ."

"We're not concerned over that," Jewel replied and winked at Bethia. "Not with our excellent wardrobe staff."

"In fact," Grady said, "we would give them to you were they not the property of Messrs. Fry and Cumberland. But as this experiment may save us the trouble of looking for another understudy, they would urge you to give this a try."

Jewel nodded thoughtfully. "Have you considered blankets?"

"Blankets?" Bethia bit her lip. That had not even entered her mind, what with it being August. But even August night temperatures could dip down into the fifties.

"We have a couple Mother brought back from India when we lived there," Jewel went on. "We never use them, and they're nice heavy cotton. I'll bring them tomorrow."

Mr. Carey looked overwhelmed. "That's too much. I can't accept—"

"Mother would be glad to know they were put to use," Jewel insisted.

"I'm afraid you're on your own as far as stockings go," Bethia said as Mr. Carey followed her up the stairs. "I'll telephone Mr. Somerset—the tailor I mentioned. He'll know where to find silk ones if he doesn't stock them himself."

The footsteps behind her fell silent. Bethia turned, hand upon the banister.

"Miss Rayborn," he said. "I appreciate your help more than I can say. But my feet will rot before I pull on a pair of women's stockings."

"For men, Mr. Carey."

"Oh." He gave her a sheepish look. "I forget this is London. I suppose one can buy them made of cheese if one knows where to look."

"I can ask Mr. Somerset about cheese stockings, if you wish."

Mr. Carey returned her smile. "Silk will be fine."

In the wardrobe room, Mrs. Hamby, Miss Lidstone, Mr. Graham, and Mr. Birch ceased chatting to gape at them.

"Mr. Carey has decided to stay after all," Bethia said. "We suspect an intolerance to wool is causing the problem."

"Ah," Mr. Birch said, nodding. "Interesting. Welcome back, Mr. Carey."

Bethia could have kissed the old man, for the discomfort eased from Mr. Carey's face. She asked the actor to have a seat so that she could look over Mr. Graham's newly hemmed trousers. Then while Mr. Birch helped Mr. Graham change behind the screen, Bethia went next door and dug out a Henrietta-cloth coat and two pairs of trousers from the racks.

It so turned out that the coat for *A Pair of Spectacles* fit nicely, if a bit tight in the shoulders. And all the trousers required was taking up two inches in the waist and letting out an inch in the hems. With no more actors to fit for the day, Bethia and the seamstresses were able to devote themselves to the task, while Mr. Carey sat in flannel wrapper and listened to Mr. Birch's accounts of his earlier years onstage at the Adelphi.

"I played one of the ruffians conscripted by Macbeth," the old man said, voice softened with fond memory. "Sarah Woolgar played Lady Macbeth. We utility actors were madly in love with her."

"Even as Lady Macbeth?" Mr. Carey teased, causing Bethia and Miss Lidstone to trade smiles over their sewing.

Mr. Birch shook a bony finger. "She was an angel backstage, young man."

"Sorry. Did she marry one of you?"

"No. Can't recall the fellow's name. He wasn't even an actor."

"I suppose that broke all of your hearts?"

"Not really." Mr. Birch shrugged. "We knew our hopes were pipe dreams. And when God sent me my own angel, I had no thought for another woman. Nor have I since she passed on after thirty happy years of marriage."

"That's so . . . so *sweet*, Mr. Birch, ha-ha," said Mrs. Hamby, dabbing her eyes with her fingertips.

He gave her a sentimental smile and did not even scold her for the laugh.

Presently Mr. Carey stood before them in the Henrietta-cloth coat and a pair of corded trousers. Miss Lidstone had even found three pairs of men's cotton stockings in the back of a cupboard drawer.

Twenty-Five

After supper in the parlour Bethia related the events of the day to her family, save Danny, who was up in Edinburgh for summer lectures. Her family shared a keen interest in such things; for years William had been bringing home stories of discoveries made in the laboratory of the Hassall Commission.

"Hard to believe the doctor prescribed lanolin without investigating further," William said, shaking his head.

"It's good you remembered what you read," Mother said. "I can hardly recall what I wore to church last Sunday. Avis has to remind me. But I can remember songs we sung on the play yard when I was but a girl."

"Will the man let you know if he's better?" John asked while rolling a tennis ball from wrist to shoulder and back again.

"I'm sure he will," Bethia replied. Mr. Carey seemed to be a grateful sort of person, who would not leave everyone in the wardrobe room wondering.

She realized, at that moment, that she owed the actor a debt of gratitude as well. For the better part of a day, she had not thought to grieve over her part in Douglas Pearce's death.

On Thursday, the day before final dress rehearsal, Mr. Carey came back up to the wardrobe room to report that his condition was improving almost by the hour.

"Last night I slept soundly for the first time in weeks," he said.

"Marvelous, Mr. Carey," Bethia said.

The actor smiled. "And I've telephoned your Mr. Somerset. He kindly directed me to a tailor near Leicester Square who agreed to make a couple of suits from Henrietta cloth, at a price within my budget. I'm going in for a fitting Saturday."

"The others will be happy to hear it."

"Do you not take lunch, Miss Rayborn?" he asked after a glance about the empty room. "May I bring you something from one of the cafés?"

"I had a sandwich from home, thank you," she said, touched and a little embarrassed by his eagerness to do something for her. "I wanted to pack up cloth remnants for the Aged Widow Society. They sew quilts from them."

"Very practical."

"I hate to throw anything useful away. And yet I tease my mother for saving wrapping paper."

He smiled again. "So does mine. May I help?"

"Oh, no thank you," she said. "After such a hectic week, I enjoy the solitude."

"Then I'll not infringe upon it," he said, taking a step back toward the door. "But if there is ever any way I may repay your kindness, you have but to ask."

Bethia shook her head. "You're not under any obligation to me, Mr. Carey. I happened to have some knowledge that was useful to you."

"You were compassionate enough to share that knowledge, Miss Rayborn," he said with voice a little thicker. He hesitated, added, "I fully believe you were an answer to prayer. I was at my lowest point when you came after me in Sloan Station."

"I saw your light under the door," Jude said softly after sticking his head into Noah's room. "Was afraid you'd fallen asleep with it on."

"You're back already?" Propped up on his two pillows, Noah glanced at the page number—37—and then closed the copy of Thackeray's *The History of Henry Esmond, Esq., A Colonel in the Service of Her Majesty Queen Anne: Written by Himself.* "Come in. What time is it?"

Jude eased the door shut and approached. "Almost midnight."

"I lost track of time." Noah nodded toward the open carton upon his chest of drawers. "Mother sent some books and two tins of ginger cake. One is for you."

"Bless that woman."

"Amen. How was the show?"

"Mark Sanger came down with hiccups onstage, poor chap. But the audience didn't even seem to notice." Quietly he lifted the ladder-backed chair from the small table that served as Noah's writing desk and brought it over to sit near the bed. "And we start rehearsals for *East Lynne* next Wednesday."

Noah grinned. "Your first speaking part."

"Well, a short one." A streak of greasepaint reflected lamplight where Jude's forehead met his grayish-brown hair. "Who would have imagined just three months ago that we would both be here—with jobs?"

"Not I. Not in a million years," Noah admitted. "I shudder when I think of how close I was to slinking back to Yorkshire in shame."

"I wouldn't have envied you that. I'm glad you're better."

"I went up and thanked Miss Rayborn today."

"Miss Rayborn?"

"The wardrobe mistress," Noah reminded him.

"Ah, yes." Jude scratched his jaw. "The name rings a bell."

"I wish you could meet her. She's quite a remarkable woman."

Jude stared at him for one, two, three seconds.

"Well, what is it?" Noah said.

"Oh no. . . ."

"It was a simple *courtesy*."

"And I'm the Prince of Wales."

Noah frowned at him. "I suppose you've taken up mind reading?"

"That's not necessary. I've seen that look on your face before."

"What look?"

"That doe-eyed look. Did you learn nothing from Olivia? You practically proposed before you knew her name."

Noah opened his mouth to deny the charge, closed it. It was an exaggeration, but only a slight one.

"And that Morgan girl," Jude was saying. "The headmaster's daughter."

"Edwina Morgan." Noah had to chuckle, but softly, so as not to incite knocks upon the walls. "We were *twelve*. And you were as infatuated with her as I was."

"*I* wasn't given licks for carving her initials on a desk. Admit it, Noah. You're a hopeless romantic. You hardly know this wardrobe mistress. It's a bit soon to be cutting out valentines, old friend."

"I'm simply grateful," Noah insisted.

Not only for discovering the source of his rashes, but for such a seemingly little thing as her hand in the crook of his arm. The memory brought a lump to his throat. She had not been afraid to touch him.

"When I was one and twenty . . ." Jude's voice broke into his thoughts. "I heard a wise man say, 'Give crowns and pounds and guineas, But not your heart away.'"

Noah groaned. "Housman?"

"From *A Shropshire Lad*," Jude replied.

Pointing to the tin beside a carton upon his chest of drawers, Noah said, "Hand me that tin. We'll have a midnight snack, and no more advice, if you please."

"You're dressed already?" Richard Whitmore said the following morning, sticking his head into Noah's closet of a dressing room.

Even understudies for the leading parts participated today, with scenes repeated after the lead actors performed their parts. Noah, clad in shirt-sleeves, waistcoat, and trousers, paused from combing his hair and admitted sheepishly. "I was the first one here."

The lead actor laughed. "I remember those days. Only a matter of time before you're a jaded old fossil like me."

"You're hardly a fossil," Noah said.

"I've the gray hair to prove it." Mr. Whitmore touched the brown bristles growing from his scalp. "Somewhere beneath this dye." He pointed to the blue-and-black striped cravat hanging from a hook near Noah's mirror. "I say, Carey, did you turn up with an extra one of those? Mine seems to be missing."

"Here, take this one."

"You don't have to—"

"I'm almost dressed." Noah handed it over. "I'll just run up and ask about the other one."

"That's awful decent of you."

"I assure you, I don't mind."

His eagerness for an excuse to go back up to the wardrobe room surprised even himself. He took to the steps with almost a lightening of his heart in his chest. Across his mind Jude's voice echoed, *"Admit it, Noah. You're a hopeless romantic!"*

Indeed, what *did* he know of Miss Rayborn, he asked himself in an attempt to tether this budding infatuation within the bounds of reality. With others in the company not exactly lingering in his presence, he was not in the flow of backstage gossip.

She was kind. That was obvious. And there was no snobbery in her character, or she would not have helped him, a mere understudy.

Intelligent. That also was obvious. Her voice was pleasing to the ears. Calm, soothing. And yes, there were those elfin blue eyes. He would not lie to himself by discounting the physical attraction. But some of the actresses—such as Lady Holt—were even more beautiful, but it was not *their* faces he was looking forward to seeing upstairs.

Mrs. Hamby was sweeping the wardrobe room and Miss Lidstone sewing a button on a coat. Noah gave the room a quick look-over while trying hard not to appear to do so. Miss Rayborn was not there.

"Ah, there you are, ha-ha!" Mrs. Hamby said. From a table she picked up the identical cravat to the one Noah had given Mr. Whitmore. "It was hanging from our doorknob this morning. Someone must have found it in the corridor."

"You really should take better care of your costumes, Mr. Carey," Miss Lidstone scolded, but in a nurturing way that was not abrasive.

"Yes, sorry. I'll do that."

The older seamstress smiled. "I was going to bring it to you on my way to the changing room. If you'll kindly wait, you may drop this coat off with Mr. Stephens and save me the trouble."

"But of course."

Mrs. Hamby beamed at him. "Miss Rayborn says you've almost recovered, ha-ha!"

"We're very happy for you," Miss Lidstone said.

"I have, thank you," Noah replied, smiling. Casually he added, "Is she not here today?"

"She went downstairs a bit ago to wait for her father and her fiancé," Mrs. Hamby replied.

"Mr. Russell isn't her fiancé," Miss Lidstone corrected. She bit off a thread and tied a knot. "But we expect her to come up here with a ring any day now."

"A girl can be a fiancée without a ring, Mildred," Mrs. Hamby said, and just when it seemed she would forget for a second time, added, "Ha-ha!"

"Not *officially*."

"*I* married without getting a ring beforehand. Are you saying I never—"

"Shall I take that coat now?" Noah said. He gave the women an apologetic look. "They'll be calling us to the greenroom."

On his way down the stairs, he muttered, "You're a hopeless something, all right."

But at least he had not reached the point of carving her name upon a desk. And his gratitude to her was no less than before. The least he could do was to be happy for her, that she had love in her life. He only hoped the fiancé—official or not—appreciated how fortunate he was.

Twenty-Six

*H*e would climb down there and join them if he could, wouldn't he?" Father said to Bethia on Friday morning. Seven rows ahead, Guy leaned over the orchestra pit to watch the musicians warm up with Chopin's Concerto in E Minor.

Bethia smiled. "But only if they asked."

Between University and working in his father's shop, Guy had never found the time to observe a dress rehearsal at the Royal Court until today. Even so, he would have to slip out in little over an hour for the Royal Opera House and rehearsal of Wagner's *The Flying Dutchman*. Father was the only family member able to accompany Bethia this time, for Danny was still in Edinburgh, William and John had accompanied Sarah to Liverpool to inspect a steam-powered ship, and Mother was nursing a summer cold.

"That trumpeter is quite good," Guy said, returning to the seventh row. He sat on the end seat, his violin case resting on the floor just inside the aisle.

"His name is Mr. Swaine," Bethia said. Onstage, Mr. Webb was showing a hammer-wielding carpenter a loose board, and the scenic designer, Mr. Bruton, was testing the pulley to the first drop scene, which depicted a summer sky, the verandah of the Bellevue Tea Garden, and some shrubbery.

"Do they ever start on time?" Father asked.

"Almost never," Bethia replied. At least dress rehearsals. "But once they begin, they'll try to time it as if it's an actual performance."

Jewel and Grady entered the auditorium through a side door.

Guy and Father got to their feet, and above the hammering and music they traded greetings and the men shook hands.

"We could have used Danny here last week, Mr. Rayborn," Grady said. "I suppose Bethia told you what happened."

"Yes," Father replied, "but I don't know if I would trust Danny to remove gallstones just yet."

Grady chuckled, and Jewel said, "Bethia's a fair doctor herself. She saved poor Mr. Carey's career."

"What is this?" Guy asked, for Bethia had not yet had the opportunity to relate the incident to him.

"It was nothing, really," Bethia said, although she had to admit to herself that she was pleased over how the situation had turned out.

"He was suffering from a severe rash," Jewel replied. "She suggested he stop wearing wool and it cleared up."

"Mr. Carey is Mr. Whitmore's understudy," Bethia explained. "I had read of wool intolerance months earlier and happened to guess that was his problem."

Grady shook his head. "The poor fellow was at the end of his rope when you helped him."

"Runs in the family," Guy said and smiled at Father.

Father smiled modestly.

A loud *thump* drew all eyes toward the stage.

"Careful, there!" Mr. Webb exclaimed.

"Sorry," said Mr. Norris, a stagehand, while righting a chair again. "But the thing's as tipsy as my uncle Luke. I barely touched it."

"Have a look at that chair!" Mr. Webb barked to one of the carpenters. "We're trying to maintain a schedule here!"

Bethia drew Jewel aside while the men's attention was drawn toward the activity on stage. "May I speak with you?"

"But of course," Jewel replied.

When they were several feet down the aisle, Bethia said, "It struck me this morning that my being out here might affect Muriel's performance. Should we move back to the balcony or—"

"Absolutely not." Jewel shook her head for emphasis while sawing sounds came from the left wing. "You've more than cooperated with her, and we're very grateful. But she can't expect you to dig a hole and bury yourself."

Bethia wasn't too certain if that was not exactly what Muriel expected.

"Besides," Jewel continued and nodded toward the stage, "once Muriel's up *there*, she's so caught up into character that she wouldn't notice the Queen herself out here."

"Very good now!" Mr. Webb said, clapping hands as a carpenter carried the repaired chair back to the set and causing a flurry of stage-hands. "Time to clear the stage!"

Muriel had to admit, if only to herself, that Bethia Rayborn was a genius at costume design. She stood to the side to study her profile in her dressing-room mirror. The simple lines and coarse brown fabric supported her role as the penniless May Edwards but did not detract from the femininity of Muriel Pearce Holt.

A knock sounded at her door.

"Come in."

The actress assigned the minor part of Emily St. Evremond, a thin girl by the name of Corrie Walters or Waters or the like, stuck her blonde head inside. "I was asked to inform you that they're waiting, Lady Holt."

Muriel took note of the "I was asked" and the politely distant expression. It seemed the cast and crew, sympathetic enough just three weeks ago to send letters of condolence up to Sheffield, had turned upon her. Why was she surprised, with every actor and actress spending time in the wardrobe room to prepare for today?

Of course, Jewel had insisted that Bethia was not the sort of person to bear a grudge or spread gossip. In other words, her other cousin was perfect.

Richard Whitmore, who unfortunately had not chilled toward her, sat looking over the playscript in the greenroom with the new fellow, Noah Carey. Muriel wondered how Mr. Whitmore dared share a sofa with him, then remembered learning through snatches of corridor gossip that he had not had lice after all.

The man was actually rather handsome, Muriel realized, now that revulsion no longer clouded her vision. Tall and broad-shouldered, with hair as dark as ink, a complexion that was no stranger to sunlight, and dark eyes. Possibly even more handsome than Mr. Whitmore.

Not that she was interested in either—Richard Whitmore, with his cloying attempts to court her, nor Mr. Carey, with his poverty.

As if on cue, Mr. Whitmore looked up and gave her a sympathetic smile, which did not mask the admiration pouring from his eyes. If she would but give him any sign of encouragement, he would be on his feet in a flash. But Muriel returned his smile with a mere cordial one and, ignoring her own understudy, Amanda Hill, took a chair off to herself. It was time to concentrate on becoming May Edwards.

That concentration was shaken onstage, briefly, toward the end of Act I.

"Two sovereigns!" she had cried when Mr. Whitmore, as Robert Brierly, placed two gold coins in her palm.

"Nay, thou'lt make better use of the brass than me," Mr. Whitmore said with a tender look that was not *all* acting. "What, crying again? Come, come, never heed that old brute. Hard words break no bones, you know."

Muriel sent a glance toward the empty rows and spotted Bethia Rayborn seated between a bearded elderly man, obviously her father, and a younger one whom Muriel did not recognize.

"It's not his hard words I'm crying for now, sir," she said smoothly, returning to character.

"What, then?" Richard Whitmore said.

Muriel allowed her voice to soften. "Your kind ones. They're harder to bear. They sound so strange to me."

With jaw set she stalked to the women's changing room, where Mrs. Allgood helped her out of the brown dress and into a blue calico for the scene to follow. Muriel spoke only when necessary to the dresser, for she burned with anger.

Some of that anger was directed toward herself. Why had she not clarified that "keeping Bethia away" also meant not allowing Miss Prim-and-Proper to smirk at her from the seventh row during rehearsal? *And while I'm still in mourning for poor Douglas!*

Back in the greenroom she fought the temptation to march into the theatre and complain to Jewel and Grady. Such a confrontation would only cast herself in a poor light and make a bigger martyr of Bethia Rayborn. A minute later Lewis stuck his head through the doorway to announce, "May Edwards!"

When the tableau curtains opened again, Muriel had stepped out onto a stage now transformed into a parlour complete with rugs, a caged canary, and framed needlework.

"There, Goldie," she said to the canary. "I must give you your breakfast, though I don't care a bit for my own. . . ."

She stayed onstage for the whole of Act II, while Corrie Walters-or-Waters came and went, then Richard Whitmore and other characters. The entire time, Muriel only glanced out into the theatre seats when Mr. Webb interrupted the acting to suggest she or someone else stand a bit farther upstage or such.

Finally, after the tableau curtains closed and the orchestra began playing their numbers for intermission, she asked Lewis how long until she was needed again.

"Fifteen minutes, Lady Holt," he replied.

"I'm stepping out for air."

The boy gave her a worried look. "But . . ."

"I'll be back."

"What are they playing?" Bethia asked.

Guy tilted his head, listened. "Mendelssohn's Fugue in D Minor."

"I don't think that light is supposed to flicker like that," Father said, pointing to a portion of the curtain.

"When did it flicker?" Bethia asked just as one section of the curtain darkened, then became illuminated again. Three rows ahead, Grady and Jewel were involved in discussion.

"I'll tell them," Father said.

"Here, Mr. Rayborn, allow me," Guy offered, starting to rise, but Father shook his head and got to his feet.

"I'd like to see how those things work anyway."

"What a hypocrite," Guy murmured when they were seated again after rising to allow Father to pass.

Bethia looked at him. "*What* did you just say?"

"Not your *father*, goose." He leaned closer. "Lady Holt. She treats you so abominably. And yet she actually had me feeling pity for her up there."

"It's called *acting*, Guy," she said dryly and felt an immediate little stab of guilt for having enjoyed hearing him speak ill of Muriel.

For even though she felt sympathy for the woman's loss of a brother and would regret her own part in the tragedy for the rest of her life, she was beginning to feel lower than human under the present arrangement—having to leave the wardrobe room well before Muriel was expected for a fitting, to pass her by in the corridors with eyes averted, and still feel the hostility coming in waves.

Forgive me, Father, she prayed under her breath. *This is a thimbleful compared to what your son endured. Please help me to shrug it off and not mind so much. Or still better, please soften Muriel's heart toward me.*

That would take a miracle, but then why pray at all if one did not believe God capable of answering?

The peace following that thought was shaken by another from some cynical portion of her mind she did not know existed. *What good did it do to pray for Douglas Pearce's safety?*

She closed her eyes, drew in an even breath. For most of her twenty-one years she had trusted that God knew best. But then, that trust was easy to maintain surrounded by people who loved her, enjoying comfort, good health, and opportunities to use her talents. A faith that was so fragile as to shatter at the first bump in the road—was that really faith at all?

Please increase my faith, Father.

Muriel passed the refreshment counter, where Mr. Birch and one of the maids were stacking cups upon a tray for the greenroom, with muffled *clicks.* Ignoring their puzzled looks, she went through the lobby, pushed open the lone unlocked door, and stepped out under the marquee. A light rain was falling. It startled and pleased her because of the clean, wet aroma of the air. Had she the liberty, she would have kirtled her skirts, run down the pavement as fast as possible, and allowed the rain to bathe away all the gloom and grief clinging to her.

A colorful poster advertising *The Ticket-of-Leave Man* hung upon the theatre wall. Such posters were scattered about town, in train stations above and below ground, on walls and lampposts. The artist had worked from a photograph she and Mr. Whitmore had posed for weeks ago, and Muriel was pleased with the blush to her cheeks and that her thick lashes seem even thicker.

He had caught the devotion toward her in Mr. Whitmore's eyes too. Any woman gazing upon that poster would envy her and assume she had not a care in the world. If only it were so!

Why wouldn't you listen to us, Douglas! she thought, her throat tightening. *He* should be inside watching the rehearsal, sitting on the front row opening night. How proud he would have been! Instead he had died in some cold place, unaware that his sister had become an actress.

"Bethia?"

Bethia turned toward Guy again. He was studying her, violin case in his arms.

"Penny for your thoughts?" he said.

She smiled and changed the subject. "You have to leave?"

"I'm afraid so." He glanced toward the stage, where an electrician was kneeling. Father and Grady watched from just before the orchestra pit, and Jewel was rustling through the playscript. "Say farewell to everyone for me?"

"I will."

But he did not leave yet. "You don't have to stay here, you know."

"I still love my work," Bethia said.

"Are you sure?"

"Yes. And mine and Muriel's paths seldom even cross." She was reminding herself of that even while she reassured him. "Don't you have to run along?"

He winced and then squeezed her hand. "Right away."

Muriel was so absorbed in thought that she did not realize the door had opened until she heard a footstep behind her. She turned. A young man was closing his coat protectively over something bulky, as if to shield it from the rain. After a fraction of a second Muriel realized he had been seated with Bethia in the dim auditorium. Blue eyes the color of sapphires were the only striking features in a rather nondescript, though nicely chiseled, face.

He nodded at her without so much as a good-day and, cradling the odd burden inside his coat, hurried toward the underground station. His boots made splatting noises against the wet pavement.

Muriel watched until he was out of sight, then went back indoors.

Mr. Birch was alone at the refreshment counter this time.

"Who was that man who just left?" Muriel asked. She gave no clue that she had seen him inside, for she did not want gossip reaching the wardrobe room that she had expressed any interest in Bethia or her companions whatsoever.

"The gentleman's name is Russell, Lady Holt," Mr. Birch replied while filling a tea strainer with leaves. The old man did not express his sympathy or even appear grateful that a lead actress would stoop to chat with him, even though he was nothing more than a glorified servant.

Though piqued, Muriel prodded some more. While she was aware that Bethia was romantically linked with a coachman's son, she could not recall Douglas ever mentioning his name. And according to Mother, a whole clan of Rayborn-Doyles lived in the Hampstead house. The man could possibly be a cousin or stepbrother or young uncle.

"His face is vaguely familiar," she prodded. "Do you happen to know what his father does for a living?"

"Living?" Finally Mr. Birch looked at her. In his gray eyes, hooded by a thatching of grayer eyebrows, lurked the expression of one who had resigned himself to giving as much information as would allow him to return to the task at hand without interruption. "I have no knowledge of his father. Why don't you ask Miss Rayborn? He's her fiancé."

Twenty-Seven

*L*ady Holt's absence for the final two-and-a-half weeks of *Lady Audley's Secret* was still being felt on the thirteenth of August, when *The Ticket-of-Leave Man* opened to a theatre only eighty-three percent filled. But word of mouth and favorable newspaper critiques increased that percentage nightly, and ten days later the production played to its first sellout audience. It would be the first of many, columnists predicted, heaping laurels upon the cast, orchestra, sets, and costumes.

Bethia was as happy as anyone at the turn of events. As soon as one production started rolling smoothly, however, it was time to start concentrating upon the one to follow. The Royal Court had staged Leopold Lewis's *The Bells* six years ago, but that was before her hiring on as wardrobe mistress. The costumes in storage were typical of rural English folk of the late nineteenth century; however, the drama was set in the early nineteenth century in the village of Alsace, near the German border, and therefore would require some influence from French as well as German cultures. For inspiration, she brought her sketch tablet to the National Gallery and studied the canvases portraying early nineteenth-century peasant life by Jean-François Millet.

Once the sketches were completed, the next steps would be to take measurements and create patterns. Muriel's appointment was scheduled for half past ten in the morning on the twenty-ninth of August. At ten past ten, Bethia took up her satchel, intent upon leaving to lessen any chance of their meeting on the stairs or in a corridor. She would walk down to Spencer, Turner & Boldero and look at cloth, she told the seamstresses.

Miss Lidstone pressed lips tight and shook her head. "It's a shame you have to coddle that—"

Mrs. Hamby cleared her throat with exaggerated enthusiasm. "Good morning, Lady Holt, ha-ha-ha!"

Bethia looked toward the doorway, where Muriel stood just inside, a white box in her arms making stark contrast to her mourning clothes. *You'll not apologize for being here,* Bethia said to herself. Not with Muriel arriving before the appointed time.

Incredibly, Muriel smiled.

"Good morning, Mrs. Hamby, Miss Lidstone . . . Miss Rayborn," she said, continuing on into the room. I picked up some éclairs from Capucine's. A peace offering, if you will."

"How lovely of you, ha-ha," Mrs. Hamby said. "Isn't that lovely, ladies?"

Miss Lidstone gave the actress a wary eye. "A peace offering, Lady Holt?"

"I realize I've been an unbearable prima donna, Muriel said, setting the carton upon the drafting table. "Especially with Miss Rayborn here."

Her eyes locked with Bethia's. "Can you ever forgive me?"

Bethia nodded, unable to speak.

"Let's go down and get a pot of tea to go with our treats," Miss Lidstone said to Mrs. Hamby.

"But we already have—" Mrs. Hamby said, then nodded owlishly. "Yes, a pot of tea, ha-ha."

When the seamstresses were gone, Bethia found her voice. "You'll never know what this means to me, Lady Holt."

Muriel smiled again and advanced to where they stood just two feet apart. "I blamed you for what happened to Douglas, as if that would bring him back."

Bethia's eyes teared. "If only . . ."

"Now, now."

Suddenly Bethia found herself in Muriel's arms.

"We must put all that behind us," Muriel said, patting her back.

"Thank you," Bethia choked. She had known love all her life: love from God, from her family, from Guy. Being on the receiving end of forgiveness felt almost as sweet. "With all my heart, thank you."

Muriel's eyes watered, and in that instant it seemed that some inexplicable cleansing freedom stretched its arms out to her, urging her to release the hatred and put it away forever.

Douglas would still be alive . . . seeped again into her consciousness from the hard knot of resentment lodged in her mind. Bethia Rayborn needed to experience the same loss her family had suffered.

Or at least as devastating a loss. As bitter as Muriel's feelings were, she was no murderer. But she had experience with breaking up a marriage. How difficult could breaking up an engagement be?

Minutes later she was stripped to her chemise and standing on the rug. The seamstresses clucked over the pastries like two hens over corn, with Mrs. Hamby inserting that ridiculous laugh that made Muriel wish she could walk over to the table and slap her.

"Please don't hold your breath, Lady Holt," Bethia said, winding the ribbon around her waist. "Hmm. You've lost an inch."

Grief will do that to you rose to the tip of Muriel's tongue, from habit. But she checked the impulse. She had been so clever, waiting over two weeks since dress rehearsal to extend the olive branch, just in case Mr. Birch happened to blather about her inquiring about the fiancé. Timing was of utmost importance, whether acting onstage or off. She would wait another week to take her revenge up another notch. *Two weeks,* Muriel amended.

"Oops . . . sorry," Bethia said.

"Mmm?"

"I believe I pricked you."

Muriel looked down at the muslin pattern pinned together at her shoulders and sides. "I didn't feel a thing."

"Every little noise the house makes," Muriel's mother said over the telephone that afternoon, "I think it's *him* coming through the door to say it was all a big misunderstanding."

"I know, Mother," Muriel said, wiping her eyes with the back of her hand. "I do the same."

"But he's never coming back, is he?"

"No, Mother."

"I wish I could die."

Muriel swallowed. "Don't say that."

Her mother's voice became smaller, almost lost. "Please come back home, Muriel. I need you."

"Mother, please . . ." Muriel kicked herself mentally for not putting the call off until tomorrow. She had to get some rest before tonight's performance. As much as she desired to comfort her mother, it was draining every bit of her energy. "We'll come up for a long visit when the show's had its run."

When she hung up the telephone, her nerves were so wound that she went to her room and lay across her mattress. She heard the door ease open, then Evelyn's hesitant voice.

"Shall I take off m'Lady's boots?"

"No." Muriel grabbed a pillow and shoved it under her chin. "Leave me alone."

Her thoughts were beginning to meld into each other like the colors on a child's water painting when a sound like a mewling kitten floated through her open window. She sat up and cocked her head, listening. The sound came again, and this time she got to her feet.

Mrs. Burles was coming from the front hall with the mail when Muriel reached the foot of the stairs.

"Lady Holt?"

"Georgiana. Is she in the garden?"

"Why, yes, your Ladyship."

With the housekeeper on her heels, Muriel hastened down the corridor and through the back door. Nanny Prescott was seated on one of the stone garden benches, an open book in her hands while Georgiana tugged at her apron, weeping as if her little heart would break. When Muriel was just a few feet away, the nursemaid lowered the book, gave her a startled look, and got to her feet. Georgiana let go of the apron and rushed toward Muriel, still weeping.

"Lady Holt . . ." said Prescott.

"What's going on here?" Muriel demanded, hefting Georgiana into her arms.

The nanny's plain face pinkened. "I beg m'Lady's pardon, but it's not how it looks."

"Sh-h-h, Mother's here," Muriel said, holding Georgiana out a bit so that Mrs. Burles could wipe her little face with a handkerchief.

To Prescott she said, "Then, what is it?"

"Miss Georgiana demands my attention every waking minute. I thought if I didn't give in to her for a half hour or so daily, she would learn to amuse herself."

"That's ridiculous!" Muriel said over her daughter's howls. "Why should she amuse herself when she has you?"

"The very idea!" said Mrs. Burles. "You're not paid good wages to ignore the child."

"I was keeping one eye on her." Prescott motioned toward a basket on the grass beside the bench. "And I brought out some toys."

Muriel had suffered just about enough frustration for one day. Georgiana continued to weep, her little face crimson, though no more tears dampened her cheeks.

"Well, you're never to do that again! Your job is to look after my daughter, not indulge yourself with novels!"

"Yes, m'Lady," Nanny Prescott said with head lowered.

Muriel turned and carried her daughter into the house, Mrs. Burles hastening ahead to open doors. She settled on a parlour chair, kissed the top of Georgiana's head and soothed, "There there, now."

After inhaling a couple of shaky breaths, Georgiana leaned against her. Muriel was not accustomed to holding her, for the child's restless energy made her nervous. Nanny Prescott had been the one to hold Georgiana in her lap most of the time during the train journeys to and from Sheffield, to prevent her from climbing over to the window and pitching herself out.

But this was rather nice, Muriel thought, resting her head against the back of the chair. Drowsiness from her unfinished nap settled over her, slowing her breathing and draining the tension from her muscles.

When she opened her eyes later, Georgiana was making faint snoring noises, and Nanny Prescott was seated on the edge of the Hepplewhite chair just inside the door. She was wearing the washed-out dark gown she had worn to apply for her position last fall, gloves, and a felt hat with a sad little cluster of drooping flowers above one ear. A faded and lumpy carpetbag listed to the right at her feet.

"Where are you going?" Muriel said softly.

"I can no longer work here, Lady Holt. But Mrs. Burles asked me to speak with you first so . . ."

"You'll abandon us without giving me time to replace you?"

"You have others here who can watch Miss Georgiana until you find someone. And as you sacked the last nanny just for giving notice, I figured I'd be leaving today anyway."

I should sack the lot of them for gossiping, Muriel thought, lips pressed tight. She did not need more strain upon her nerves. "Have you also heard that I didn't give the last nanny a reference? You saw how many others applied for your position. Just how do you expect to find another one?"

Nanny Prescott closed her eyes briefly, nodded. "I have that other letter from Mrs. Godfrey. I've saved my wages. I'll get by until I find something."

Muriel was all set to dispute that point when Georgiana drew in a deep breath and shifted in her lap. With a pointed glance down at her sleeping daughter, Muriel said, "Do you care nothing for *her* happiness?"

"More than you can know, Lady Holt," the nursemaid said calmly. "And that's why I must leave. I'm with Miss Georgiana every waking minute. But I can no longer in good conscience stay here as simply her older playmate. I taught her to use a fork and brush her teeth. May I not teach her some strength of character?"

Strength of character indeed! Muriel thought. A lofty term, coming from a woman whose only previous experience was rearing siblings and pigs. "She's but three years old, Prescott."

Nanny Prescott's sloping shoulders rose, fell. "I learned from my own brothers and sisters that it's the lessons we learn young that stick with us. How will Miss Georgiana develop patience—and a keen imagination—if she's not left to her own devices now and again? How will she cope with having to share a schoolmistress's attention?"

It was only because her child slept in her lap that Muriel was forced to keep her temper in check. Somewhat. She was drawing breath to inform Prescott, but calmly so, that she did not appreciate a lecture on child-rearing from someone who had never parented her *own* child, when memories of her miserable friendless two years at the Ryle Day School gave her pause. She had marched through the gates expecting the same royal treatment she received at home, only to discover she was not the only Princess of Belgravia.

Some of the logic of what she was hearing slipped past her defenses.

"It's just that it breaks my heart to hear her weep so," Muriel admitted, startled at herself for being so candid with a servant.

Prescott nodded sympathetically. "Rarely has Miss Georgiana the occasion to weep, Lady Holt. The others will confirm that I'm kind to her, if you'll but ask them. But if shedding some tears early—while I'm close at hand to make sure she's safe—will save her from more serious tears later, is it not worth it?"

Muriel had no opportunity to ponder that question, for Georgiana stirred, sighed, and sat up. Damp tendrils of her still-baby-fine hair curled about her ear, where she had leaned against Muriel. Blinking, the child seemed to be trying to get her bearings.

"Good afternoon, Georgiana," Muriel said.

Georgiana turned her little face up, blinked at her, and then looked across the room. "Where nanny going?" she asked with worried tone, pointing toward the carpetbag.

"Nowhere," Muriel replied, and gave Prescott an imploring look.

"Lady Holt, I cannot stay under—"

"Do you promise you'll always stay right there with her?"

"Of course I will."

Any misgivings Muriel still suffered were silenced for the moment when Georgiana climbed down from her lap and hastened across the carpet to tug at the handles of the carpetbag. "Nanny not go. I help nanny put away."

Just before leaving for the theatre that evening, Muriel went up to the nursery. A tray of used supper dishes sat upon the table where the child and nanny ate their meals. Georgiana sat upon Prescott's lap in the rocking chair while Prescott read from *The Butterfly's Ball*. The child turned up her cheek for Muriel's farewell kiss and then fastened her blue eyes again to the open picture book.

"Read story?" she said to her nanny.

Relieved that she had not allowed her temper to drive Prescott away, Muriel was nonetheless struck by the same little pang that came whenever it was obvious that Georgiana was closer to her nanny than herself.

On her way back downstairs she reasoned away the hurt by reminding herself that every child in Belgravia was reared by a nanny. One had only to walk in Green Park on a sunny day for proof. But when Georgiana became old enough to do things with her—to shop, attend theatre, and the like—she was positive that their bond would strengthen. More like friends than mother and daughter. Just like her relationship with her own mother had been.

"You're moving up in the world are you, Mr. Carey?" Miss Lidstone asked on the last day of August, between Mr. Birch's calling out measurements from behind the screen.

When *The Bells* opened in four weeks, Mr. Carey would be playing the Clerk of the Court in Act III. He would also continue as Mr. Whitmore's understudy, as Mr. Hicks was still recovering. In the event that Mr. Carey would be called upon to assume the lead role for an evening, one of the utility actors would fill in for the minor role.

"I'm moving up indeed," the actor called over the screen.

"And his back is as clear as a baby's bottom!" Mr. Birch volunteered.

"Mr. Birch!" Miss Lidstone scolded, while Mrs. Hamby dissolved into giggles.

Bethia would have covered her face with her hands were she not holding a pencil and notebook. It was time to speak with Mr. Birch about some of his irreverent remarks, as amusing as they were.

"I'm sure your back is just as attractive, Mr. Birch," she heard Mr. Carey say.

"Ah, now, you wouldn't want to go laying money on that!"

"Congratulations on your new part," Bethia said when the actor came back out in his street clothes—a suit of tweed-looking Henrietta cloth.

"Is it a big part, Mr. Carey, ha-ha?" Mrs. Hamby asked.

The actor smiled at her. "Not quite. My lines add up to exactly forty-two words."

Miss Lidstone walked over to him, reached up to tweak his cheek. "We're very proud of you."

"Why, thank you," he said, blushing but looking pleased.

"I wonder why he's so poor?" she said after he left. "Surely he made some money on the York stage."

Mr. Birch shook his head. "Most regional theatres pay the local actors pittance. They wait tables or wash windows between jobs."

"I have it on good authority that he spent his life savings on his fiancée's funeral," said Mrs. Hamby, but with sentimental expression and no mirth to the trailing "ha-ha!"

"And whom might your 'good authority' be?" Mr. Birch asked.

Mrs. Hamby drew up her short stature. "Mrs. Shore overheard Mr. Dalton saying it to Miss Hill, I'll have you know."

"Ah, well then, that's as good as a sworn-in jury."

"Let's get back to work, shall we?" Bethia said amiably. But firmly.

*G*ood evening," Bethia said to the seamstresses outside the Royal Court on Friday the second of September.

"And to you," Miss Lidstone and Mrs. Hamby replied in unison, followed by the latter's nervous titter. Ordinarily Bethia would accompany them to Sloan Station, but she was having supper with the Russells tonight and then accompanying them to the Royal Opera House for the production of *The Flying Dutchman*. The nearest underground railway stop to Bond Street was Victoria Station, but she would still have to walk a mile after that, so she planned to take a hansom instead and was headed for the stand a half-block down when she heard her name.

"Miss Rayborn?"

Bethia turned and spotted Muriel exiting a black coach trimmed in silver as her driver held the door.

"Yes, Lady Holt?"

"I was hoping to catch you," Muriel said, hastening toward her with black-gloved hands outstretched.

Returning her smile, Bethia pushed the strap of her bag up her arm so that they could clasp hands. It occurred to her to wonder why Muriel had not simply gone inside to look for her. She had to go inside anyway to get costumed up for tonight's performance. But she did not rack her brain over it. She was so grateful that the enmity was a thing of the past and so hopeful that it would stay that way, that Muriel could have clog danced upon the theatre steps and Bethia would not have questioned her.

"You know how it is—a maze inside with all those nooks and

crannies," Muriel said, as if reading her mind. "I was afraid I would miss you entirely. Are you in a hurry? May we sit in my coach for a quick chat?"

Flattered as she was, Bethia glanced at her wristwatch and replied, "I'm sorry, Lady Holt. I'm on my way to catch a cab. I've plans for the evening."

"Then my driver will take you wherever you'd like to go."

"Thank you, but—"

"And now you have time for our chat," Muriel said, linking an arm through hers. "I promise to detain you but a minute."

Before Bethia quite knew what was happening, she was seated inside the coach. "Just a turn around the Square, Ham," Muriel said to the driver as the door closed.

And then Muriel smiled across at her. Even in mourning dress she was beautiful. As the wheels started moving, she said, "I've invited some of my neighbors for tea on Thursday, before rehearsals start up again. I've not really gotten on well with them, but many were kind enough to send their condolences to my family when Douglas—"

A chill ran down Bethia's back. Her smile froze.

"Now, now," Muriel said, leaning forward to pat her arm. "That's water under the bridge, dear. And that's *not* why I abducted you. I thought some music would be a lovely background for visiting—but nothing as overbearing as an ensemble, mind you. Some light classical, very subdued, for an hour and a half at the most."

It did not seem that Muriel was extending an invitation to the tea, for she had mentioned neighbors. Still, Bethia sent up a quick prayer of thanks for the miracle of the two of them sitting and chatting like old friends. Or at least on the *surface* like old friends, for she would continue to feel a slight uneasiness in Muriel's presence until the emotional wounds from Douglas Pearce's death were not so fresh.

"I had thought to hire one of the musicians here," Muriel went on, "but then recalled hearing that your beau plays violin for the Royal Opera House."

"He plays piano and flute as well," Bethia said modestly, for Guy was, after all, *her* beau. Still, it pleased her to have an excuse to point out his accomplishments. "But his scholarship was for violin."

"You must be very proud of him."

"I am," she admitted. The reason for Muriel's drawing her apart clicked in her mind like an electric light bulb. She wanted Guy to play for her tea. But for hire, or was she asking a favor? Were she herself the violinist, she'd offer to play in a heartbeat, simply out of indebtedness. But she had no right to be volunteering Guy's limited time.

"I probably shouldn't ask this. . . ." Muriel bit her lip.

Bethia's shoulders stiffened. "Yes?"

"Does he possibly hire out for private affairs? I would pay, mind you."

"As long as they don't conflict with rehearsals and perform-ances," Bethia replied, relaxing again. "He helps out in his father's shop, but those hours are flexible."

"Hmm. Do you know if he's rehearsing Thursday afternoon?"

"I'll be happy to ask," Bethia said, ignoring a faint warning voice in her mind. What was there to be afraid of? "I'll be seeing him shortly."

"Also, please ask if ten pounds would be adequate compensation. My late husband always handled such details, so I'm woefully igno-rant of them. If that's not enough, I'll be happy to pay more."

"I'm sure he'll think ten pounds most generous."

The coach had come to a stop outside the theatre again. Muriel leaned to give her a quick embrace. "Thank you. This will be my first time to entertain since . . . well, you know, and I do so want this to be special."

Bethia smiled. "You're welcome, Lady Holt."

"It's Muriel, if you please," she corrected. "And you'll be *Bethia* to me. After all, we're practically related.

"Thank you," Bethia said to Muriel's coachman on the pavement outside Russell Saddle and Tack. She held out a crown. "And please accept this."

"I couldn't, Miss," he replied while eyeing the coin with an expression that suggested otherwise.

"I would consider it a favor," Bethia said. "You saved me a lot of inconvenience."

"Well . . ." He grinned at her, took the crown, and pocketed it. "Thank you, Miss."

As she neared the door to Russell Saddle and Tack, it opened and Lottie stepped outside. "Whose coach?"

"Lady Holt's," Bethia said, linking arms with the seventeen-year-old. "You remember, the actress who played Lady Audley? By the way, I've tickets for *The Ticket-of-Leave Man* in my bag."

"Thank you!" Lottie stepped ahead to open the shop door. The bell tinkled, and Mr. Neale paused from polishing a saddle to raise a smeared rag in greeting. Bethia smiled back.

"How are your studies?" she asked the girl as they walked through the curtained area.

"Intense." The girl drew in a breath, and out flowed a high note, "*Ma, me, may, mo, mu . . .*"

"One day we'll have two reasons to visit the opera, yes?"

"That would be nice." Lottie paused at the foot of the staircase. "How is your family?"

"Very well, thank you."

"And John?"

Hence, the reason Lottie waited. She was blonde and pretty, but whenever the families got together, sixteen-year-old John barely seemed to notice her. *I should advise her to carry a football,* Bethia thought. "He's well. I'll mention that you asked about him."

The girl brightened. "Thank you."

Upstairs, the rest of the Russell family greeted her, save Guy, already at the opera house. Penny Russell cooked the family meals, though she sent the laundry out and had a day maid in once a week to polish furniture and floors. She ushered everyone to the table and served boiled knuckle of veal with rice, turnips, and potatoes, followed by baked apple pudding.

There was no time to tidy up, so Bethia helped the girls carry the dishes to the kitchen sink while Mrs. Russell put away the leftover food. Twelve-year-old Sharon was brushing crumbs from the cloth when Mr. Russell came back upstairs to say he had a hired coach waiting. They sat like sardines in a tin, but not unbearably so, with Bethia sharing a seat with Lottie and Sharon.

The Royal Opera House in Covent Garden had a handsome slab-faced exterior with Corinthian columns and was huge enough to seat thirty-five hundred persons. Because the tickets Guy had procured were complementary, they were located up in the amphitheater stalls, but that did not hinder Bethia's enjoyment of the story of the Dutchman doomed to sail the seas for all eternity, landing only once every seven years until redeemed by the love of a faithful woman.

"You were the best violinist," Sharon said when Guy joined them afterward.

He tweaked her cheek, winked at Bethia. "There were eight violins. How could you tell me from the others?"

"I'm your sister. I could tell."

Because of the late hour, Bethia's father had already arranged to send the coach from Hampstead to meet her after the opera. "Let us deliver you home," she said to the Russells.

Stanley Russell declined the offer. "We're in opposite directions. We'll hire another coach."

Guy walked Bethia down Bow Street while his family waited for the queue of carriages for hire to snake its way toward the front of the Opera House. Quickly, Bethia related her conversation with Muriel.

"I would rather not, Bethia."

"You'll have rehearsal?"

"Actually, we won't." They reached the coach. Guy exchanged greetings with Hiram, opened the door, and turned to her again. "But I don't care to meet her."

"She's been trying hard to make up for the past." The memory of Muriel's embrace was still pleasant. "She's brought pastries up to wardrobe three times now."

"I don't know, Bethia. . . ."

"She would pay ten pounds."

His dark brows lifted. *"Ten pounds?"*

"She actually offered more if that's not enough," Bethia said. "It seems very important to her to make a good impression on her neighbors. And this could lead to other engagements, you know."

And so it was settled. He agreed to telephone the Holt residence in the morning.

"But for us, not *her*," he clarified. "For the deposit on our house."

"Why don't we meet for lunch Monday?" Jewel said in Muriel's dressing room a half hour before curtain the following evening. "Just the two of us. It's been ages."

Though Dorothy, the makeup artist, had just left with her greasepaints, Muriel picked up a hare's foot and dusted her cheeks lightly. "Where?"

Jewel blew out a quiet breath of relief and smiled at her cousin in the mirror. Muriel would not have agreed so quickly had she any inkling of an ulterior motive. She was about to suggest Giovanni's but reconsidered. Too great the chance of running into some of the cast or crew. "Let's go to the Savoy. Then we'll hop over to your house so Georgiana doesn't forget her old cousin."

She had not seen the child since just after the memorial service, another reason she and Muriel should get together, and another reason she should not feel an iota of guilt.

"The Savoy?" Muriel said. "Can you spare the time?"

"I'll make the time. Mr. Fisher will be showing us his scene sketches for *The Bells* at eleven, but that usually takes less than an hour."

"Then we'll come for you at half past one."

"That's not necessary. I'll take a cab and meet you."

Muriel turned upon her stool and arched a perfectly shaped brow. "Jewel, of what use is having a rich cousin if you can't enjoy some pampering now and again? And lunch will be my treat, by the way."

A knock sounded at the door, accompanied by Lewis's voice. "Greenroom, please, Lady Holt?"

"I've followed the cab as far as I could! I saw them get out, and lost them at the last turning. If I could only keep them in sight—if he could but hear my voice—Robert! Robert!"

Every seat and box were taken, so Jewel and Grady had settled onto stools in the dress circle corridor to peer discreetly through the back curtain.

"Do you hear that?" Jewel whispered, pushing her eyeglasses up the bridge of her nose.

He smiled and nodded. She did not have to explain that she

referred not to Muriel's brilliant heart-tugging plea onstage but to the sounds of weeping in the audience. Every sniff, every honk into a handkerchief, was music to their ears.

She smiled at Grady during the standing ovation. He winked back. They turned their attention back toward the stage, where, amidst the applause and *bravos,* Mr. Whitmore let go of Muriel's hand and took two steps backward to join in the applause. Jewel watched her cousin soak up the applause, glowing, and felt a twinge of wistfulness. What would it be like to be on the receiving end of such adoration?

"Here, dearest, give me your stool before the corridor fills," Grady said over the roar, a hand resting lightly upon her shoulder.

Jewel smiled and got to her feet. But of course she knew how it felt. And Grady's love for her would continue long past the point when Muriel's admirers found some other object of affection on some other stage.

May that be years and years away, Jewel thought—and not only for her cousin's sake. The receipt ledger had come to life again, like a sickly person after taking a tonic.

Muriel's most steadfast admirer shepherded Jewel into his dressing room after she congratulated him on his performance. Grady was not along, having been summoned to the mezzanine-level refreshment stand to look at a faulty shipment of chocolates.

"I heard you're meeting Lady Holt for lunch tomorrow," Mr. Whitmore said, closing his door.

"That news is already circulating?" Jewel said. "I believe that's a record for speed."

"Thin walls." Smiling, he knocked upon one lightly for emphasis. "And for speed, the record was set last year when Susannah Laws was overheard boasting to a visitor that she could act circles around anyone in the company—especially Charlotte Steel. We froze her out after that."

"So *that's* why she went over to the Lyceum," Jewel said, folding her arms.

"I had no fondness for Charlotte." The actor shrugged. "And we're all conceited in our own ways. But anyone foolish enough to admit it deserves what she gets."

"Why weren't Mr. McGuire and I informed?"

The greasepaint upon Mr. Whitmore's cheeks creased about the corners of his smile. "Well, you're management. You think *everything* reaches your ears?"

"I'm actually glad it doesn't," Jewel said with a feigned shudder. The hums and drones of conversations just outside the door reminded her that she needed to be out in the corridor chatting with patrons, congratulating other members of the cast. "Now that you mention management, I really must be—"

"Wait!" He gave her a pleading look. "I don't quite know how to ask this, but will you hint around to Lady Holt, find out what it is I'm doing that repels her?"

"I'm sure you don't repel her, Mr. Whitmore."

"But I don't attract her either. She's completely indifferent toward me. If I could just know what I'm doing wrong, that would be a tremendous help."

"Well, you realize she's been in mourning for almost two months."

He nodded soberly, ran a hand through his dyed hair. "Yes, of course. And I'm deeply sorry over her brother. But she's paid me scant notice from her first day here. I don't think that has anything to do with it."

"You feel *that* strongly for her?"

She had to ask, even though the word that he was smitten with Muriel *had* reached management's two sets of ears. Over the years she had witnessed a succession of admiring ladies upon the actor's arm, and she had doubts to his staying power in any relationship. The fact that she was Muriel's cousin gave her the responsibility for questioning his motives.

"I love her, Mrs. McGuire," he said earnestly.

The tremor in his voice was touching. Then again, Muriel said to herself, he *was* an actor. Not that Mr. Whitmore, for all his faults, would deliberately attempt to deceive her. But self-deception was the most powerful of deceptions. Actors spent years stepping back and forth over the line separating fantasy from reality, and sometimes that line became blurred in the mind.

"Are you quite sure, Mr. Whitmore? Or could it be that her indifference presents a challenge?"

"I've never been more sure of anything. You'll help me, won't you Mrs. McGuire? Drop a hint? Be my detective?"

She gave it some thought while he stared at her with love-sick eyes. At length she had to shake her head regretfully. "It wouldn't be right, Mr. Whitmore . . . going behind her back. We aren't children on the grammar school playground. The only way I can oblige you is to ask her directly, admitting that I'm inquiring upon your behalf."

His eyes widened with panic. "No, please—"

"Then you could do it yourself. She doesn't bite."

At least not since she was a tot. According to Mother, she and Aunt Phyllis once did not speak to each other for weeks over some teeth marks. Jewel automatically rubbed her arm, even though she had no memory of the event.

Mr. Whitmore was shaking his head, expression crestfallen. "I just can't. Not yet, anyway."

"I'm sorry I can't help you. But may I offer some advice?"

"What is it?" he asked with pathetic eagerness.

She had to take a second to decide how to phrase this without slandering her cousin. "Lady Holt is quite used to having men admire her. You might try cooling your ardor."

"And you think that would work?"

"I'm afraid I can offer you no guarantee," she admitted.

From the corner of her eye Jewel noticed the usual stares, nods of recognition, murmured conferences that Muriel drew as they followed the maître d' in the Savoy's vast dining hall. No doubt many recognized her from the stage, which would explain the sympathy in many expressions, for Mr. Shaw's column had praised the beautiful young actress *"whose dedication to London theatre patrons and to her fellow cast members inspires her to trade mourning gown for May Edward's rustic costume."*

Thankfully those mourning clothes seemed to inhibit any autograph seekers, so they were able to study the menus in peace.

"Grady is considering holding over *The Ticket-of-Leave Man,*" Jewel said after the server left with their orders—Jewel's, lamb cutlets and French beans; Muriel's, curried grouse and bread sauce.

Muriel raised the netting from over most of her face to secure it to the crown of her hat with a pin. "I promised Mother a visit when it closes, but I suppose she can wait a little longer."

She gave Jewel a guilty look. "I'm actually a bit relieved. It's so gloomy up there. Mother hasn't work to distract her, as I have. And with her physical limitations, she has long days just to sit and think."

"I'm so sorry."

Her cousin shrugged. "Well, I'm glad she has Bernard and Agatha close by, and your mother still calls on her regularly. Let's change the subject, shall we? I lose my appetite when I'm sad."

"Very well," Jewel said and ceased folding the napkin in her lap into triangles to try to think of a subject that would not give away the reason she had asked Muriel to lunch. But impatience got the best of her, and she blurted, "You're having a tea Thursday?"

"Why, yes," Muriel replied, clearly not taken aback, almost as if she had anticipated the question.

So much for subtlety, Jewel thought. "I see."

"I hope you understand why I didn't invite you," Muriel said. "It's for a few of the ladies on the Square. I thought it would be nice to become better acquainted with them before we plunge back into rehearsals. How did you find out?"

"Bethia's delighted over your having hired Guy Russell to play. But . . . you've never done anything like this before."

"I beg to differ. I tried to have a party for Georgiana, remember?"

"And what makes you think the same thing won't happen?" Jewel said carefully.

"I wasn't famous then," Muriel said with a dry smile. "But to give my neighbors credit, some showed their support after Douglas passed on. I'd like to repay them."

Now Jewel was confused. For the past three weeks, ever since Muriel's first peace offering to Bethia, a vague, nebulous suspicion had anchored itself to Jewel's mind. But when she discussed as much with Grady, he reasoned that the death of a loved one often prompted a person to reflect upon his own philosophy of life.

"Why not give her credit for wanting to change, until you have reason to suspect otherwise?" he had said.

The fact that she was *Muriel* was reason enough to suspect otherwise. Jewel had not said this to Grady, however, but decided to wait for the other shoe to drop.

But was this the shoe? Or did the shoe even exist? Could Grady possibly be right?

She cleared her throat. "Grady and I appreciate how pleasant you've been toward Bethia lately. More than you can know. But why Guy Russell, of all people?"

"Of all people?" Her cousin blinked at her. "You speak as if he plays for pennies on street corners. You've said he's gifted, and I can afford quality."

"Yes, but . . . are you quite sure you've *completely* forgiven Bethia?"

"I beg your pardon?"

"Because if you haven't, I wouldn't want her to get hurt."

"And how would my hiring Mr. Russell hurt her, pray tell?" Muriel asked, folding her arms.

Jewel shifted her weight in her chair, glanced away.

"Well . . . ?"

Please don't make me spell it out, Jewel begged silently.

Her cousin gaped at her, shook her head. "I can't believe this, Jewel. You're afraid I'll try to steal him away from her for spite? And a man I've never met?"

Lamely Jewel said, "Well, it could happen in spite of you. Men fall in love with you all the time."

"And this is why you asked me to lunch." Muriel's tone was flat.

Jewel drew in a breath and held it, saving it for carrying out just the right reply. When none rose in her mind, she attached to it the feeble words, "*One* of the reasons, yes. But it's just as true that I wanted to spend time with you and Georgiana."

Muriel's stare was so piercing, so wounded, that Jewel steeled herself for an outburst. To her utter surprise, her cousin lowered her eyes to stare at her gloved hands clasped upon the cloth.

"I suppose I deserve that."

"Now, I didn't intend to dredge up old—"

Her cousin shook her head. "Father once said there is never quite enough glue to repair a shattered reputation completely. Mother and I mocked him behind his back, but I understand now what he meant."

This isn't going as well as I'd hoped, Jewel thought. If only they were at the Royal Court instead of the Savoy; Mr. Webb could shake his head and say "Once again, and this time read the *correct* lines!"

They would start over, chatting of the cool early-September breezes outside, or of how quickly Georgiana was growing, or of how nice it was to have the theatre full again. Instead, she had blundered, practically accused Muriel of some nefarious plot for which she had no evidence.

She broke up a marriage, rose defensively in Jewel's mind. Muriel would have to answer to God for that. But the liability did not rest solely upon her shoulders. An indulged and naïve fifteen-year-old could not have inflicted such damage without Lord Holt's willing participation.

And Guy Russell and the late Lord Holt were as different as Whigs and Tories. He would play his violin and place his wages toward the terrace house in Kensington. And Muriel would impress her neighbors, who would recommend Guy to their circles of acquaintance, thereby leading to more engagements and more money put aside for the marriage nest egg.

This was a *good* thing. Muriel was indeed paying Bethia a favor.

You've been reading too many playscripts, Jewel said to herself. She leaned forward to take Muriel's hand. "I'm wrong, Muriel. So wrong. Please forgive me?"

Her cousin squeezed her hand and waved away her apology with the other. Tears shimmered in her eyes. "There is nothing to forgive."

"But there is. You're doing a good deed, and I go and practically accuse you. I'm so ashamed."

"Then I forgive you, if it makes you feel better," Muriel said, averting her eyes. "And you'll forgive *me* if I say this conversation is beginning to bore me. Now, may we talk of something else?"

Twenty-Nine

A perfect setting, Muriel said to herself, picking up a petit four from a tray on the table and popping it into her mouth. Cottonlike clouds suspended in a Wedgwood-blue sky, the garden awash in color with frothy pink and white gypsophila, canary yellow aster, delicate lilac buddleia, and velvety red clematis. The garden had not suffered under the sole attention of Mr. Watterson, she had to admit.

The servants were all starched and ready, with Joyce standing unobtrusively just outside the back door waiting for the signal to bring out the tea, and Mrs. Burles inside watching the front door. They were actors in her playscript, playing their parts without even being aware of doing so.

But the thought of having Georgiana here this afternoon had disturbed her, for reasons she could not quite fathom; hence, she had sent her with Prescott to the Zoological Gardens. A pang of regret had struck her as she watched Ham hold open the coach door for them. Georgiana had had to be prompted by her nanny to cease babbling over the animals she expected to see long enough to turn her little cheek up dutifully for a farewell kiss.

You can always stop this foolishness and go with them, a little voice had prodded. She could leave payment for Mr. Russell's trouble with Mrs. Burles. The wavering had lasted only a second. The zoo would always be there, and she had put too many plans into motion to back out now.

Besides, it was far from foolish to avenge poor Douglas's death. She had but to imagine him trembling and coughing up sputum on a cot in a mission hospital, tended by strangers, and her resolve was strengthened. No one had the right to treat any Pearce the way Bethia Rayborn had treated her brother.

Muriel congratulated herself for her restraint. She certainly could inflict a lot more pain, should she desire. But she would not go so far as to *keep* this Mr. Russell once she had snatched him away. As if she wanted him! She would allow him to go whimpering back to Bethia once her point had been made.

Her only regret was that Jewel would be livid, especially after being assured that she had no plans for revenge. Her cousin had to bear some of the blame, Muriel reminded herself, for refusing to discharge Bethia from the theatre.

She had no fear of being sacked herself. Not with a full house every performance! And besides, if the scenario she had orchestrated moved along as planned, her fingerprints would not be evident upon the playscript. Just a simple transference of affection. It happened all the time.

"Lady Holt?"

Joyce's voice. Muriel turned and met the blue eyes of the young man who had dashed out into the rain from the steps of the Royal Court. He was dressed formally, in black tailcoat and trousers, white waistcoat cut low over pleated white shirt, a white bow tie at the collar, white gloves. Short brown hair sprouted from his head in all directions like picta grass, and a faint ridge plowed the sides from the top hat he carried. Untidy as his hair was, it gave him a rather endearing look, as that of a small boy who has to be pinned down by a nanny to be groomed.

"Good afternoon, Mr. Russell," Muriel said, taking three steps forward. "Thank you for agreeing to play."

"Thank you for asking, Lady Holt." His right hand held the violin case. He did not tuck the top hat under his left arm to be prepared in case she should she offer her hand. Indeed, there was something very akin to mistrust behind the polite expression. Muriel smiled to herself. Not since auditioning for the role of Lady Audley had she come across any sort of challenge. This would almost be amusing.

The violin case he held prompted a memory.

"So that's what you were carrying," she said.

"I beg your pardon?"

"Forgive me . . . I was thinking out loud. The day of dress rehearsal, when you left the Royal Court you were shielding something from the rain with your coat."

"I had to dash to my own rehearsal," he said, hefting the case a bit.

"I'm glad you haven't rehearsal today. That worked out nicely."

But of course it had, for before she even set the date for the phantom party, she telephoned the office of the Royal Opera, identifying herself to the theatre manager as the wife of a Mr. Braedeker from the *Cornhill Magazine,* who wished to photograph the empty theatre interior for an article he was writing. Naturally she would ask rehearsal and performance schedules before making an appointment.

She wondered if the magazine would receive an irate telephone call from the theatre manager this afternoon.

"Would you care for some refreshments before my guests arrive?"

"No, thank you." He glanced about the garden. "Where shall I . . . ?"

"Here." She led him past the table and past a semicircle of six chairs. "By the rose trellis, if you please. There's a bench there, if you'd care to sit for now. Have you a music stand?"

"I brought no music," he replied. "Miss Rayborn said you specified light classical. I committed several pieces to memory during the course of my schooling—Rossini, Mozart, Haydn, and the like. More than enough to fill a couple of hours."

"I'm impressed," she said. And not just with his repertoire. Even knowing of his University degree and seat in the Opera, she had expected his speech to be more common, as befitting the offspring of servants. But his was as cultured as that of any of her peers.

For the fraction of a second he seemed on the verge of a smile. But with a blink of the eyes the somber expression resumed itself. "Thank you. I'll tune my violin now, if you please."

"By all means."

He walked over to the trellis and leaned down to open the case, while Muriel loitered about the garden, straightening a chair here, inspecting the table there. Mr. Russell was absorbed in drawing the bow across a string, listening, tightening or loosening a peg. He might as well have been alone for all the attention he paid her, but still she played the part of the anxious hostess. Mr. Webb would be proud of her for staying in character, she thought.

"Please ask Mrs. Burles if anyone has arrived yet," she said to Joyce, even though the housekeeper would naturally bring such a person through the house.

"Yes, m'Lady."

Muriel waited on the edge of the terrace. When Joyce returned to answer in the negative, she allowed herself an uncertain smile.

"Ham delivered the invitations on Monday. I'm quite sure I wrote the correct date on them. But do you think I gave enough notice?"

The maid, unused to being asked for advice, looked at her as if she had chewed and swallowed a May bug. "I don't know, m'Lady."

Muriel nodded. "They'll be here. It's just such a pretty day . . . everyone moves a little more slowly."

She had no idea what she even meant by that. But that was good. The excuses people made to save face were usually feeble ones.

"Yes, m'Lady."

As long as she was playing a part, she had to play it to the fullest. It was important that the servants be convinced as well. She went inside and approached Mrs. Burles in the foyer, put on an anxious expression. "No one yet?"

"I'm sorry, your Ladyship."

Muriel reached for the doorknob. "I'll step outside and . . ." She turned to the housekeeper. "Or would that make me look too eager?"

"I expect it would, your Ladyship. Shall I?"

"Yes . . . no. That would be the same as my looking." Allowing herself a little frown, raising her chin a bit, she added, "If they're snubbing me again, I won't give them that satisfaction."

In the garden again, she was pleased to notice the helpless concern in Mr. Russell's expression. She gave him a brave, quick smile, mindful not to pay him *too* much attention, and wandered over to one of the chairs. Sitting sideways, she draped her arms about the back and rested her chin upon her clasped hands.

Presently Mrs. Burles came outside, looked about, and approached. "It's half past two, your Ladyship."

"No one is coming," Muriel said dully.

"It doesn't appear so, your Ladyship."

"I thought they had changed their minds about me." Muriel sighed and brushed a gloved fingertip beneath her dry eyes. She could feel Mr. Russell's eyes upon her as she got to her feet. "I suppose it's time to bring everything inside. What pains me the most is that all of you went to such trouble for nothing."

Mrs. Burles's eyes widened as had Joyce's earlier, but she covered her surprise and said, "Yes, your Ladyship."

Muriel turned toward Mr. Russell, now approaching.

"And I'm sorry that your time was wasted, Mr. Russell. If you'll accompany me inside, I'll draft your cheque."

"That's not necessary, Lady Holt."

"I insist. You came out here prepared, whether or not you had the opportunity to play."

He shook his head. "Really, I'd rather not."

She pressed fingertips against the base of her neck and gave him a look that suggested a struggle to maintain composure. "I had high hopes for this afternoon, Mr. Russell, and it's turned sour. Cheating you out of your just compensation would just be heaping guilt upon the disappointment I already feel."

"Very well," he said finally. "With the understanding that the next time you need a musician, you must allow me to play—for no fee."

"That's very kind of you." Dishes rattled at the table, where Mrs. Burles and Joyce and Gladys, the scullery maid, were packing up trays. Muriel gave them a thoughtful look, then turned again to the musician. "But you know, you could earn your wages today after all. The afternoon is still young. And it's a shame that you went to all the trouble of tuning your violin for nothing."

"Would you like me to play?" he asked, his smile not quite masking the trace of puzzlement in his blue eyes.

"If you please. But wait." To Mrs. Burles, stacking teacups and saucers, she said, "Please leave those and ask everyone inside to come out here. We'll have our own party."

She smiled to herself at the lightning-quick look that passed between Joyce and Gladys. Mrs. Burles, more clever at hiding her astonishment, sent the scullery maid inside for the others. Minutes later, Mr. Watterson was bringing out a chair under each arm, and Mrs. Arnold the cook, Evelyn, Joyce, Gladys, and Mrs. Burles were awkwardly placing little sandwiches and cakes upon dishes.

"Here, I'll do the pouring," Muriel ordered with a smile when Mrs. Arnold touched the handle to the teapot. "I've already had mine."

At her urging the servants sat upon the chairs, rigid, balancing dishes and saucers with cups upon knees. Muriel slipped into an end seat. They were all looking expectantly at Mr. Russell. He obviously sensed that a concert would be more appropriate than background music to nonexistent conversation, smiled, and took a few steps closer.

"Franz Joseph Haydn's Symphony number eighty-eight, first movement."

He tucked the violin into his neck and drew the bow across the strings as if bow and violin were extensions of his body. After Haydn, he played Bach's Violin Concerto in E Major. The music was as moving and sweet as a lullaby. Still playing her part, Muriel sent an occasional wistful look toward the garden wall. Once she willed tears to her eyes, blinked until they traveled down her cheeks, then wiped them with the back of her glove.

The servants nibbled on sandwiches and pastries, balancing them upon knees again to applaud each piece. Mr. Russell played some Mozart and then lowered the violin during the applause. "Have you any requests?"

After a second of silence, Mr. Watterson cleared his throat and said, "That was pleasing to the ears, sir. But we don't know much fancy music."

Mr. Russell gave him an almost tender smile, and Muriel wondered if the gardener reminded him of his father.

"It doesn't have to be classical," he said, tucking the violin beneath his chin again. The first floating notes of "Come Back to Erin" caused exchanged smiles and nods, and Mr. Watterson's foot to start tapping.

"Do you know 'Listen to the Mockingbird'? Gladys asked timidly.

"I'll give it a try," Mr. Russell replied. His forehead furrowed as he drew the bow across the strings for a couple of short strokes. And then the song, every note perfect.

Mrs. Arnold asked for "Silver Threads Among the Gold," and Joyce, "What a Friend We Have in Jesus."

"And you, miss?" Mr. Russell asked Evelyn.

She asked for "Grandfather's Clock," and during the song wept quietly with her head upon Mrs. Arnold's shoulder. Muriel's lips tightened. That was the trouble with servants. One could purchase a corset at Harrod's without even knowing the shop assistant's name, but servants invariably insinuated their own private dramas into a household. Everyone sent the girl sympathetic looks, so Muriel had to do the same lest Mr. Russell, the son of servants, assume she had no feelings toward her own.

Mrs. Burles, in an obvious and successful effort to lift spirits again, said, "Do you know 'Waxie's Dargle,' Mr. Russell?"

He winked at her. "I'll play it if you'll sing it."

"Oh, no," she said with a shake of the head that made her top-knot quiver.

"I'll sing it," Gladys offered and broke into a slightly off-key soprano.

"Says my old one to your old one,
'Will you come to Waxie's dargle?'
Says your old one to my old one,
'Sure I haven't got a farthing.
I've just been down to Monto town,
To see Uncle McArdle,
But he wouldn't lend me half a crown,
To go to the Waxie's dargle!'"

"Very grand!" Mr. Watterson exclaimed amidst the applause when the song was over.

Gladys rose to give a little curtsey, and Mr. Russell bowed and said, "Thank you. You were a lovely audience."

"I'm glad the neighbors didn't show!" Joyce blurted.

"Joyce . . ." Mrs. Burles said with a worried glance at Muriel.

"That's quite all right, Mrs. Burles," Muriel said, hoping Mr. Russell was paying attention. "I'm glad as well."

As the servants cleared the table and Mr. Watterson started carrying chairs to the terrace, Mr. Russell went over to the bench to put the violin in the case. Muriel waited one second, two, three, then followed.

"I can see why you made the Royal Opera, Mr. Russell."

He latched the case and turned to her. "It's very kind of you to say so, Lady Holt."

"Is that an expensive violin?"

"Not at all. I found it in a secondhand shop years ago and had it restrung and refinished in Bologna."

"You do wonders with it. And how is it that you know so many songs from different categories?"

"I inherited my mother's ear for music," he said almost apologetically, as if fearing he might sound boastful. "Once I've heard a tune, I can fairly well play it. And studying music for most of my life helped build a repertoire."

"We made you up a plate, Mr. Russell," Mrs. Burles said, approaching with dish in hand. "And will you have tea?"

"I can't stay, but thank you," he replied. "We've a performance tonight."

"So have I." Muriel looked at her wristwatch. "But it's only half past three. You've time."

"I really must leave."

Muriel thought she detected the slight hesitation before his reply, but decided not to take advantage of it. "Very well. I'll draft that cheque now. Please come with me."

He accompanied her through the house and into the parlour, where her writing desk had occupied a corner since yesterday, when she decided it would be too obvious to ask him to follow her upstairs to the morning room. Raising the lid, she said, "Do have a seat, Mr. Russell. This will take but a minute."

"Thank you, Lady Holt."

From the corner of her eye she watched him look about and settle in the nearest chair, hat upon the chair arm and violin case upon the floor. She had left the door open, so as not to arouse any suspicion of her motives. The servants would be using the kitchen stairs for carrying in trays and dishes. If any were to come onto the ground floor, they would know better than to disturb her without good reason.

"That was very kind of you . . . what you did for your people," he said, standing again as she rose from the chair.

"I'm only ashamed that it took a snubbing from the neighbors to make me think of it," she said with a sad smile. "But it's an ill wind that blows no good, yes?"

She crossed the carpet and handed him the cheque.

"Thank—" he began and glanced at the face of it. He held it out to her. "Lady Holt, I can't accept this."

"You must, Mr. Russell."

"But it's twice what we agreed upon."

"You earned it. You were a friend today, when I desperately needed one. Jewel says you're saving for a house for yourself and Bethia. Put that toward it, and you'll make me very happy."

With obvious reluctance he folded the cheque and slipped it into his coat pocket. "I meant what I said about playing again—free of charge."

"If I ever have friends enough to entertain, I'll remember that," she said dryly, holding out her hand.

He thanked her as he took her hand. Upon releasing it, he picked up his hat and violin case. But he did not move. "Forgive me, Lady Holt, but why don't you leave here? There are people all over London who would be honored to have you as neighbor."

"Sheer, stupid stubbornness, Mr. Russell," she replied. She raised her hands, dropped them. "How else can I explain? We moved from this neighborhood when I was eight. Even though that was seventeen years ago, people have long memories. My father is remembered as an insurance salesman. It was common knowledge that it was only an inheritance from my grandfather that allowed us to live here."

"But now . . ."

"Yes, now I have a title," she said with a little nod. "One I did not come by rightfully, Mr. Russell, if truth be known. But I was young and naïve. I'm sure you've heard the story."

He actually blushed. That amused her. She could not recall Sidney ever blushing.

"You may not understand this," she went on, aiming the arrow where she imagined to be his most vulnerable spot, "but there is this drive in me to prove that I'm as good as anyone else. Truthfully, I'm not even certain if it's to those others or to myself I must prove it. I only know that it can't be done by running away."

In the silence that followed, his eyes glistened. "I understand more than you can know, Lady Holt."

She stared for a minute, asked softly, "How so?"

"My parents were servants. I realized at a very young age that no matter how hard they worked, we occupied the lowest rung in the social ladder. And I can't remember *not* being driven to prove myself."

"But weren't some of the Doyles and Rayborns servants themselves?" she asked innocently, though knowing the answer. "Surely that would have removed any class barriers between you."

"I speak of Britons in general, Lady Holt," he said with faint edge to his voice. "Mr. Rayborn was kind enough to pay for my music lessons when I was a boy."

"I see." She walked over to the sofa and nodded toward the chair he had occupied so briefly. "I should very much like to hear more, Mr. Russell. Can you not stay a bit longer?"

He blushed again. "You don't want to hear me complain."

"You don't strike me as a complainer, Mr. Russell." Muriel sat down, smoothed her gown over her knees. "And it's those resentments that fuel our drives. It's been so long since I've met a kindred spirit. Please help me to understand how you felt those class constraints even as a child."

Awkwardly he sat, his violin case upon the carpet again. "Little things," he began at length, tapping the ends of his fingers together as if unaware of doing so. "Schoolmasters whose praise and punishment varied, for the same accomplishment or infraction, according to the social status of a student's family. Watching shop clerks abandon assisting my parents in order to bow and scrape to some well-dressed *swell* just entering the shop. My sister wearing cast-off clothing."

Would those be Bethia's cast-off clothes? Muriel wondered. To ask would make it obvious that she was attempting to drive a wedge between them. But if the clothing was indeed from Bethia, and it had festered in his mind this long, perhaps it was not so much a matter of driving the wedge as nurturing it so that it would grow.

"Is that why you took up music, Mr. Russell?"

"Not at all, Lady Holt. I've always loved music. It was when I was twelve when I recognized it as a means to gain the respect I so craved." He gave her a thoughtful look. "What about you and acting?"

"It is the same," she replied.

And now that they had established a connection, it was time to send him off. Better that *she* be the one to bring a halt to the conversation, lest he regret having revealed so much and resent her for coaxing it out of him. The best web to catch a fly would be woven of invisible subtle strands, not obvious ones.

"Speaking of acting," she said, rising again, "I'm afraid it's time I begin preparing for tonight's performance. But I enjoyed our chat immensely, Mr. Russell."

———

"Look! He opens his eyes!"

Muriel kissed the forehead of the man cradled in her arms, raised her face again.

"Robert, speak to me!" A sob, pause. "It's May—your own wife!"

Richard Whitmore gazed up at her. "My darling, I'm glad you're here! It's only a clip on the head. It was all my game to snare those villains."

There would be another standing ovation tonight, Muriel thought as she lovingly stroked the actor's dyed hair. One could predict so by the number of sniffs coming from the rows.

"You see?" Mr. Whitmore said, reaching up to touch her cheek. "There may be some good left in a ticket-of-leave man after all!"

They held that pose as the heavy green curtain floated downward with slow and solemn folds, then Mr. Whitmore bolted up to his feet so swiftly that Muriel fell backward. Her petticoat saved her from any injury, save to her dignity.

"Good gracious!" she said above the roar as he helped her to her feet. "Did you have to do that?"

"Sorry," he said with a sympathetic grimace.

The applause intensified, meaning the actors playing minor parts were taking bows in front of the curtain. It was time to prepare for their turns. Instead of offering his arm as usual, he turned and strode toward the wing.

Who put the bee in your bonnet? she wondered, recalling how he had ignored her in the greenroom before the performance. She did not have the opportunity to ask, for it was time to step out for bows. He took her hand as if by rote, they strode out onto center stage, smiling and looking overwhelmed at the standing ovation, then bowing. He let go of her hand to step forward and applaud the orchestra, and then, as usual, swept his arm toward her. She curtseyed, head lowered, and then he bowed again. Then the whole cast joined hands for one final bow.

Offstage, Richard Whitmore congratulated every actor but her. It was only as he was heading for the dressing rooms that he sent her a look. A glance over his shoulder, actually, and in a vague sort of way, as if just looking back in general and not at anyone in particular.

Muriel smiled as understanding dawned upon her. She had spent enough time in school yards to have heard of "playing hard to get." *I just hope he keeps it up,* she thought.

But that was not to be, for the following evening he knocked at her dressing room door as she was wondering whether to bother with changing her left stocking, for her disproportionately long big toes tended to work holes into the tips. Not that it would show, but a toe poking through frayed silk was not the most pleasant sensation.

"Have you a moment?" he said after opening the door wide enough to look through the gap.

"Just one," she replied. "What is it?"

He stepped into the room and closed the door. He was in costume, save the hat the character Robert Brierly was to wear in the opening scene. Uneasily, his eyes full of longing, he said, "I must apologize, Lady Holt, for knocking you down last night. And for my rudeness afterward and in the greenroom."

"It was only an accident, Mr. Whitmore, but thank you," she said with an impersonal smile. And so that he would not assume she paid attention to him in any manner, thereby encouraging his tedious efforts at courtship, she added casually, "And I wasn't aware of any rudeness."

Pain washed across his aristocratic face. "What is it I've done to make you dislike me so, Lady Holt?"

"I don't dislike you at all," she replied, feeling a little sorry for him in spite of herself. "It's just . . ."

"Just what?" he said, and it seemed he held his breath after the words left his mouth.

Muriel sighed. She did not wish an unpleasant scene, especially when they would be called to the greenroom any second, and she needed this time to get into character as well as into a more comfortable stocking. But with him standing there, practically offering his heart to her on a platter, should she not take advantage of the opportunity to nip this infatuation in the bud?

"I'm not interested in any sort of courtship with *any* man, Mr. Whitmore. I apologize if anything I've done has led you to believe otherwise."

He winced and looked away, then back at her. "But outside of work, you hardly know me."

In the bud, Muriel thought. Hoping that her regretful expression would prove that she was not indifferent to his sadness, she softened her voice and said, "Nor do I wish to, I'm afraid. And if you please, Mr. Whitmore, I really must finish dressing."

Thirty

Standing on the parlour rug of the Hampstead house Sunday afternoon, John tugged on his earlobe.

"Sounds like . . ." Sarah said.

John nodded, then grimaced theatrically.

"Frown!" guessed Danny, home from University for the fortnight before Michaelmas Term was to begin.

"Anger!" Sarah said.

"Scowl?" said Guy.

John pumped his head, this time more enthusiastically.

Bethia sneaked a worried look to William, Mother, and Father. The other team was getting close.

"What sounds like scowl?" Sarah asked. "Hmm. Fowl?"

"Howl?" Guy guessed.

"Owl?" said Danny, prompting more nods from John.

"The owl . . . the owl . . ." Sarah clapped her hands sharply. *"The Owl and the Nightingale!"*

"That's it!" John exclaimed.

"That's five to two," Danny reminded Bethia's team.

"It's not over," Father reminded *him*.

The game of charades continued for well over an hour. The team comprised of Father, Mother, William, and Bethia ultimately won by a single point, the final subject being George Eliot's *Felix Holt, the Radical*, which the other team had been so certain would stump them.

They had not reckoned upon Father striking forefinger against thumb, Bethia guessing *flick*, William extending it to *flicks*, Father making motions that the word should be drawn out, and Mother coming up with the title.

"Remember, I'll not be by next Sunday," Guy said as he and Bethia walked arm in arm up Cannonhall Road afterward. As usual, William had offered to drive him back to Bond Street in his runabout, as Hiram had Sundays off, but Guy was just as content to take the underground railway.

"I remember," Bethia said. "Will her neighbors come this time, do you think?"

"She believes they will. In fact, that was how she realized she had written the wrong date on the invitations. A neighbor she happened upon in the Square said she was looking forward to the eighteenth."

"That's quite a leap . . . from eight to eighteen."

Guy smiled. "She said the date had been stuck in her mind for weeks, as it's when her brother's wife's baby is due."

"Bernard." Bethia smiled as well. "I didn't realize they were expecting. How lovely."

"I'm relieved, actually," Guy said. "What with her overpaying me that first time."

"Yes, of course."

She understood how a person could absently write an incorrect number. In fact, Girton College had had to return a cheque to Father because he had written it for the amount remaining in his banking ledger instead of the amount of tuition, an overpayment of over seven thousand pounds.

But to compound a mistake a half dozen times?

It could happen. Once the first invitation was written, then the other five would be copied by rote, without much thought. Bethia had been around actors and actresses long enough to know that an artistic temperament and the ability to focus on mundane tasks did not always go hand in hand.

And besides, what was the alternative? To believe that Muriel had engineered this so that she could have Guy over twice? To what end? If she wished him to come to her house twice, she simply could host two teas and hire him both times.

"Lady Holt says an acquaintance of hers is interested in lessons," he said.

"Lessons, Guy? Isn't that a step down for a concert violinist?"

He gave her a sidelong look. "I polish saddles and bridles too, remember? How is giving lessons any more of a step down?"

She blew out a breath, aware of how snobbish she had sounded, aware that the difference between his and her upbringings would always be, if not a barrier between them, a third presence that sometimes nudged its way between them without invitation. It mattered little that her own mother had once been a servant. Her family possessed wealth, his did not. "You know I didn't mean it that way, Guy."

"What's wrong, Bethia?" he asked as they turned down Heath Street.

She would not have jumped upon the lessons had the idea not ultimately originated from Muriel Holt. It was time to confess her concern. That, or continue suffering doubts. If the foundation for their marriage was to be total honesty, as Guy had said before, she did not want to start having to weigh her words before they even made it to the altar.

"It's Muriel," she admitted. "I'm not quite sure what to think of this attention she's giving you."

"Attention? She's simply hiring me to play at her tea." He squeezed her hand. "And as I recall, *you* talked me into accepting that first engagement."

"I just didn't realize it would lead into another quite so soon."

"But I explained the mistake. It was supposed to be—" Guy stopped himself midsentence, studied her face. "You wouldn't possibly be jealous, would you?"

"No," Bethia replied at once, then bit her lip. That wasn't true.

Gently he went on. "Because you've owned my heart since we were children."

"I have?" she said.

"You know very well you have." He gave her a knowing grin. "But I'm *very* flattered that you were jealous."

Bethia could not quite bring herself to smile at his jest. "She's . . . very beautiful."

"So are you, Lilly." Not breaking stride, he released her hand to give her shoulder a brief squeeze. "But I would love you if you were homely as a hat rack. Because you have the most beautiful heart of anyone I know."

His words, the comforting gesture put her fears to rest. Two women on the opposite pavement put their heads together disapprovingly. Bethia moved her eyes from them. Avoiding even the appearance of evil had always been easy, what with having parents who instilled in her a respect for God and herself and the family name. But if she allowed a stranger's frown to become her barometer for evil, she would have never gone to a women's college, which many British still considered detrimental to society, or taken the job at the theatre, which still more considered Sodom and Gomorrah.

"I'll telephone you afterward and let you know how it went," he said, taking her hand again as they continued down Heath Street.

"You don't have to do that."

"Then I'll telephone just to hear your voice."

She smiled. "That would be nice."

———

"Are you quite sure she's not bored?" Muriel whispered. Georgiana, on her knees beside a pail, swirled the water with a stick so that a handful of leaves raced in circles inside the rim.

"She's in her own little world, m'Lady," Leah Prescott whispered back. "Her little mind is turning just like that water. Those leaves have become boats . . . or perhaps ducklings, in her imagination."

"Do you think she's bright, then?"

Smiling, the nursemaid replied, "I know she's bright, m'Lady."

The surge of pleasure Muriel felt from hearing those words was attached to an equally strong surge of guilt. Rehearsals for *The Bells* were to begin tomorrow, and she had spent every spare minute of Monday and today going over her lines.

"After *The Bells* runs, I'm thinking of taking some time off," she said impulsively, for the thought had not entered her mind until that very minute. And the very second it left her lips, she knew she would not do so. She could not afford to have some understudy or, worse, a known actress, replace her and possibly become even more popular. Even six weeks without the approval of an audience was unthinkable.

"Very good, m'Lady."

Muriel pretended to concentrate upon her daughter again. She did not care to see the awareness in Leah Prescott's small brown eyes. She was relieved when Joyce came out to the terrace to announce a telephone call from Gleadless.

"A boy?" Muriel said when Bernard finally stopped enthusing long enough to allow her to react. "How is Agatha?"

Her brother's voice calmed. "I'm afraid she had a tough go of it this time. She's quite weak."

"I'm sorry. Is there any danger. . . ." She could not finish, even though she was not particularly fond of Bernard's wife. Death had done enough damage during its first visit to the family.

"Not if she stays in bed until the doctor says she's well enough to move about. I'm spooning beef tea into her on the hour. And she's—" his voice broke— "she's *radiant*, Muriel. I'm so proud of her."

"But of course. What will you name him?"

He chuckled. "Probably Norman. We'd like to wait a bit and see if he grows into it. He doesn't look like a Norman."

"What does a Norman look like?"

"Well . . . like Father."

Muriel had to smile. "Why not name him Douglas?"

The pause that followed was long enough for her to have an answer.

Sharp anger tweaked in her chest. "Or better yet, why don't you forget we ever had a brother? He'll never have a son to carry his name, you know."

"That's not my son's fault," Bernard said tightly. "And I'll not brand him with a family tragedy. I loved our brother just as much as you did, Muriel. He was my best playfellow most of my life. But it's time you stopped making a martyr of yourself."

"Don't you mean a martyr of Douglas?" she seethed.

"No, of yourself. I think you relish playing the suffering sister. Don't you get enough attention onstage?"

"That's absurd, Bernard."

"Is it?" he said. "It looks that way to me."

"Well, just because you're a vicar doesn't make you all-wise."

"I'll be the first to admit that." A sigh came over the line, and then his voice again, softer. "I just want you to have a good life,

Muriel. And you can't do that as long as you wear the past like a hair shirt. Don't you see?"

"Yes," she replied, just to bring an end to the conversation.

A pause, then, "Are you sure?"

"Quite sure." Her chest still burned, but she managed to inject enough calm into her voice to congratulate him and to ask him to give Agatha her best wishes. When she replaced the receiver, she sank down into the sofa cushions and rested her cheek against the arm. She almost envied Bernard his ability to put aside all that happened to their brother and concentrate upon his profession and family. She simply could not do likewise, for that would be the ultimate betrayal. But after she made Bethia Rayborn truly sorry, perhaps it would be easier.

———

"I'm going out for some lunch," Bethia said in the open office doorway on Wednesday afternoon. "May I bring you anything?"

"What happened to your sandwich?" Jewel asked.

"Well, Lewis happened to it." Rehearsal was as intense for the callboy as for any of the cast and crew, for he had to become familiar enough with the timing of the script to have the actors ready for their appearances with no delays and yet not too early as to cause congestion in the wings.

"The boy knows you for a soft touch," Grady said.

Bethia smiled and nodded. "I'm going to ask Trudy to pack two from now on. I should have thought of it months ago."

"We've not had lunch yet," Grady said, pushing his chair back from the desk. "Let's all go to Giovanni's."

"Yes, let's." Jewel got to her feet as well. "Before rehearsal's over and the seats are all taken with *theatre* people."

Mrs. Giovanni took their orders—pizza pies for Jewel and Bethia, ravioli for Grady. They sat at a round table in the center. The café was doing a brisk business, with conversation humming all about them.

Grady was saying how they would definitely postpone opening night for *The Bells* until the end of October, when the corner of Bethia's eye registered movement. She automatically glanced to the table at her right. Mr. Carey was pulling out a chair across from a another young man.

"Have you been waiting long?" Mr. Carey was saying.

"Only ten minutes or so," the other gentleman replied.

"Good afternoon, Mr. Carey," Jewel said.

Mr. Carey looked over at all of them and smiled. He stepped over to offer his hand to Grady. "Good afternoon. Mrs. McGuire, Miss Rayborn, Mr. McGuire. May I introduce my good friend Jude Nicholls?"

That prompted Mr. Nicholls to rise from his chair and another round of greetings and handshakes. Grady nodded toward the empty chair between himself and Bethia and started pushing his own closer to Jewel. "Why don't you pull up another and join us? That table's no bigger than a postage stamp."

"Thank you. But we wouldn't wish to impose."

"Nonsense," said Jewel. "This is a special occasion. We've never seen you in here."

"We're celebrating." Mr. Nicholls pulled his chair over and settled in between Bethia and Jewel. "And you never see Noah in here because he's too poor to eat anything but lodging-house soup."

"Jude . . ." Mr. Carey scolded, but his frown was such that Bethia would wear while admonishing Danny or John. Disapproval of the words spoken, but genuine affection for the speaker.

It had little effect upon Mr. Nicholls. In fact, he winked at Bethia. This intimacy from a stranger would normally have unsettled her. Instead, she surprised herself by smiling.

"What are you celebrating, Mr. Carey?" Jewel asked.

"My first rehearsal for my first speaking part, Mrs. McGuire."

"First speaking part in *London*," his friend corrected. "And I've just concluded rehearsing my first speaking part . . . in London. We open in two nights at Daly's."

"Ah, *East Lynne*." Grady folded his arms over his thick chest. "Well, I hope it's a bomb, naturally."

Bethia and Jewel chided him, but all three men chuckled. Mrs. Giovanni came to take Mr. Carey's and Mr. Nicholls's orders.

"You simply *must* try the pizza pie, Mr. Carey," Jewel said.

He nodded. "That's why we're here. I've heard so much about it."

"Are you from Yorkshire as well, Mr. Nicholls?" Bethia asked after he had ordered.

"I am, Miss Rayborn. Does my accent give me away?"

"Actually, you haven't much of an accent." She looked at Mr. Carey. "Neither have you."

"My mother's family moved from Bristol when she was thirteen," he explained. "She never really picked up the accent, and hence, neither did I."

"I lost my accent when we were in theatre at Oxford," said Mr. Nicholls. "I had to have the audience understand what I was saying."

"As well as professors," Mr. Carey reminded him.

"You both went to Oxford?" Bethia hoped her surprise was not too obvious. Oxford was for the sons of the wealthy, or at least comfortable middle class. But William had worked his way through as a servant, so anything was possible.

"We graduated from Corpus Christi College, in fact." said Mr. Nicholls. "Noah with honors, me by the skin of my teeth."

"Jude is actually brighter than I am," Mr. Carey said, "but he would freeze up for examinations."

Mr. Nicholls nodded.

Grady leaned forward, elbows upon table. "You know, before I left Ireland, I assumed all Englishmen sounded alike. I know that to be far from true now, but I confess I'm not sure that I would recognize a Yorkshire accent."

A spark lit Mr. Nicholls's eyes. In a singsong voice, he said, "Wherst tha bin last neet?"

"I beg your pardon?" Grady said.

"I said, where have you been last night?"

"And we've words you won't hear down here," Mr. Carey said. "Such as, well, *gloppened*."

"Which means . . . ?" Bethia asked.

"Surprised." He smiled at her. "I was *gloppened* to notice you beside us."

"And you invited us to share your *mickle* table," said Mr. Nicholls, "because ours was so small."

Even though everyone was smiling, a sheepish look stole over Mr. Carey's face.

"Do forgive our rambling on," he said. "We couldn't wait to leave Yorkshire, but we do get homesick at times, as is obvious."

"No apology is necessary," Jewel said. "It was quite entertaining. Do you hear from your families often?"

Mr. Nicholls did not reply. Mr. Carey gave him a glance that seemed tinged with some sadness and replied quietly, "My mother and I exchange letters once a week or so."

Recovering from the melancholy that had briefly descended, Mr. Nicholls turned to Bethia and smiled. "Noah has always been considerate of his mother. He'll make some fortunate woman a good *mmph*!"

The latter was blurted with a little jump of the shoulders, as if he were suddenly seized by an attack of dyspepsia. Or as if someone had kicked him beneath the table. The only logical person was Mr. Carey. Bethia glanced at him. The actor's countenance was as bland as cream.

"I understand why you're so enamored with Miss Rayborn," Jude said on Sloan Station platform for the underground train that would carry them to Leicester Square. "I'd go after her myself if you weren't my best friend."

"Sh-h-h!" Noah hissed, even though they had parted company with the McGuires and Miss Rayborn at the theatre.

"Sorry to disappoint you, old man," Jude said, lowering his voice. "She didn't follow you."

Noah glowered at him. "She has a fiancé, as you know. I didn't appreciate your hinting like that in front of her."

"And *I* didn't appreciate that kick. There is very little cushioning over the shinbone, you know."

"You had it coming. And I'm not enamored. Can't a man *like* a woman without romance entering the picture?"

"Of course he can."

"Are we only allowed friendships with fifty percent of the population?" Noah asked, picking up steam.

"Perish the thought!"

"So, *there*."

"So, there!" Jude echoed.

They stood in silence on the platform, both sets of hands in pockets, both sets of ears attuned to the faraway whistle, both sets of eyes watching the tunnel. Presently Jude turned to Noah again. "Too bad about the fiancé, though."

Noah could not help but grin. "Lucky bloke."

Thirty-One

On Saturday evening Noah wondered why Richard Whitmore had yet to appear, now that orchestra music from the opening theme floated into the greenroom.

A figure stepped through the doorway, but it was only Lewis. Lewis, wearing a worried expression. Beckoning him. "Mr. Carey, if you please?"

"Of course."

Out in the corridor, Mr. McGuire was hastening in his direction from the stairs. "You'll be playing lead tonight, Mr. Carey."

"Is Mr. Whitmore ill?" Noah asked. They had exchanged greetings in the corridor just an hour ago, and the actor had seemed hale and hearty, if a little flush.

"He's . . . feeling out of sorts."

Noah glanced at the staircase. "Can you delay the curtain for a little while? Perhaps some broth would—"

Mr. McGuire shook his head. "Won't help."

Lady Holt was summoned out into the corridor and took the news stoically. But as Noah escorted her into the wing, she murmured, "Are you quite sure you know your lines completely, Mr. Carey?"

"Yes, Lady Holt."

"Very good." She smiled, but the warning in the violet eyes canceled out any warmth in her expression. "See that you pay attention to your cues out there. Because if you embarrass me, I'll do my best to have you sacked."

Once he got over the shock, he opened his mouth to inform her that he had played the part of Robert Brierly some forty times on the York stage, could play it blindfolded, in his sleep, juggling, or with whatever handicap she would care to choose.

But then he realized that saying so would only soothe the uncertainty she must surely be feeling over sharing center stage with an understudy on a Saturday night. After the threat she had just delivered, he rather liked the idea of her being uncertain.

He allowed anxiety to creep into his expression, because he was, after all, an actor. "I'll try my best, Lady Holt."

"See that you do," she said.

"Just remind me . . . what are my cues?"

He left her gaping like a pike, his practiced ear having picked up his very first cue onstage, the voice of the James Dalton character saying, "Ah, here's my pigeon!"

"Aye! Nobody will say Bob Brierly craned while he could keep't going," Noah said, striding out to drop into a chair. The confusion in the audience was almost palatable. Some murmurs reached his ears.

Pretend you're back in York, he thought, and his momentary stage fright left him, replaced with the confidence that came from practice.

The applause was quite healthy as the tableau curtain closed for intermission, giving Noah hope that mass members of the audience had not slipped out during the first two acts. He wouldn't have noticed if they had, so much had he absorbed the character of Robert Brierly.

"Good job, Mr. Carey!" said Mr. Webb, pounding his back. Members of the cast congratulated him as well, with the exception of Lady Holt, who made a beeline for her dressing room. It all felt very good, better than he would have imagined.

Mrs. McGuire actually gave him a sisterly embrace in the corridor. "You saved the show, Mr. Carey."

"Thank you," he replied, smiling. "I'm just going to run up and look in on Mr. Whitmore."

"That's very kind of you. But Mr. McGuire took him home."

"Is there anything I can do for him?"

Mrs. McGuire lowered her voice. "Just pray he pulls himself together."

He got the message. His heart went out to the man, who was generous with acting advice toward a mere understudy and was one of the few not to shun him during the itching phase. He wondered if the coldness Lady Holt displayed toward Mr. Whitmore, in the face of his infatuation, had anything to do with this. Another reason to dislike her, not to mention the unkindness she had displayed toward Miss Rayborn. The rumor mill's latest was that Lady Holt had patched things up with Miss Rayborn, but Noah remained skeptical. He knew firsthand how effectively a layer of beauty could hide a core of cruelty.

Lady Holt gave him still another reason to dislike her as they stood in the wing again, waiting their cues for Act III.

"It appears you knew your cues very well after all, Mr. Carey," she said in low voice. "I suppose you think that was very clever."

He looked at her to see if she was joking, in the friendly sardonic way he and Jude sometimes made sport with each other. There was no evidence of that in her stone-cold expression. This time he made no reply, but reached up with his left hand to scratch his right shoulder vigorously. Her violet eyes widened, and she took a step away from him.

Act III sailed by as if on wings, the cast delivering their lines as if forgetful that over six hundred people were watching from the seats. There was no standing ovation, save from a handful of souls who sat down again quickly when they discovered themselves to be the only ones. But the applause was hearty. It was only as Noah was taking his bows that he allowed himself to cast aside the needful illusion that he was on the York stage.

I'm in London, he thought while tears coursed down his cheeks. *Father, you can take me now and I'll be satisfied that I've lived a good life.*

When the final curtain closed and the applause was melding into sounds of rustling feet and conversation, members of the cast congratulated him and each other.

"Good job!" said Corrie Walters, giving him a quick sideways embrace.

Lady Holt stepped closer, and for a maddening second Noah imagined she would do the same. Instead, she gave him a chill little smile and said, "Before you think yourself too high and mighty, Mr.

Carey, you might remember that this is our first night in three weeks *not* to have a standing ovation."

The dart hit its mark in Noah's chest. The only variable in tonight's performance was him. As his shoulders deflated, he took note of the dislike in her eyes. Or was it mirrored from his own?

"How does it feel," he asked, "to discover that they were rising for Mr. Whitmore all along, and not for you?"

If looks could have killed, he would have been a heap of ashes. She turned and walked away. Whether or not she could have him sacked frightened him not one iota. He had not endured poverty and physical torment just to kowtow to a spoiled prima donna. Not with some thirty-five other theatres in London.

———

"Mother, I have guests arriving in an hour," Muriel said into the telephone mouthpiece on Sunday afternoon. She felt as fatigued as if she had not lain in until almost ten. In spite of having to orient herself to working with a new lead last night, and with very little notice, she had delivered a fine performance. So had said Mr. Webb, who ought to know. And he was the *only* person to say so, with everyone else in the company vying with each other for a turn to pound that cheeky sheep farmer on the back as if he had played Macbeth for the Queen. She hoped he had bruises the size of saucers this morning.

And now, her mother's petulant voice.

"All I said was that wet-nursing one baby after another would ruin her figure," her mother went on, as though Muriel had not reminded her twice already that she did not have time to chat. "Besides, she's too weak."

"But that's her decision, Mother," Muriel argued, hopefully to hasten an end to the conversation. "And why should a minister's wife need worry over her figure?"

"Well, I tried to help by insisting Sally come stay with us for a couple of weeks. Florence could look after her just fine. But Bernard says they don't want her to feel as if her brother displaced her. As if she would know. She's but fourteen months old!"

"I really must finish dressing," Muriel said, winding the telephone cord about her forefinger. "Why don't you sit out in your garden? I'll ring you again after my guests leave."

"No you won't."

Muriel closed her eyes, filled her lungs again. "Yes I will."

"You'll forget." A sniff, and then her mother's voice became more brittle. "I don't even feel as if I have family anymore. Douglas is gone, Bernard is wrapped up in his family and church, and you are—"

"I'm coming for a nice visit between shows." A three-day, two-night visit, actually, but it was better than nothing.

"In two weeks, yes?" her mother said.

"Well, later. Grady says we'll be running this one until the twenty-second of October."

She braced herself, but silence followed, as if her mother had to gather up her strength before dissolving into hysterics. An idea flashed into Muriel's mind, and she spoke it impulsively.

"Why don't I send Georgiana and her nanny in the meantime?"

The advantages would be three-fold, Muriel realized. Not only would her mother be mollified, but she would not have to invent outings—such as today's to the Botanical Garden—so that Georgiana and Mr. Russell would not be at the house at the same time. And she would be relieved, at least for a while, of guilt over not spending enough time with Georgiana. Her mother would dote over her.

"You would do that?" her mother said in a small voice.

"The country air would be good for her."

"You haven't still got that nanny with eyes like a monkey, do you?"

"Mother, Prescott is very capable. I'll put them on the train Wednesday."

The voice on the other end of the line strengthened dramatically. "That will be lovely, darling. Now, go prepare for your tea. That's nice that you're establishing friendships with your neighbors."

Mr. Russell arrived at ten of two, giving Muriel very little time to speak with him. Her guests arrived almost en masse: Mrs. Fiske, Mrs. Griffen from next door on the west and her niece Miss Davy, Mrs. Postgate from across the Square and her sister Mrs. Scott, and Mrs. Farmer, who knocked at the door yearly collecting donations for seamen's widows.

Conversation flowed more easily than Muriel would have imagined, against the backdrop of Mr. Russell's soothing music. Muriel *enjoyed* herself more than she would have imagined, considering that she had only invited them because she needed a half-dozen props, the minimum amount necessary to hold a realistic social gathering.

They were full of questions about the theatre, such as was she nervous when she auditioned for that first part, how did it feel to have the attention of so many people, and how long did rehearsals go before a production was considered ready?

"Is Mr. Whitmore as charming in person as he is onstage?" Mrs. Postgate asked, and her subtle tone made it obvious that she was really asking if the love scenes were not just acting. The anticipation that came over the other five faces gave evidence that they were wondering the same.

"He's very charming," Muriel replied. "And a good friend. I hope he finds a nice little wife one day." Just in case Mr. Russell could hear her over the sound produced by the strings near his ear.

"Thank you, Mr. Russell," Muriel said after her guests had left with declarations of having had a lovely time. "Your music lent elegance to the whole little affair."

"It would have been an elegant affair without me. But thank you, Lady Holt." He hesitated. "And I'm glad you were mistaken over why no one came last week."

"So am I." She gave him a cautious little smile. "And now I wonder if I might persuade you to stay a little longer? My servants enjoyed your impromptu concert so much last week. I rather hinted to them that I would ask again. I'll pay extra, of course."

"I would be honored. But I'll not accept payment."

"Mr. Russell . . ."

"We had an agreement, Lady Holt."

"*You* had an agreement," she corrected, wagging a finger at him. "I don't recall having any part in it. And being the gentleman that you are, will you not allow the lady her way?"

He smiled. "If you force a cheque upon me, I'll accept it—being the gentleman that I am—but I'll not cash it."

"Oh, very well." Muriel sighed. "You're a stubborn man, Mr. Russell. But I do admire your integrity. We'll speak more after your concert."

Having been warned this time, the servants quickly abandoned stacking dishes at Mrs. Burles's urging and filled the chairs. This time they were not so timid about singing along to tunes they requested, such as "Hares on the Mountains" and "Sweet Lovely Joan." The warbling was quite awful, Muriel thought, with only Joyce and Mr. Watterson able to maintain pitch. But it was worth the discomfort to her ears when Mrs. Beckingham's bemused face appeared and then disappeared above the wall.

"I would like to do something for Gladys," Muriel said as they sat with cups of tea on the parlour sofa. He remained adamant about not accepting payment, even though he had stayed another hour for the servants' sake.

"She's the one who sang 'Waxie's Dargle' last week," Muriel continued and leaned her head thoughtfully. "Whatever in the world is a *dargle*?"

He smiled at that. "I'm not sure myself."

"Oh well . . . after you left, she said she would give anything to be able to play an instrument and bring such joy to a gathering. I have not brought this up to her for fear of disappointing her if you're not willing, but I wonder if you would consider giving her lessons?"

It would be like throwing money down a well, but she was consoled by the thought that the lessons would last only for as long as the lesson she would teach Bethia Rayborn.

"*She's* the acquaintance you mentioned to me last week?" Mr. Russell asked, clearly a little surprised.

"Yes." Muriel allowed her expression to soften with sentiment. "I do not take my blessings for granted, Mr. Russell. I realize I'm compelled to do something for someone less fortunate. And Gladys has had a difficult life."

She had not actually found the *time* to ask the scullery maid her background, but it would stand to reason that any sixteen-year-old willing to take a job standing in a kitchen washing dishes would have had a difficult life.

"But before I proceed further," she went on, "I must ask you, as one who, well, is familiar with servitude. Will my providing lessons make her feel as a charity case? Because it might not be worth it."

"I'm afraid she won't be able to avoid feeling that way, no matter how you couch your offer," he said frankly. "But if she desires to play music, it's worth it.

"Then, that answers my question," Muriel said. "And I'll be most delicate. Will you teach her, for ten pounds per lesson?"

He stared at her. "Lady Holt, I couldn't accept that in good conscience. She would need three lessons per week, to start."

"You sell yourself too short, Mr. Russell. I've never believed in cutting corners. If I'm going to hire someone, I'm going to hire the best. And if someone is the best, he deserves to be paid well."

Again Mr. Russell seemed at a loss for words. When he finally spoke, it was to say, "I think you sell yourself too short as well, Lady Holt."

She stared down at her teacup as if herself lost for words. She could have taken advantage of the moment, perhaps confessed some attraction to him, but the same instinct that had helped her win Sidney at such a young age caused her to maintain a businesslike attitude.

That did not mean she had to put aside her femininity. Softly, she said, "That means more than you can know, Mr. Russell, hearing you say that. Will you consider teaching Gladys? It would mean so much to her."

"It will be a privilege," he replied, and when she raised her eyes to his again, he smiled. He suggested that ten in the morning on Mondays, Wednesdays, and Fridays would not conflict with his rehearsal and performance schedules. A jolt of disappointment over having to rise early hit Muriel until she reminded herself that she would not actually have to be present during the lessons, just afterward.

But not for the first week. He must not suspect that the lessons were for any reason than her generous nature.

"Have you a violin she can use?" he asked.

Muriel blinked at him. "Won't you bring yours?"

"She'll need one for practicing. I still have my first one. It's fine for a beginner. She may borrow it."

"Thank you, Mr. Russell."

You've missed your calling, she said to herself as his footsteps faded in the corridor outside the sitting room. She should be writing playscripts instead of acting from them.

"Three times a week, m'Lady?" The scullery maid appeared to be constrained from hysterics only by the fact that Muriel could sack her in an instant.

"Actually you'll have to practice every day as well," Muriel said.

"But I don't *want* lessons, if you please."

Muriel sent a bewildered look to Mrs. Abbot, who began stirring a kettle with renewed vigor, as if she had not slowed to eavesdrop. So eager was Muriel to see the results of her magnanimous gesture that she had made a rare visit to the kitchen instead of sending for Gladys. And only to have the stupid girl throw back in her face the offer of a lifetime?

"Do you understand I've offered Mr. Russell thirty pounds weekly? *Thirty pounds!*"

"That's very generous of m'Lady," Mrs. Abbot said reprovingly from the stove.

At having two now against her, Gladys put her hands to her cheeks. She was a plain girl, with dull-looking dark blonde hair and crooked gray teeth. Between sniffs, she whimpered, "Begging m'Lady's pardon, but my Sunday school teacher once tried to give me piano lessons and it was hopeless. All those sharps and flats. . . . Please, m'Lady."

Muriel's patience evaporated. But maintaining control of her voice, she said, "I'm sure violin is easier. It's smaller. You may have an hour to rethink this, Gladys. If I were kindly offered the choice of learning music instead of slaving in a kitchen three hours a week, I believe I would have sense enough to accept."

And Gladys would accept, Muriel knew as she left the kitchen. It was all written out in the playscript in her mind.

$\mathcal{P}$lease allow me, Miss Rayborn," Noah said when he happened upon her at the foot of the backstage stairs Monday.

She was wearing a Gibson Girl white blouse with puffed sleeves that tightened from elbow to wrist, a wide brown leather belt, and blue skirt. "Thank you, Mr. Carey," she said, handing him the tray holding a pink Minton teapot with steam rising from a chipped spout, and four mismatched cups. "And congratulations on your performance Saturday. I wish I would have been here to see it."

"That's very kind of you to say."

She smiled and turned, one hand upon the banister. He waited until there were four steps between them and followed, so as not to crowd her. Her honey-colored hair was caught in a green ribbon at her collar, and the ends curled and bounced against her white blouse. A little lump caught in his throat. He imagined Jude shaking his head.

"Were you nervous?" she asked, turning her chin to speak over her shoulder.

"Not as much as I would have been had I more warning," he replied. "But it helped that I've played the part before."

"I would imagine."

"How are fittings progressing?" he asked.

She turned briefly again to give him a frustrated little smile. "We've misplaced a shirt, somehow. But I'm sure we'll find it shoved out of place in one of the costume-room racks. And rehearsals?"

"Very well. I enjoy watching what started out as chaos, shape up into a fluid piece of work."

"You sound like my cousin."

"I'll take that as a compliment," he said.

Again, the smile over the shoulder. They had to squeeze to the side when a couple of prop men descended, one carrying a floor lamp, the other a crate of some sort. After trading greetings with the two, Noah and Miss Rayborn were silent until they neared the wardrobe room's open door.

"I'll take it from here, thank you," she said, reaching for the tray. "You had best get along to rehearsal. Oh, Lady Holt sent us up some pastries. Would you care for one to bring along?"

"No, thank you." He thought of jokingly cautioning her about poison but discarded the impulse before embarrassing her and himself. "And I hope you find the shirt."

"While Noah Carey's portrayal of Robert Brierly did not measure up to the mark set by such icons of the stage as the late Sir Henry Irving and Richard Whitmore, the understudy performed quite admirably, considering that the role was thrust upon him only seconds before curtain, due to Mr. Whitmore's sudden illness."

Mr. Birch looked up from Mr. Gatcomb's column in the Thursday issue of *Illustrated London News*. "He was drunk as Zeus."

"Mr. Birch, please watch what you say," Bethia admonished. Final fittings were being conducted as planned, meaning someone could walk through the door at any minute. The last person she wanted to hurt was Mr. Whitmore, for whom the denizens of the wardrobe room felt a particular fondness. He was treading the boards again after that one absence, his performances as fine as ever, but his personality backstage more subdued than she had ever seen it.

I would give anything to have him play the pillow trick again, she thought.

The head attendant nodded somberly and continued reading aloud.

"My own absorption into the drama at the Royal Court was

hindered by a nagging suspicion that I had seen Mr. Carey onstage in a lead role some months ago. The catalog of theatres ran through my mind, until memory served notice that it was the Royal York Theatre, not in London at all.

"I rang the friend I was visiting those ten months ago, fellow newsman Mr. Horace Beard, of the Yorkshire Post, and was informed that Mr. Noah Carey goes by another title in Yorkshire, the Earl of Danby, himself being tenth in a line of succession dating back from an appointment by Charles II."

"My word!" Miss Lidstone exclaimed with hand to her bosom.

"And we thought he was poor, ha-ha-ha!" said Mrs. Hamby.

"Mrs. Hamby . . ." Bethia warned.

"Titles do not always mean money," Mr. Birch said. The three were like a trio of dogs reluctant to give up a choice bone before picking all the meat from it. "You've heard the saying 'land-rich, purse-poor,' haven't you?"

"Is there more, Mr. Birch?" asked Miss Lidstone.

"Quite so." The newspaper rustled as the white-haired man brought it back into his line of vision.

"Wait." Bethia went to the door and peered out. No one lurked. She closed the door and had the wry thought that there were actually *four* dogs in the room. "Do lower your voice, Mr. Birch."

"At my urging, Mr. Beard sought an interview with a Mr. Bryant, stage manager of Royal York Theatre, and learned that Lord Danby was a competent lead actor who simply aspired to test his talent on the London stage. By probing more deeply, namely by buying pints for some of the cast and crew after a show, Mr. Beard learned that Lord Danby's sudden move may have had more to do with having had his heart broken when the daughter of a York physician called off their engagement only weeks before the wedding date.

" 'She simply realized she no longer loved him,' said the physician, who asked that his family name not be published. 'Her mother and I advised her that it was kinder to break an engagement than to go through a wedding without truthfully being able to pledge one's love.' "

"Poor Mr. Carey," Bethia said.

"I'll wager she broke it off because she realized he had no more money," Miss Lidstone said. "The little opportunist."

"How do you think he lost it, ha-ha-ha," said Mrs. Hamby, but with no mirth.

"He doesn't strike me as a gambler," Mr. Birch said. "That's how most of the titled lose their fortunes. Gambling and high living."

"That's none of our business," Bethia reminded them but in the following breath said, "Please do go on, Mr. Birch."

Mr. Birch cleared his throat.

"I caught up with Lord Danby outside Royal Court Theatre on Wednesday, as he arrived to rehearse a minor part in Leopold Lewis's *The Bells.* 'I desired to try for success on the London stage based upon my own merit,' the actor said when asked why he concealed his title. He declined to comment upon the statement by his former fiancée's father, nor would he explain the apparent poverty that has reduced him to lodgings in a house for struggling artists off Leicester Square.

"Fellow lodger Mr. Rigby, who plays the part of the shopkeeper in *The Pink Dominoes* at Toole's Theatre, expressed surprise to learn of Mr. Carey's title. 'He's just like one of us, poor as a beggar's cat.' Mr. Grady McGuire, manager of Royal Court Theatre, expressed likewise surprise but declined to speculate further. 'Mr. Carey is a talented, hard-working actor and a decent fellow,' he said. 'That is all that concerns us here.'

"Mr. McGuire also wished me to announce that the run of *The Ticket-of-Leave Man* is extended until the twenty-second of October, after which Leopold Lewis's *The Bells* opens upon the twenty-ninth."

"Naturally we were stunned," Jewel said in Kensington Sunday afternoon, as she and Grady, Bethia and Guy passed around dishes of roast rib of beef with horseradish sauce, French beans, boiled potatoes, and baked apple pudding from the Red Lion Inn.

She had put aside her reticence to discuss work while at home, for as she said, "It's not every day you learn you have an earl working as an understudy."

"Two more reporters have telephoned since that Thursday edition." Grady dropped a dollop of horseradish sauce upon his beef. "Another knocked on our office door. Everyone is intrigued."

"But Mr. Carey doesn't wish to speak with them," Jewel said. "Not after that Mr. Gatcomb caught him by surprise."

"Why not, do you suppose?" asked Guy. "Wouldn't that sort of—" he held a serving spoon poised over the dish of French beans as he searched for the word— "*mystique* be good for a stage career?"

"The article also made much of his being poor," Bethia explained.

Guy winced. "Then I can understand his reluctance. Poor fellow."

On their way to the underground station again, Bethia asked Guy how the past week's lessons had gone. She had hoped he would mention them during the walk from Kensington Station, where he had met her. Perhaps he felt as Jewel and Grady did most times—loathe to spoil rare leisure times with discussions of work. And Guy worked longer hours than she, with his various obligations.

He sighed and ran a hand through his hatless dark hair, adding to its natural unruliness only a little less than the September wind was already doing. "It's too early to judge, but I suspect she has a tin ear. Learning notes and scales isn't enough. To play strings, you *have* to have that ear for music."

"Perhaps that will come," Bethia said.

"I doubt it. You either have it or you don't."

"At least she has the desire to learn."

"I wish she had the desire to practice more." He frowned. "I confess I got a little frustrated Friday and asked if she was *positive* she wanted to play the violin. She started weeping, begging me not to give up on her. What can you do with that?"

"What does Muriel have to say?" Bethia asked, despising herself for going so low as to hope she would discontinue the lessons so that Guy would not be going to her house thrice a week.

He gave her a sidelong look. "Bethia, I haven't seen Lady Holt since Sunday past. The housekeeper lets me in and pays me afterward."

She wished now that she had not asked. The comfort his answer provided was overshadowed by the smallness she felt.

———

On Monday the sounds from the parlour seemed more tortured

feline than from any instrument made by man. Muriel opened the door at two minutes until eleven.

"This weekend, I'd like you to practice drawing your bow across each string," Mr. Russell was saying patiently to Gladys. Patiently, but with a weariness that indicated he had repeated this request before. "Listen closely so that you can tell them apart when I play them."

"How is she progressing?" Muriel asked, stepping into the room as the long-case clock began chiming the eleventh hour.

Mr. Russell smiled at the scullery maid. Instead of the formal clothing he had worn while performing at her teas, he wore a suit of tan tweed that suited his brown hair. "Quite well, Lady Holt."

"Very good, Gladys." Muriel gave her a warm smile. "You may leave now."

The girl avoided her eyes as she left the room. Muriel closed the door and went over to the sofa, where Mr. Russell was latching his violin case.

"How is she really doing?"

He gave her a worried look. "I feel as if I'm stealing your money, frankly."

"Hmm. The money is my least concern, Mr. Russell. But why don't we talk about it over breakfast?" She smiled. "Or early lunch, if you'd rather call it that. It's all set up."

"That's very kind of you, but I have to prepare for rehearsal."

"I see." Muriel sent a pointed glance toward the long-case clock, silent again except for the ticking. "So 'preparing for rehearsal' doesn't include having a meal?"

"Well . . . I have . . ." He smiled sheepishly. "I just wouldn't wish to impose."

"I'll be glad for the company," she said, linking an arm through his. "And we do need to discuss Gladys's lessons, yes?"

"This is my little refuge," she said as he followed her into the morning room. "I have most of my meals here or in the garden. A dining room seems so vast and formal when one dines alone."

"Does your daughter not take meals with you?" he asked, looking at the blue plates over the mantelpiece.

"Of course," she said quickly. "Most times. But with our schedules so different, that's not always possible. She's up in Sheffield, by the way, or I would introduce you. My mother is having a difficult time dealing with my brother's death, and I thought Georgiana would bring her some comfort."

Her reply was more than his simple question required, but she felt compelled to explain. And then she changed the subject by motioning toward the round table near the window overlooking the garden. "Shall we?"

Not knowing how long it would take to convince Mr. Russell to join her for a meal, nor wishing to have servants bustling about serving, she had instructed Mrs. Abbot to prepare cold foods. A joint of roast beef, two veal-and-ham pies, stewed pears, two small molded cabinet puddings, jam puffs, and slices of smoked Cheshire cheese graced the tablecloth.

"All this for just the two of us?" he asked, pulling her chair from the table.

She sat and smoothed her skirts. "I wasn't sure what you'd like, so I asked Mrs. Abbot for a bit of everything."

He was seated across from her now. Puzzlement entered and left his eyes, as if he had entertained the thought of asking how she could have been so certain that he would stay.

Because it's written in my playscript, she answered silently.

Her first order of business was to convince him to continue tutoring Gladys. "She's a shy girl. She may be too nervous in your company to pay attention to the notes properly. Why don't we give her some time?"

He smiled. "Very well."

Muriel returned his smile and held out a dish of cheese. "Are any of your family as musically inclined as you are?"

Taking two slices, he replied, "Some are. My mother sings at church, and my sister Lottie just began her second year at the Royal Academy of Music. But my younger sister, Sharon, can't sit still for music lessons. She's more like our father."

"Well, he must have some very good qualities, being able to run a business as he does."

"Quite so," he said. "Thank you."

"Tell me more about all of them," she said and forced herself to pay attention, even though she could quite identify with the younger sister.

Thirty-Three

As long as she lived, Muriel thought, she would never take a standing ovation for granted. She drank in the applause and shouts of *bravo!* through every pore, blowing one final kiss to the audience as the curtain closed again. She was so caught up in the moment that she gave Richard Whitmore a euphoric smile, though she regretted it for the cautious hope it brought to his expression.

But she had other things to attend and turned from him with a little parting wave. The members of the orchestra would be leaving through the stage door shortly, for they did not have to get out of costume or makeup. "Will you ask one of the violinists to my dressing room?" she asked Lewis.

The callboy gave her the same adoring look that lurked in Richard Whitmore's eyes. "Right away, Lady Holt!"

She lingered in the dressing corridor only as long as courtesy demanded. Six bouquets of roses vied for space upon her dressing table and floor. She was loosening the braids from her May Edwards hair when the knock sounded.

"Come in."

The door opened. "Lady Holt?"

She swiveled upon her stool to smile at a middle-aged man with thinning auburn hair slicked straight backwards from his forehead. She recognized him from the orchestra, of course, but could not recall his name. "Thank you for coming, Mr. . . ."

"Kirk, Lady Holt," he reminded her. "Hubert Kirk. Mrs. McGuire introduced you to my wife and me at the opening night party."

"Oh yes, now I remember." She rolled her eyes prettily. "Forgive me, Mr. Kirk. If I forgot my lines as frequently as I forget names, I wouldn't be here. Do close the door."

He obeyed and stood just inside, wearing an expression of being flattered that she should wish to speak with him, mingled with fear that she might pounce.

You've absolutely nothing to worry about, she thought. "I would like to buy a violin for the orchestra of my brother's church. A gift. But knowing nothing of them, I fear I'll be taken advantage of if I merely walk into a shop. Please enlighten me, Mr. Kirk. What's the best money could buy?"

"Why, a Stradivarius, in my opinion," he said, visibly relaxing enough to prop an elbow against the door. "Some would argue a Stainer. I would give all of my teeth for either."

"How much do they cost?"

"I doubt you could find either one for less than five thousand pounds."

That wouldn't do, she thought, even though she could well afford it. Why spend so much on a man she did not intend to keep?

"Could I get one that you'd give *some* of your teeth for, for less than five hundred pounds?" she asked.

"Absolutely, Lady Holt," he replied. "Johann Hellmer, from Prague, made some fine instruments. I saw one last week in Finny and Yates on Regent Street. Four hundred and sixty quid, and the tone's as mellow and clear as a brass bell."

"Do you think it's still there?"

"Without doubt it is. Most musicians I know can't afford that, and even rich folks wouldn't get one that pricy for children's lessons."

That was all she needed to know. "Thank you, Mr. Kirk," she said, turning to take a pencil from the beaker on the dressing table. She had no paper, so she tore open a packet of dressing pins over the drawer. "Will you write it all down for me so I can ring them tomorrow? They'll deliver it to the house, won't they?"

"Wouldn't you want to look at it first?"

"I don't know violins from violets," she shrugged. "You said it's a good one. I trust your judgment."

He looked flattered and did as she asked. When he handed her the paper and pencil again, she thanked him by insisting he carry home to his wife as many bouquets as his arms would hold, which happened to be four.

"By the way, Mr. Kirk, there are people here who are acquainted with my brother," she said, opening the door for him. She gave him her most compelling smile. "I would hate to have his surprise spoiled. Will you please not mention our chat to anyone? It's very important to me."

In mid-nod he paused, grimaced. "Some of the musicians heard Lewis ask me to your dressing room. They'll ask me about it for sure."

"Hmm." She was annoyed at herself for not taking that into account. The simplest answer seemed best, and he carried the proof of it in his arms. "Just say your wife and I got on well at the cast party, and I wished to share my flowers with her."

"Why, that's very kind of you, Lady Holt," the musician said, as if already forgetting the flowers were now merely props for an excuse and not some gesture of friendship.

Muriel knew enough about backstage gossip to know that he would not be able to keep their conversation secret indefinitely, roses or not. But she was only concerned with stalling the flow for a few days. And even then, she had Bernard as an unwitting alibi. Those were the best kind, she was learning.

———

"Now remember, no personal questions," Bethia warned the seamstresses and Mr. Birch on Thursday the twenty-ninth of September after a glance into the corridor.

"We'll be the soul of tact," Miss Lidstone promised.

"The *souls* of tact," Mr. Birch corrected.

Even though Mr. Carey had played the lead in *The Ticket-of-Leave Man* twelve days ago and was assigned the minor role of the Clerk of Court in the upcoming *The Bells*, he was still an understudy for the moment, making him one of the last actors to be fitted.

He appeared in the doorway two minutes later, bearing a tray with teapot and cups. "Miss Ainsley just made a fresh pot, so I thought—"

"You're not supposed to be bringing us tea, Lord Danby!" Mrs.

Hamby hastened over to him, her voice filled with alarm.

Wonderful! Bethia thought, intercepting Miss Lidstone's dry look.

His face fell. "Please, Mr. Carey would suit me better."

"Thank you, Mr. Carey," Bethia said as Mrs. Hamby took the tray. "Tea is always welcome up here."

Mr. Birch's stooped figure rose from the drafting table stool. "If you'll step behind the screen, Mr. Carey."

"Wait, please."

He had said it softly, but exclaiming it would have caused the same effect. Time froze. Everyone stood still as statues, waiting.

"I assume you've all read the article."

All eyes went to Bethia. She nodded.

"You've all been exceptionally kind to me," he said. "I believe I owe you an explanation."

Bethia looped her measuring ribbon over her neck, raising her beribboned hair to fall over it. Having spent the last several days in the 'hurry' frame of mind, she realized it was no longer necessary. She looked at Mrs. Hamby, lining up cups and saucers on the drafting table. "Shall we talk over tea? I'm sure we have another cup up here somewhere."

The chairs dragged over from sewing machines and odd parts of the room formed a circle. Easier to balance cup and saucer upon a knee than sit at the table that rose to chin height when seated in an ordinary chair. *Or chest height for Mr. Carey,* she thought, smiling at her own silent joke.

"I didn't intend to deceive anyone," he said after swallowing a mouthful of tea. "I just chose not to mention my past."

"I desired to try for success on the London stage based upon my own merit," Mr. Birch quoted from memory.

A shadow of vexation crossed Mr. Carey's patrician features. "I didn't say any of that. That reporter made me sound like a pompous . . . person."

"What did you actually say to him, Mr. Carey?" Miss Lidstone asked.

He looked at her. "I said 'Go away or I'll flatten you on the spot!'"

"Did you, Mr. Carey?" she said with eyes wide, while Mr. Birch chuckled so hard that he had to set his cup up on a corner of the drafting table.

"No." The actor smiled sheepishly. "But I thought it. He stuck to my side like a tick, from Sloan Station to the theatre door."

"Then, why *did* you conceal your title?" Bethia asked.

"Actually, for the reason 'quoted' in the article, though in not so grand terms. I simply wanted to see how far my talent alone would carry me." He shook his head. "My talent and prayer, to be precise."

Bethia's admiration for Mr. Carey grew as she remembered her own early employment at the Royal Court, when she insisted that Jewel and Grady keep to themselves that she was Jewel's cousin. Word had eventually leaked out, though she faulted neither for it. She had learned between then and now that secrets flitted about in the backstage atmosphere like spores, reproducing wherever they landed.

She was also touched that he would mention praying, something Guy could never say in the presence of others, though she was certain that he prayed. Admitting thus, for Guy, would be admitting that he could not succeed on his own. They were somewhat alike, the two men, in that they were driven to prove themselves. Only, because of Guy's background, he had a deeper pride issue.

Mrs. Hamby was studying him intently. A dangerous sign, and sure enough, she said, "The article says you're poor as a beggar's cat, Mr. Carey. Ha-ha!"

Time froze a second time. But once the look of surprise wore off Mr. Carey's face, he laughed and everyone else laughed until he sloshed tea upon the lapel of his coat.

"That description is entirely accurate," he replied, pulling a folded handkerchief from his pocket. "For as long as she lives, my mother has full financial control of the estate my father left me."

"Here, I'll do it." Miss Lidstone took it from him and dabbed at his coat. "Will she not share any of it with you?"

"Nothing would please her more. But then . . ."

"*I desired to try for success on the London stage based upon my own merit,*" Mr. Birch quoted for the second time.

Mr. Carey sent him a smile. "I couldn't have said it better myself."

Once all cups of tea were drained, Bethia got to her feet and the others followed suit. If they sat about chatting any longer, someone was certain to bring up the matter of the former fiancée. She glanced at Mrs. Hamby, who even now seemed to be mulling over something.

The costume coat fit Mr. Carey's broad shoulders perfectly. The hem of the trousers had somehow escaped pressing, but Miss Lidstone would attend to that before they all went home. Bethia accompanied Mr. Carey into the corridor and to the staircase, fearful that if she brought up the subject that had dominated their tea party again in Mrs. Hamby's hearing, the word *fiancée* would be given air.

"I appreciate your being so candid with us, Mr. Carey," she said with voice lowered slightly. "But I hope you felt no pressure to do so."

"It's sort of a relief to get it out," he said. "I suppose I can only comfortably be who I am."

She smiled, reminded him, "Unless you're onstage."

"Unless I'm onstage," he echoed. His brown eyes softened over his smile, the way Father's did when he leaned his cheek for a good-night kiss, the way Mother's did sometimes in the mirror whenever Bethia brushed her hair. And suddenly the look was gone, the eyes opaque as mahogany buttons. His feet shifted. "I should go now. Good day, Miss Rayborn."

"Good day, Mr. Carey."

Shame about the fiancée, Bethia thought on her way back to the wardrobe room. It was not her place to judge someone she had never even met, especially without being informed of the situation from both sides. But, she thought, a woman who would decide she did not love Mr. Carey must be exceptionally hard to please.

"Please give Gladys another week," Muriel said to Mr. Russell on Friday. "She so desperately wishes to learn."

She had persuaded the musician to accept her invitation to the Savoy for lunch this time, stating Bethia would understand that it was a reward for his not giving up on the lessons. But she had a feeling he would not even mention it to her.

The awe Mr. Russell had been attempting to conceal in his expression ever since they walked into the restaurant faded briefly into sobriety. "You know, Lady Holt, she would be more suited to piano, if she's that desperate. Not having an ear for music would not be such a liability, as the notes on the piano cannot be made sharp or flat by the press of a finger."

Because he was unfamiliar with the menu, Muriel had ordered prawns with lobster sauce for him, fowl *à la béchamel* for herself. Most of the remaining space upon the cloth was taken up by side dishes—artichokes *à l'Italienne,* stewed mushrooms, potatoes *à la maître d'hôtel,* cauliflower with parmesan cheese, baked tomatoes, broiled mushrooms. She leaned forward and stretched out her arm with half an artichoke heart impaled upon her fork. "I insist you taste this. They seem like sweets to me."

After a hesitation he leaned forward and opened his mouth. He chewed self-consciously, swallowed, and smiled. "Very good."

"Would *you* consider giving Gladys piano lessons?"

"I'm sorry," he said a little tersely.

Muriel realized why she had offended him. Piano lessons were usually given by dowagers needing a genteel way to maintain a life-style no longer supported by a fat bank account. Not fitting for a man with pride.

She wasn't too alarmed. She smiled across the table, aware that she looked especially beautiful today. Just because a woman wore mourning clothes did not mean she had to give up elegance. The black cloth only intensified the ash-blonde and golden waves rippling over her shoulder to her tiny waist. Nor did it mean she had to give up dabbing the intoxicating scent of Fougere upon her neck and wrists.

"No, you definitely weren't meant to teach piano. You're still concerned over wasting my money. May I be frank with you, Mr. Russell?"

"Please, Lady Holt."

"Thanks to shrewd investments my late husband made, there is more in my account than I can spend in a lifetime. I do not say this with any pride, mind you, for I did nothing to earn it. I don't know a stock certificate from a bill of sale. So even if the lessons turn out to be a waste of money, it won't cause a hardship. And I would have afforded Gladys some pleasure."

He sat silent, chewing a bite of pigeon pie, digesting her little speech. "What's it like?" he asked at length. Cautiously, as if against his better judgment.

"What's what like?" she asked, though she knew.

"Having more money than you can spend."

Her eyes locked with his. "It's quite nice, Mr. Russell. I can afford to be charitable to people like Gladys. And it allows me to give gifts to people I admire."

Muriel lingered at her dressing table that evening at the Royal Court. Jewel knocked and stuck her head into the room. "Good, you're still here. I had to explain to a reporter that after a show isn't a convenient time to be pressing for an interview. I just wanted to congratulate you on another excellent performance."

"Thank you," Muriel said, turning again to her mirror to wipe rouge from her cheek. "But I don't mind giving an interview."

Not tonight, when she needed an excuse to linger.

Her cousin stepped on inside and closed the door. "He actually was asking for Mr. Carey. Because he only played that one perform-ance, most reporters haven't *seen* his face, so it's useless to hover about the stage door at night. Especially when he avoids them."

"Oh," Muriel said flatly. It was not too long ago that *she* was the biggest novelty at the Royal Court.

The mirror revealed the uneasiness in Jewel's reflected face. "They're intrigued about his being an earl and the like. I'm sure the attention will temper off soon."

"No doubt the publicity is good for you. Why does Mr. Carey avoid reporters?"

Muriel asked the question simply to mask her feeling of disap-pointment, not because she gave a whit about "His Smugness." She would *never* address him as Lord Danby, she thought, even though an earl was only outranked by a duke and a marquise on the peerage scale, and Sidney's title as baron fell at the very bottom. *He may outrank you,* she said to herself, *but you don't live in a crumbling lodging house or lurk about the greenroom hoping someone falls ill so you can act.*

"He wants to be judged by his talent," Jewel said. "Not some melodrama they've cooked up about his background."

"Hard to do when you rarely walk out onstage," Muriel said flippantly.

She halfway expected to see Mr. Russell outside the stage door, but she was not surprised when he was not among the half dozen people seeking to have their playbills inscribed. There were those who would recognize his face.

Can you see me now, Douglas? she thought as the coach clattered down fog-shrouded streets. *Will you rest easier after she has paid?*

Whether he would or not, she had no way of knowing. As for herself, untroubled sleep was becoming a thing of the past. She felt as if she were walking downhill, taking bigger and bigger steps to stay balanced, unable to stop. A little part of her said that only letting go of her obsession with Bethia Rayborn's crime would bring her peace. But having already stepped out onstage, she had to play her part.

She was glad Georgiana was up in Sheffield. The idea of her being under the same roof, albeit a different floor, was disturbing. A warning sting came to her eyes. She blinked and tried to comfort herself by allowing her mind to travel back across the highlights of this evening's performance. The audience had loved her, as usual. Their goodwill flowed up onstage like a serene river, sustaining her. If only she could find a way to bottle that goodwill, she thought, she would have it for the low times.

Mr. Russell was seated on the top step of her house, a fog-blurred form eerily illuminated by the light over the door.

"Shall I see you to the door, m'Lady?" Ham asked after helping her to the pavement, eyeing the figure, who was now standing.

Muriel could see the violin case through the fog. She had paid a courier boy to deliver it to the flat above the saddle shop on Bond Street at five so that Mr. Russell would not have the opportunity to come out here until the Royal Opera and the Royal Court let out. "No. I'm fine," she replied.

"I can wait."

"No."

He climbed back into the driver's seat. Hooves clattered down the street on their way to the mews. Muriel walked toward the door.

"Lady Holt," her visitor said. He was still dressed in white tie and tails. The violin case rested in the crook of one arm. The top hat was still perched upon a step behind him.

"Good evening, Mr. Russell." Even though she was an actress, it would have been silly to pretend surprise. "How was the opera?"

"You know that I cannot accept this."

They stood only three feet apart. Close enough for her to see the confusion in the young man's face, even though darkness hooded his eyes.

"Then you'll disappoint me," she said, taking a step closer.

Hesitation, then, "I love Bethia."

Softly, Muriel said, "Of course you do."

For you, Douglas.

"But you *like* me. Isn't that so, Mr. Russell?"

Thirty-Four

*W*hat say you to a couple of steaks, now that we have a little more pocket money?" Jude said as he and Noah walked away from St. Andrew's on Sunday the ninth of October.

Their finances were a bit healthier now that Jude had a minor speaking role and Noah was rehearsing for one. But Noah had to pass, regretfully. "I'm saving for another suit. I'd like to give back the clothes I borrowed from wardrobe as soon as possible. But you go."

His friend shook his head. "We would be foolish to pass up the only non-soup day at the lodging house anyway. But when we've claimed our success we'll have steak every day."

"Except the days we have lobster," Noah said, absently kicking a small stone.

"And pheasant." Jude kicked it next.

The sun overhead pleasantly warmed an afternoon as crisp as a fall apple. A fine day for being out-of-doors, Noah thought. "Why don't we walk out to the embankment later? All I plan to do is write home sometime today."

"Don't you have to study?"

Noah tapped his temple. "I have it all down."

Not only his forty-two words, but Mr. Whitmore's lines as well. Having already acted *The Ticket-of-Leave Man* in York meant Noah had only to read over the playscript now and again to refresh his memory, giving him ample time to study ahead for *The Bells.*

"How is Miss Rayborn?" Jude asked. They had caught up with an older man and woman strolling at a leisurely pace, and so to file past them meant leaving the stone in its new habitation.

Noah scowled at him. "Engaged. As if you didn't know."

"All's fair in love and war, you know," Jude persisted, like a gnat that refused to be fanned away from his ear.

"Why do you come out with these things?" Noah asked. "Two months ago you were quoting poetry about guarding my heart."

"You obviously didn't listen. So now I have to help you win her. Besides, I rather liked her. She thought I was witty. I could tell."

They had reached the lodging house. Noah opened the door and paused. "I appreciate your looking out for me, but do pay me the favor of letting this drop, will you? It's a lost cause."

Jude shrugged, but with understanding in his dun-colored eyes. "Whatever you wish, big fellow."

————————

Bethia raised the lid of the rosewood davenport in the parlour that was shared by all members of the family, even though each bed-chamber had a writing table. Danny had only been away two-and-a-half weeks, but by the time a letter reached him, another week would have passed. She knew from experience how welcome was news from home. And in the parlour, she had family input.

"Tell him John has Mr. Lamb for calculus," Sarah said.

Sarah says that John has Mr. Lamb for calculus, Bethia wrote.

"The macaroons," Mother reminded, crochet needle spearing and looping white yarn through a half-completed baby blanket, a gift for a neighbor up the road who was expected to deliver by Christmas.

Mother and Trudy made macaroons for you Friday. They will take longer to reach you than this letter, so expect them any day.

"And the pens." This from William, at the chess table with Father.

"What brand were they?" Bethia asked, her own pen to the side over the blotter. After he replied, she wrote *William enclosed two Jointless Lucky Curve pens.*

She looked to her father, who lifted his eyes from the chess board. "Remind him that we love him."

Bethia smiled. She admired her father for so many things. His thirst for knowledge. His faithfulness toward Mother. His wry humor. His godliness. Integrity.

But his sweetness she appreciated most. It was a shame that the adjective was used primarily for the praise of little girls with curly hair and lace dresses, for it was just as endearing in the soft lines of an aged face.

Father says to remind you that we love you.

The tears that would bring to Danny's eyes would last only for a few seconds, and then he would blink them away and go about his studies with the usual quiet confidence that came from knowing his moorings were secured firmly in the harbor of loving family. She knew that from receiving such letters herself.

Included with her own words was the news about Mr. Carey's being an earl. Danny would never admit it, but he enjoyed hearing what was going on backstage. She addressed and stamped the envelope, but left it and the letter on the open desktop. Guy would want to add something, if only a greeting.

She returned to share the sofa with Sarah, who was reading a copy of Henry James's *What Maisie Knew*. A second later the telephone rang from the lamp table. Her half sister reached for it.

"Oh, good afternoon, Guy." She smiled at Bethia. "Yes, she's right here."

They had to trade places, for the cord only reached so far. Settling in her corner of the sofa, Bethia positioned the earpiece and spoke into the mouthpiece. "Hello . . . Guy?"

"Hello, Bethia. I'm afraid I'll not be able to see you today after all."

"Are you all right?" she asked.

"Fine, Lil—" he began, but cut off the endearment and said with hurried voice, "I haven't quite committed this . . . this Shamus O'Brien piece to memory. I'm going to have to spend some time on it before tomorrow's practice."

"Guy . . ." Deflated, she sank back into the sofa. With his and her busy schedules, she so looked forward to their Sunday afternoons. But at least he seemed to be recovered from the bad cold that kept him away last week. Wise of him to stay indoors out of the rain, lest it develop into pneumonia.

"I know. I'm disappointed too. But I'm the newest violinist, remember? I have to pull my weight."

"They didn't teach it at University?" she asked, for it was not like Guy to admit unfamiliarity with any piece of music.

"Teach an opera by an English composer?" The chuckle that came through the earpiece seemed a trifle forced. "There would have been riots in Bologna."

"Is everything all right?" Mother asked as Bethia stood the telephone back on its table.

"He has to practice," Bethia replied and smiled, for both parents studied her with concern in their expressions. Sometimes it was as if her forehead were made of glass, allowing them to read her thoughts. Or most accurately, her worries.

Guy has never lied to you, she reminded herself. If his voice sounded a little odd, it was probably from frustration with the piece of music he was learning.

That, and from the disappointment of not being able to see her, of course.

———

"Please, Mr. Whitmore," Jewel said on Wednesday the twelfth of October, two hours before another rehearsal for *The Bells* was to commence. "Please . . . you can't *seriously* think of leaving."

The actor gave her a regretful look from the chair facing Grady's desk. As soon as he broke the news, Jewel and Grady had abandoned their own chairs to flank either side of him.

"Don't think I enjoy the thought of leaving, Mrs. McGuire. You're like family. But it's time I moved on. Drury Lane Theatre has offered me *Hamlet*."

Grady passed a hand over his face. "*The Bells* opens in seventeen days. You signed a contract."

"Which is no longer binding, since you set back the date."

"We've never had to draw up new contracts after holdovers before."

"But you should, according to my attorney. Once the opening date changes, the contract has to be renegotiated."

That was correct, Jewel realized. With Royal Court being smaller than the Strand theatres, and with so many cast and crew staying on year after year, they had made the mistake of taking for granted that it would always be so. Of treating the business as if it were a small family concern.

Messrs. Cumberland and Fry would not be happy. She and Grady would most certainly lose their positions. Grady groaned, his mind clearly having reached that same conclusion. "We'll be ruined."

"That's simply not so." Mr. Whitmore shifted in his chair. "Look how you weathered Mrs. Steel's leaving. You have Mr. Carey. He's quite good, you know."

"He's not *you*," Jewel said.

"*I* wasn't me when I first came here. Everyone has to start somewhere. And look at the publicity he's already generated. Think of how it will look on posters and playbills." He made corners in the air with thumbs and fingers, as if forming a poster. "*Lady Holt and Lord Danby* at Royal Court. Drury Lane can't even boast *one* peer, much less two."

We should never have hired Muriel jumped into Jewel's mind and stuck. And now, this rumor that she had inquired about purchasing an expensive violin. Not for one second did Jewel believe Muriel's explanation that it was to go to Bernard's church. But when a person so adamantly protests her innocence, as Muriel had done, what could one do? Accuse her of lying?

"I have to ask this, Mr. Whitmore," she said. "Is this because of Lady Holt?"

He met her eyes, stared for a second, and said with voice a little softer. "What do you think?"

"We'll let her go," Grady said. "If your contract is void, so is hers. You're an institution here."

The actor shook his head. "I've signed a contract with Drury Lane, Mr. McGuire. I can only stay until *The Ticket-of-Leave Man* closes. As long as you don't extend it again."

There was a hesitation, during which he seemed to labor over whether or not to say something.

"What is it, Mr. Whitmore?" Jewel asked.

He sighed. "You might ask her to be more discreet."

"Over what?" Grady asked.

"Mr. Graham and I spotted her with Miss Rayborn's fiancé having lunch at the Savoy on Sunday."

"He's giving violin lessons to her maid," Jewel said, grasping at

358   Lawana Blackwell

straws even while knowing they were only straws.

Mr. Whitmore cocked an eyebrow at her. "I don't wish to be crude, Mrs. McGuire, but it was obvious that *somebody's* getting lessons in *something* other than the violin."

"I'll kill her," Jewel muttered, pacing the floor.

"You can't even mention this to her," Grady said, taking her into his arms. "Not until we've drawn up a new contract and gotten her signature."

She stepped back so she could see his face. "You can't be serious."

"I have to be." His voice was calm, but the gray eyes were filled with the same emotions raging through Jewel. "We can't have her walk out. It's not just our jobs that would be affected."

He was right, she realized. The Royal Court could ill afford to lose two leads. They may as well tender their resignations.

"What about Bethia?" Jewel asked. "She should know."

He nodded somberly. "We have to consider that it may have been bitterness speaking with Mr. Whitmore. Or that Mr. Russell will come to his senses, if there is something more. We could make a bigger mess of things if we jump in feetfirst. Wait until you've had the chance to talk this over with Muriel. *After* she signs her contract."

"Then, when can we have it drawn?"

"I'll see."

He went to the telephone and rang the theatre solicitor, Mr. Kahn, while Jewel paced the floor and blamed herself for everything, beginning with making peace with Muriel when Lord Holt died.

"He's visiting family in Lincolnshire and won't return until late Tuesday," Grady said, replacing the receiver.

Jewel's rage expanded to include Mr. Kahn until she forced herself to see reason. The old contracts were drawn and signed. He had performed his duty as assigned to him.

Grady came over to hold her by the shoulders and leaned his head against hers. "I'm going to have to ask you to put this aside for now, love. As much as it hurts. We've lots to do and little time."

"Ah, there you are, Mr. Carey," said Mr. Birch when Noah stepped into the lobby. "Rehearsal is canceled today. But the McGuires would like to see you posthaste."

"Thank you," Noah said. *Mr. Hicks must be returning.* That meant he would lose his understudy job, for his contract still contained the clause that the position was as temporary fill-in. Would they keep him on just to play Clerk of Court? Or would Mr. Hicks be assigned that role as well?

Father, help me to bear whatever comes, he prayed under his breath.

The door swung open. Mr. McGuire stood in the gap, as somber as a mortician.

"Come in, Mr. Carey."

Mrs. McGuire sat at her desk. She had obviously been weeping.

Moved by her pity for him, Noah forced a smile, as Mr. McGuire closed the door. Forced himself to say, "Really, it's quite all right, Mrs. McGuire. I was aware coming in that it was only temporary."

Husband and wife gave each other looks Noah could not decipher. And then Mr. McGuire broke into chuckles that shook his stocky frame, so much so that he had to back up to his chair and sink into it.

Mrs. McGuire's expression softened somewhat. "Do sit down, Mr. Carey," she said as her husband wiped his eyes. "We asked you in here because there may be a casting change for *The Bells.*"

"Yes, I understand." Noah sat down and wondered if Mr. McGuire had possibly lost his faculties and why his wife did not seem alarmed. "Mr. Hicks is returning."

That prompted another chuckle from Mr. McGuire. Grinning, he said, "This has nothing to do with Mr. Hicks. If we can't muster up a proper lead actor for *The Bells* very soon, you're it."

Noah took a moment to cycle that last statement through his mind, and still he did not grasp it. "I'm afraid you've lost me. What about Mr. Whitmore?"

Mr. McGuire sobered. "He'll be leaving when *The Ticket-of-Leave Man* closes to play Hamlet at Drury Lane. He recommended you, and that carries a lot of weight with us."

"We would have to insist you use your title professionally," Mrs. McGuire added. "You would have to be known as 'Lord Danby.'"

"That's all you think I have to offer?" Noah said with heart sinking. "My title?"

"We do not," she said. "We know you have talent."

"But the title will help draw an audience," Mr. McGuire admitted. "We can't stay open without audiences, Mr. Carey. After they're in their seats, the rest is up to you and the others."

Noah mulled this over. He had grown used to *Mr. Carey* from cast and crew. Might they think he was putting on airs if that were to change suddenly? "You wouldn't insist the others address me by the title, would you?"

"Not if you'd prefer they didn't," said Mrs. McGuire after husband and wife exchanged bemused looks.

"Do you agree, Mr. Carey?" Mr. McGuire asked.

He smiled at the both of them. "There is another word in the Yorkshire vernacular. *Eejit*. That's what I would have to be to turn this down."

Once the office door closed behind him, he eased open the greenroom door. Empty. He stepped inside, eased the door shut again, and got down on his knees. It seemed fitting that this should be the place to send up his first prayer of thanks.

"You really thought you were to be sacked?" Jude asked Noah that evening as they sat over bowls of oxtail soup before returning to their respective theatres for evening performances.

Noah paused from blowing on a spoonful. "I was convinced of it once I got a look at their faces."

"When will they let the others know?"

"At tomorrow's rehearsal. Mind you, it's not carved in stone."

"They'll never find someone on such short notice." His friend shook his head in wonder. "Incredible!"

"Then, it's all right with you?"

Jude cocked an eyebrow at him. "Why should I mind?"

"Well, you came down here before I did."

"I'm overjoyed! In fact, I would plant a kiss on your ugly mug right now if it wouldn't make Mrs. Savill throw us out." He looked over his shoulder, lowered his voice. "I suppose you'll be looking for a better place to live."

"Hmm. I hadn't thought of that." Noah had grown used to near poverty. The fact that he would earn much higher wages, if this opportunity came to pass, had not sunk in. "It would be nice to sleep on a mattress that doesn't dip in the middle, wouldn't it?"

"Absolutely." His friend still smiled, but the light in his eyes had faded a bit.

"But I'll not move unless you come with me," Noah said.

Jude shook his head. "That's very good of you. But I won't do that until I can afford to carry my weight."

"But—"

"*You* of all people should understand that."

"Then I'll wait until you can," Noah said. "It's only a matter of time. Besides, it would be wise to build up a nest egg for a while. There's no guarantee that I won't bomb."

"As if!"

Noah raised a finger as if he were a schoolmaster making an essential point. "But you'll indulge me in this one matter, or I'll never give you a moment's peace over it."

"What matter?" Jude said, eyes narrowing suspiciously.

"When my wages rise, I want to buy new beds for our rooms."

He expected an argument, but Jude smiled. "Will you throw in sheets without holes?"

Noah smiled back. "That goes without saying."

The landlord's wife walked by the table. "Don't talk so much. Eat your soup. Others will need the table."

The other members of the cast were clearly stunned to hear Mr. McGuire's announcement the following afternoon. A couple of the actresses wept. Lady Holt remained stone-faced.

Did they resent him? Noah couldn't fault anyone who would. Here he was, the newest member, and an understudy at that, landing the plum role. *Possibly* landing the role, his mind amended.

But he should have remembered how theatre people were used to rolling with punches, for there were handshakes and claps on the back when Mr. McGuire left the stage.

"Congratulations, Mr. Carey," Miss Rayborn said in the corridor after rehearsal. She looked as fetching as ever, even with the simple lines of her gown—gray, with burgundy pinstripes and burgundy ruffle down the bodice.

Knowing he should not ask, but unable to resist, he said, "If this *does* come to pass, will you come watch?"

She smiled. "I missed the last time. But I'll not miss this one."

The way she said it warmed his heart, but she could affect him the same way by commenting upon the weather, he supposed. "Thank you, Miss Rayborn."

Again she smiled. "What are friends for?"

He was surprised in that he was not crushed by this. Later, he realized why. Just because a deeper relationship was not possible did not mean he should sulk and miss out on the gift she was offering. Friendship with a good person was still a marvelous thing.

Thirty-Five

*W*hen Guy had not appeared in Hampstead by four o'clock on Sunday the sixteenth, Bethia rang the Russells' flat.

Lottie answered the telephone, and after an exchange of greetings said, "He said he was going to your house."

"When did he leave?" Bethia asked.

"About noon." A pause, then, "Is John there?"

"He *was*. Sarah and William are taking him back to school."

"Lottie?" sounded in the background. Mrs. Russell's voice.

"Are you quite sure Guy said he was coming here?" Bethia asked.

"I'll ask Mother."

She heard murmuring, then Mrs. Russell's voice again, this time more clearly. "Bethia? Isn't Guy over there? That's where he said he was heading."

"He isn't here." Bethia shrugged at her parents, gave them a smile that conveyed nothing was wrong, apparently just a misunderstanding.

"Perhaps he decided to run an errand first and got detained."

"Yes, that's probably what happened," Bethia said into the mouthpiece. "Shall I have him ring you?"

"Yes, please." A half second passed, then, "No, never mind. He doesn't like being treated as a child. Do give our love to your family."

"It's not like Guy to be thoughtless," Mother said at the supper table three hours later.

"Perhaps you should ring over there again," Father said.

Bethia shook her head, wishing she had waited until the family was clear of the parlour before ringing the Russells. She had caused them to worry over what was probably nothing. Any minute now she would be summoned to the telephone, would hear his voice.

After supper she settled on the sofa with a copy of Grossmith's *The Diary of a Nobody*. Light reading, but it would be useless to attempt anything that would require strenuous concentration. Even so, her eyes wandered through many a paragraph that her mind did not absorb. The longer the telephone sat mute, the more she could not help but wonder. Did what was beginning to seem like evasive behavior on Guy's part have anything to do with Muriel Holt?

The following morning she stepped from Sloan Square Station into daylight, groggy from lack of sleep.

"Bethia."

"Guy!" she exclaimed, hand to her heart, then smiled. "You almost gave me—"

The smile died when she noticed the gravity in his expression. "What's wrong?"

He looked away for a second, again at her. "Will you come with me?"

"Where?"

"I hired a coach," he said with a nod toward the vehicle, team and driver waiting, just a few feet away. Bethia had paid it no mind, for traffic was simply part of the topography of London.

"Very well," she said. He stood as rigid as a sleepwalker while holding the door. No supporting hand upon her back as she stepped up into the coach or even companionable touch upon her coat sleeve.

"Where are we going?" she asked when he was seated in the seat facing hers and the coach jolted slightly into movement. She wondered why he did not smile. If he would but smile, everything would return to normal.

He turned his face toward the window. "Just across the Square."

Automatically looking through the same window, Bethia spotted Mrs. Hamby and Miss Lidstone nearing the doors to the Royal Court, probably commenting to each other on the pleasantness of the mid-October morning.

"I didn't know where else to go," Guy said, still not looking at her.

Bethia had never considered herself a genius, but she read books, even had earned a college certificate. And she had known Guy from her earliest memories. He would not waste money on a coach just for privacy if he did not have a serious discussion in mind. The lack of any intimacy in his demeanor could mean only one thing.

"So it's true," she said dully, as ice spread through her stomach. "Muriel."

He turned to her. The whites of his eyes were pink, making the irises seem even bluer. "We've fallen in love."

"Guy . . ." Tears stung her own eyes. "Muriel is leading you on out of revenge toward me. Can't you see that?"

"She said you would say that. There's a side to her that few people know, Bethia. It's as if we're soul mates, if that makes any sense."

"It makes no sense at all. I love you. For years, you've said you love me."

I *still* love you, Bethia," he said thickly.

She shook her head. "But you love her more."

He looked away again.

"After knowing her for how long?" Bethia asked. The tears clinging to her jaw turned cold and dropped upon the front of her coat. "Five weeks? Six?"

"How can I explain how she makes me feel?" He wiped his cheeks with his coat sleeve. "This is so awful, Bethia. You're such a good person. I would rather *die* than hurt you."

"And yet you still live," she said with dark dryness. "Why couldn't you do this out at the house? I never knew you to be a coward."

He winced as if she had slapped him. "You're so protective of your parents. I just assumed you would rather . . ."

"I can't believe you don't see how Muriel's using you."

"You're wrong, Bethia." The coach rocked to a gentle stop across the Square from the theatre. Pathetic earnestness filled Guy's expression. "She feels as bad about this as I do, if that's any consolation."

He's serious, she thought, staring at the face she had thought she knew so well. Serious, and deluded. Every hollow space inside her face felt impacted with concrete. She pulled a handkerchief from her handbag, wiped her eyes and cheeks and blew her nose, then reached for the door handle.

"Very well, Guy. Have a good life."

"Wait . . ." Finally he touched her, a restraining hand upon the sleeve of her coat. "Don't go like that, Bethia. Please. We have to talk."

She shook his hand away. "What more is there to say? You've taken leave of your senses. And I don't want to be with anyone who doesn't want to be with me."

Pain caused her to hurl that at him. But if he would speak her name with any tenderness and regret in his voice, take back his dreadful words, she knew that she would throw herself into his arms. When he only sat rubbing his forehead, she was glad for what she had said. She would not beg him to love her. He did not have a monopoly on pride.

"Please, Bethia," he said from inside as she stepped to the pavement.

Pedestrians and traffic seemed to be moving behind the gauze curtain used for nightmare scenes at the Royal Court. Irrationally, she was stung by the coldness of the milieu, that people could continue with their usual routines without heed to the devastation of a human being in their vicinity. *You can't go to work like this,* she thought. Nor take the underground home. She could tell from the heat in her skin that her face was splotched, and her stinging eyes were already beginning to swell. Not that she gave a whit about her appearance, but she could not abide the curious and even sympathetic stares of strangers.

She turned and almost collided with Guy, exiting the coach.

"You don't need this any more," she said, moving aside so he could pass without their touching. When he was out of the way, she stepped back inside. "Give the driver my address."

"Yes, of course," he said from the door opening. His face was anxious. Whether he was anxious for her or anxious to get over to Muriel and say that the deed was done—or both—did not really matter anymore. "And I'll pay him."

Bethia drew in a breath. "Don't you *dare.*"

While the wheels rolled she was grateful for curtains to draw over the windows. She wept and allowed Guy's words to run though her mind again and again, as if by dissecting them she would be able somehow to make sense of the situation.

At length her mind paused at his statement about her parents. She indeed wished to shield them from this. They would not be able to bear seeing her this way. But how would she explain coming home? And how could she *not* go home, when it seemed the coach could not reach Hampstead soon enough?

She forced her grief-dulled mind to plot. She would signal the coachman to stop just before the carriage drive, and then she'd go around the back of the house. If she met Jack, the gardener, on the way to the terrace door, she would simply explain that she felt a little ill. Which she did. Ill at heart. By the time word spread to other servants and then her family, she would hopefully have had at least a couple of hours of privacy in her room.

"Are you sure you want out in the road like this, Miss?" the coachman, bearded and stocky, said as she dropped a sovereign into his hand on Cannonhall Road. It was far more than the fare warranted, but she did not possess the energy even to care.

Bethia averted her burning eyes from his compassionate ones. "Yes, thank you."

He tsked his tongue, shook his head. "Men are such rakes."

She did not believe that. But it felt good to hear it anyway.

Her plan worked. The only sign of Jack was the metallic sound of some garden implement being sharpened in the potting shed. And she didn't meet anyone on the servants' staircase in the back of the house. As she eased her bedchamber door shut, she was grateful that the bed was made, which meant Susan had already cleaned.

For at least an hour, perhaps two, she lay sideways with the pillow shoved under her neck, stirring only whenever the handkerchief needed to be put to use.

Why, Father?

She swallowed. The stuffiness of her face caused her ears to pop. *I haven't been perfect, but I've tried to do the things that would please you.*

It was not always easy, either. She had loved Guy for so long. His kisses, his embraces left her so lightheaded that it had sometimes been tempting to rationalize going further.

Sounds of movement came from the bedchamber on the west side. William would still be at work for hours, and the bedrooms on this side had apparently been cleaned for the day. She took a chance that the person was Sarah and got up. She slipped through the neighboring doorway without knocking.

Her sister stood at her chest rumbling through a drawer and muttering to herself.

"I *know* it's here."

"Sarah?"

Sarah jumped, then smiled, exhaling, just as Bethia had done earlier. "Oh, Beth . . ." The smile froze. "What's the matter?"

With throat raw, Bethia told her. Her sister held her while she wept some more.

"That's why he stopped coming around," Sarah said, rubbing Bethia's back. "I could just strangle him!"

Bethia did not believe that either, but again, it felt good to hear it. She stepped back to wipe her eyes again. "Do you know where Mother and Father are?"

"They're out for a walk on the Heath."

That meant the parlour was free and clear, at least of parents. "Will you ring Jewel for me? I'm afraid she'll call here, if she hasn't already."

"Certainly." Her sister's lips pressed together. "Shall I inform her of what their *star* has done?"

Bethia rested a hand upon Sarah's arm. As comforting as it was to have her older sister want to fight her battles, she could not allow blame where it did not belong. "This isn't Jewel's fault, Sarah."

Sarah gave a reluctant sigh. "I suppose not."

"Just say that I don't feel well."

Which was again the truth, if an understatement.

"And please don't mention Muriel to Mother and Father," Bethia went on. "I don't want them to know the sordid details."

"Very well." Sarah gave her an understanding look. "But you may not be able to hide that from them forever."

"At least I can try."

"They're stronger than you think," Sarah pressed. "I think it makes them feel small when we shield them from our problems."

"Please," Bethia said, barely capable of managing the *immediate* situation. "Will you just keep that part to yourself, for now?"

Sarah embraced her again. "But of course. Poor baby."

She washed her face and came down at lunch to break the news, which turned out to be the worst possible time, because Trudy's fried whitings lay on the dishes practically untouched. The reason she gave was that Guy no longer loved her, which was certainly accurate, despite what he had said to the contrary. Her swollen eyes made it impossible to convince them that she was weathering this just fine. But fortunately, her tear ducts had somehow decided independently that they needed rest, so at least she wasn't dripping all over the tablecloth.

Bethia could not drag herself out of bed when the long night finally grayed into dawn. Having the opening of *The Bells* delayed meant that all costumes were fitted and ready, save some minor nips and tucks and loose buttons that the seamstresses could take care of without her. During one of her half-asleep, half-waking moments she wondered if she should ring Jewel. The thought of having to rise and go to the parlour settled the matter. She would stay here, wrapped in a cocoon of anguish. Jewel would just have to assume she still did not feel well.

Thankfully, family and servants did not disturb her, though she sometimes heard whispering in the corridor.

Her thoughts this morning were no clearer than yesterday's, except for one issue. She forced her mind to see reason, even though her heart would rather attach blame. God had not caused this. He did not make sport with his children's lives as if they were chessmen, granting affection here, withdrawing it there. This was Guy's doing. Muriel's doing.

Close to noon she could no longer ignore the hunger pangs that somehow traveled up to her brain through the great ache in her chest. She dressed, washed her face, and went down to lunch. Mother and Father were solicitous, worried. Even William had chosen to stay home. Everyone walked about as if there had been a death in the family.

But she was able to eat, a little. The vegetable marrow soup warmed her aching insides.

"Jewel rang," Mother said quietly. "She said you should take the rest of the week off, that the seamstresses are managing fine. And she reminds you that the theatre's closed next week until Friday's dress rehearsal, so you'll have opportunity for a good rest."

Bethia lowered her spoon and caught Sarah's eye. Her sister nodded back, a silent message that, yes, Mother had informed their cousin of the breakup.

"Will you resign?" Sarah asked in her room later.

"No," Bethia replied, though she would have said otherwise yesterday. "Muriel's already taken Guy. I won't hand my job over to her. She's not going to win everything."

"But that means you'll have to see her."

"Then I'll see her. I won't be the first person to have to work with a disagreeable person."

Sarah folded her arms. "*Disagreeable*, Bethia?"

She was right, Bethia thought. So ingrained was the habit of trying to say the charitable thing that it was the first adjective that rose to her lips. A more appropriate one came to mind right away. "Very well then . . . *evil*."

One of the many last-minute tasks that Jewel had to attend to was arranging for Mr. Whitmore's farewell party after Saturday night's closing performance of *The Ticket-of-Leave Man*. She was glad to have something to occupy her mind besides Muriel's treachery and Guy Russell's inconceivable stupidity.

Or at least to *attempt* to occupy her mind, for anger seeped into even thoughts so unrelated as the wording on the cake.

"Madame?" said the proprietor of Capucine's.

Jewel blinked at him. "I beg your pardon. I'd like *Parting Is Such Sweet Sorrow* written beneath the name."

"And the name is Richard Whitmore?"

"Yes," Jewel said. "And if you can manage, include *From Your Friends at Royal Court*."

The fact that Aunt Naomi did not mention Muriel over the telephone this morning was not surprising. But no one had to draw Jewel a picture. She walked back to the theatre encompassed by a storm cloud of fury. Passersby could have all worn clown suits for all the notice she took of them.

New contracts tomorrow, she thought. Then she would tell Muriel exactly what she thought of her. She could hardly wait. She would spend all evening thinking of choice words, perhaps even writing them down, lest she forget. And surely Grady, given his rough upbringing, could supply some she had never even heard of.

Her steps slowed. But was raging at Muriel the best action to take?

Mentally she traveled back through the years to their childhoods, when even strangers would stop Aunt Phyllis to comment on Muriel's beauty. As she grew into young womanhood, her cousin carried the hearts of what seemed like all of Sheffield's young men on a string. All that attention, and yet it never seemed enough. In fact, she never seemed happier than when she had stirred up a row, between herself and her parents, brothers, cousins, servants, strangers—it did not matter, just as long as she occupied the center of that maelstrom.

Had Muriel ever outgrown that? Was *that* really why she chose to stay in Belgravia, even when most of her neighbors snubbed her? Because now and again it brought on a confrontation? Was that why she encouraged the attentions of Lord Holt, a married man, because she knew most of her family would be outraged?

The fact that Muriel had loved Douglas was beyond question. But Jewel began to wonder if her obsessive drive to punish Bethia had less to do with revenge and more to do with needing to be once again in the center of outrageous attention.

"But she gets standing ovations every night," Grady said when she voiced her theory back in the office.

"And she loves that," Jewel said. "But I don't think that's enough for her. There is no turmoil in having strangers rise and applaud, and she knows the vast majority will return to their own lives with little or no thought of her until some later performance. Muriel was weaned on chaos. It's what she's used to."

"That's no excuse for what she did."

"No, of course not. But it helps me understand that showing her the rough side of my tongue would be giving Muriel just what she wants. I'm the *last* person to want to give her what she wants right now."

"The second-to-last person, you mean." Grady corrected.

"Yes." Jewel picked up the telephone. "I'll see about Bethia now."

Sarah answered and said, after an exchange of subdued greetings, "She's out in the garden with Father and Naomi."

"How is she?"

"Mmm . . . not so well. But I'm glad she's staying home and doesn't have to face . . . anybody."

Even over the telephone, Jewel could discern the restraint it had taken for Sarah not to say Muriel's name. Father's side of the family was always mindful of hers and Catherine's positions in the middle.

"She should take as long as she needs," Jewel assured her. "We'll manage."

"I'm sure she'll return to work when the new production starts," Sarah said. "She's trying to prove to Father and Naomi that this hasn't destroyed her. And who knows? Perhaps getting back into her old routine will help her. Even with . . ."

Again, she left off the name.

Thirty-Six

"We could marry next week," Guy said after a second farewell kiss in the morning room. "Please, Muriel."

She brushed a bit of lint from his sleeve, smiled. "I'm not ready."

His brows drew together in an agonized expression. "Is it because you fear I'm after your money? If so, we'll go to a solicitor, have him draw up some sort of legal document giving me no rights to it. And I'll be wealthy in my own right one day. I promise."

"It has nothing to do with money."

"Then, what is it?"

"I'm still in mourning," she said a little reprovingly. "I *did* find out I lost a brother just three months ago."

"I'm sorry. Of course." His sapphire eyes shone. "It's just that I love you so much. When we're apart, you're all I think about."

"I love you too."

Gladys's hopeless lessons had ceased a week ago, at great relief to the scullery maid, but Guy still came over those three days, and at other times when both schedules allowed. They had been back to the Savoy twice since that first time.

She stepped back so that he would loosen his arms and touched the tip of his nose. "But it's off with you now. I have to leave soon. Grady wants me to sign a new contract."

At her dressing table, she allowed Evelyn to twist tendrils of her hair into clever little curls about the crown of her head. Would Bethia choose today to return? Muriel had a strong feeling she would not resign. After all, she did not resign when asked to keep her distance after Douglas's memorial. That was fine. What good was revenge if she could not witness its effect firsthand?

Her only regret was that Jewel would be furious. But probably not for too long. Her cousin's loyalty to Royal Court Theatre was the one ace Muriel held. After all, Mr. Whitmore's leaving meant that the success of future productions rested in *her* hands. The insufferable Lord-of-the-Sheep may be getting some attention in the newspapers, but *she* had proven herself onstage. Once the novelty of him wore off, everyone would see that it was *her* devoted followers who kept the theatre filled.

And Bethia could have her beau back fairly soon. Already Muriel was growing a little weary of his company. If she cared about having someone follow her about with lovelorn eyes she would have encouraged Mr. Whitmore. Or bought an Irish Setter.

"We had the playbills delivered to the rehearsal room," Jewel said to Mr. Birch in the office. "Please get Lewis to help you count them into stacks. We've appointments all day for contract signings."

"I'll see to it right away," Mr. Birch said, but he continued to stand just inside the door.

At length Grady said, "Is there something else, Mr. Birch?"

"We're wondering—upstairs—how Miss Rayborn is faring?"

"She plans to return after the break," Jewel replied.

"Well, that's good. The best remedy for a broken heart is to keep busy."

The elderly man turned toward the door, but Jewel was on her feet and at his side before he could touch the knob.

"Wait." She took hold of his coat sleeve. "What do you mean?"

Not *how did you find that out,* her initial thought, just in case he was merely guessing and was seeking confirmation from her.

He gave her an indulgent, yet sad, smile. "How long have you been employed here, Mrs. McGuire? The walls talk. And it seems her fiancé has been seen about town with a certain actress."

"Oh dear," Jewel said. She had known, of course, that word would spread, but she had hoped that *The Bells* would be well under way first. The cast and crew were far fonder of Bethia than Muriel, and there were sure to be repercussions.

Repercussions that Muriel deserved, but such backstage dramas had a way of affecting performances in actors less disciplined than Mr. Whitmore and Mrs. Steel.

The elderly man leaned his head thoughtfully. "We believe—upstairs—that the future will eventually be brighter for our dear Miss Rayborn. It is obvious to us that Mr. Carey has a fondness for her. He's a decent fellow, very thoughtful. And he has no liking for a certain actress, so there would be no danger there."

"Everyone is fond of Miss Rayborn, Mr. Birch," Grady said. "Not just Mr. Carey."

"Yes, that's so." Mr. Birch nodded. "But there is fond, and there is *fond*."

Jewel waved the elderly man out of the office. Gruffly, but gently, she said, "You three have too much time on your hands up there."

"Does this mean the lead for the run of the play?" Mr. Carey asked after signing his name to two contracts—one for himself, one for Grady's file. "Not temporarily?"

"That's what it means, Mr. Carey." Grady affixed his own signature to the contracts. "You read it yourself."

"I didn't quite trust my eyes," the actor admitted.

"How do you feel, Mr. Carey?" Jewel asked.

He returned her smile. "As if this is a dream, Mrs. McGuire."

"Well, being that I'm in your dream, kindly arrange it so I don't have to wear these," she said, touching the wire rim of her eyeglasses.

"And make me taller," Grady said.

All three chuckled at this, and then Mr. Carey sobered again.

"Miss Lidstone said Miss Rayborn's not feeling well. Is it serious?"

"She actually plans to return after the break," Jewel said evasively, though she wondered why she bothered. If the news of the breakup was already out, it was just a matter of time before it reached Mr. Carey's ears.

"I'm glad."

Mr. Birch is right, Jewel thought, catching the relief in the actor's expression.

"I know what you're thinking," Grady said after Mr. Carey left the office.

She raised eyebrows. "And just how do you know that, pray tell?"

"Because I was thinking the same thing. But we've got to stay out of it, love."

Jewel nodded. The last thing Bethia would be interested in was another romance. Instinctively she knew this to be so, even though she had had no experience with affairs of the heart until Grady entered her life. But, given that her cousin hopefully would recover from this over time, what could it hurt to have a friendship already established with a decent man such as Mr. Carey?

If he truly loved Bethia, he would not have fallen in love with me. They weren't officially engaged.

I had the best of intentions when I hired him for my party. I didn't expect this to happen.

I've been so lonesome since Sidney died. Would you begrudge me a little happiness?

Remember, I'm your cousin too.

In the coach, Muriel mulled over which arguments would be most effective in the shouting match that was certain to happen. She stepped up to one of the theatre doors just as it opened from the inside. Mr. Carey's tall frame was garbed in a heavy tan cotton jacket, with large pockets and pinstriped black linen trousers.

"Good afternoon, Lady Holt," he said, stepping back to hold the door with one hand, removing bowler hat with the other.

"Thank you."

Odd that he did not use his title. She would rather give up her diamond rings than her title. And even odder was the gossip that he lived in poverty when he had the means to live lavishly. Halfway through the doorway she noticed the top third of a book sticking up in his pocket.

"The Time Machine?" She paused, looked up at him "You read science fiction, Mr. Carey?"

"Sometimes," he replied with a glance down at the book. "My mother sent me *War of the Worlds,* and I enjoyed it, so I bought this one on my way in."

"I wish I would have known. I could have lent it to you."

He looked surprised, and indeed, Muriel could hardly believe the words had come from her own mouth.

"Why, that's very kind of you, even so," he said and smiled.

"I've lots more books," she said, surprising herself again. But after all, if they were to be working closely together, it was probably best that they at least be able to hold a pleasant conversation. As long as he did not carry it to extremes.

Like Douglas.

The thought shook her. She pushed it from her mind, substituting the more accurate *Like Mr. Whitmore.*

They wished each other good-day, and as she drew closer to the office, she was glad for the civil exchange for another reason. Bethia was well liked. Once word got around that she had taken Guy from her, Jewel and Grady would not be the only people furious. She could weather that storm as well as she had weathered any others in the past, but it would surely be easier with a friend or two on her side.

Nice eyes, she thought, recalling how his smile had caused them to crinkle at the corners. *I wonder why I never noticed before?*

While Jewel worked at her desk, Grady thanked Muriel for coming and presented two identical contracts—one for her, one for the files. He explained that new contracts were necessary because of the delayed opening of *The Bells.* Muriel signed both without reading, for legal language was not her forte. But she was confident that Grady and Jewel would not abuse her trust.

Even now, when they were obviously angry with her.

"Thank you," Grady said, signing and then handing over her copy. His smile seemed pasted on, and his gray eyes could have been peering at a wedge of cheese for all the animation therein.

"You're welcome," Muriel said. She looked over at Jewel, penciling in a notebook. "I spotted one of the new posters outside. It's very nice."

Her cousin raised her head and smiled. Politely. "Yes, we're pleased."

Neither Jewel nor Grady rose to escort her from the office. Muriel stood in the corridor, looking back at the closed door. There was more to this than a mere unwillingness to ruffle the feathers of their biggest star. The coolness in Jewel's eyes suggested that they were simply co-workers forced to associate, not family.

She'll get over it, Muriel assured herself on her way back to the coach. But her steps were heavy. If Jewel would have shouted and railed, she could have defended herself, justified her actions. How did one defend oneself against politeness?

"Oh, there you are, your Ladyship," Mrs. Burles said when Muriel walked into the house. "Mrs. Pearce is on the telephone."

The last thing Muriel wished to do was chat over the telephone. But with Georgiana still up in Sheffield, she had to make certain nothing was wrong.

"It's that nanny . . . Prescott." The voice coming through the line was as brittle as ever. "She's too strict!"

Muriel drew in a deep breath, eased it out. "Mother, I'll be there in four days. We'll talk about it then. I have to go."

"You don't really need me for these contracts, do you?" Jewel asked.

Grady smiled at her. "Do give Bethia my love."

Forty minutes later she was having tea in the Hampstead parlour with Uncle Daniel and Aunt Naomi. Sarah had gone to the shipping office, Aunt Naomi said, and Bethia was riding her bicycle out on the Heath.

"I'm surprised," Jewel said.

"She said she needed the fresh air," Uncle Daniel said from his chair. "I suspect it's for our benefit, to distract us from worrying over her."

"As if *that* would be all it took." Aunt Naomi shook her head. "I wish Bethia didn't feel she has to shield us. Sometimes its as if she's the parent and we're the children."

Uncle Daniel gave Jewel a sad smile. "I suppose that's what happens when your parents have been old for most of your life."

"You've never seemed old to me," Jewel said. "You have to remember, Bethia's nature has always been nurturing. That's one reason she excels at her job." She set her empty cup and saucer upon the tea table and rose. "I need to get back to help prepare for tonight's show."

Even though she asked the two to keep their seats, both rose for embraces. Uncle Daniel apologized for the coach being away and attempted to give her money for a cab as if she were still twelve years old. Rather than feel insulted, Jewel liked the feel of being parented.

"The underground is quicker," she said, kissing his bearded cheek and leaving before he could drop coins into her palm for that as well. She met Bethia pushing the bicycle up the carriage drive. A moment later, the bicycle was lying on the soft ground and they were in each other's arms. Over her cousin's shoulder, Jewel spotted the gardener taking a couple of steps toward them, hesitating, then retreating to the back garden.

"I still feel as if I'm walking about in a dream," Bethia said, stepping back at length to wipe her eyes with her fingertips.

Jewel recalled Mr. Carey saying the same thing earlier, but under happier circumstances. "I'm so sorry, Bethia."

Her cousin shrugged, wiped her face again. "I vacillate between feeling sorry for myself and disgust at my own weakness."

"You're anything but weak," Jewel said. "But I wish you wouldn't put up such a brave front for your father and mother. It makes them feel helpless."

"I know," Bethia sighed. "That's what Sarah says. But this has broken their hearts as well. I can't bring myself to add to their misery by wailing on their shoulders."

"That's why you kept Muriel's part in this from them?"

Bethia gave her a tight-lipped nod.

"I hope you realize we would sack her if we could afford to. She has us over a barrel, and she knows it."

"I realize that, Jewel," Bethia said somberly. "I don't blame you and Grady at all."

Jewel embraced her again, patted her back. "But I'm glad you're coming back to work. Somehow, she's not going to win this thing."

———

Father, help me through this, Bethia prayed under her breath as the family coach rocked gently to a halt on Saturday evening. If this were not Richard Whitmore's final performance at the Royal Court, she would just as soon pass.

William, dressed in tails and top hat, hopped out and turned to offer his arm. "Ready, ladies?"

Sarah, closest to the door, stepped out first. The claret red velvet gown she was wearing was striking against her fair complexion, like red roses mixed with white. Bethia wore sea-green silk enlivened with strands of gold and had allowed Avis to fashion her honey-brown hair into ringlets after very little persuasion on Sarah's part. In the back of her mind was the thought that Guy would be here, at least at the party afterward. By looking her best, she would cause him to regret his action, perhaps even ask to return to her. She did not linger over that hope for too long, however, for one devastation was as much as she could manage for now. Foolish to invite another one.

Her parents had declined to come along, even though Jewel had sent enough tickets to the house for the whole family. She had not pressured them. If Guy did attend the party, it would be difficult enough to hold her head high without having two sets of parental eyes sadly and helplessly focused upon her.

"Why don't you go first?" Sarah said to William in the aisle of the orchestra section, nudging her husband down their row of seats so that she could sit on Bethia's left. Bethia soon realized why. When Muriel walked out onstage, Sarah scooped up Bethia's hand and held it tight. She forced herself to endure by focusing on Mr. Whitmore's performance, recalling his antics in the wardrobe room, his ready smile in the corridors. How such an endearing man could love Muriel was a mystery, but at least he had the sense to get away from her.

You'll make a fine Hamlet, she thought.

Thirty-Seven

*T*he afterglow from the standing ovation had disintegrated into uneasiness before Muriel even reached her dressing room. She had acted her heart out, and yet the only recognition she received within the company were the obligatory polite congratulations from Jewel and Grady. Even Mr. Whitmore had been distant, and she had the uncomfortable feeling that it was not some ruse to win her heart this time.

And the pleasant working relationship she had envisioned between herself and Mr. Carey was not likely to happen. Stony silence was his only response when she asked, in the greenroom, if he had started *The Time Machine.*

Back propped against the door, she listened to the hum of conversation, the clicks of heels and rustles of skirts in the corridor. When the theatre was cleared, everyone would drift over to the rehearsal room for the farewell party. Suddenly she was glad that Guy Russell had refused to meet her here after the Opera House let out, despite her pleading and tears and even empty promise to reconsider his marriage proposal. She could no more walk into the rehearsal room with him at her arm than fly. She could no more walk into the room *alone* than fly.

Eight or nine bouquets of roses made the dressing room heady with scents. Glass covering the favorable reviews cut from magazines and newspapers reflected light from the electric bulb. All this time she had convinced herself that approval from audiences and critics mattered far more than that of the cast and crew. But the audience and critics would be in their beds within a couple of hours, while cast and crew were still soaking up goodwill and friendship from each other.

The revenge she had so longed for was as bile rising in her mouth. Yes, she had succeeded in paying Bethia Rayborn back. But at what cost to herself? Bethia was probably at Mr. Whitmore's party this very minute, being coddled by Jewel and Grady and others who knew—and Muriel had to assume everyone knew by now, judging by all the cold shoulders and openly hostile looks this evening. And meanwhile, she was trapped in her dressing room. Trapped by her own stupidity. Why could she not have been content with quiet hatred? Why spin such an elaborate and obvious plot, which only served to make a martyr of the person she despised?

Finally the corridor quieted. She changed into her black gown without removing her stage makeup. She was glad she would be leaving for Sheffield tomorrow, and not just because of Georgiana. She needed to get away from London, from the whole theatre environment. To think. Or still better, *not* to think. It was thinking that had brought on all this misery.

Someone knocked at her door just as she was picking up her handbag from her dressing table. So, Guy had decided to come after all, she thought. She was not surprised. He was pathetically anxious to please her. She turned the doorknob with a sardonic smile, picturing the relief that would come to his face when she informed him she did not care to attend the party after all.

"I thought you weren't—"

For a disorienting fraction of a second she gaped up at the tall figure in the doorway.

"I spoke with your young Galahad," Mr. Carey said, brown eyes cold upon her. "He decided to leave."

There was no point in asking of whom he spoke. "You've never even met him."

"No, I had not had that pleasure," he said cynically. "Someone pointed him out to me in the lobby."

She could just picture Mr. Birch whispering in Mr. Carey's ear, or perhaps even the seamstress duo whispering in both ears. If only he would stand aside! The corridor seemed empty. Dare she try to push past? Surely he would not lay a hand upon her.

"What did you do, threaten violence against him?" she said,

feigning a bravado worthy of the stage. She regretted that she had offered to lend him books, and especially regretted having thought he had nice eyes. "We can have you arrested, you know."

"I simply invited him to leave. He didn't seem keen on the idea of staying anyway."

He was clearly not intimidated by her. To Muriel this was quite unsettling. In fact, she felt small under his unrelenting stare.

You don't have to justify yourself to him! she thought. And yet she found herself saying, "I'll have you know I changed my mind about attending the party before you even knocked."

His expression did not soften. "A wise choice, Lady Holt. You would not have been well received."

It was crushing to hear it spoken aloud, even though the same thought had passed through her mind minutes ago. The hollows of her face began stinging, a warning of tears soon to come. Still, she was compelled ask, "Why do you take it upon yourself to insinuate yourself in my business?"

"Because I can't sit by and watch a good person be mistreated by the likes of you," he replied.

Don't cry, don't cry, don't cry! she ordered herself. It did no good, for her eyes brimmed.

If he was moved at all by her tears, it did not show upon his granitelike face.

Muriel swallowed. "I thought we were going to be friends."

Finally he stood aside to allow her to pass. Voice flat, he said, "I would sooner be friends with the devil."

Muriel's heels clicked upon the steps. She held her skirt gathered in one hand for faster flight, her handbag in the other.

He loves her dawned upon her halfway down the stairs.

Mr. Carey was nothing to *her,* she reminded herself. But it only served to prove her morose thoughts in the dressing room. Bethia, Miss Pure-as-the-Driven-Snow, would come out of this on top, whether or not Guy became part of her future again.

Lewis stood at the stage door, idly tossing and catching a ring of keys.

"Do you need an escort to your coach, Lady Holt?" he asked. Even *his* expression was one of polite disinterest, though surely he noticed her tears. "There are a couple of reporters milling about."

"No," she replied. "Just unlock the door."

The only signs of life in the street were horses, tethered to a queue of carriages and coaches, and standing like statues in the semi-darkness. She heard laughter from the right. A half dozen or so men in livery clothes were visiting near a streetlamp halfway down the block.

I'll dock him a day's pay for this, she thought, setting out in that direction and ignoring the faint voice of reason that told her Ham would not have expected her out so early.

A man appeared at her side. "Lady Holt?"

"Yes, what is it?" she snapped.

"I'm Mr. Gatcomb with *Illustrated London News.*" Extraordinary white teeth flashed beneath a dark mustache. "You were magnificent in there this evening, as usual."

"Thank you." Glad for the lack of lighting upon her face, she said, "Now if you'll excuse me."

But he continued along beside her, holding pencil and a small notebook. "Would you pay me the favor of a brief interview?"

"I'm sorry. Later."

Then, if you please, may I impose upon you for the names of the people present at Mr. Whitmore's farewell party?"

"I'm obviously not there. How would I know?"

She had covered half the distance down the block, was close enough to see the lights from a half dozen coachmen's cigarettes. Undeterred, the reporter said, "May I ask why you're not attending the party, Lady Holt? *You* aren't thinking of leaving the Royal Court as well, are you?"

"It's possible." Actually, the thought had not entered her mind, but he had touched a nerve. Her pace increased, his as well. Up ahead Ham looked over his shoulder, tossed his cigarette, and started advancing.

"And why is that, may I ask?"

"Because the wardrobe mistress is a heartless trollop who killed my brother."

The reporter's white teeth formed two gaping rows beneath the mustache.

"Lady Holt?" Ham said, joining them. "Forgive me, I didn't expect—"

"And how did that happen, Lady Holt?" Mr. Gatcomb cut in, leaning closer as if fearing he would miss a word.

Muriel ignored him and looked at Ham. "Take me home now."

According to Jewel, Mr. Whitmore had requested that the party be a private affair, limited to those closely associated with the Royal Court Theatre and their families. He wished to relax in the company of his old friends one last time, without the intrusion of patrons, reporters, and even dignitaries. Messrs. Cumberland and Fry and their wives were present. Mrs. Steel put in a surprising and touching appearance, long enough to present the actor with an oil painting of the acting team based upon a signboard of their earliest production together, Dion Coucicault's *The Willow Copse.*

"May we leave once I've had the chance to say farewell?" Bethia asked Sarah and William.

"But of course," William said.

The two hovered near her, and Bethia did not mind. Fortunately, Muriel had yet to show herself; therefore, it looked as if she would not have to see Guy tonight, after all.

Only for Mr. Whitmore's sake was she even here. But every sympathetic look, each quiet embrace from crew and cast members, brought her again to the brink of tears, and more importantly, took attention away from where it rightfully belonged this evening.

During a rare moment when the actor was not surrounded by well-wishers, she stood on tiptoe to kiss his cheek and promised to come see him at Drury Lane. "But you mustn't tell Grady," she added, surprised that she could joke even mildly.

He squeezed her shoulders and murmured into her ear over the conversations and laughter and piano music, "Just remember the title to another Shakespeare play . . . *All's Well That End's Well.* It's hard to imagine now, dear girl, but I have a strong feeling one day you'll see this was for the best."

The elbow in Noah's side jostled the beaker of punch in his hands. "What—?"

"I've been looking all over for you!" Jude said. "Where in the world did you go?"

"I had an errand," Noah replied. "I'll tell you about it later."

"Well, I just overheard Miss Rayborn saying farewell to Mr. Whitmore. If you hurry you can catch up with her before she leaves."

Noah shook his head. "I'm not going to take advantage of the situation."

He could not fault Jude's eagerness to have him rush into the void her fiancé had left. That same hopefulness had come over him when Mr. Birch first whispered the news. Until he realized how devastated she must be.

Help her through this, please Father, he prayed under his breath.

"Noah?"

"Hmm?" Noah blinked, a little surprised Jude still stood before him.

Jude blew out his cheeks. "I *said* I don't see how simply chatting with her is taking advantage of any situation."

"Well, it is." Noah sent a glance across the room. "Miss Walters is looking over here."

Jude made a motion as if to turn and look but then stopped himself. Stiffly, he said, "Are you quite sure?"

"You must have made quite an impression on her. You didn't show her the wiggle-your-ears trick, did you?"

"As if!" his friend snorted, and lowered his voice. "Is she looking now?"

Noah's height served him well for peering across crowded rooms. The utility actress, thin as a rail but still feminine, with brilliant amber curls and upturned nose, lingered near the piano. When her eyes met Noah's, she gave him back a little sheepish smile and shifted her eyes toward the back of Jude's head.

"She is," Noah replied. "Why don't you go back over there?"

Jude smiled. "She seems a nice girl."

"A very nice girl. Now, go invest a little time in your own love life, for a change."

———

Waiting outside Muriel's house, Guy cut an elegant figure in his black tailcoat and white waistcoat, but his expression was as wretched as she imagined hers to be. "I tried to meet you."

"I know," Muriel said.

"Did you see her?"

"Let's go inside."

He followed her into the house. In the parlour, she dropped into a chair instead of the sofa so that he would not be able to sit near her. When he stood awkwardly inside the doorway, she said, "Will you close the door, or do you want the servants listening?"

Either way, she realized she did not really care. What was one more morsel of gossip after the feasts she had already provided for them?

He did as she asked and then walked over to stand in front of her chair. After a hesitation, as if he did not quite know what to do with himself, he lowered himself to one knee.

"I didn't go to the party," Muriel said.

"You didn't?" His shoulders sagged visibly. "Thank you, Muriel."

"It wasn't for your sake." She realized she was being cruel, but after suffering such cruel treatment herself all evening, it felt good to lash out. "I simply changed my mind."

Guy studied her face, blue eyes lifeless. At length he said, "I've always prided myself on not being easily manipulated. But you've been using me from the beginning, haven't you?"

Muriel drew in a long breath, let it out. "I'm sorry, Guy."

A tortured moan rose from his throat. "Sorry?"

"I was so angry I couldn't think straight. Douglas—"

"I don't want to hear about your pathetic brother!" he snapped, but then he seized her hands and pressed them to his chest. "But you've come to care about me, Muriel, haven't you? Even a little?"

She pulled her hands from his desperate grasp but said as gently as she could manage, "I'm sorry, Guy. Please go away. Perhaps she'll take you back if you ask her."

So little had he meant to her that she was surprised at how hard she wept when he was gone. She could not stop associating the look upon his face as he begged her to love him, with that on Douglas's as he mourned over Bethia's lack of affection.

You didn't send Guy a hateful letter, she reminded herself.

No, what she did was worse. She had cultivated the affection of a young man and then cast him off when her plan did not produce the euphoria she had anticipated.

Bethia never pretended to love Douglas. As for the letter, would not she herself have sent a far more scathing one to Richard Whitmore had he followed her about town and even out of town?

Douglas was your brother, she thought in an attempt to shut out the accusations grinding away at her mind.

It worked for only a second, for on the heels of that came the reminder that Guy Russell had sisters who probably cared just as much for *his* well-being.

Thirty-Eight

*M*ummy!" Georgiana cried, pitching her little body into Muriel's arms on Sunday.

"Hello, sweetheart." Muriel kissed a rosy cheek and picked up the package lying on the parlour sofa cushion. "Look what Mother brought you."

For the half hour that followed, Georgiana alternated between sitting in her lap, hopping down, playing with her new doll, demanding having *The Land of Long Ago* read aloud, and climbing down before Muriel was halfway finished.

"Where is her nanny?" Muriel asked as her already-strained nerves were bristling beneath her skin.

Georgiana brightened. "Where is Nanny?"

"I sent her on an errand, sweetheart, remember?" Muriel's mother said gently, then pulled the bell cord. Florence came straightway.

"Come, Miss Georgiana," the maid said. "We'll have a tea party."

Georgiana shook her head. "Don't want to. Want Nanny."

"How about if we go into the kitchen and ask Cook to make biscuits?"

"Chocolate?" Georgiana asked.

"Yes, dearest," Muriel's mother replied.

Muriel waited until the door closed after the maid and child, and turned to her mother again. "What sort of errand?"

Her mother hesitated, and then the corners of her mouth dipped into a righteous frown. "I discharged her."

"You *what?*"

"She was too strict. She forced Georgiana to help tidy the nursery. I telephoned you about it, but you wouldn't make time to speak with me."

"Mother." Muriel groaned as the little bit of stamina she still possessed drained from her pores. She did not even have the strength for a decent fit of anger.

"I never made *you* do servant's work," her mother said defensively. "Nor the boys."

"Perhaps you should have."

"And just what do you mean by that?"

"I don't know what I mean." Muriel kneaded her forehead. "Perhaps, just perhaps we would all be happier."

"Nonsense. Bernard's happy."

"Well, bully for Bernard."

"Don't use vulgarities, Muriel," her mother scolded. "And *you're* happy."

"Well, bully for me."

She forced herself out of bed at nine Monday morning, padded to the parlour in her wrapper, and asked the telephone operator to connect her with the offices of *Illustrated London News.*

"Mr. Gatcomb isn't in yet," said the male secretary who answered. "I believe he's looking up leads for a story."

That sounded ominous.

"I expect he'll be here after lunch," the voice went on. "Would you care to leave a message?"

"Yes, this is Lady Holt from the Royal Court Theatre. I will appreciate your informing Mr. Gatcomb that he must disregard an accusation I made against a certain person in the heat of anger Saturday evening. Tell him I was mistaken. He'll know what you mean."

"Very well, Lady Holt. Shall I have him ring you?"

"I'm not home. But do give him the message."

"I'll deliver it personally. And might I say my wife and I enjoyed seeing you in *The Ticket-of-Leave Man* last month."

"Thank you." Next, she telephoned her house.

"Has Prescott telephoned or come by?" she asked Mrs. Burles.

"Why, no, your Ladyship," the housekeeper said. "Isn't she there with you?"

Yes, silly me, she's standing right here at my elbow. Muriel restrained herself from voicing the sarcastic comment because excellent housekeepers were hard to find. "No. If she shows up at the house to collect her letter of reference from Mrs. Godfrey, please ask her to stay. Tell her it was all a mistake that we'll straighten out when I get home."

There was a hesitation, then, "She keeps the letter in her handbag, your Ladyship."

"Why would she do that?"

"Ah . . . can't say, your Ladyship."

Muriel grimaced. Mrs. Burles knew exactly why, and so did she.

"Well, if you hear from her at all before I arrive home, ring me here."

With the children grown and her mother practically housebound, Muriel's parents had no more need of a coach and driver. Her father either walked or took an omnibus the one mile to the offices of Sun Insurance. Therefore, on Tuesday Muriel hired a coach for her mother and herself to visit Bernard and his family. She left Georgiana in Florence's care, fearing the strain upon Agatha. That's what she told herself.

The vicarage was of mellowed gray stone, situated across from Holy Cross Church in the village of Gleadless. Six-week-old Norman Pearce lay nestled in Agatha's arms in the small parlour, his wisps of lashes resting upon his cheek.

Muriel leaned close to weave her fingers through the infant's fine brown hair. How she envied him his untroubled sleep! "I thought only girl babies were supposed to be sweet."

"So did I," Agatha confessed, smiling. She was still pale and gaunt, but she and Bernard had assured Muriel that she was gaining strength by the week.

Bernard had cooked lunch, roasting venison a parishioner had given them with potatoes and carrots from another parishioner's garden. The loaf of bread and a chocolate cake came from the village bakery.

392 * Lawana Blackwell

"It's just until Agatha gets on her feet again," he said at the table. "I'm sorry it's so plain."

"No, it's delicious," Muriel lied, teeth grinding a bite of venison so dry that it refused to disintegrate. Afterward, while Agatha put Sally and the baby down for naps and Mother dozed in a chair by the fireplace, Muriel asked her brother why the parish did not provide a cook.

"It's a small parish," he replied. "When I was hired, we were informed there were just enough funds for a day maid or cook. Agatha knew how to cook, so she decided she would rather do that than clean. We did all right until this latest pregnancy."

"I'd like to hire one for you."

Bernard glanced at their mother. "That's very kind of you, Muriel," he said with voice low. But I can't accept your offer."

"But why? I can easily afford it."

He rose from his chair and went over to the hall tree to take down her cloak. "Come, let's take a turn about the village."

They strolled together, her hand tucked into the crook of his arm. Smoke rose from chimney pots of stone, brick, and half-timbered houses flanking the lane. Pine needles crushed beneath their feet, and browning clematis vines against picket fences gave off pleasant, earthy autumn aromas. Fortunately, most villagers were either at work or school, or were kept inside by the late-October chill, so there were no interruptions from parishioners desiring to chat.

"Mother and Father have already offered. But I can't put Agatha under that obligation to her in-laws. Mother . . ." Bernard winced. "Well, she tends to meddle."

"Does she?" Muriel said dryly. "All the more reason you should allow me. I'm the last person to offer you advice. If I ever *do*, you should do just the opposite."

His hazel eyes gave her a sidelong look. "What's wrong, Muriel?"

She sighed. "I did something . . . very bad."

"What sort of thing?" he asked.

"Just . . . something. Everyone despises me now. Even Jewel."

Mercifully, he didn't press for details. Nor did he make light of her remorse by assuring her that Jewel could never despise her.

"I love my work. But it's hard to bear the cold looks." She

sighed. "I wouldn't have thought I would have minded so much."

He patted the hand tucked into his arm. "Well, you have to make amends."

"I tried that once before." She could not bring herself to admit to him that they were not genuine. "It . . . didn't keep. No one will believe me this time."

"They will eventually, if you stay constant. Nothing showy or grand, mind you. No flattery. Just ask forgiveness of whom you need to and repair what you can of the situation."

She gave another brittle laugh. "*No* one is going to forgive me. And as far as repairs go, I doubt that this can be undone."

Even if Bethia decided to forgive Guy and take him back, how could she help but wonder if another betrayal lay in the future?

"That doesn't absolve you from trying," Bernard said. Again the sidelong look. "You take too much upon yourself, Muriel. You don't have to go it alone. God can move people's hearts."

Uh-oh. She hated it when he changed from brother to minister.

"But you have to give Him *yours* first," he went on.

His voice was soothing, his tone nonjudgmental, his eyes warm. Strong was the temptation just to turn herself over to the prompting she could feel within her.

And then the moment passed. Bernard may not judge her, but he did not know the half of what she had done. God knew it all, and as little as she knew Him, she knew He was not pleased. Better to hide from God until she could at least make an effort at amends. Better to confess sins in the *distant* past than those so fresh that the repercussions were still ringing in her ears.

"Muriel?" her brother said.

She turned her face from him long enough to blink once, twice, clear the sheen over her eyes. "When we come back for Christmas," she said, "we'll talk again then."

"Christmas . . ." he said sadly.

"I promise." Muriel nudged his side. A playful gesture to cover up the heaviness of her heart. "It's only two months away. Meanwhile, let's talk about hiring that cook."

———

Bethia was certain it was quite by accident that Muriel and Guy had chosen a relatively *convenient* time to send a cyclone through her life. The seamstresses had managed fine without her last week, and now, with the Royal Court closed until Friday's dress rehearsal, she did not have to stir from the house if she did not wish to. Mostly she kept to her room. She found it impossible to lose herself in the pages of a novel, but did manage to sketch several costumes for Dion Boucicault's comedy in five acts, *London Assurance,* which was to follow *The Bells.*

On Wednesday morning, nine days after the breakup, she was relieved to have the house to herself—at least as far as family was concerned. Her father had left for a meeting of his camera club, her mother and Sarah were helping plan the sponsors' Christmas party at St. Matthew's Home for Foundling Girls, and William was at work. For a few hours, she did not have to put on any sort of brave front.

She was seated by her bedroom fireplace, combing hair still damp from her bath, and trying to pay attention to chambermaid Susan's account of a cousin's witnessing a monkey loose at Regent's Park, when Claire Duffy came to her room. The housekeeper was a Rub-enesque woman of sixty-three who still moved with the grace of a ballerina. There was nothing graceful about her stiff posture at the moment.

"Mr. Russell is downstairs. *Guy* Russell."

A surge of joy automatically lifted Bethia's spirits.

Mrs. Duffy's scornful voice brought them back down to reality. "Shall I send him packing?"

In her most fierce Cockney, Susan said, "Shall I box 'is ears for you, Miss Rayborn?"

"No, thank you," Bethia said, though grateful to both women. It felt good to be reminded, once again, that she had allies. "Please have him wait in the parlour."

With Susan's grumbling assistance, she changed from her dressing gown into her white blouse and burgundy wool skirt. She refused to follow her initial impulse toward the blue silk, one of Guy's favor-ites because it complemented her eyes. Her hair hung damp down her back as she walked downstairs. He was standing at the fireplace in the parlour.

"Hello, Guy." *Dignity,* a voice said inside her mind. She may not have Muriel's exotic beauty, but she could maintain dignity if it killed her.

"Bethia." Guy advanced across the carpet.

Fearful that he would attempt to embrace her, Bethia took a step backward. He noticed and halted obligingly. Shadows lurked beneath his eyes.

"How are you?" he asked.

"Why are you here?" she asked in return. He had given up the right to know how she was keeping. And there was too much history between them to go through the motions of social niceties.

He nodded and said in a hollow voice, "I'm so sorry, Bethia. You were right about Muriel. I couldn't even see her flattery for what it was."

There was nothing she could add to make that any more true, so she simply waited.

"Mother and Father . . . the girls," he went on. "They were so angry at me. They miss you."

The thought caused warning needle pricks beneath her eyes. Bethia blinked, willing tears away. "I miss them too."

"Perhaps you could stop by one day? Visit them?"

"One day." It would have to be a long while from now, but she could not see herself simply forgetting the Russells were part of her life since her earliest years.

"Thank you." He wiped his eyes with the heels of his hands, looked up at her again, and blurted, "I never felt good enough for you."

"What?"

"You were always so perfect. And I held it against you instead of appreciating—"

"Don't say that," Bethia cut in.

"I can't help but say it!" A sob broke his voice. "I miss you so much, Bethia. You always understood me better than anyone. I've no right even to ask, but can you find it in your heart to forgive me?"

For days she had dreamed of this, his asking her to take him back, promising faithfulness for the rest of their lives. The wall between them consisted only of memories of his lies—and of her imagination's tormenting pictures of him in Muriel's arms. How easy it would be to destroy that wall. One step forward on her part, and life could go on almost as before.

It was the *almost* that gave her pause. For the immediate now, that would be good enough, surely better than walking about with the knot of pain in her chest. But what of the years to come? Did she really want to settle for an *almost* trusting relationship, just to keep from being alone?

If Guy had never been born, would her destiny be to wander through a life devoid of meaning? Or did the fact that she had devoted so much of her life to him mean that she had failed to notice other worthwhile paths branching out during her journey?

There are always other paths passed through her mind.

She cleared her throat, looked at the face she had loved for so long. At some point the love had become such a habit that she ceased to evaluate its merit.

"I promise you, I'll never even so much as look at another woman," he was saying.

"It's not just 'the other woman' that's the problem," Bethia said, having realized it herself just seconds ago.

"Then what is it? I'll do any—"

"The violin Muriel bought," Bethia cut in. "It wasn't for Bernard, was it? She gave it to you."

She was guessing, but the flush that passed over his face was her answer.

"It's . . . ah . . . I'll get rid of it. *Anything*, Bethia."

The fact that he had not thought of doing so on his own saddened her more than anything. "You said I was perfect," she said. "I'm not. Far from it."

He closed his eyes, opened them. "Yes, you are."

"No, I'm not." She shook her head and said gently, for she could still be moved by the misery in his expression. "But Guy, I do deserve better."

"Bethia?"

"Just a minute, Mother." Bethia wiped her eyes and blew her nose again. She tucked the wadded handkerchief beneath a bolster, stood, and brushed the wrinkles from her skirt.

"Come in."

Her mother opened the door and entered. Father followed.

Oh no. Blinking as if just awakening from an afternoon nap, hoping the red splotches that were surely on her face could pass for pillow marks, she said casually, "How were your mornings?"

"Claire says Guy was here," Mother said without answering her question.

Father's spectacles magnified the worry in his green eyes. "He asked you to take him back, didn't he?"

"He says he made a mistake," Bethia replied.

"A mistake?" Father shook his head. "Evading someone you professed to love because you haven't the courage to admit some misgivings . . . That's not a mistake. That's a character flaw. And as fond as I was of Guy at one time, it doesn't bode well for a good life in the future."

You don't even know the half of it, Bethia thought as Muriel's face flashed before her mind's eye.

"What did you say to him?" Mother asked.

The tension in the room was palpable. They were so afraid that she would ruin her future. "I forgave him."

"You did?" Mother said, face falling as if she would weep.

Bethia rubbed her mother's back and met her father's worried stare. "And then I asked him to leave."

———

"Have you seen the marmalade?" Jewel called, moving jars and bottles about in the kitchen cupboard Thursday morning.

"It's here at the table," Grady called back.

"Not the orange. I want to try the quince we bought yesterday."

"I brought it to the table. And your tea's getting cold, love."

They shared two newspapers over breakfast—the *Times* and *Illustrated Morning News*. Jewel heaped quince marmalade upon her toast, stirred sugar into her tea, and scanned the *Times* front-page article concerning the growing tension over France's claim to the left bank of the Nile. "Has there ever been a time when we and France weren't at each other's throats?"

She looked up when her husband did not even humor her with a distracted "Hmm?"

Grady was gaping at the newspaper open before him as if reading his own obituary.

"Grady?"

"Oh no . . ." he groaned.

She reached over to touch his arm. "Grady, what's wrong?"

Finally he raised his color-blind eyes to her bespectacled ones. "She's broken the camel's back this time, love."

Thirty-Nine

*T*elephone, Lady Holt," said Muriel's mother's chambermaid, Priscilla, whose cleaning duties had been extended to the parlour now that Florence was acting as nanny.

Prescott! Muriel thought. Hopefully, the nanny had decided to look for a new situation in Sheffield instead of London and had remembered that she would be here this week. With Georgiana alternating between frenzied activity and weeping for her nanny, Muriel did not know how she would manage her on the train this afternoon. And she could not ask Florence to come for the ride. The maid could hardly get the child to obey without bribes.

"It's Mrs. McGuire," Priscilla went on.

Another reason for hope, Muriel thought. Jewel ringing her, even if only to remind her of tomorrow's dress rehearsal, meant her anger was cooling. Perhaps somehow word had reached her that Guy was no longer a part of her life.

Perhaps the situation can be repaired after all, she thought. If not back to the way it was before, at least patched well enough so that everyone she had hurt could eventually put this behind them.

She closed the parlour door, picked up the telephone from its table. "Hello, Jewel?"

"Muriel."

Just the dead, flat way her cousin said her name made Muriel lower herself to the edge of the sofa. "Yes? What is it, Jewel?"

"Mr. Gatcomb devoted his column to you today."

Muriel's blood chilled. "Oh dear."

"How *could* you—"

"I can explain," Muriel cut in, her speech as rapid as her pulse. "I said something about Bethia in the heat of anger that I realized later wasn't true, but I rang his office Monday, and his secretary promised to tell him I'd made a mistake."

"Muriel, he did some digging, found Douglas's obituary, and then nosed around Sun Insurance. That led him back to the Royal Court. We've a lot of employees. I'm sure it wasn't hard to find someone to talk."

"I'll sue, Jewel! I'll demand a retraction! It wasn't fair how Mr. Gatcomb ambushed me that way right after . . ." The full weight of the situation hit Muriel like a slap in the face. "Bethia will never forgive me now."

"Bethia?"

Muriel swallowed. "I said she killed my brother and . . . that she was a heartless trollop."

She heard the sigh through the earpiece, her cousin's resigned voice again. "Muriel, Mr. Gatcomb obviously couldn't resist finding out what you meant. Gossip sells newspapers. But it doesn't libel *Bethia*. It puts the blame where it belongs."

"Where it belongs," Muriel muttered.

"It's all here. Some of Douglas's former co-workers saying how he ignored his job to follow Bethia about. A maid up at Girton College even confirms that. And then it goes on about how you blamed her when he died and . . . seduced her fiancé."

Hard to breathe, Muriel thought, a hand to her throat, where her pulse fluttered like mad. *You had everything! Why couldn't you sit back and enjoy it instead of causing such chaos?!*

". . . Frye and Mr. Cumberland," Jewel was saying. "Grady and I agree."

Twin tears trickled down Muriel's cheeks. "Agree what?"

Another sigh. "It's over, Muriel. There is a clause in your contract forbidding you to cause the Royal Court any adverse publicity. And you're not likely to find work in any other London theatre."

"Jewel, you can't do this!" Muriel shook her head, as if her cousin could see her. "*The Bells* starts in two days! What about the posters? I'll visit Mr. Gatcomb personally and demand a retraction!"

"You can't retract the truth, Muriel. And now I have to get back to work."

————

"It's good to see your appetite improving," Daniel Rayborn said when Bethia went to the sideboard for seconds during lunch.

"Thank you, Father." As she spooned beets onto her plate, she wondered why something so delicious had tasted so vile to her as a child. But she had no time to ponder this question, for she heard footsteps and turned to see Jewel walk into the dining room with a folded newspaper in her hand.

"Why, Jewel!" Mother said. "What a pleasant surprise."

Father got to his feet. "And you're just in time."

"No, thank you. I can't stay."

Still, Jewel waited until Bethia was seated, then pulled out the chair across from her and unfolded the newspaper. "Have you seen the *Illustrated London News?*"

"Why, no," Father said. "We take the *Times* and the *Chronicle.*"

Something about the way Jewel looked up at her caused Bethia a sensation of faint nausea. But why?

"I'm afraid there is something I need to read to you." Jewel pushed her eyeglasses up her nose and cleared her throat. " 'It seems the stage is not the only place where dramas are acted at Royal Court Theatre. . . .' "

Five minutes later, Mother and Father were giving Bethia stricken looks.

"Why didn't you tell us about Muriel?" Mother asked.

Bethia lowered her head. "Well . . . it was such an ugly story."

She could not bring herself to look at her cousin. And yet, how long could she have hidden something printed in the *newspaper?*

"Do you know how that makes us feel?" Father said. "Being shielded from unpleasantries, like children?"

"Her motives were always pure," Jewel reminded them, folding the newspaper again.

"We realize that," Mother said and turned to Bethia once more. "Perhaps we could have helped you. We may be old, but we've gained some wisdom over the years."

They were right, Bethia realized, looking at the dear faces. "I'm sorry. I just never wanted to worry you."

"We worry *more* when we can't believe that you're doing as well as you say." Father sighed. "I didn't inform my parents of every minute in my day when I was your age. But please, never carry a burden like that alone again."

"Yes, of course. Really, I'll be more mindful in the future."

Jewel smiled wearily. "Forgive me, but now that I've dropped in and ruined your meal, I have to get back to work. We've dress rehearsal tomorrow. And we've let Muriel go."

"You have?" Bethia gaped at her cousin. As little as she cared for Muriel, there were jobs at stake. Jobs belonging to good people. "Are you sure you want to do that?"

"Absolutely. We can't tolerate that sort of publicity."

"Is her understudy up to the task?" Mother asked.

"She knows her lines." Jewel pushed out her chair. "But Grady has an idea he'd like to try first. Please pray that it works."

"I'm not sure I'm up to this," Bethia said the following morning as her father opened the front door. Past him, she could see Hiram waiting in the carriage drive with the coach. "I didn't sleep well last night. I'm a little tired."

Mother put a hand upon her arm. "You'll feel more energetic when you see the results of all your hard work."

"But what if there are reporters?"

She had a strong feeling there would be, what with this morning's *Times* confirming that Lady Holt had been fired from Royal Court. There was speculation over the success of *The Bells* with *two* understudies in the leads, but the article did embellish Mr. Carey's— or Lord Danby's—riches-to-rags-to-riches story. Perhaps just the novelty of it would keep ticket sales at least healthy enough to keep everyone employed.

In spite of herself, she managed to feel a sliver of pity for Muriel. Mr. Gatcomb's article had painted her as a conniving, vindictive opportunist. She was certainly that, but the tiny grain of guilt for her own part in Douglas's death still existed in Bethia's conscience, and she could not help but wonder how different things might be had she not sent a certain letter.

"If there are reporters, you just refer them to me," her father said.

Bethia had to smile. "I'll refer them to you."

Indeed, four reporters with notebooks, two photographers with cameras, and apparently about a half dozen passersby were gathered around the steps of the Royal Court. None paid attention to Bethia and her parents, for on the top step, between Grady and Jewel, stood Charlotte Steel. She was as beautiful as ever, even in the ordinary brown poplin gown designed for Muriel in the role of Catherine, the burgomaster's wife.

". . . yes, our little Michael is almost four months old," the actress was saying while reporters scribbled into notebooks and photographers snapped cameras. "I agreed to return only for the run of *The Bells,* so after today there will be no morning rehearsals to compete with my time with my son."

"What will you do for a lead actress when Mrs. Steel leaves, Mr. McGuire?" a reporter asked.

A smile softened Grady's bulldog face. "We've time to plan for that. In the meantime, we appreciate Mrs. Steel coming to our rescue."

"But she only has a day to learn her part," Mother whispered.

"She's played it here before." Bethia sent a little wave toward Jewel, who was looking over tops of heads in their direction.

Jewel winked back.

That's why they made the announcement out here, at this time, Bethia realized. Any reporter interested in *her* part in Muriel's drama would jump on the bigger story.

Thank God for family! she thought. Frustrations and all.

Inside the theatre, sounds of instruments being tuned rose from the orchestra pit. The stage was set up as the residence of the village burgomaster, with table and chairs, sideboard with china, stove and kettle, candles and clock. Through a false window, snow was falling, or rather, Sunlight soap flakes were being shaken by a prop man on a hidden ladder. Mr. Webb was in his usual dress rehearsal frenzy.

"May I remind you that the morning is ticking away?" he was saying to propmen and carpenters.

As Bethia moved up the aisle with her parents, she noticed two people sitting in the sixth row: a young man and a woman with a gray chignon beneath the brim of a forest-green felt hat. The man looked over his shoulder, got to his feet, and moved out into the aisle.

"Miss Rayborn, I was hoping you would be here," Jude Nicholls said.

"It's good to see you again, Mr. Nicholls." Bethia introduced her parents, and Mr. Nicholls introduced them all to the woman, Lady Danby.

Mr. Carey's mother, Bethia realized.

"Lady Danby is Noah's mother," Mr. Nicholls explained, as if Bethia were the only person in London who did not read newspapers.

"How do you do?" Lady Danby said, moving into the aisle as well. She was plump and matronly looking, with soft cheeks and warm green eyes, and said she had been staying in the Grand Hotel, Charing Cross Road since Monday.

"Noah has been showing me the city."

"The tablecloth hangs longer on one side!" Mr. Webb's voice boomed. "If you'll but take a few steps back you'll *notice* such things!"

Before Bethia could remind her parents exactly who *Noah* was, Mother stepped closer to take the hand Lady Danby offered and said, "Your son is the one who went from understudy to lead. Bethia told us all about him."

At this, Mr. Nicholls sent Bethia a smile that apparently was supposed to convey some deeper meaning.

Bethia gave him an odd look. *What is it?* she said with her eyes, but he just continued smiling.

"How proud you must be," Father was saying to Lady Danby.

"I am." She offered her hand to him. "But I'm sure you know how it is with mothers. I was proud when he no longer had to wear nappies. But speaking of proud . . ."

She turned to Bethia and did not offer her hand but stepped closer and squeezed her shoulders gently. "You must be terribly proud of your daughter. Wool intolerance! Who would have imagined?"

"It was just something I read," Bethia said, but not minding the embrace, for it seemed only natural to extend the fondness she had for Mr. Carey toward his mother.

"Well, you gave my son a new lease on life. I've heard your name many times this week."

Mr. Nicholls flashed Bethia another loaded smile.

Strange man, she thought.

"Curtains!" Mr. Webb barked.

"Would you care to sit with us?" Lady Danby asked as the green curtain floated downward.

"We would be delighted," Mother replied. They filed into the row: Mr. Nicholls, Lady Danby, Mother, Bethia, and Father. Jewel and Grady entered, sent waves, and hurried to the second row.

The orchestra began playing Clara Schumann's "Drei Romanzen". Presently the curtain opened upon Mrs. Steel, seated at a spinning wheel. The play was essentially a study in remorse, of a burgomaster who sees nightmarish visions of a Polish Jew he murdered for his gold. Mr. Carey's role as Mathias the Burgomaster was therefore pivotal to the success of the production; he would have to be convincing as a man hiding inner torment behind a cheerful exterior.

Mr. Graham stepped out onto the stage in his role as Hans, a tenant of the burgomaster, with his wife. "More snow, Madame Mathias, more snow!" he exclaimed, taking off his hat and brushing away soap flakes.

"Still in the village, Hans?" said Mrs. Steel as Catherine.

Bethia thought, *If only Mr. Whitmore were here!* It would be like old times.

Still, she leaned forward a bit when Mr. Carey passed behind the fake window, then came through the door. Over his shirt and trousers he wore the long cloak of Strasburg cloth she had hemmed herself. Completing his costume were an otter's skin cap Mrs. Hamby had found at a secondhand shop, gaiters, spurs, and riding whip.

"It is I," he said warmly.

She sent up a quick prayer that he would be able to fill Mr. Whitmore's formidable shoes. Somewhere before the second act, she forgot to evaluate Mr. Carey's every movement, every syllable, and began simply enjoying the performance. He had ceased being Mr. Carey or Lord Danby and became Burgomaster Mathias. She caught the smiles Jewel and Grady were giving each other.

During intermission, while the orchestra played, Mother and Lady Danby chatted quietly. Soon the rehearsal began again and moved along wonderfully. The final scene was horrific and yet moving, for driven mad by his own guilt, the burgomaster imagines a rope about his neck and strangles to death in the presence of his loved ones. As the curtain lowered, Mother was holding Lady Danby's hand, and both sets of eyes glistened. Beyond Lady Danby, even Mr. Nicholls was wiping his eyes.

"Excellent!" came Mr. Webb's voice through the curtain. "Mr. Robbs, I must remind you to watch your timing, and Thomas, the snow needs to fall at a more consistent rate, but all in all it was excellent!"

Jewel and Grady came over, drank in the compliments, then apologized for having to hurry backstage to speak with the cast. There was no reason for Bethia and her parents to linger, so they bade Lady Danby and Mr. Nicholls good-day.

"Oh, but won't you please allow me to repay you, in a small measure, for your kindness to my son?" Lady Danby said. "Noah and Jude want me to try some new Italian dish at a restaurant nearby. Do say you'll join us."

Both sets of parental eyes went toward Bethia. The message in both was clearly *Are you up to this?*

After almost two weeks of brooding about the house, Bethia was beginning to feel like a tortoise out of its shell. She would never have come had her parents not coaxed her.

But then, had she not enjoyed herself?

Why not? she thought. They had already informed Trudy they would take lunch somewhere in town and arranged for Hiram to return for them at the theatre at two. What did she have to lose but some brood time, which she would probably make up for in the wee hours tonight?

Forty

*I*t was impossible to descend into another blue mood while watching people have pizza pie for the first time. Not only was Lady Danby a novice, but the dish was new to Bethia's parents as well.

"You may just have to give up and use your fingers, Mrs. Rayborn," Mr. Carey advised as Bethia's mother attempted to fork away a small piece she had sawed apart with a knife only to have the cheese stay attached to both pieces like elastic.

"Like this." Corrie Walters demonstrated, piling strings of cheese atop a slice, then biting off the end. Mr. Nicholls beamed at her as if she had invented electricity.

They all praised Mr. Carey's dress rehearsal performance, as did members of the company who stopped by the table. He was quick to deflect some of those compliments toward Miss Walters' performance as well as to Bethia's costume designs. When Mother asked if Mr. Carey was nervous over sharing the stage with Mrs. Steel, he admitted that his hands where shaking during the earliest scenes.

"Well, you certainly hid it well," Father said.

By this time, it was obvious that no one felt inclined to mention the reason for the abrupt change in casting, so Bethia was able to let down her guard and relax. Sincerely, she said, "I agree. You should have seen the smiles Jewel and Grady were giving each other."

Mr. Carey blushed but looked appreciative. "Thank you. I'll remind myself you said that when I'm onstage tomorrow evening."

From the way he was looking at her, it seemed he wished to say something else. But then the moment passed. Mother asked Lady

Danby when she planned to return to Yorkshire.

"Monday morning." She sighed. "I had forgotten how big London is. We've visited but a third of the places circled in my guidebook."

"And what were those places?" Father asked.

"Let's see. Westminster Abbey, of course, and the British Museum. The Guildhall and Saint Paul's." She smiled across the table at Mr. Nicholls. "We especially enjoyed watching Jude in *East Lynne* at Daly's."

"It's just a small part," he said modestly.

"You'll not have small parts for long," Lady Danby predicted. "You were simply wonderful."

"Wonderful," Miss Walters echoed.

Noticing Mr. Nicholls's eyes glistening again, Bethia wondered why he made no mention of his own family visiting him.

"Don't go encouraging him," Mr. Carey teased, as if aware of the melancholy coming over his friend. "He's vain enough."

His friend smirked at him, but with a lighter countenance.

Mr. Carey ground some pepper over his remaining slice of pizza pie. "I'm trying to convince Mother to stay longer. I can still show her about in the mornings, after the show opens."

"I'm afraid when you're my age, your joints start longing for their own bed again after a week," Lady Danby said. "And *you* need to be able to concentrate upon the show, no matter what you say. I'll simply have to save the rest for future visits."

"Next time, you must stay with us, Lady Danby," Mother said. "We've plenty of room."

Father nodded. "Hampstead is quite lovely. We're a stone's throw from the Heath."

"Why, how kind of you to offer." Lady Danby looked surprised and pleased. "We have a Constable painting of the Heath in our sitting room. It's actually one of the places I circled in my guidebook."

"Then, come for lunch tomorrow," Mother said.

"Oh, but you mustn't feel obliged. . . ."

"Not at all," Father said. "It would be our pleasure. Let's lunch at eleven so we'll have a little time to explore."

Mr. Nicholls made a polite little clearing of his throat. When

Mother looked at him, he lifted his eyebrows and gave her a hopeful smile.

Mother smiled back. "We would love to have *all* of you, of course."

Definitely a strange man, Bethia thought. But he was growing on her now that she had been allowed that brief glimpse beyond the glib facade. She glanced at Corrie Walters's radiant face and smiled to herself. *Not only on me.*

"You don't mind, do you?" Mother asked her in the coach. "They were quite pleasant, and after all, they *did* treat us today."

"I don't mind."

"You seemed to enjoy yourself," Father said.

"I did." No information of monumental importance had passed back and forth. But that was just what she needed. An outing with people with whom she could relax, even laugh. And, she realized, Guy had visited her thoughts only three or four times. On those occasions, the pull of regret was noticeably lighter.

I'm going to be happy again, she realized, incredibly. Just days ago, no one could have convinced her of that.

Lady Danby and Mr. Carey, Mr. Nicholls and Miss Walters arrived early enough for a tour of the house. Trudy, always delighted to justify her huge kitchen, prepared thick grouse soup, roast sirloin of beef, and fillets of turbot *à la crème*, along with assorted vegetables and a baked plum pudding.

After lunch everyone—Sarah, William, and John as well—shrugged into coats and hats and strolled some of the footpaths of the Heath. Their visitors asked questions of Bethia's family, such as what were William's responsibilities at the Hassall Commission and Sarah's at Blake Shipping, about John's studies, and whether they missed Danny terribly. They covered but a fraction of the whole 480 acres, since Mr. Carey, Mr. Nicholls, and Miss Walters needed to be at Royal Court and Daly's by five, but they saved enough time for hot chocolate in the parlour.

"Where will you take your mother tomorrow?" Sarah asked Mr. Carey.

"Church, and then the Tower of London," he replied. "And

hopefully a boat ride down the Thames, if there is enough daylight left over."

John had maneuvered an ottoman close to Miss Walters's chair. In a moss green gown, she looked like a golden-haired fairy queen. He glanced at her for any sign of awe as he said, "Did you know that my grandfather wrote a book on the history of the Tower?"

"Why, Mr. Rayborn!" Lady Danby turned to him. "We're being entertained by an author?"

"Well . . ." Father sat between Bethia and Mother on the sofa. Even from the side, Bethia detected the pleasure in his expression and smiled to herself.

Mr. Nicholls leaned forward a bit in his chair, eyes narrowing with thought. "*Now* I remember why your name struck a chord. We read a text on the bubonic plague our second year at Oxford. Did you, perchance . . ."

"He wrote it," John answered for Father with a glance at Miss Walters. When the actress's attention was focused upon Mr. Nicholls, his shoulders fell.

Now he knows how Lottie feels, Bethia thought. Poor Lottie! The families would probably never be as close as before.

"We've an extra copy of the Tower book in my library," Father said to Lady Danby. "Would you care to have it?"

She smiled. "You must have read my mind, Mr. Rayborn. I was wondering if the bookshops would be open before time to board my train Monday. It would make interesting reading on my way home."

"I'll get it," Bethia offered, rising.

Mr. Carey got to his feet from the settee he shared with his mother. "May I tag along? I'd like to see the library again."

In silence Noah accompanied her down a corridor. She looked as fetching as ever in a dark coral-colored dress with tiny blue flowers, her honey-brown hair hanging down to the blue sash at her waist. After opening the library door for her, he stepped back. She entered and snapped on the electric light. The room spoke of unostentatious comfort, with its worn leather chairs and oak shelves groaning with books. Notebooks and several texts, papers, and pencils lay upon a table in the center.

"My father's research," she explained when Noah picked up a

copy of the *Domesday Book,* a census of Norman Britain commissioned by William the Conqueror in the eleventh century. "He's writing a history of Hampstead."

"He's thorough, isn't he?"

"To the most minute detail."

"As you are with costumes."

She wrinkled her nose. "Actually, I take a shortcut here and there."

He put a hand to his heart, affecting shock. "I'll never believe that."

"Sorry to disillusion you. But I'm not such a stickler for detail that I'm willing to give up the sewing machines for time periods before they were invented. And good paint can make wooden buttons look like gold."

As she turned away to scan the shelves, he said, "Shall I look on another wall?"

"No, thank you. It'll be here somewhere. Ah, here it is."

She handed him a thick red clothbound copy of *A History of the Tower of London,* by Daniel Rayborn. "Will he mind if we ask him to inscribe it?" Noah asked, absently running fingers along the etched gold lettering.

"Why, that would please him."

They had no more reason to linger. He would have to hurry before he lost his nerve. Again.

"Miss Rayborn, this is asking a lot, and you're probably sick to death of us by now, but I reserved three front-row orchestra tickets for tonight's performance last week, when I assumed my uncle and aunt would be accompanying my mother to London. Is it possible that you and someone in your family would consider sitting with her?"

"Tonight?" she said a little uneasily.

"Or I'll ask your parents or the Doyles, if you're not up to it. I should have mentioned this yesterday, but . . ."

His words trailed and hopes sank a little, for she seemed on the verge of declining. But then she said, "I remember promising to come the next time you played lead. And Lady Danby shouldn't have to sit alone. I'm sure someone will be happy to come along with me."

She even smiled and added, "From the looks of it, it may be John."

"Thank you," he said. "You, your family . . . you've been so thoughtful. It's added tremendously to Mother's visit."

"She's a lovely person."

It seemed she would move toward the door. But she looked up at him again. "May I ask a personal question, Mr. Carey?"

"You may ask me anything," he said, then mentally kicked himself for the thickness of his voice. He cleared his throat, as if to convey some physical reason. She apparently had not noticed, seeming to be preoccupied with how to phrase her question.

"How long . . . did it take you to recover completely when your fiancée left you?"

Noah cleared his throat again, this time to stall for time. "Ah . . ."

She shook her head. "Forgive me. I don't know what I was thinking."

"No, really, it's all right." He blew out his cheeks. "You see, that newspaper article was not correct. *I* broke off the engagement."

"I see," she said. But it was as if a curtain had dropped between them. As she turned toward the door, Noah automatically moved a hand to touch her shoulder but restrained himself.

"Please wait, Miss Rayborn."

She turned again.

"I broke it off because my fiancée and I did not agree on a moral issue that was important to me." It sounded pompous and lofty to his own ears, but under the constraint of his promise to Miss Spear, he could think of no other way to word it. Still, he could clarify one point. "There wasn't another woman, or anything of that sort."

She had winced at the *other woman* reference. "You read the article too?"

"You've no reason to be embarrassed, Miss Rayborn." Once again sentiment touched his voice, but there was nothing he could do about that. "Everyone grieves for you. You're like the younger sister we all wish we could protect."

Her face clouded for a brief second, then her expression eased a bit. "That's actually a comforting thought, Mr. Carey. I've rather dreaded the thought of returning to work, but yesterday was quite nice. And being back among my friends is probably the best tonic."

"I *know* it is, Miss Rayborn."

"And it will be easier on my parents as well, with my not brooding in my room."

Noah affected a sigh. "Being loved is such a burden, isn't it?"

"Thank you." She smiled. "For reminding me that I'm still loved."

More than you know, ran through Noah's mind.

When Bethia mentioned the invitation after their guests left, the family seemed relieved that she would consider still another outing. John declined, apparently having given up on winning Miss Walters's heart. Since Mother and Father had seen the dress rehearsal, they declined as well. But William, who always enjoyed an opportunity to pamper Sarah, encouraged her to accompany Bethia.

By the time Hiram brought the coach around that evening, the two had managed to look smart enough for an evening at the theatre without spending hours dressing. Sarah wore a gown of plum silk trimmed with Havana brown embroidery, and her blonde hair was caught up in a low-crowned marquis hat. Bethia had chosen her pearl-gray cashmere with narrow black stripes and a wide black sash but decided against a hat, liking the look of how Avis had styled her hair into a long braid twisted around a comb at the crown of her head.

Lady Danby was waiting near the will-call window at Royal Court. "How dear of you both to come on such short notice. I hated the thought of having no one with whom to share Noah's debut."

"We're happy to be here," Bethia assured her.

Mr. Birch appeared to lead them to their front-row seats. When the curtain rose on Charlotte Steel, faint murmuring came from various spots in the theatre. Obviously, not every patron had read the newspapers or noticed the last-minute corrections penned inside the playbills. Presently Mr. Carey strode into the setting, quirked a self-effacing but warm smile at the actress, and said, "It is I!"

If he was nervous, it did not show. Bethia had wondered, given the lack of animosity—real or pretended—between Mr. Carey and Mrs. Steel, if there would be enough convincing romantic tension between them, but both pulled it off extremely well.

Well enough for a standing ovation as the final curtain lowered. Realistically, she figured Mrs. Steel's presence was the cause. Mr. Carey clearly knew it to be so, for during final bows he stepped back and applauded her as enthusiastically as did anyone else. But Bethia was happy for him, that he would always have the memory of seeing his mother weeping quietly on the front row.

As the theatre was emptying and the cast changing, Bethia, Sarah, and Lady Danby went up to the wardrobe room. "My word," Mr. Carey's mother said, eyeing the row of hats upon a shelf. "What a wonderful place to work. This reminds me of my grandmother's attic. My sisters and I would spend hours playing dress up."

"Bethia never grew up," Sarah teased. "She's found a way to be *paid* to play dress up."

That made Lady Danby laugh. Bethia made a face at her sister. "You wouldn't consider it 'play' during final fittings."

"Noah says you work very hard," Lady Danby said.

Bethia smiled, a little surprised at how much he seemed to speak of her to his mother. When they left the staircase, Mr. Carey was pacing the office corridor. "Ah, there you are," he said. "I was worried you might have given up on me and decided to run away. A reporter for the *Stage* asked for a photograph with Mrs. Steel onstage."

All three women complimented his performance. He thanked them, saying he surprised himself by being less nervous tonight than for rehearsal. "It was so kind of you to keep Mother company," he added to Bethia and Sarah. "Will you be our guests for a late supper at the Cavour?"

"I'm afraid we'll need to get back," Sarah replied straightaway. "We sprang this outing on our coachman at the last minute. He's probably very tired."

Mr. Carey seems a very decent man," Sarah said as the coach carried them northward up gaslit streets.

"He is," Bethia said.

"And he's fond of you."

When Bethia opened her mouth, her mind was unable to send

down any protest. She had noticed *something* these past two days, some meeting of his mind and hers on a level beyond casual conversation. Had it gone on even before this weekend, or had her life been too preoccupied with Guy to notice?

"I'm not ready for another romance," she assured her sister.

"Are you sure?"

Bethia caught the unease in her expression and nodded. "I know it's best to wait until I'm completely over Guy."

Sarah shook her head. "I'm not speaking of waiting until you're 'over' Guy to allow another beau in your life, Bethia. I'm suggesting that you not even entertain the *possibility* of another romance for several months."

"Why is that?" Not that Bethia had set her sights on Mr. Carey or any other man. But she knew the natural order of life. People courted, married, and started families. She *wanted* children and to carry on the traditions handed down from her parents.

"We were all very fond of Guy," her sister said, touching her arm. "And he was such a natural part of your life. I didn't even realize until he was gone that we rather considered you *half* a person. I think you even thought of yourself that way."

Again Bethia opened her mouth. And again her mind refused to cooperate. Had not she weighed almost every decision she made on whether Guy would approve? Even when he was miles away, she had carried him around with her, a presence always in the background of her conscious thoughts.

"I'm afraid that once Guy is out of your system completely," Sarah went on, "you'll allow Mr. Carey . . . or someone else to become that other half, and you'll never have experienced the joy of just being Bethia. And if you spring out on another path too quickly, you'll miss out on the added joy of waiting and trusting God to give you direction."

The *path* imagery brought back Bethia's thoughts three days ago, when Guy came to the house. She had prayed for guidance by rote since childhood, but had she ever actually waited for God to light the way first? It seemed, looking back, that she had included Him only in the difficult decisions, those without obvious answers. For the most part, however, she had decided what to do and then assumed

God would give his stamp of approval simply because she was a Christian.

She turned to Sarah. "You're a good sister."

"As are you," Sarah replied, but then gave her a worried look. "But does that mean you don't agree with what I'm saying?"

"No, it makes perfect sense." Bethia sighed. "I may just have to ask you to remind me sometimes. The thought of being alone is still a little frightening."

"Alone? You still have God, your family and your friends. *And* . . ." Sarah slipped her arm about her shoulders and squeezed. "You have Bethia Rayborn—who is on her way to becoming a whole person in her own right."

Amidst the recent upheaval to her life, Bethia had devoted little thought to her upcoming twenty-second birthday. She certainly did not link it to Father and William and John setting out on some vague errand after church the following day, for the first of November was still two days away.

Minutes after she heard the coach in the drive again, Danny walked into the parlour as if he had just stepped out for a second.

"Happy birthday, sister."

She let out a cry of joy, got to her feet, and hurried across the parlour. He embraced her sideways, with his right arm looped around her, because his left arm held a small towel-wrapped bundle against his chest.

"Your lectures?" Bethia said.

"My professors gave permission, and some friends will share their notes. But I'll have to leave Tuesday morning."

And then the bundle barked.

"He's a Skye Terrier," Danny said as family gathered around. "Like Greyfriar's Bobby."

Bethia had heard the true story of the little dog who kept watch over its deceased owner's grave until its own death fourteen years later. A statue was even erected in his honor in the heart of Edinburgh. She held the long-haired animal up to her chest and laughed while a pink tongue bathed her chin. Sarah scratched its ears, and Bethia smiled at her. Her sister had warned her against another romance so soon, but she had not warned her against puppies, and she was smitten.

"What's his name?" she asked Danny.

"That's for you to decide."

Bethia studied its intelligent face. "Scotty, I think."

Forty-One

*T*hree weeks into *The Bells* run, the wardrobe room staff were already preparing for *London Assurance*. The only lead cast member *not* to be measured for costuming would be Mrs. Steel.

Jewel had confided to Bethia that she and Grady hoped the lead actress would change her mind once she stepped out onto the boards again. Still, public speculation over who would take her place added to the favorable columns devoted to *The Bells*, and the Royal Court was holding its own against the larger theatres on the Strand.

"I would have thought you would be leaving that lodging house," Bethia heard Mr. Birch say to Mr. Carey behind the screen on the sixteenth of November. The actor had requested the last appointment for the day so that he could await delivery of two beds and mattresses.

"I'm waiting for a friend's situation to improve so we can share a flat," Mr. Carey said. "Jude Nicholls is his name. He's a member of the cast at Daly's."

"Ah . . . I remember him very well from Mr. Whitmore's party."

Miss Lidstone closed the hood on her sewing machine and sent Bethia and Mrs. Hamby a sage look. "He was the fellow chatting up Miss Walters."

The actor's eyes appeared above the screen. Good-naturedly he said, "If you please, Miss Lidstone . . . he happens to be a decent man."

"Did I say he was not?" she snapped defensively.

Mrs. Hamby was picking change out of her handbag to slip into her pocket for Sloan Station. "And when will your friend's situation improve, Mr. Carey, ha-ha!"

The eyes appeared again. "Sometime after January. He's won the part of Captain Ardale in *The Second Mrs. Tanqueray*."

Presently Mr. Carey walked out from the screen in street clothes. Miss Lidstone said in a mild offering of appeasement, "How does it feel to have your portrait on posters all over town, Mr. Carey?"

Mr. Carey smiled at the older woman. "Better than a poke in the eye with a sharp stick, Miss Lidstone."

When the chuckling abated, the staff gathered up umbrellas, coats, hats, and handbags. Bethia set her notebook upon the drafting table and said in her most businesslike tone, "Will you stay another minute, Mr. Carey? I'd like to speak with you."

"But of course, Miss Rayborn."

All three of her co-workers' movements slowed noticeably. But when there were no more items to gather, they traded reluctant good-byes and filed out of the room, Mr. Birch closing the door in deference to the stove. Mr. Carey smiled down at Bethia, attentive.

"We received a package from Lady Danby yesterday," Bethia said. "Three Wensleydale cheeses and a dozen jars of wild rowan jam. Mother is writing to thank her, but it was such a lovely gesture that I wanted you to know how surprised and pleased we were."

He did not react at first, then leaned his head to study her. "That's it?"

"Well, yes." She felt a little sheepish, having to explain, and nodded toward the closed door. "You know . . . well . . . how people here speculate. If they learned your mother sent gifts . . ."

Mr. Carey's eyes crinkled at the corners, betraying an effort to hold in a smile.

"Do you find that amusing, Mr. Carey?" Bethia said with a small dose of Miss Lidstone's testiness. She had been on her feet most of the long day and was not inclined to be made sport of.

"No, not at—" he began, but stopped his head in midshake. "I'm sorry, Miss Rayborn, that's just not true. I'm delighted to hear that about my mother. But I confess the thought struck me that Mr. Birch and the others are probably speculating all the same."

"Oh dear." She put a hand up to her forehead. "I acted on impulse, but of course you're right."

"They'll have us engaged," he said. "Not that I *mind*."

"Mr. Carey," she said as heat stole through her cheeks.

"Forgive me." He gave her a pensive little smile and echoed her own words. "I acted on impulse too."

One month had passed since Guy asked Bethia to step into the coach outside the theatre. The sharpness of the hurt had worn to a dull ache, and even that was subsiding as she realized more and more how incompatible they really were, at least for marriage. With the lessening of pain came sharper clarity. Sarah was very right. It was too soon to encourage another romance. Even one with Mr. Carey, who caused her to smile every time they came across each other in corridors or the wardrobe room.

To cover her embarrassment, she went over to the stove and closed the damper. "I don't want you to miss your supper," she said lightly. He only had two hours before time to return for tonight's production. She took her handbag from the cupboard ledge while he walked over to the copper urn by the door and lifted out her umbrella.

"This is yours?" he asked.

"Yes, thank you."

When she joined him at the door, he cleared his throat. "May I say something?"

"Of course, Mr. Carey," she answered and found herself holding her breath.

A trace of hopefulness came to his smile. "I've no wish to frighten you, like Lady Holt's brother did. And I realize you need some time to recover from the obviously insane former fiancé. But would you be adverse to going out for lunch with me some Sunday? I'll invite Jude and Miss Walters if that will make you more comfortable."

Bethia's mind began racing. *How to say this?*

It was enough hesitation for hopefulness to fade from his smile.

"It was just a thought," he said, and nodded. "I understand."

The resignation in his voice disturbed her. She could not leave this conversation hanging in the air, incomplete, with the potential to cause future awkwardness or even misunderstanding between them.

Looking up at him, she asked, "What *do* you understand, Mr. Carey?"

"Well . . . that I shouldn't press for anything beyond friendship."

Courage please, Father, she prayed under her breath. *And the right words too!*

"I treasure that friendship," Bethia said. "It's just that I can't encourage anything beyond that for the time being."

"Yes, I under—" He paused, and a brow lifted warily. "For the time being?"

"Yes. For the time being."

"Then, you're not saying you would be averse to a social outing with me . . . *one* day?"

She nodded. "That's exactly what I'm saying."

A little smile quirked the corners of Mr. Carey's mouth. "Have you any idea how long 'for the time being' will be?"

"I'm afraid I don't," she admitted, thinking, *Where's Sarah when you need her?* "Months? A year, perhaps? So, if you're not inclined to wait, I understand."

"Oh, I'll wait," he said, but then a dent appeared between his dark brows. "Just one thing, Miss Rayborn."

"Yes?"

"When you know for certain that 'for the time being' is over, will you give me some sort of hint? You see, I've no wish to become a pest, but a man needs to know."

"I'm not sure if I can promise that." She gave him an apologetic look. "Gender roles and such."

"Then how will I . . . ?"

She took the umbrella from his hands. "You're an intelligent man, Mr. Carey. I suppose you'll just have to figure that out."

They were halfway down the last flight of stairs, Mr. Carey a few steps behind Bethia, when Lewis came bounding up the steps, two at a time. "There you are. The McGuires would like to see you."

"Both of us?" Mr. Carey asked.

"Just Miss Rayborn, sir."

Bethia said farewell to Mr. Carey at the foot of the stairs. Grady was standing outside the closed greenroom door, hands in trouser pockets, expression anxious. He gave Lewis some coins for some meat pies up the Square and motioned Bethia aside, away from the greenroom.

"Muriel's in there with Jewel," he said with voice low. "She asked to be allowed to beg your forgiveness, but we warned her that that would be up to you."

"Is she asking to come back?"

Grady shook his head. "She knows very well that's impossible."

"Do you think she's sincere?"

"I do." He gave her a wry smile. "But then, she was a clever actress."

"I'll see her," Bethia said.

Curiosity was the chief reason. This was unfinished business. She could not help but wonder what Muriel could possibly have to say. When she realized Grady was not following her into the room, she closed the door behind herself and turned. Jewel and Muriel rose from a sofa.

"Thank you for agreeing to see me, Bethia," Muriel said.

To Bethia's relief, Muriel did not lunge at her to snivel on her shoulder. But something about the setting was not quite right. She realized it was the gown Muriel wore, of muted amber and nutmeg plaid, with red threads running down the squares. Only four months had passed since Douglas's memorial. The customary time period for mourning a sibling was six.

Muriel followed Bethia's eyes. "Bernard said it would help put the past behind me."

"Oh."

Jewel moved away from the sofa. "I'll give you two some privacy." As she passed, she patted Bethia's arm. Bethia moved on into the room, stopping about six feet from the other woman.

"I know you expect a scene," Muriel said quietly.

That was exactly what Bethia expected and was the reason she was so stoic. One show of emotion on her part had the potential of setting off an avalanche of hysterics. And with Muriel's proven ability to produce tears six nights a week on cue, how would she know if they were genuine?

"There is nothing I can say that will ever repair everything I did," Muriel continued. Her eyes lustered. She blinked and stood straighter, as if willing tears away. "But I would like for you to know that the hatred I directed toward you—and others—is now directed toward myself. I've no right to ask, but one day I hope you'll find it in your heart to forgive me."

"What about Guy?" Bethia said.

"I spoke with him yesterday." Muriel's violet eyes closed as if the memory was painful, and then opened. "He said you won't have him back."

"I have you to thank for that."

When Muriel's eyes glistened again, Bethia shook her head and said, "That wasn't a dart. I *realize* you meant to hurt me. But God helped me glean good from the tragedy. Guy and I weren't meant to be together."

Muriel drew in a sigh. "He's terribly hurt, still. I was hoping . . ."

"Perhaps good will come out of this for him too, eventually."

"I pray for that every day."

When Bethia stared with suspicions aroused anew, Muriel gave her a little self-conscious smile. "If one is determined to destroy one's life, it's convenient to have a minister in the family. I was almost suicidal until Bernard read to me of the woman at the well. Now I'm trying as best I can to make amends to everyone I've ever hurt—you, Guy, Milly . . ." Again the self-conscious smile. "But you haven't all day, have you?"

In spite of herself, Bethia allowed her stony facade to soften. Just a bit. "I'll always regret sending Douglas that letter."

"You had cause," Muriel said. "But if you want forgiveness, it's absolutely yours."

"Thank you."

Muriel bit her lip. "Will you forgive me?"

"Yes," Bethia said without hesitation. And in spite of herself, she advanced and embraced her former enemy.

"Oh, thank you!" Muriel gushed, squeezing Bethia's shoulders hard.

Having spent twenty-five years with little or no remorse for any of her actions, Muriel was still in awe over how being on the receiving end of forgiveness felt like a cool cleansing stream flowing through her mind.

And having granted *others* forgiveness even fewer times in twenty-five years, she wondered why she never noticed how heavy a burden bitterness was to carry around day after day.

"What will you do now?" Bethia asked, sharing the sofa with her.

"I've bought a cottage up in Gleadless. That's where Bernard and his family live. I'll be meeting with a land agent tomorrow afternoon to put the house here on the market."

She had other loose ends to tie as well. Two of the servants, Ham and Evelyn, had family in London and did not wish to relocate, so she needed to write up character references for the hiring agency and withdraw some money from the bank to tide them over. And the detective she had commissioned over the telephone would be stopping by the house at six. "I have to go now," she said, squeezing both of Bethia's hands.

"I'm glad you came," Bethia said.

"Oh, so am I!" Muriel said as relief welled up within her again. She hesitated. "Perhaps we'll be friends one day?"

"Perhaps we will," Bethia replied. Not a definite *yes*, but she was smiling as if the notion did not repulse her.

The detective, a Mr. Fowler, had been highly recommended by Henry Godfrey when Muriel telephoned Northamptonshire to ask if Leah Prescott had returned to her former home. Mr. Fowler walked with the aid of a cane and looked as old as the pyramids, but he had the information she had sought.

"She has not found another nursemaid position," Mr. Fowler said, leaning forward on the cane even from the parlour chair. "I'm certain that her having no *recent* character references was a factor. She's working at a factory, stitching gloves twelve hours a day."

"But why don't you have her with you?"

He shook his wizened head. "She flatly refused."

"I'll change her mind," Muriel said. She realized pride was a sin but did not think God minded confidence, as long as one could back up one's words. Another question she would have to ask Bernard. Thank God he never seemed to tire of them!

But at least her brother had more *time* for her questions, now that he no longer had to cook.

"Will you direct me to her now?" she asked.

"Tomorrow. We don't want to be caught in her neighborhood after dark."

"But she'll be at work tomorrow."

"Sunday, then."

"That's four days away."

Patience was another virtue Muriel was still in the process of learning. And she was not quite *there* yet.

She came up with a solution that was against her natural inclination to sleep late. At six o'clock the following morning while Mr. Fowler waited in the coach, she and Ham watched workers file through the entrance of a smoke-darkened brick building in Spitafields, Troughton Fine Glovers. Out of the fog still shrouding the cold street walked Leah Prescott carrying a lunch pail.

Muriel ran toward her and held her by the shoulders, ignoring the curious stares and murmurs about her. "Prescott! I'm so glad we found you!"

"Good morning, Lady Holt," said Georgiana's former nurse-maid, but gently trying to step back out of her grasp. "I'll be late for work."

"But I need you! Please!"

The small brown eyes revealed no sign of emotion. Indeed, Prescott's voice was almost lifeless as she said, "You can hire another nursemaid."

"Yes, I can." Muriel nodded. "But I need more than just another nursemaid. I need you to teach me how to rear my daughter."

A wistful look washed over Prescott's plain features. "Do you really mean that?"

"With all my heart." Smiling, Muriel leaned down to take the pail from her hand. She set it on the pavement, where surely someone else would take advantage of it. "You don't need that. Let's go collect your things. I've a lot to do today. And the sooner they get done, the sooner we return to Georgiana."

Forty-Two

On the fifth of June of the following year, Noah Carey let out a low groan as he stepped up under the marquee of the Royal Court Theatre. After not having picked up a sword since University, he was taking lessons for Thomas and Scott's _The Swordsman's Daughter,_ in which he would play a Parisian fencing master.

The soreness would ease away before the production opened in six weeks, he was assured by the tutor hired by the theatre. Sir Julius Stacey was an obvious sadist who enjoyed pushing to the limit the four cast members under his instruction. But the dashing swordplay onstage would be worth a little muscle pain.

Mr. Birch met him in the lobby with expression somber. "The McGuires ask that you stop by the office, Mr. Carey."

Déjà vu struck Noah. The last time Mr. Birch had delivered such a message, the McGuires informed him that he would probably replace Mr. Whitmore. But now that he was the Royal Court's lead actor, there was no place to go but down.

Don't be a pessimist, he thought on his way down the corridor. God had blessed him more than he could have imagined. And as of four months ago, he was perfectly teamed with a lead actress, twenty-two-year-old Jessie Bateman, a veteran of theatre since playing Cobweb in _A Midsummer Night's Dream_ at the age of twelve.

But the McGuires' expressions were as somber as Mr. Birch's had been. Noah sat down in the extra chair and asked, "What's wrong?"

Mr. McGuire traded glances with Mrs. McGuire. "Mr. Rigby says the managers of Prince of Wales Theatre were looking for you at the lodging house."

Noah nodded, weaving fingers over one propped knee. "I heard the same. But I wonder why they went out there? I've not lived there for months."

He and Jude shared a tidy flat on Seville Street, just two blocks south of Hyde Park.

"In fact," Noah mused aloud, "I wonder why they took it upon themselves to look me up at all."

Again the husband and wife sent looks to each other. Mrs. McGuire said, "The word has been out that they're looking for a new lead actor. And they informed Mr. Rigby you had contacted them."

"To ask when tickets will be available," Noah explained. "My mother is coming when *The Swordsman's Daughter* opens, and she also wishes to see *An Ideal Husband* at the Prince of Wales."

"Ah . . . I see." Mr. McGuire's frame eased in his chair.

Mrs. McGuire smiled. "So you're still content here?"

"Content to stay here as long as you'll have me."

"That will be a long time!" Mr. McGuire assured him and got up from his chair to pound him upon the back.

Noah winced, and smiled. "Careful now. Fencing lessons."

Bethia was relieved to hear the door open. Mr. Birch was aware that costume measurements for male cast members were to commence, and she was beginning to worry that he would be late. "The tea is still hot," she said, turning from her sketches at the drafting table.

But it was Mr. Carey who stood inside the doorway.

"Thank you, but I've had tea," he said. "Where is everybody?"

"Mr. Birch is on his way up," she replied but realized that if that were so, Mr. Carey would have seen him. "Miss Lidstone and Mrs. Hamby are at a wedding."

Mrs. Hamby's younger sister Flora was the bride. Miss Lidstone would return some time after lunch, but Mrs. Hamby was taking the day off.

Not that it was any of Mr. Carey's business, she reminded herself.

"Well, I can't take your measurements without Mr. Birch," she said coolly. "Will you come back in a little while?"

"Certainly."

"Thank you." She turned to her sketches again, picked up her pencil.

But she did not hear the door open again. She waited three seconds, four, then looked over at the actor. "Is there something else?"

He gave her a rueful look. "I guess you've heard?"

"Yes," she replied. Why deny it?

"You don't think it's a good idea?"

She slammed down her pencil, harder than intended. "What I think isn't the issue, Mr. Carey. But Jewel and Grady took a huge chance with you. I suppose I'm just sadly disappointed in your lack of gratitude."

"I see." His broad shoulders rose and fell. "It's just that Mother is so fond of Oscar Wilde's work."

Bethia stared, bemused. The course of this discussion had suddenly taken a turn, leaving her standing on a corner. "What does that have to do . . ."

"Well, I can't rightly take her to see *An Ideal Husband* without tickets. So I rang the Prince of Wales office, and for some reason they're out looking for me." A corner of his mouth quirked. "They must be frightfully expensive, if their own managers are out delivering them."

It took Bethia a moment to grasp what he was saying. "Then . . . you're not planning to leave here?"

"Goodness, no. But it's very admirable . . . the loyalty you have toward the McGuires."

"Jewel's my cousin," she reminded him.

Mr. Carey nodded, studied her. "Is that the only reason you were disappointed?"

Bethia realized she had two choices. Coyness, which would put him under the burden of trying to coax an answer from her somehow. Or straightforwardness. As she could expect Mr. Birch to stroll in any second, she opted for the latter.

"It wasn't the only reason," she said quietly. "I didn't want you to leave."

The actor smiled. "Does that mean 'for the time being' is over?"

"It is, Mr. Carey. It has been for a couple of weeks."

"A couple of weeks? But why didn't you say something?"

"I really tried." Bethia returned his smile. "But you know how it is. Gender roles and such."

"Please connect me with Lady Danby in Danby-dale, Yorkshire," Noah said into the telephone mouthpiece the following morning in the flat he shared with Jude. Only, Jude would be moving out in two months, having purchased a little terrace house in Kensington.

It was one of the best things he ever did, Noah thought, encouraging Jude to write his father of his engagement to Corrie Walters. Not only did Sir Thaddeus send a cheque for a thousand pounds with the advice that Jude should get a bit of real estate and not throw money into the ash can by paying rent, but he expressed his intention to come down for the August wedding. It was as close as Sir Thaddeus could come to apologizing. Jude was happy, hence, so was Noah.

"Good morning . . . Noah?"

The hopefulness in her voice made him smile. "Yes, it's me, Mother. And I need your advice."

"Yes? About what?"

"What should I pack for a picnic lunch Sunday afternoon?"

"You're going to *cook*?"

"I'm going to try," he said.

"For how many people?"

"Two."

"Well, now, that depends. If it's just to be you and Jude, roast beef sandwiches will suffice; a couple of Scotch eggs and a tin—"

"Why would I want to go on a picnic with Jude?"

His mother's sigh carried over the line, all the way from Yorkshire. "I understand now," she said. "That was my cue to ask with whom you're going on this picnic. Correct?"

"Not exactly." He smiled again. "That was your cue to *guess*."

"Miss Rayborn," she said without hesitation.

"Why, yes. But how is it that you were so certain?"

"I wasn't," she confessed. "That was wishful thinking. I know how fond you are of her. Is it really so?"

"We're going to Regent's Park."

"I'm happy for you, son," she said warmly. "And I'm happy for Miss Rayborn. You deserve each other."

He felt like a small boy being praised for reciting the alphabet. A pleasant feeling, no matter that he was two years shy of thirty. Jesting lightly, he said, "It's just our first date, mind you."

"Then you should have a good restaurant pack your hamper," she said. "You'll be wanting a second date, won't you?"

————

With the last day of December falling on a Sunday, there were no grand-scale celebrations to mark the close of a century. The title of Vicar Streatfield's sermon in Christ Church was *The Year of God's Favour*, based upon readings from Ecclesiastes and Saint Luke. After services at their own churches, Noah, Jewel and Grady, Catherine and Hugh and their sons, and Jude and Corrie Nicholls came to Hampstead for lunch.

Afterward everyone gathered in the parlour, children on pillows or ottomans upon the carpet. Somewhere during the course of conversation and singing, Noah sent Bethia a covert glance. He casually left the room while Danny was playing the opening notes to "Long, Long Ago."

Bethia waited until the beginning of the second stanza to hand Scotty down to Nicholas Sedgwick's eager arms and get to her feet.

> "Do you remember the path where we met,
> Long, long ago . . . long, long ago?
> That's when you told me you would not forget,
> Long, long ago, long ago."

She met her father's eye on her way to the door. He simply smiled and continued singing. She smiled back.

"There's a fire lit in the sitting room," Noah whispered in the chill corridor.

Bethia shook her head. "Not there."

She had a strong feeling about what was coming. What other explanation could there be for her turquoise birthday ring disappearing from her jewelry box one night three weeks ago, only to reappear the following night after she had frantically searched every inch of her room and even retraced her steps? If her premonition were to prove correct, she did not want it to happen in the same room where she had spoken of the future with Guy.

"The library," she whispered.

The room was cold, but she did not mind. The warmth in Noah's dark eyes as he took her in his arms was enough. "I love you, Bethia."

"I know that," she said. "I love you too, Noah."

He kissed her and then got down on one knee. "I can't imagine any way I would rather begin a new century than with your promise to be my wife. Say you'll marry me?"

"I'll marry you," she said, smiling down at him.

From his pocket he took a black velvet box, opened it. She moved her turquoise ring to her right hand and allowed him to slip the engagement ring onto her finger. It slid easily, of course. She lifted her hand. A cluster of seven octagonal diamonds was encompassed by twenty-four smaller diamonds and set in gold.

"Do you like it?" he asked.

As before, she would have been content with a far more modest ring. His *actions* were what proved how much he cherished her. But he was watching her face anxiously, and she would not scold him for such extravagance for anything.

"It's beautiful," Bethia said, watching the facets reflect light.